Malak sprang to his feet to block the advancement of his karmic twin. The two men stood unmoving as they studied each other. For many lifetimes their paths had not physically crossed, yet in every other way they had been intimately linked.

"Malak." Dethen's bass tone conveyed his contempt. "Step aside, little one. I have a use for the young girl."

Malak could not stand his brother's gaze. The black, soulless depths of his eyes terrified him; their invulnerable, brutal strength was tremendous. He suddenly felt frail and utterly insignificant.

"You'll have to step over my corpse, brother." His voice tremored slightly with the rush of adrenaline in his veins.

Dethen smiled, a patronizing and sinister gesture. "That is not a problem, little one."

Forthcoming by D. A. heeley

Ronin (Book II of the *Darkness and Light* trilogy)

Lilith

Darkness and Light:
Book I

D. A. heeley

1996
Llewellyn Publications
St. Paul, MN 55164-0383

FIRST EDITION
First Printing, 1996

Cover art: Lissanne Lake
Cover design: Tom Grewe
Editing and book design: Darwin Holmstrom
Layout: Virginia Sutton

Library of Congress Cataloging-in-publication Data
Heeley, D. A., 1971-
    CIP data filed
    ISBN 1-56718-355-7 (Trade pbk.)

Printed in the United States of America

Llewellyn Publications
A Division of Llewellyn Worldwide, Ltd.
P.O. Box 64383, St. Paul, MN 55164-0383

Dedication

For my karmic twin, Ravi. Though we may not be related in flesh, in spirit we are forever entwined. Our relationship is beyond this plane, beyond any words or expressions I can find. It simply is. Nothing can taint your light or subdue your spirit: you are one of life's warriors, a true saint-soldier. Though at times we are separated by race and culture, by space and time, I am always with you. I will always be here for you, even through incarnations yet to come, just as we've been there for each other in lives gone by. This book is for you, my twin sister, with eternal love.

Thanks to my close friends for help in writing this book: Adam, Dev, Paul and the beautiful Jane. Thanks also go to ex-workmates Gary and Paul, and to my karate instructor, Mark Robertson, for teaching me many of the techniques presented in this book.

Author's Note

Darkness and Light is a fantasy trilogy set within the doctrine of the Hebrew Qabalah, a work of fiction entwined with a factual philosophy. *Darkness and Light* is composed of three novels: *Lilith*, *Ronin*, and a third novel, as of this writing untitled, but with the working title *Ipsissimus*, which is the highest grade a magus may obtain. The trilogy follows Malak, an Adept of the White School of Magick. His story is analogous to the evolution of man, relating his Fall, Regeneration, Rebirth (self-realization), and God-realization. It is a tale related in many mythologies, most notably in Christ, but also in Osiris, the Phoenix, Krishna, Lugh, Baldur, and others.

The glossary at the back of *Lilith* lists words the reader may be unfamiliar with. The essay beginning on page 263 is a brief explaination of the Qabalah for those interested in the philosophy behind *Darkness and Light*. I've also included a recommended reading list on page 277, should the reader wish to learn more about the subject. These books may be of interest to the open-minded reader.

I am always ready to accept any questions or comments from readers. I can be reached via the publisher or by e-mail on the Internet at dheeley@kether.demon.co.uk.

Grace has been defined as the outward expression of the inward harmony of the soul.

—Hazlitt

Enya
Yesod of Yetzirah
The Aeon of harmony

Amethyst rays crept around the silhouette of the Celestial Tower as the sun began its lethargic rise into the sky. Seated on the translucent crystal causeway was the Magus, his eyes glowing with a supernatural brilliance that no sun could ever match. His face was hawk-like and predatory, an imperfection he kept to remind people of his human origins.

Children and adults were clustered about him on the causeway, eager to share the dawn with him. Though the Magus had no favourites, room was always left beside him for the beautiful dark-haired woman who had been so close to him in human life.

As the sun rose above the Celestial Tower, one of the men started to play a pipe. Its haunting notes hung in the air, making the precious moment with the Magus even more magical.

The Magus dropped his gaze from the sky to look at the children before him.

"You have come to hear the Story?" he asked.

"Yes! The Story!" they whispered with excitement.

The Magus' smile rippled through the crowd, washing away cynicism and pessimism wherever it touched.

The nearest child took the Magus' hand. "Is this the story of how you became God?" he asked, his eyes wide with awe.

"We are all God," said the Magus. "It is only that I have realized it, and cast away my false beliefs."

"Is it like throwing off your coat?" asked another child.

The Magus smiled again. "Just like that. Only it can take a long time to learn how to cast away beliefs, because we mistake them to be our true selves."

The child looked puzzled.

"It is like thinking your coat is really your skin," the Magus said. "Just as you think you are only a child, when in reality you are everything." He looked up to speak to the whole crowd. "You are all of God. I am the Aleph and Tau, the Alpha and Omega, the very essence which flows through the multiverse. In time you will realize that you are too. All of you will make the journey I have made, and perhaps one of you will eventually sit where I am now and talk as I am."

The Magus's gaze lingered on the beautiful dark-haired woman beside him before continuing.

"I will tell you the Story in a moment," he said. "It is my story, but also the story of many others, and in the end it is the story of every man and woman who ever lived. For though every journey is unique, the destination is always the same. Just as we all spring from All That Is, we must surely return to it.

"I will tell the Story from all sides, because in a way I was all the people involved, and I still am. All experience and all knowledge is mine to share with you, if only you knew how to listen. But you must learn yourselves, for life itself is your teacher. This is what you will learn from the Story. Sit at the feet of your life, and it will teach you. Learn about your life, and you learn about yourself. Master the inner, and you master the outer. These are among the highest teachings."

"Tell us the Story! Tell us!" said one of the children.

The Magus bowed his head and started to speak. His melodious voice was haunting beyond any instrument, its soothing tones gliding through the morning air. He spoke and the world shimmered as the people began to live the eternal Story he told…

Part
I

Eden

Every man and every woman is a star. Some fall. Some burst into dust.
Some shine on steadily through the long, dark night. We start them off,
we Masters, by handing them a candle.

—Aleister Crowley

Remember all ye that existence is pure joy, that all the sorrows are but as shadows; they pass and are done, but there is that which remains.

—Doctrine of the White School (Aleister Crowley)

And when the true horror of the creation of the world was realized, the Lord cowered in shame from his sin. The three mightiest Adepts sought him out. The first Adept saw the Lord's shame, and covered it walking backwards with a white sheet. The second Adept saw the Lord's shame, and covered it walking sideways with a yellow sheet. The last Adept saw the Lord's shame and burst into laughter; the robes of the final Adept were black.

—Doctrine of the Black School

False imagination teaches that such things as light and shade, long and short, black and white are different and to be discriminated, but they are not independent of each other; they are only different aspects of the same thing, they are terms of relation, not of reality. Conditions of existence are not of a mutually exclusive character; in essence things are not two but one.

—Doctrine of the Yellow School (Lankavatara Sutra)

There is no coming to consciousness without pain.

—C. G. Jung

We do not see things as they are. We see them as we are.

—The Talmud

Enya
Yesod of Yetzirah
The Aeon of Dreams

A distant flash of violet lightning illuminated Dethen's figure against the black void of the night sky. A colossal physique, standing almost seven feet tall, his robes flailed about him in the severe, gusting wind. He radiated an aura of power and knowledge, yet there was a suffocating blackness centred around him, choking off light and hope wherever it touched.

His face was hawk-like, though not completely unhandsome. Aged far beyond his thirty years, deep black bags accentuated his eyes. Scars and deep lines of suffering crossed his face to produce a dramatic and intimidating effect. His jaw was strong and clean shaven, his hair black and short, neatly and efficiently kept.

However, it was his eyes that drew people's attention. The irides were black, the pupils fathomless holes, barely visible against the ebony visage. A flame flickered in their depths; it was impossible to tell if it was a reflection of the lightning or a cold fire burning within the pit of his soul.

He held out his arms, sensing the tension from the oncoming storm; the reek of ozone permeated the air. He could feel turmoil in the elemental forces eddying about him. The sounds of the crashing ocean and rioting wind blocked out all other noises. Enya was entering a period of intense imbalance and chaos: the protective forces were weakening. The knowledge was enough to bring a thin smile to his sober face.

Two bulky figures loomed out of the darkness behind him. Clad in black, studded-leather armour, Roruch and Janus both bore the distorted symbol of a lightning bolt on their breast. This was the symbol of the Black School; next to it was Dethen's personal sigil, inlaid in silver. They were each armed with a *wakizashi* short sword, unheard of on Enya; there had been no bloodshed for two millennia.

Dethen's gaze raked critically over his troops. When he spoke, it was quietly, yet his voice cut sharply through the background noise.

"Follow me."

He set off toward the sea cliffs that hovered at the edge of his vision. The soldiers exchanged anxious glances in the gloom before following, shells and pebbles crunching under their heavy boots.

The cliffs were limestone, probably two hundred feet tall. They were jagged and treacherous, interlaced with caverns and fissures. Dethen strode confidently toward his target: a small, semi-concealed cave entrance. He climbed the slope to the opening.

"Roruch. A torch."

"Yes, Master." Anticipating the demand, the captain was ready with the lighted torch in seconds. Dethen took it without speaking; the flame danced precariously on the wind, animating malevolent shadows against the cliff face.

Dethen slipped through the tight tunnel entrance, holding the scabbard of the *katana* that hung from his belt. Though he wore several layers of robes, his athletic build was obvious. He moved with a feline grace that made the trailing Roruch and Janus look awkward.

They moved slowly through the cavern in single file, stooped over. Chips of quartz and mica glittered seductively in the torch light. The floor was broken and uneven, but very soon the passage enlarged, beginning to slope steeply upward.

The two soldiers pushed on after their master, fighting hard against the slope while attempting to maintain a grip on the slippery floor. Dethen moved with ease, never slipping or slowing when moving across difficult footing. Roruch was beginning to struggle when the natural limestone suddenly gave way to a much harder and more polished material. It was smooth and crystalline; the tunnel's shape also became more regular, indicating an artificial element. A water mark could be seen at the boundary, where the waters of the ocean reached. A thin coating of luminous fungi cast an eerie green light along the passage.

Carved carefully into the walls on either side was a hexagram:

the Seal of Solomon. Inside each hexagram was the Oriental symbol representing the balance of yin and yang. Underneath the Seals
were Hebrew letters and Egyptian hieroglyphs. Only an Initiate
would be able to read them.

Dethen paused to run his eyes over the runes, and nodded soberly.

"We are here," he said, his voice tinged with alien emotion. "This
is the Yellow School sanctuary. Ahead is the Chamber of the Magus.
We must be careful."

"Master? The *Magus?*" Janus's throat closed as he tried to pro-
nounce the word. "We are going into the temple of the God-man?"

Dethen's ebony eyes narrowed. Roruch drew in a sharp breath
and Janus moved back a step.

The moment lasted a fraction of a second, and then Dethen
seemed to relax. When he spoke, his voice was caustic: "I have been
summoned by the Magus himself, and I have responded. No stranger
has intruded upon this shrine for two thousand years." He moved to
within inches of Janus' face. "The Magus is omnipotent. Bring no
fear with you, soldier, for here your fear will be projected. It will take
on a form of its own. And here, even my power is limited."

Janus swallowed hard, transfixed by the abysmal black stare.
"Yes, Master."

Dethen's scathing gaze held Janus for a few seconds longer, as
a hawk might study a rabbit. Then he turned dismissively and
continued forward. Janus avoided Roruch's glare: to question the
Master was taboo. Roruch could feel his own apprehension turning
to fear as they followed. His eyes ran across the ancient hieroglyphs;
even to him they seemed to spell out a dire warning.

They travelled for several minutes in silence, a silence broken
only by the dripping of water. Even the sound of the ocean didn't
penetrate this deeply into the cliff-side. The passage they followed
remained unchanging, which only increased the tension, but they
could feel intensifying currents of energy flowing through the tunnel.

Dethen pushed on, immune to the fear and tension the others
felt. The air thickened and vibrated as if alive. It parted obediently
for him but smothered the soldiers like glue, making it difficult to
breathe. It tried to force them backward, resenting the intrusion of
the uninitiated into its lair.

The soldiers of the Black Guard were veteran warriors, not
easily frightened, but magick was a force they could not see, combat,

or understand. Helplessness was the one condition they loathed.

Roruch and Janus began to hear voices, quiet at first, but increasing in strength. The voices whispered terrible and perverted notions. Ethereal hands and claws reached out for their skin, desiring their life force and heat. Roruch felt fear rising within him. Cold sweat lubricated his body beneath his armour, freezing him to the marrow. His pulse hammered in his ears, and he felt as though he was breathing through cotton wool. Dethen didn't seem to be suffering, nor did he acknowledge the anguish of his troops. They were useful to him only in proportion to their resilience: weakness was unforgivable.

Small side branches began to appear on both sides of the passage. They were unilluminated and forbidding; neither of the soldiers cared to theorize what lay down them. Many sloped vertically, and it seemed that the whole cliff-side was impregnated by the lair.

Suddenly Janus gave a choked cry and collapsed. Roruch watched as he writhed on the floor, fingers clawing at his throat as he started to asphyxiate. Dethen tilted his head as the man fell, but didn't slow his pace. Roruch grimaced and followed suit. He knew the power that Dethen commanded, but the soldier's weakness proved he wasn't worth preserving.

Dethen's attitude seemed poignant to Roruch; he felt he would collapse himself at any moment. His strength and willpower were being sapped by the icy claws that pierced his body. He gritted his teeth and pushed on.

The two men passed over a dozen side exits. Dethen neither slowed nor deviated from his course. As he came level with the next passage, their presence was directly challenged for the first time. Dethen's senses detected his opponent just in time to react.

He twisted his head sharply. An adolescent lunged at him from the darkness with a short sword. The assailant's thrust was crude and badly timed: the youngster obviously lacked proficiency with his weapon. However, Dethen was a master swordsman and was deadly with his own. He slipped fluidly to the side of the attacking blade. With perfect co-ordination and lightning speed, he drew his katana from its sheath and struck. The blade sliced through the boy's wrist; his hand dropped to the floor, still grasping the sword. The dull ring of metal striking stone echoed through the damp, suffocating atmosphere.

The boy screamed in shock and pain, clutching the severed limb to his chest. The blood flowed in merciless quantities, staining the front of his white cotton robes a deep red. He staggered back against the wall, his eyes beginning to dilate and glaze over. Dethen wiped his blade on the adolescent's robes; they identified him as a neophyte, the lowest level of temple initiation.

The boy's body shivered and convulsed. Dethen took hold of his head, staring deep into his eyes. Roruch shuffled nervously on his feet, straining against unseen demons in the air. The youngster blinked several times and his eyes dilated further. His body went limp and he seemed oblivious to his surroundings.

"Where is Ghalan?" Dethen asked, his voice harsh and emotionless.

The boy blinked again and looked groggy. Dethen's iron will raped the contents of his simple mind, flicking aside any inner strength that the boy still posessed like an annoying insect.

"Where is the Magus?" he asked again, his voice now sharp and edged with menace.

But the neophyte was barely conscious, and unaware of all except the frigid yet inviting embrace of death. Dethen frowned and pulled back from the boy to hold him at arm's length. He skimmed his aura, scanning through the mental body. He smiled grimly as he located the desired information. As he had thought, the Magus was expecting him. He gently laid the boy on the ground, crossing the adolescent's arms across his chest.

He turned to his captain. He gave the soldier a hard stare as he realized the difficulty he was having in standing.

"I will go on alone from here," Dethen said. "Await me by the entrance."

Roruch didn't hesitate. He saluted smartly and accepted the torch Dethen handed to him. The neophyte had been aware of their approach due to the torch light, and Dethen wanted no disadvantage in further encounters. He did not expect any, though. Ghalan had summoned him. He stared in amazement as the body of the neophyte began to disappear. His eyes glittered with dark humour: the attack had been merely a test. As poor as it had been, very few people on the plane of Enya could defend themselves against violence of any kind.

Dethen waited for Roruch to disappear from sight. He needed time to prepare himself; he had waited three lifetimes for this moment.

After focusing himself he turned and continued his trek down the passage, now relying upon the unearthly illumination of the fungi. He walked for several minutes, never losing track of his environment for a second: his awareness was always centred. His breathing was perfectly regular, using the full capacity of his lungs.

Eventually he discerned the outline of a single figure in the distance. Behind it was a faint glow. He pressed on, pushing back his cloak to gain better access to his sword.

The light intensified as he approached. Soon he could make out details of the figure: its robes were yellow, and around its neck it wore a lamen containing a large topaz. The topaz glittered like a golden diamond in the dim light. As Dethen closed within twenty yards, he noticed the distinctive and extended aura surrounding the figure, marking it as an Adept.

Dethen halted a few feet before the figure, scrutinizing it carefully. The hood of the outer robe was pulled across the head, but he could now tell that it was a woman. The Adept pulled back her hood and regarded him with a dispassionate look. Her hair was blond and short, the pale face boyish and elfin but radiant with health. Her hands were clasped formally before her.

"I am Soror Chani of the Adeptus Minor grade, Sentinel of the Yellow School. Who seeketh the Chamber of the Magus?"

She waited for his reply, holding his gaze remarkably well as his black eyes bored into hers.

"I am Frater Dethen, Adeptus Major and Master of the Black School. I have been summoned by the Magus himself for an audience."

Dethen was impressed by her strength of character: she held his gaze for several seconds before lowering her head in submission.

She stepped aside. "Please, enter the Chamber."

Sixty feet down the corridor, Dethen could see that the yellow light spilled from a room. With a nod of acknowledgment, he strode toward it.

Less than a dozen yards before the entrance, he was forced to stop suddenly. Almost too faint to be seen, a green sheet of ethereal matter stretched across the passage before him. Flickering sparks of scarlet danced across its surface, and hovering behind it, like a half-formed shadow, was an artificial elemental.

He realized immediately that the ethereal sheet was connected to the elemental plane of fire. To walk through it would cause the elemental to attack instantly; this would cause insanity in most men as it assailed their mind. The elemental waited menacingly, a billowing cloud of murky red gas. Dethen could tell from its grim countenance that its creator was powerful. It was also well-masked: his ethereal vision strained to see it.

He slid his hand to the hilt of his katana and carefully withdrew it. Forged over two thousand years ago, *Widowmaker* had accompanied him through three lifetimes. The blade was jet black, yet had a strange lustre to its surface. It vibrated gently as it was withdrawn; the blade had a hunger possessed by no other sword. It was forged from mithril silver, which was intrinsically magical on Enya. The blade was keen enough to cleave through stone.

The sword's hilt resembled black onyx; it was smooth and highly polished. Inset into the hilt were protective runes of the Enochian tongue, said to be the language of the angels themselves. Set into the pommel of the sword was a rounded garnet, its colour a deep blood red. Instead of glittering, the gem sucked in all light that fell upon it. It was instantly discernible as the sword's source of power.

Dethen thrust the katana into the ethereal field. It vibrated as it eagerly absorbed the energy, adding it to its own great reservoir. After so many centuries with its owner, the sword was completely attuned to his aura, and had developed a sentiency of its own. Its goals and desires were exact replicas of its master's, and it communicated its feelings to him empathically.

The ethereal field dimmed in intensity, the sparks dying away. As soon as the field disappeared, the elemental started to move. It was uncertain of which direction to go. It zigzagged back and forth along the corridor, unsure of its task now that it had been released. The entity was totally lacking in intelligence, having been created for a specific purpose: to attack anyone who crossed the ethereal barrier.

Dethen stepped forward carefully. He stopped dead as the elemental paused, then launched itself at him like a javelin, aiming straight for his head. He shifted his sword into a ready position and waited a split second before side-stepping, slicing through the entity as it streaked past.

He felt a surge of heat travel up the katana, and *Widowmaker* gave a whine of discomfort. The fire elemental dissipated with a cry of relief.

Dethen nodded in satisfaction as the pitch of his psychic hearing dropped. He sheathed the satiated *Widowmaker* and strode boldly forward into the Chamber of the Magus.

The Chamber was perfectly square, each side exactly forty-five feet long. The temperature was warm and comfortable. An eerie golden light was present, but had no obvious source; it shifted and flowed with the astral currents. The walls were a luminescent grey and seemed to be immaterial. The east wall, which exhibited a bright yellow equilateral triangle with a horizontal line through it, shimmered and rippled with power. The north wall showed the same symbol, but this was black, and the triangle was inverted. The south wall displayed a radiant red triangle; the west wall the same, but the icon was blue and inverted.

Dethen received the impression that he had crossed into another plane, completely removed from Enya; knowing the power of the Magus, he realized that this was possible. Centred prominently on the floor was the *Sigillum Dei Aemeth,* the Enochian Holy Pantacle. It was instantly recognizable: the pentagram surrounded by a heptagram, itself contained within a circle. The seven unknowable and unpronounceable Enochian names of God interlaced the disc, woven amongst the names of the greatest archangels. The whole symbol pulsed with incredible force, and Dethen knew that it was a true reflection of the might it represented. He was truly in the presence of Divinity, even if it was only a minute fraction of the Infinite.

For a brief second, he had an urge to fall to his knees in adoration, but he viciously fought down the impulse: he had no love for God, just as God had no love for him.

Seated within the *Sigillum Dei Aemeth* was Ghalan, the Magus, dressed in a yellow robe with his body locked into perfect posture. His aura shone brilliantly; there was a sphere of pure white light above and around his head. Dethen was overawed; he knew this was his Kether chakra, Ghalan's direct link to the Divine.

Despite his obvious spiritual health, Ghalan's eyes were closed and his breathing almost undetectable. Dethen was shocked by his physical condition: he was obviously on the very edge of death. Ghalan's face, like Dethen's, had the distinctive hawk-like appearance of the family, yet it was now pale and drawn. His head was bald, and his once unruly grey beard was now pathetically sparse. Through his robes it could be seen that his limbs and bones were wasting away; he could no longer hold his back straight.

Dethen bowed with great respect to his old teacher before crossing the chamber to kneel before him, just outside the *Sigillum Dei Aemeth*. Ghalan stirred and opened his eyes. They glowed with such intensity that even Dethen could not withstand their stare.

"Ah you are here, my son. You are not too late."

Ghalan's voice was incredibly weak, and Dethen had to strain forward to hear him. Although it had been over twenty centuries since they had been father and son, the karmic link between them was so strong that they still considered themselves related, even though they had never crossed paths since that lifetime—not since Ghalan had crossed the Abyss to become the Magus of Enya.

"I received your summoning whilst in the spirit vision, Master."

The Magus smiled as he studied the aura of his one-time student. Dethen's character had changed greatly: the emotional intensity had been replaced with a cold, indomitable will. Two further incarnations had increased his power a hundred-fold. Dethen had pushed himself to the limit in all things, driven by the sinister karmic vow that had bound him for three lifetimes.

Ghalan gave a chuckle, which turned into a long wheezing cough. Dethen moved to help him, but stopped quickly as he saw the old man's warning glare. He could not enter the circle; to do so would shatter his body and mind. He stared contemptuously at the circle boundary, considering the Divine essence it channelled.

One day I will face you, and you shall answer to me for the abomination of the world.

Ghalan controlled the convulsive wheezing. He looked up to Dethen's expression, which almost bordered on concern.

He smiled. "So, there is a vestige of humanity left in you."

Dethen's face darkened. He had never been reputed for his sense of humour.

"Why have you summoned me, old man?"

"Ah, I can see from your eyes that you suspect, my son. And you are right. For two thousand years I have reigned on this plane. ...but now my time is due."

"There is to be a new Aeon?" Dethen's voice was calculating, and insidious.

Ghalan let out a shallow sigh and nodded.

"The end of the Aeon of Dreams has drawn nigh. For two millennia, my word has controlled and protected every aspect of Enya. My presence on this plane signifies peace, harmony and balance. And yet this has now become the balance of stagnation. My influence is already dwindling; it will remain for barely a week."

"There is to be a new Magus?"

Ghalan nodded.

"It is time for another to walk the path of the Abyss. To reach the spiritual heights, one must first pass through the path of ultimate spiritual darkness and pain. And for myself, I must make the transition to Ipsissimus. The power of the Godhead beckons."

Dethen smiled grimly, his hope realized.

Ghalan continued: "Without a Magus, this plane will be without protection. It will change from a plane of dreams to a plane of nightmares. A new Magus must be put in place. Therefore, it is time for the battle of duality to recommence. It will be vicious, and only the strong can hope to survive. The White and Black Schools must wrestle for the seat of the Yellow School....and only one Adept from each School is eligible."

"Malak and myself," Dethen said.

The Magus nodded. "Karma dictates that you are the only two. I had summoned Malak also, but he is too late. I trust you will not exploit this unexpected advantage?"

"I need no advantage. My twin brother is of no consequence. I am the stronger! He wastes his time playing with faeries and undines," the black mage snarled. "His precious White School is a pathetic sham."

Ghalan's face had a knowing look to it.

"You are the strongest, Dethen. But Malak has the greatest potential strength of all. He has yet to mature. Your brother was, and yet will be, my teacher."

Dethen frowned, not understanding what he was attempting to imply.

"What does that mean? Malak is weak!"

Ghalan smiled. "And yet shall you defeat him? Only one can become Magus, but only together may you pass safely through the Trial of the Abyss."

"Lies!" Dethen snarled, an edge of uncertainty in his voice.

Ghalan chuckled. He leaned forward, his eyes burning with supernatural intensity. When he spoke his voice was incredibly weak, yet there was an ominous ring of prophecy to his words.

"Only through death can the twins be reunited...."

He smiled serenely. Dethen frowned; the old man's tone was deeply disturbing.

The body of the Magus suddenly shuddered and convulsed. The glowing Kether centre above his head flared brighter and descended his body to immerse it completely. There was a tremendous crack of thunder and a high-pitched howling of released pressure. Dethen was caught by an immense blast of wind. He huddled against the floor, shielding his eyes with his arms.

The noise and chaos gradually subsided. Dethen opened his eyes and stared in bewilderment. He was sitting at the end of a passage: the Chamber of the Magus was gone. Enya was without a Magus.

In Budo-kai, the difference between a Master and a young warrior is one of ideals. The warrior is proud and thinks he is powerful; in reality he is nothing. The Master knows he is nothing, and this realization helps him to become something.

—The Bushido, Way of the Warrior

Enya
Lokhi Region
The Enchanted Forest

A single naked figure stood unmoving in the centre of the forest clearing. In natural stance with head bowed and eyes closed, his breathing was barely detectable.

The amethyst sky brightened into an exquisite pink hue as the dawn sun slid into view over the treetop horizon. Rose-coloured rays gently and amorously massaged the lethargic landscape, and the world gradually awakened from slumber.

Malak inhaled a huge lung-full of air, and exhaled slowly. He was in a state of *zanshin*, acutely aware of everything around him. The wind rustled the blue-green leaves of the trees, blending with the splash of the nearby waterfall. Creatures scuttled through the foliage and birds praised the new dawn in harmony. His olfactory revelled in the subtle smells of the pine, oak and cedar. He could almost feel the nearby trees in the gentle air currents that caressed his bare skin.

At over six feet in height, Malak was not a short man by Enyan standards. His physique was sturdy but not overly impressive: the muscles were lean and well-defined, though not intimidating. Straight, shoulder-length black hair framed strong hawk-like features; the resemblance to his twin brother was obvious. Malak's eyes were a deep blue, compassionate with a firm gaze, but they contained a superficiality which recent maturity had not quite exorcised.

He focused his vision ahead to gain maximum benefit of his peripheral sight. The pitch of his psychic hearing altered; the frequency was now almost imperceptibly high. This signalled the arrival of his incorporeal friends. He gave a nod to his invisible companions, and then slipped into *yoi*.

His training partners materialized, solidifying from the air. There were three, as always. Two opponents circled in front of him, while the other approached from the rear. They all wore identical apparel: full-bodied scarlet robes that covered every appendage from head to ground. Their faces were concealed within dark hoods, and although two of them held weapons, there were no hands visible—the weapons glided along of their own volition.

Without a word the three assailants advanced in an attacking paradigm. Without moving or blinking, Malak monitored their approach. He could clearly see the first two attackers, both advancing at forty-five degrees to his direction of vision. One was skillfully spinning a *bo*-staff, while the other was unarmed. He could hear the rustling robes of the attacker behind him.

Suddenly the rear opponent attacked. Malak instantly analyzed the sound as a sword slash. He performed a forward roll toward the unarmed opponent in front of him.

The sword attack sliced through vacant air. Malak found his feet and blasted a side kick into the kneecap of the unarmed assailant. The figure collapsed onto the dislocated knee. Malak slammed a roundhouse kick into his head, hurling him across the clearing. The assailant landed hard and diffused into the air a moment later.

Malak spun around. The other two opponents had recovered their wits. They circled him, gaining an angle of 180 degrees. His vision flicked between them, looking for an opening in their defenses. They closed in, one wielding a wakizashi, the other a *bo*. Malak licked his lips. They intended to attack together.

The contender with the bo-staff closed in, spinning his weapon to form a defensive shield. Malak knew that his only chance of survival was to attack, and he had much more chance against the staff than the sword.

He lunged forward. Surprised, his enemy paused momentarily but recovered. He changed the path of the *bo* to strike, but Malak anticipated the blow. He caught it double-handed, lessening the impact on his unprotected hands and allowing his momentum to carry him forward into a head-butt. His aggressor staggered backward, losing his grip on the staff. Malak spun into a back kick. His heel landed square in the pit of his enemy's stomach, dropping him instantly.

Malak jabbed viciously with the staff into his opponent's ribs and heard a satisfying splinter of bone.

He turned sharply as the final attacker charged from behind. He twirled the staff into a ready position. He knew that he now possessed the advantage: in combat against a sword, a bo was always the superior weapon.

The wakizashi sliced diagonally down at him. Malak parried the blow with one end of the staff and crashed the opposite end into his aggressor's skull. There was another sickening crunch of bone as his skull collapsed. The empty scarlet robe fell to the ground.

Malak slid back into natural stance and dropped the bo-staff. He waited as the three piles of scarlet robes began to glow and shimmer. They rose up, gradually forming humanoid shapes; the bo by his feet reappeared in the clutches of its owner. They took up positions around him to reproduce the equilateral triangle. Malak gave a bow of appreciation, which they returned respectfully.

The figures scintillated and rapidly diffused into the air. Within a few seconds, the pitch of Malak's psychic hearing returned to normal. He knew that he should continue training for another half hour, but as usual, his heart was not in it. Natural talent was what he relied on, rather than the uncompromising and relentless practice of his twin brother.

He crossed to the edge of the small clearing and wiped his sweat with a towel. Listening to the sounds of the forest, he donned his deep purple robe. On his left breast, the silver symbol of a pentagram glittered in the early morning light. As he dressed, he frowned in puzzlement at the sounds around him: something seemed amiss. Although most of the usual forest sounds were present, there was a subtle anxiety in the atmosphere. Such tension was extremely rare on Enya, so he wasn't sure he could trust his senses. Also, he knew that he was feeling uneasy within himself. His mission to the Magus had put him on edge. He vividly remembered the lucid dream that had summoned him several days ago.

He shrugged and banished the issue from his mind. He retrieved his katana reverently, and laid it naked on a navy cotton cloth. *Retaliator* was stunning to behold. It was undoubtedly the finest sword on the Outer Planes, matched only by its twin. The blade shimmered with a supernatural blue light that fluxed as he moved it. The hilt was of clear quartz, but it fractured the light like a huge diamond.

Embedded beneath the quartz were sigils of the Hebrew God-Names and Archangels; the sigils were magically forged from lapis lazuli of the most intense blue. The blade, inscribed with magical runes of protection and beneficence, was honed to incredible sharpness, an edge that would never dull or nick.

The pommel of the sword was formed from a blue star-sapphire, half the size of a man's fist. Here the katana's power was concentrated. It glistened and sparkled as he studied it. The sword represented his link to his Higher Self, epitomizing the philosophy of the White School.

He wrapped the katana in the cloth, tied it securely and carefully slung it over his back. There hadn't been occasion to use the weapon for many centuries.

Taking a last look at the clearing, he prepared to return to his mount. Again he received a perception that something was wrong, but this time he could sense the direction it emanated from: the stream. He paused, then moved forward toward the disturbance. He felt that it was close.

He moved through the light airy undergrowth, parting the vegetation before him. He had no concern about nettles or thorns: such things did not grow on the dream-like plane. The sound of the splashing waterfall increased in volume as he approached. He pushed on, feeling he was very near. Well-defined emotions—pain, fear, and frustration—filtered through, and still he saw no visible signs.

He was within thirty feet of the waterfall now, although it was completely obscured by the green-blue undergrowth. The sky above behaved strangely. It ebbed and flowed with subtle colours; the air was distorting.

He almost trod on the source of the negative emotions. In a section of dense foliage, a young hawk was flapping insanely on the ground, one of its wings hopelessly broken. Its eyes were wild in panic and frustration, its breathing rapid.

He sighed, cursing his own paranoia: there was nothing to fear here. He knelt before the bird, which accepted his presence without further agitation. Empathy for animals was a rare gift with which few were born, but creatures always accepted Malak.

He cupped his hands above the hawk. The bird gradually calmed as he spoke, pushing the negative emotions from its aura with his own. He closed his eyes to concentrate and breathed deeply, focusing on the Kether chakra above his head. A sphere of pure white light flickered into life, its brilliance like burning magnesium. He channelled the energy down through his body and out through his hands. The broken flesh and bones of the hawk's injury started to knit back together. He worked for several minutes until the hawk's aura was entirely healed.

He reached down to pick up the bird, which now lay contented. As it spread its wings to a span of several feet, it gave a cry of thanks and launched itself into the air, circling above the trees to show its appreciation.

Looking up, Malak realized why the sky was in motion. He pushed himself toward the waterfall, parting the undergrowth and kneeling to gain a lucid view. The sight was breathtaking.

The crystal-clear water cascaded down a twelve-foot drop to the rocks below, throwing up a fine mist of spray. From the spray there reached out a beautiful rainbow, indigenous to Enya. Its nine-coloured spectrum shimmered sensationally in the cool morning air. It formed a great bridge, arcing up to the heights of the sky, where its intensity gradually faded. Pale yellow and blue globes of light spiralled around it, as the sylphs and undines frolicked about the wavering image.

Malak drew in his breath sharply. The elementals weren't the only creatures taking an interest in the rainbow. Wading in the shallow water below the waterfall, a unicorn was enjoying the refreshing spray of the mist as it studied the arcing colours above it.

Like all unicorns it was androgynous, with sublime elegance, but with the muscle tone of a stallion. Its coat was pure white, radiant with health. Its mane was wild, and tinted silver. A horn spiralled up from its forehead to form a keen point. Its whole body radiated magical energy. The creature was majestic; there was no other fitting description. It stood perfectly still, gazing up at the rainbow with an alien intelligence.

There was a rustling noise behind Malak, and he turned to glimpse Lena stealthily approaching. He smiled knowingly. He knew that his wife would adore the scene. He put a finger to his lips and beckoned her forward.

At her physical peak, Lena was incredibly beautiful. Her figure was tall and slim, curved perfectly in the right places. Her long, straight, black hair shone with amazing vitality. Her face was delicate, stunning, and lightly tanned. Her eyes were a very dark brown, deep and alluring. She wore black robes with a silver pentagram, the symbol of Adepthood in the White School.

She quietly moved toward him, her feet gliding across the forest surface. Kneeling down behind him, she kissed him, wrapping her arms around his neck in a warm embrace.

"What is it?" she whispered.

Malak pointed his finger at the unicorn, which was now rearing up on its hind legs in elation and appreciation of the rainbow. She gasped and squeezed him tighter, her face full of delight. Lena's love of living creatures was one of the aspects of her personality which Malak loved dearly. Although she didn't possess his unusual ability, she loved them passionately.

"I want one," she moaned, her face set in a mock expression of discontent.

Malak grinned. "You've got no chance!"

"And why is that?" she demanded.

"Well, you know the legend…"

She raised her eyebrows, conveying that she didn't, and also that he was on dangerous ground.

"Well, you know, only the pure and innocent can approach them."

Lena frowned, and then realized the insult. Her arms tightened around his neck. "Do you want to live to see Ghalan?"

Malak grinned. "Only kidding! You can let go of my throat now."

"Only the pure and innocent can approach them, huh?"

"That's what Dahran said. And their eyes reveal the future. They can sense what will happen to you."

Lena released her husband and crawled forward towards the waterfall. She parted the last of the undergrowth and crept to the edge of the stream. The unicorn started and turned to face her, its exquisite eyes like liquid mirrors. Malak watched in fascination as Lena stretched out her hand, being careful to keep her eyes downcast. The creature shuffled nervously; it stared at her for a few seconds before splashing forward to nuzzle her hand.

Lena cried out in delight. "Malak, come down. She's accepted me, look."

Malak pushed his way toward them, moving slowly.

"Don't you startle her, now," Lena warned. "And keep your eyes down. It's dangerous to look into their eyes."

The unicorn watched carefully as Malak approached, but didn't flinch when he reached out his hand to stroke its head.

"He's beautiful," he said, knowing the words to be an understatement even as he said them.

The unicorn reached forward to nuzzle his forehead and Malak moved back in surprise.

"Malak, don't look into her..."

Time shuddered to a standstill as his gaze locked with the unicorn's. For a moment it was as if he was the unicorn, gazing at a young man as yet untainted by the trials of life, and then came the images, so quick and terrible he could hardly register them, yet they seemed to last an eternity. He screamed and fell back in slow motion. A single image was left burned into his mind, and it horrified him. He saw himself as he would be: twisted and warped, destroyed by evil. With terrible certainty, he knew that the appalling fate was almost unavoidable: the events were already in place.

The unicorn reared up before him, attacking him with its front legs. Malak gasped as he saw the fear in its eyes. He protected his head with his arms as he fell back. When he hit the ground, time reverted to normal and he saw the unicorn gallop off.

"Malak! Malak! What happened?" Lena shouted as she pried his arms from his face.

Malak was almost too shocked to speak. He stared at his wife in bewilderment. "I think it took a dislike to me."

"That's impossible! All animals like you!"

Malak shook his head. "It is not me that it fears, but my future self. Something terrible is going to happen."

Lena opened her mouth to argue, and then stopped as she saw the haunted look in her husband's eyes. She saw there a shadow of what he had experienced, and it terrified her. The two lovers stared at each, daunted by a ghastly foreboding.

Pleasure is the disease. Pain is the cure.
—Doctrine of the Black School

Discipline is the education of the soul.
—Doctrine of the Yellow School

Enya
Wilderness Region
Black School
subterranean lair

The three senior Black Adepts sat facing each other in lotus posture, heads bowed and eyes closed. Other than the slow, rhythmic sound of synchronized breathing, nothing broke the tranquillity of the underground chamber. The cold blue light of the filtered oil lamp was constant, and their bodies were absolutely motionless. Time stood still; even the air seemed dormant.

Felmarr was shocked when Dethen spoke, but he didn't alter his position. It would be inappropriate to do so before his Master.

"Leave us, Old One."

As always, the Black Master's tone was neutral and unemotional, yet conveyed an incontestable authority.

Bal rose smoothly from his position, with only a slight creak of joints. As he walked toward the door, Dethen spoke again.

"Guard the entrance. Allow no one to enter."

"Yes, Master." Bal's tone was unquestioningly obedient.

The heavy, lead-lined door closed with a resounding crack.

Dethen was silent once Bal had gone, and Felmarr wondered what was about to occur. He felt a surge of egoism: he knew that more than any other Adept in the Order he had the trust of the Master. If Dethen had something to say, it had to be very important indeed, because Bal was fanatically loyal to his Master. Indeed, he was actually Dethen's genetic father. Upon his impending death in his last incarnation, Dethen had given instructions to Bal to copulate with a slave girl at a specific time after his demise.

In this way, Dethen had chosen favourable astrological aspects for his birth. He had also informed Bal of how he should be raised as a child, to facilitate maximum physical strength and complete return of past-life memories and thus his identity. Bal had performed his appointed task well, and had gained from Dethen one thing he gave in extremely sparse amounts: respect.

In the same manner, Dethen had facilitated Felmarr's own rebirth into the Order. In his previous life, he had been Dethen's apprentice, and the Master had reclaimed him in the present one. Though he had yet to retain full memories of his past life, he was at least partially aware of his identity. At twenty years of age, he still had several years of development before him.

His appearance was closer to thirty years, however. His face was quite boyish, yet the suffering and experience on it aged him considerably. His skin was dark, and his eyes were brown, the gaze intelligent and severe. In every way, he tried to emulate his Master, in whom he saw no imperfection.

"It is an important time for us," Dethen finally said. "The restrictions have been removed, and our Purpose is now in sight."

Felmarr heard a rustle of material as Dethen lifted his head. Felmarr followed suit, and opened his eyes to hold the Black Master's gaze. This was something that had taken many years to accomplish. Dethen's eyes drew him in, like a steel web snaring an insect. The knowledge and experience behind the black stare terrified Felmarr, yet he held it with awe: he craved that wisdom.

"Ghalan?" he asked uncertainly; he knew of the journey his Master had recently completed.

Dethen nodded. "Ghalan has transcended to the Godhead. His protective influence on Enya is already dwindling, and the Boundary is weakening. Without his presence, the barriers to physical magick are collapsing."

"I don't understand, Master. Ghalan is the Magus. How can he leave, and how can Enya survive without him?"

He felt himself being drawn into Dethen's eyes; the chamber slid back and forth in his peripheral vision. He fought to retain consciousness—he would not disappoint the Master. Dethen's eyes were black holes that drew in all and from which nothing ever escaped. Rarely did he lower his guard, even when alone with his apprentice.

"Ghalan has risen to the First Glory, and his place must now be filled by another."

"I believed the Magus to be immortal," Felmarr said, confused; it was everyday knowledge that Ghalan had reigned on Enya for two thousand years.

Dethen smiled humourlessly. "That he was, yet his allotted time is over. It was once well known that a Magus rules for only two millennia, yet the fact is not now known even by Adepts. But ignorance does not alter reality, and the time of a Magus is limited.

"A Magus heralds the beginning of a new Aeon, and there have been two of these on Enya. The first Magus was of the White School, and his power gave shape to Enya. Hence, it was known as the Aeon of Creation. He formed the plane according to the lower plane of Malkuth, casting its structure out of the plastic material of the astral. As you know, without a Magus present, the plane will gradually disintegrate into the materials which form it.

"The present time is the Aeon of Dreams, presided over by Ghalan."

Felmarr bowed his head in thought, assimilating the new information. In personal terms it affected him little—he would simply continue to obey his Master to the utmost of his ability.

"Then who shall be the next Magus?"

"Only my karmic brother and I are eligible. One of us must pass the Trial of the Abyss."

"Then you shall be the next Magus!" Felmarr declared with conviction. "Malak is weak and naïve. He is only a boy!"

Dethen sighed. "My path has not crossed with Malak's for three lifetimes, and whereas my power has increased tenfold, he has yet to retain that which he once possessed. The battle will not be fair on him. He is young, barely a man. Once we were twins, but in this life he is ten years my junior."

"Malak will fight you for the Seat of Magus?"

"Perhaps. I think maybe he will not bother us. He is content in his gullible paradise." Dethen's voice was bitter. "I have no wish to harm my brother: remember that he was once one of us, a Black Adept, and may be again. But if he opposes me…"

Felmarr winced involuntarily at the menace in Dethen's voice.

"He will not stand a chance, Master! No one can stand against you!"

Dethen bowed his head and closed his eyes. For a fearful moment,

Felmarr thought he had been offended. But the Black Master was in deep thought: it seemed that he was mentally wrestling with something. Some minutes later, he spoke again.

"I fear no man, Felmarr."

Felmarr frowned, uncertain of the conversation's change of direction.

"This is well known, Master. Yet you are feared by all."

Dethen nodded and his face twisted into a spiteful leer against himself.

"To become Magus, one has to cross the Abyss. In the Trial of the Abyss, an Adept must pass Chronzon, the Dark One."

Felmarr shuffled uneasily at the name, then silently cursed himself for lack of control. When he replied, his voice was almost a whisper.

"Is it not our Purpose to defeat the Dark One?"

"No," snapped Dethen, "it is our Purpose to destroy the Demon utterly! His Power is terrible, and His evil beyond measure. He exploits an Adept's weaknesses and turns him against himself."

Felmarr's eyes widened as he recognized fear in his Master's voice. The revelation shook him to the core: he could not envisage a power capable of doing this. But he knew that Dethen's will was indomitable and his faith in him was absolute.

"You shall defeat Him, Master."

Felmarr's tone was annoyingly confident. Dethen was aware of the opinion his apprentice had of him, and did not approve: his goal was not to be respected or worshipped. The opinions of others were irrelevant.

"Do you not realize that no one is perfect? Everyone has weaknesses and complexes to overcome. It is transcending these limitations that matters. Strength is the goal. Only with strength will I become Magus, and only as Magus can I achieve the Purpose!"

"Yet you have no fears or weaknesses, Master!"

Dethen smiled bitterly at his apprentice's naiveté. His eyes clouded in remembrance of his harrowing past.

"No I haven't," he said. "Only the Dark One…"

⮐⬥⬥⬥⮑

Seth stood impatiently as his hands were tightly bound behind his back. His eyes were fiery with battle lust as he prepared for his ordeal.

For two years he had pitted himself against the best fighters on the plane, and he had survived. Now he would receive his prize: graduation into the Black Guard, the most elite fighting force ever to exist on the plane. He simply had to pass the initiation test to reach his goal, and then the glory would be his, with luxuries undreamed of.

Before him was the passage that would take him forward to his glory. He tingled with excitement.

He frowned uncertainly as Roruch started to tie a blindfold across his eyes, but submitted as he felt the captain's iron grip on his shoulder. Although he had little idea of what challenges lay ahead, he had not expected to be blind.

Still, he was sure that the test would not be too severe: his skill and strength would see him through. The one thing he knew was that he was expected to fight in single combat, and he had chosen to fight unarmed. He was sure that he could not possibly lose this: he knew that he was strong enough to match many of the Black Guard even now.

When Roruch had finished tying the blindfold, Seth felt him move around to stand before him. He knew that the captain was studying him.

Look and weep, he thought with satisfaction. He said nothing however—Roruch was one man whom he would not wish to anger. The heavily built captain had an intimidating presence. His head was shaved bare, and a four-inch knife scar stretched over the top. His face was hard and experienced, and one eye was covered by an eye-patch, having been gouged out many years ago.

"You are ready?" Roruch asked gruffly.

"Aye."

There was an impatient arrogance in Seth's tone, but Roruch ignored it. He had received the same manner from every candidate who had walked this path. It was satisfying to know that the great majority of them were now dead. He wondered briefly whether this one would survive. Seth was very strong in mind and body, but he knew that survival was still unlikely. The elite label applied to the Black Guard was not an unjustified one.

"If you are ready, then I will explain the only rule of the test," he said. "It is quite simple. Do not yield. Survive the test without yielding and you pass. Understand?"

"You mean that's it? There are no other rules?"

"Do not leave the Circle of Blood, or your life is forfeit. We do not expect cowardice from Black Guard candidates. This is clear?"

"Aye," Seth growled, unhappy that his courage was in any way being questioned: he feared nothing.

He heard footsteps approaching from the direction of the initiation chamber, and then a voice he didn't recognize.

"The Master is ready, captain."

"Then the initiation shall begin."

Seth was led along the passage. As he walked he became conscious of the choking, martial smell of unrefined tobacco. It intensified as they walked, burning his trachea as it entered his lungs.

He was dimly aware of passing through an entrance, and the atmosphere suddenly changed. There was power here, dark and forbidding. Death tainted every molecule of the air. Fear was present, but also bravery.

Seth was pushed forward; a stone doorway crashed shut behind him. He was within some kind of enclosed chamber. From the brightness entering his closed eyelids, he knew the room was well lit. The smell of tobacco was so strong he had to fight the urge to gag.

Heat washed briefly over him as he was led forward; it seemed part of the floor was on fire. Tension gripped the atmosphere and his skin crawled. He was sure that he was being intensely observed by something fearful, something more than human. After a few more steps, Roruch's grip on his shoulder indicated he should kneel. The gesture of humility did not come easily to him, but he didn't try to resist.

Although he could hear no physical sounds, the chamber had a subtle frequency that pressed in on him like a suffocating sheet. Adrenaline surged through him as he fought against it. He also fought his own rogue emotions. Eventually the painful, limbo-like state was broken by a voice.

"Unbind the prisoner."

The voice was deep and harsh, devoid of emotion and yet sinister in a subtle, daunting way.

Cold steel touched against his wrists before the knife freed his hands. He flexed them to return his circulation. Roruch removed the blindfold and retreated from the area. Seth blinked rapidly against the light.

He was in a pentagonal chamber. The walls were each decorated with a creature: an ox, a lion, an eagle and a man. The final wall was inscribed with a white circle, dissected by eight spokes. In each of the five corners was placed an incense burner, and these were the source of the throat-rending tobacco smoke. A single shelf ran around the perimeter of the chamber, and upon this were over a hundred human skulls. They were equally spaced and meticulously clean, and seemed to be trophies. He swallowed hard as he realized the fate of his head should he fail the initiation.

The majority of the space in the chamber was usurped by a large circle, traced in blood on the stone floor. This was where Seth found himself kneeling. Seventy-two black candles were studded around the perimeter of the circle. Behind him, outside the circle, Roruch was sitting cross-legged and facing away from him.

Seth's eyes widened at the sight directly before him. Seated on a bare, undecorated stone throne was a huge man dressed in black robes. His gaze was black, darker than anything Seth had seen. It bored through his body and soul as if they were insubstantial. He couldn't hold the gaze for a second without flinching. This man wasn't simply putting forward an impression of power: he truly possessed it. He was not concerned with the perceptions others had of him.

Although he had never before seen him, Seth was sure that he knelt before the Master of the Black School. Seated at Dethen's feet was an old man, also robed in black and possessing a piercing gaze. To either side of him sat three more Adepts, all hooded and masked. Ripples of dark power emanating from the group flowed through the chamber. Seth wondered where the final Adept was: though he had paid little attention, he was sure that there was supposed to be nine.

"You are here to seek initiation into the Black Guard, the defenders of the mighty Black School of Magick," Dethen intoned. "As you know, you cannot fail the initiation and survive. A rebirth of some description is therefore inevitable: your old self will die."

Seth knelt, silently listening to the Master's words. He could feel an uncomfortable tension in his solar plexus every time he was spoken to, and he was torn between fear and anger. Dethen's gaze conveyed the insignificance with which he viewed the candidate, and it was more than Seth's ego could take. It enflamed him with wrath toward the Adept on the throne and the servants at his feet. He would show them when combat commenced.

"The purpose of this initiation is for your benefit," Dethen continued. "It is to show you the meaning of true power. You have battled against many opponents in your journey to this moment. But you must now learn your own limitations, and learn respect for those who will command you."

Seth sneered to himself: he could have no respect for the Adepts who hid behind the might of the Black Guard, commanding them as if they were strong themselves. He remembered with anger the Adept who trained the soldiers, a man whom the Black Guard treated with awe and great respect. The thought sickened him: he had seen nothing impressive from the young Adept. He realized that the Adept was not one of those seated before the Master.

Dethen spoke again, and it seemed as though the Black Master had read his mind: "To persuade you of the ability of your masters, I give you the chance to pit your skills against Frater Felmarr, who I'm sure you are acquainted with."

He made a gesture with his hand, and Seth almost fell over as the kneeling form of Felmarr materialized six feet in front of him. He instantly recognized him to be the Adept who trained the Black Guard. He also realized that the Adept had been kneeling there all the time, and had somehow concealed himself. He had heard tales of the Adepts' ability to play mind-tricks, and work acts of sorcery. He also knew that only a powerful Adept could perform such feats.

Felmarr flowed to his feet like water, his movements smooth and purposeful. Realizing his intention, Seth also rose and began to circle around his opponent. He blocked out all external stimuli, concentrating solely on the Adept before him. Felmarr's eyes were a deep brown, his gaze steady and unnerving. Seth thought he could see the slightest flicker of the Master's strength within them.

From the Adept's movements, Seth realized that he had been wrong in his assumption: there was no doubt that Felmarr was a fighter. It could be read in the poise of his physique, and the perfect concentration on his face. He was a different kind of fighter than Seth had met before; there was no trace of aggression to be seen.

Seth slid into a flexible stance, shifting slightly more of his weight onto his back leg, and raised his arms to form a guard. Although he didn't expect much trouble, he didn't want to underestimate his opponent by leaving himself open to attack. He feinted a couple of times with his hands, but Felmarr didn't react. He simply continued to circle his opponent slowly, his hands by his sides and his feet in natural stance.

For over a minute the opponents psyched each other out, and Seth became extremely anxious. He was not used to waiting in a combat situation: battles usually lasted for a few seconds, until a telling blow landed and the affair was ended. Felmarr's gaze greatly unnerved him—his mind became groggy after holding it for more than a few seconds.

Mind tricks! Let's see how you handle a real battle, Seth thought.

He lunged forward with a vicious hook punch. Even though he moved at full speed, Felmarr slid fluidly under the movement and behind him. Seth realized his mistake in over-committing the technique, but the Adept did not attack from behind. Felmarr allowed him the split second necessary to regain balance and spin around.

The slow circling recommenced. Seth noticed that Felmarr's look was in no way patronizing, nor was there any hint of satisfaction at the minor humiliation. He had to admit that the Adept had surprised him, but he was still not too concerned; although he was very sharp, Felmarr's build was too small to do significant damage to a man of Seth's size.

He could feel the stern, judgmental gaze of the observing Adepts, and it infuriated him.

How dare they judge me!

He feinted, and immediately followed through with a powerful front kick, aimed at his opponent's solar plexus. A split second later, he followed the kick in with a double punching combination.

Felmarr moved with incredible speed, slipping to the side of the kick and hooking his arm underneath to catch it. His head slid to the side of the first punch. He caught the second with a forceful grip. Before Seth could react, Felmarr moved his leg behind his opponent's supporting leg and slammed him to the ground.

He flowed smoothly out of range as his challenger struggled breathlessly to his feet. Seth was shocked. He had not believed that such a combination of speed and power was possible. The Adept seemed ready to counter almost before the attack was launched. It was also becoming obvious that Felmarr was playing with him— twice he had passed by the opportunity to end the confrontation.

As he found his feet again, he noticed a glance pass between Dethen and Felmarr. Dethen gave a brief nod, which Felmarr returned in understanding. Seth was suddenly aware that playtime was over. He would now be fighting for his life.

He lunged forward, his body forming the *kiash* of a roundhouse kick. The movement proceeded no further. Felmarr skipped forward to catch him with a side kick under the jaw. The chamber reverberated with the thunder of his *kiai*, as every muscle of his body focused into the technique. Seth's jaw instantly shattered. The power of the kick blasted him backward, causing him to flip in the air and land heavily on his front.

His vision failed. He desperately struggled to cling to consciousness. The pain flowing through his jaw, head, and the top of his spine was immense. He knew that the technique had almost broken his neck.

A thick river of blood ran through his mouth, and he could feel several dislodged teeth. He could not spit them out. The mere thought of moving his jaw horrified him. It hung open, all muscle control lost. His head felt as if it would explode. An incredible pressure pushed in upon him and he could hear phantom voices shouting abuse.

Seth wanted nothing more than to collapse, but this would be to yield and his life would end. He fought to regain his vision, which manifested as sparkling lights. It then came into focus as red and blue pin-points of a surreal reality. Not feeling in control of his body, he slowly pushed himself to his feet. His mind had almost failed him, and he was now functioning purely on reflexes.

He vaguely distinguished the figure of Felmarr only a few feet away, and he threw himself forward to attack. There was a sickening crunch as the Adept's palm hand struck him in the chest, breaking his sternum. His lungs collapsed and his heart ceased its rhythmic beating as his organs absorbed the impact of the blow. He wasn't aware of falling, but the ground hit him hard a second later.

He writhed in excruciating pain, unaware of everything now except the agony, and the pressing need to breathe. He considered rising, but quickly rejected the idea because he knew that he was on the verge of death. The action would only bring more punishment. He whimpered quietly as pain racked his body, his heart still beating erratically.

Felmarr stood over Seth's body, watching as he coughed blood and bile onto the stone floor. As usual, he felt a dark satisfaction at his triumph. He enjoyed cutting the arrogant down to size. Seth would not rise again—the fight had been taken out of him. He smiled at the irony of the situation: if he had risen once more, Dethen would certainly have graduated him. It was mental strength, more importantly than physical, that the Black Guard sought.

Felmarr looked over to Dethen. The Black Master nodded soberly.

Seth felt a final flare of pain in his temple as Felmarr's knuckle drove the sphenoid of his skull into his brain. Then came a welcome release as the dark, velvet grasp of death seized him.

*In order to learn Truth, you must first
unlearn untruth.*

—Zen Maxim

What doesn't kill us, makes us stronger.
—Doctrine of the White School[1]

Enya
Lokhi Region
The Enchanted Forest

Lena reined Raven to a halt and patted the back of his neck
with satisfaction. She lovingly stroked his black glossy coat
as she waited for Malak to catch up.

Raven was a huge, hot-tempered stallion. He had once been completely wild, but she had trained him. He was not tame, however.
He allowed no one other than Lena to mount him, and permitted
only Malak to approach him. His speed and power had never been
matched by any other horse, and Lena was sure that it never would
be. She had originally fallen in love with him due to his coat colour.

She turned as Malak pulled Gemma to a halt beside her. She
smiled and raised her eyebrows. Malak shook his head in mock
dismay.

"It's that damned horse," he pleaded, slumping forward to lean on
Gemma's neck.

"We could always swap horses, and try again…"

"You know he'll throw me off before I'm in the saddle!"

It was his own riding ability that worried him, rather than Raven's
reaction to him. He knew the stallion would accept him.

"Oh," said Lena, feigning surprise.

Malak smiled and scanned their environment. The forest was at
its most beautiful as spring slowly gave way to summer. Pink sun-
light filtered through the airy blue-green canopy, illuminating the

---

1 Quoted from Nietzsche

golden bark and evergreen undergrowth below. Malak inhaled deeply, then sighed in contentment. The air was thick with the sweet smell of dark orchids, which were scattered in clumps across the forest floor. Their deep purple hue was a pleasing contrast against the undergrowth.

"We're at the boundary to the inner forest," Lena said. "We've veered off course. Oaklan must be over there somewhere."

Malak followed the direction of her finger and nodded. Their brief chase through the undergrowth had pushed them well off the trail. The leaves of the trees before him were a slightly different shade than the ones behind. He knew that the leaves would gradually change to a blue-violet toward the centre of the woodland. The Enchanted Forest was avoided by Enyans, but Adepts knew that only the inner forest was sacred. Within this was the centre of the plane: the Rose Circle that formed a link between Enya and the other planes of existence. No one had trespassed onto its sacred soil for many centuries.

Lena felt the first sensations of rain on her face. Within a few seconds, the forest floor was bombarded with huge droplets, bouncing their way through the leaves. She threw back the hood of her robe and shook her long black hair free, enjoying the sensation as the rain cascaded down.

Malak silently watched her. He had been with Lena since their early childhood, when they had both been raised by her father, Dahran. They were undoubtedly soul mates: they were now enjoying their third incarnation together. They had first met when Malak was son to Ghalan, over two thousand years ago. To Malak, Lena was such a creature of joy and beauty. She possessed all the best qualities of a child, but none of the worst. Though often stubborn, her heart was completely unselfish. Her elegance blended uniquely with her beauty and fiery determination.

Lena realized that he was watching her and smiled. As always, Malak could see that her feelings for him were identical, though she was more effective at concealing them when necessary. She shook her wet hair and rearranged it more comfortably. The short shower was now abating.

"We should go. It will soon be dusk," he said.

Lena nodded. "We should reach Oaklan before then."

Malak nudged Gemma gently forward, and Raven fell in behind, snorting at the insult of having to follow a mare.

As the couple reached Oaklan Village, the deep amethyst sky was darkening. The air was filled with bird song, and the nocturnal grey squirrels were stirring from their languor. They skipped from tree to tree, pelting the magicians with nuts and acorns. Their mischievous laughter flitted back and forth through the treetops as they played games of bravery, approaching as close to the humans as they dared.

The games abruptly ended when one squirrel strayed too close. Malak slung an acorn into the trees, knocking a rodent from the tree branch it clung to. It gave a yelp of surprise, but caught itself on a lower branch as it fell. The strange laughter abruptly ceased and a score of squirrels suddenly disappeared.

Malak laughed good-humouredly. "They'll think twice next time."

Oaklan was relatively small, but had existed for centuries. Malak fancied that he had an impression of it from a past life, but as always the recollection was very hazy for him.

There were a dozen houses scattered loosely around a beautiful copper plated well, which was studded with semi-precious stones. The houses were single story, large and spacious. The designs were elegant and pleasing to the eye. Many were as old as the village, yet they were all well maintained.

The magicians guided their mounts to the largest house, near to the well. Outside was a post, especially placed for visitors' horses.

Strangely, there were no people around: the village seemed deserted.

"You know, I don't understand why Dahran wanted us to come here," Malak said. "When I told him of my dream, he was adamant that I reach Ghalan as quickly as possible. This will cost us even more time."

"Hmm. My father has been acting strangely since you told him of the dream. He acts as if he thinks it is the end of the world or something," Lena said.

"Dahran doesn't need a reason to act strange. He does that well enough already."

"Malak! You're just irritated because he drives you so hard in your training."

"Hard? He drives me to exhaustion, and then has the cheek to call me lazy! Anyway, I still think it's strange that he wanted us to stop off here."

"I think it must have something to do with Jeshua. He wants us to see Jeshua again."

"Huh. Now there's another strange one. That old man makes me uneasy. I wonder why he wants us to see him."

Lena shrugged. "Come on, we'll soon find out."

In front of the Adepts, the tip of the sun bowed from sight behind the horizon-line of trees. Behind them, the huge waning disc of the moon was now visible, its sheer size intimidating. They dismounted and tethered their horses.

Jeshua's front door was open, though this was not unusual in Oaklan. There was still no sign of life, however. Lena looked at her husband and frowned.

"The setting sun," he whispered, pointing to the west.

The muffled sound of chanted prayer drifted through the doorway. They waited for a few minutes until the sound trailed away. Malak rapped on the door frame. Within a few seconds an extremely venerable, but sprightly man appeared in the doorway. His eyes were a sharp blue, full of dry humour; there was a surreptitious but profound wisdom locked in their depths. His head was bald with the barest remains of white hair.

"Hello, Jeshua. How are you?"

"Lena!" The old man took Lena's hand and kissed it. "Ah, as pretty as ever, I see!"

He grinned as Lena rolled her eyes to the sky. "And still hates for it to be mentioned, I see. I suppose you'd still rather be a warrior than an enchantress?"

He chuckled as he saw the light of desire appear in Lena's eyes.

"Aye, I thought as much," he said. "And Malak," Jeshua said, his tone more formal and more lacking in affection, "are you well?"

"Quite well, Jeshua, quite well," Malak said, shaking the old man's outstretched hand.

"Well, come on in, both of you. You must be exhausted!"

Jeshua took their travelling cloaks from them. "Tara! We have guests!"

A girl of about seventeen appeared. Her face broke into a shy smile as she recognized the magi. Tara was moderately pretty, with long blond hair and a round, slightly plump face. Malak remembered her as Jeshua's great great granddaughter.

Tara bashfully took the travelling cloaks from Jeshua and left the room to stow them away. Her gaze lingered on Malak before she disappeared through the doorway.

"Anyway, I'm sure you're both hungry after your journey through the forest," Jeshua said. "I hope that you'll both join us for supper."

"We'd love to," Lena said.

Jeshua nodded appreciatively. "But first I'm sure you'd like to bathe. It must be two days since the last village, and those robes are soaked through. I'll get Tara to prepare a hot bath."

<hr />

The atmosphere was tense in the small dining room after the group finished their meal. Jeshua sat on one side of the table, Malak and Lena on the other. Scanning the beautifully sculptured oaken table, Malak noticed that there was no meat on it and that the goblets contained water, rather than the traditional wine. He realized that Jeshua had arranged this: the old man had once been an Adept at the Celestial Tower and was familiar with the restrictions placed upon White Adepts.

Jeshua raised his goblet. "I would like to propose a toast to two of the Guardians of Enya, Lord Malak and Lady Lena!"

Malak exchanged an embarrassed glance with his wife, uncertain whether he had detected sarcasm in the old man's voice. Though they received such treatment in other villages, he had not expected it in Oaklan. He was apprehensive about Jeshua's sincerity. Self-consciously, he followed Lena's lead and joined the toast.

There was an uncomfortable silence for a few moments before Malak spoke. "Jeshua, don't you miss your days as an Adept at the Tower?"

The old man smiled at him, a gesture that was not entirely friendly. "My dear Malak, forgive the cliché, but I miss the White School like a hole in the head."

Malak frowned, taken aback by the answer. "You no longer believe in the philosophy of the School?"

"Theory and practice are two very different concepts. Just because I love the philosophy behind the School, it does not mean I love the School itself."

"You think the School has betrayed its principles?" Lena asked as she slowly buttered a slice of bread.

Malak noticed that Tara followed the conversation very carefully as she ate.

"What would you say differentiates the Three Schools of Magick?" Jeshua asked.

"You know of the Black School?" Malak was surprised. "The White Council doesn't even acknowledge its existence. They recognize only the White and Yellow Schools."

Jeshua's eyes glittered with dark amusement. "I know far more than you would give me credit for, Malak. About many things. But come now, answer the question. Would you say that the Schools vary in the magical techniques they employ?"

"The magical techniques are essentially the same. The Schools only vary in their approach and their underlying philosophy," Malak said.

"Ah. Interesting. I'm pleased that you see that."

"But the Schools would differ in the techniques they were prepared to use," Lena said. "The Black School would use any means to achieve an objective, whereas the White School would never knowingly harm anything."

"And the Yellow School doesn't have objectives," Malak interjected, half in jest.

Jeshua smiled thinly. "So what do you consider the purposes of the Three Schools to be? What are their objectives?"

"The Yellow School has no objectives, as far as we are aware," Lena said. "Their whole philosophy is based on non-interference with the universe. Since they consider themselves a part of the universe, they do not believe they can affect it. Free will is an illusion to them. They seek to gain all knowledge of the universe by crossing the Abyss."

"And the Black School considers free will to be real, but views life as the ultimate practical joke, designed by a cruel and malicious creator. Their Purpose is to destroy the manifest universe, destroying the Life Cycle and the prison of reincarnation, which they seek to escape at all costs," Malak said.

Jeshua nodded. "A fairly good description. Now what of the White School?"

Malak shrugged. "The White School is the only one which has contact with the people, which it is sworn to protect and to offer guidance to. The philosophy takes a delight in the joy and variety of life, welcoming problems as challenges rather grieving about them. Each individual Adept seeks growth and expansion of consciousness. The ultimate goal is to cross the Abyss, becoming one with All That Is."

"And do you think that the White School lives up to these dignified and lofty ideals?" Jeshua asked.

"Of course," said Lena.

The old man raised his eyebrows. "You can see Iysa and the rest of the White Council taking a joy in life? Both of you are on the Council, and you must know the others well. You can see them casting aside their politics and valiantly battling for the common people of Enya, laying their lives down if necessary?"

"Well…" Malak looked at Lena. "I guess that's difficult to imagine. But the role of the School has changed in this Aeon. In the first Aeon the White School ruled, and the Magus protected the plane and people. But now it is the Aeon of Dreams: the Yellow School rules and there is no need for our protection. Besides, there is nothing to defend them from on Enya. It is the plane of dreams, after all."

"Really? Nothing to defend from, eh? And what about your karmic brother Dethen? You consider him to be harmless?"

An uncomfortable silence washed over the table. Malak glanced at his wife, who was always distressed when Dethen's name was mentioned: she loathed him vehemently, and rarely suffered even his name to be spoken.

"Well?" said Jeshua.

Lena's face was stoic, her eyes hard. It was obvious she was anxious, yet Jeshua seemed determined to press the point. Not for the first time, Malak felt a growing annoyance with the old man.

"Dethen could not do any real damage because of the Magus," he said. "Ghalan's influences protects us all."

"And Malak's brother cannot control himself, never mind anything else," Lena said, her voice quiet and carefully controlled. "He is wildly emotional, and that will always be his weakness. He has no discipline, no self control."

"No self control?" Jeshua's voice was almost goading. "It had been three lifetimes since either of you have even laid eyes on Dethen. I think, perhaps, he may have changed since then." He leaned forward, his eyes intense. "Perhaps he had changed a great deal."

Lena glared at him, a fierce raking glare which always accompanied her mounting wrath. It was a look which could stop most people in mid-sentence, but Jeshua ignored it completely. Malak gripped her hand under the table, a reminder that she was a guest in Jeshua's house. He saw her jaw line harden as she controlled her fiery temper.

"It's true, Dethen could have changed a great deal," Malak conceded. "Now, may we conclude this discussion amicably and move onto a more pleasant subject of conversation?"

"Ah, so you admit that your brother is a potential threat," Jeshua said.

Malak's own temper began to fray now: he was not prepared to see Lena upset by anyone, no matter what status they had once held. "Yes, damn it! If you say so. But as I said, the Magus would prevent him from doing anything serious."

"And if the Magus was no longer with us?"

"This is stupidity!" Lena snapped. "The Magus is immortal!"

Jeshua sighed. "Dahran is right, you both have much to learn. But at least it's not entirely hopeless. I'm told that Iysa doesn't even believe in the Magus. She thinks it is a story for children." His tone was subdued and reflective.

"You patronize us," Malak growled.

Jeshua shook his head. "That is not my intention."

"Then what is your intention?" Lena demanded bitterly. "Why did my father ask us to come here? To be insulted? You may not know, but we are on a journey to see the Magus, even now."

"I know more of your mission than you do, Lena," Jeshua said. "And as for Dahran, you are aware that we have been friends for many years?"

"Yes, I know that. You were Master of the Council when my father was young."

"Master! Oh, no," Jeshua seemed surprised. "I was never Master of the Council. The competition was too good."

"Really?" Malak's interest had been piqued. "I thought you were. So who was it that foiled your ambitions?"

Jeshua smiled. "Well, it was you of course. In your last incarnation, you were Master of the Council. And in the one before that. But don't worry, you didn't foil my ambitions. I was quite willing to follow you, and so was everyone else."

Malak frowned. "I have vague memories of being on the Council in my last life, but I didn't know that I had been Master."

"You do not remember? That is a shame. I remember you and your wife very well. You were married even then, of course."

"So, in your current life, you knew me in my past incarnation?" Malak asked. Though he remembered very little of his past lives, Malak knew that he had been born approximately fifty years after his last death.

"That's right. I am even older than I look, you know."

"What was he like?" Lena asked, her temper now back in check.

Jeshua leaned back and stretched; a smile played across his face as he cast his mind back. When he spoke, there was fondness in his tone. "You were an extremely powerful and intimidating figure, and yet you were full of serenity and compassion. You were very different in those days."

"But I'm still me!" Malak protested.

"You still have half of those qualities. I don't doubt the merit of your compassion. But you are lacking in strength. You are a boy who thinks he is a man."

Malak felt an incredibly strong urge inside him, pulling him away from the table. He stood up sharply, feeling physically sick.

"Excuse me, I must go."

He lurched away from the table and out of the room. Jeshua followed him with a level, unflinching gaze.

"I must go after him," Lena said worriedly. She stood up.

"I'm sorry, Lena. Your father and I agreed that it was necessary. He must be awakened to himself," Jeshua said.

Lena stared in disbelief. "You did this to him?"

"It is why Dahran sent you here. He must regain the strength he once had."

She scowled. "Excuse me," she spat sharply.

———◦◦◦◦◦———

Malak burst through the doorway into the hall. In the dark, he rummaged furiously through his saddlebags and equipment. Within a few seconds he found the source of his desire. *Retaliator* hummed voraciously, pulsing with a deep, intense throb. Her rhythm perfectly matched his heartbeat. The azure light of the star-sapphire illuminated the hallway.

Memories from previous decades flowed back to Malak. They came so quickly he was barely able to register them. They were recollections of himself, yet he felt stronger and more purposeful, far exceeding the limits he thought he now had. Yet his other self was tantalizingly beyond reach: as always, a person he always strove to become, but never lived up to. Too much was expected of him!

Retaliator was attempting to communicate with him, an event that had never before occurred in his present life. She was impressing images of his brother upon him. He saw that Dethen was preparing to unleash havoc upon Enya. His twin had strengthened himself to an unassailable status, and was preparing to strike.

Malak struggled to digest the knowledge. Dazed, he wondered how *Retaliator* could know such information. He suddenly remembered, that like himself and Dethen, *Retaliator* and *Widowmaker* were irrevocably linked. Just as Malak and Dethen were once twin sons to Ghalan, the swords were twins that had been forged by the Magus.

A patch of darkness across the room suddenly moved. Malak spun around in shock, *Retaliator* upraised. He relaxed as he recognized the hard green gaze of his familiar.

Bast was like a long-haired panther, with a powerfully muscled feline body and silver-white whiskers. Her eyes were twin pieces of jade; they contained an incomprehensible and alien intelligence. Though he hadn't seen the familiar since entering the forest, she was never far from him. Their unusual relationship was induced by Malak's natural empathy for creatures, both natural and supernatural. Bast had accompanied him through all three of his incarnations on Enya.

As he stared into her eyes, he could see there an accusation. Though he knew it to be an illusion, she seemed to be mocking his physical and mental weakness. His mind spun uncontrollably from the effects of the drug. He shook his head and looked at her again. She seemed to be talking to him, directly through his mind.

The time is near…The time is near…

Fear coursed through his veins. He whirled around to leave the hallway. Behind him, Lena was just entering the room.

"What's wrong, Malak? Are you all right?"

Her voice was full of concern, but she stopped dead as she saw the naked blade of *Retaliator*. Malak lowered the weapon. Though he was groggy, he was lucid enough to remember his wife's phobia of swords.

"Are you all right?" she repeated. She took hold of his arm and tried to make eye contact.

He dizzily shook his head. "I must go and strengthen myself. Already it is too late!"

"But you are strong. What's wrong?! What has Jeshua done to you?"

"Guardians of Enya! What a farce! The White School couldn't even defend itself! I must go before my brother comes. He will destroy us all!"

"Malak, you're scaring me!"

"The time is near…"

"What?!"

"I must go."

He moved to leave, but she wouldn't release her grip.

"Stay with me, Malak. Please, you're scaring me!"

He shook her off and strode for the door, mumbling incoherently about Dethen.

Lena stared in dismay as he strode from the house, heading for the depths of the forest. She looked at Bast, who watched her master with curiosity.

"Follow him," Lena said. "And keep him out of trouble."

The familiar tilted her head to one side, and then loped through the door after her master.

The contacts of matter, O son of Kunti, giving heat and cold, pleasure and pain—they come and go; they are impermanent. Endure them bravely.

—Bhagavad Gita II:14

Taking as equal both pleasure and pain, gain and loss, victory and defeat, gird thee for the battle.

—Bhagavad Gita II:38

Enya
Thenyan Region
The Celestial Tower

As he fell, Dahran awoke with a start. Confused, he struggled against a gripping paralysis. The harder he fought the more strongly he was bound, and gradually he realized he was experiencing astral whiplash. He deepened his breathing and slowed his pulse. Little by little his muscles subdued to his will.

The memory of his astral experience returned as he lay motionless. With it came the unwelcome knowledge he had learned.

Soon he would die. There could be no mistake: his prophecies never failed.

He felt no fear. For years he had lived as an empty shell, mourning the death of his wife. But a terrible foreboding had settled upon him. Enya was in desperate peril: with his own death would come the death of countless thousands.

Normally he was conscious in dreams, but this one had occurred deep within his unconscious mind. The dream had no tangible forms to grasp but the emotions had left a deep impression. It had not been a whimsical dream: it had been purposefully sent to him. He had been intentionally drawn deep into the astral plane to receive important knowledge. And the knowledge burned within his mind like a venomous thorn.

He rose unsteadily, swinging his feet to the floor. His knees creaked as he stood up.

You're getting old, he thought.

This wasn't strictly true. His age of seventy-two wasn't unusual on Enya. His joints were plagued by arthritis from sixty years of martial arts, often performed with poor technique when young.

Stiffly, he walked over to the wash basin and looked in the mirror. A shock of white hair covered his head and an unruly beard concealed most of his face; his mouth was almost lost in the mass of hair. His eyebrows were thick and bushy, and a pale complexion completed the sloppy, dishevelled appearance. Only his eyes suggested he was not what he seemed. They were a vivid blue with a strong, unwavering gaze.

As he washed he tried in vain to force from his inner eye the image that plagued him. The figure was tall, dark and extremely sinister, the black eyes haunting. Dahran had been a fearsome warrior in youth, and was still greatly respected. But he could never compete with the dark, compelling power that flowed from Dethen.

He knew the image had not arisen spontaneously. Dethen posed an incalculable threat to the stability of Enya. Dahran feared for the safety of Lena and Malak. His daughter and her husband were distressingly close to the lair of the Black School, but were oblivious of the fact.

He wondered whether Jeshua had made a difference to Malak's psychology. The young Adept was strong and energetic, trustworthy and compassionate. But Malak was still only a shadow of his true self. Due to the interference of the White Council, his life thus far had been very sheltered.

This was no fault of his own, but time was short. Malak remembered Dethen as extremely influential but emotionally unbalanced. However, that had been three incarnations ago, when Malak had defeated his twin in a personal feud.

Dethen had had two lifetimes in which to perfect himself. And Dahran had seen the result. Dethen had more power than any man should be able to wield. Driven by a powerful but unknown motive, he sought to destroy the Tree of Life. And behind him he now had the Black School. Dahran doubted whether anyone could stop him.

When Malak's past life memories returned, the White Council would quake in fear. They had interfered with his life so much, they would be very disfavoured when he claimed his seat as Master of the Council. Yet how long would the change take to occur? Time was of the essence.

Dahran walked over to his chamber's single window. Far below,

the gentle waves of Mishmar Lake buffeted against the crystal causeway, which was the only approach to the Celestial Tower. In the
background were the misty blue-violet peaks of the Wyrmspine
Mountains. The closest of these formed the valley in which Mishmar
Lake resided.

The air outside shifted and flowed, slowly changing through the
colours of the spectrum. It seemed that the Tower was adjusting its
dimensional relationship to Enya. Dahran frowned. He knew this
to be unlikely. Suddenly he realized that it was the vibrational rate
of Enya that was changing. For some days he had been trying to convince the Council that the power of the Magus was waning. He had
been unsuccessful, but now he had proof.

He turned toward his wardrobe, his mind set on a new course
of action.

———————◦◉◦———————

Dahran leaned heavily on his staff at the bottom of the spiral staircase. He waited for the stabbing pain to subside from his joints
before walking on, not using his staff for balance. A vestige of pride
had survived through his old age.

He walked across the landing toward a set of heavy oak doors.
Inlaid upon the doors was a gold cross, the symbol of the Inner
Order. He frowned as he saw the single guard posted outside. He
straightened his back as he approached.

"Why are you guarding that door, neophyte?" he asked gruffly.

The guard looked uncomfortable. "I will have to ask you to leave,
Lord Dahran. I have orders from the Master of the Council to
admit no one."

"Have you indeed?"

Dahran's tone was caustic. The guard made a point of studying
his feet.

"And why is this?"

"There is an important meeting between the Council and one of
the Royal Families, Lord."

Dahran's eyes blazed with anger. "Stand aside, I need to see the
Council."

The neophyte shuffled uncertainly on his feet. "Lord, I was
instructed to use all means at my disposal to stop anyone entering,
and your name was specifically mentioned."

Dahran glared at him. "Young man, if you don't open this door immediately, I will use all means at my disposal to kick you across the length of the landing! I am the longest standing Council member, and I don't take kindly to meetings that I don't know about! Stand aside."

The neophyte snapped to attention. "Aye, Sir!"

He opened one of the doors. Dahran waited as he stepped inside and announced his presence.

A frigid female voice cut through the air: "I ordered no interruptions…"

"I'm sorry, Master, but Lord Dahran insisted…"

Dahran stepped into the room. He quickly scanned it, noting that all twelve Council members were present except himself, Malak and Lena.

Iysa stood up. "That will be all, guard. I shall speak with you later…"

"Yes, Master." The neophyte quickly backed out of the chamber.

Iysa was forty years old, yet looked barely thirty. She had a cold, heartless beauty with a pale complexion that was smooth but lifeless. When she spoke to Dahran her irritation was poorly concealed; her eyes were narrowed in displeasure.

"Lord Dahran, we did not wish to disturb you. Please, feel free to join our meeting. This is Princess Yahra of Gorom, our honoured guest."

Seated at the position of honour was a young lady. Her air of arrogance was instantly apparent. She looked to be barely twenty, with a girlish face and undeveloped figure. She wore a long azure dress, studded copiously with jewels and trimmed with platinum. It looked incredibly expensive, and utterly tasteless.

Seated next to her was a dark-skinned bodyguard with an oversized physique. He was dressed in ceremonial chain mail and had a mace bound to his belt. Dahran frowned as he saw this. It was highly unusual; even ceremonial weapons were a breach of conduct in most social gatherings. He doubted whether the guard would have any idea how to use the weapon: very few men possessed such knowledge.

Dahran gave the princess a brief nod and turned back to Iysa. He immediately felt the hostility emanating from the royal envoy. She had obviously expected more than a simple acknowledgment.

"Iysa, I need to address the Council. And in private." Dahran said, his eyes lingering on the princess; Yahra's eyes ignited with anger.

Though Iysa had had many disputes with Dahran, they had never yet had a full confrontation. She feared his fiery temper too much for that, as did the other Council members. Dahran avoided a full conflict because she had too much control of the Council, even if they were young charlatans, with no discipline or magical knowledge whatsoever.

But Iysa was unimpressed with the casual use of her name at an official function. Council members were traditionally addressed as "Lord" or "Lady", but Dahran had never been one for officialdom.

"I don't think this is the time for such an address," she said through clenched teeth. "The princess is an extremely important guest. I'm sure your information can wait."

Her eyes locked with Dahran's sharp blue gaze.

"No, damn it, it can't wait! I have information which the Council must consider!"

Iysa rolled her eyes to the ceiling. "I hope it's not another faerie story about the waning power of the Magus. We're all intelligent people here. We don't involve ourselves in myths turned out for the common masses."

Dahran turned livid with rage. "I was an Adept before you were born. How dare you patronize me! I'm telling you that Ghalan has transcended, and that the Black School is preparing to strike! Do you know nothing of the history of Enya?"

Iysa absorbed his outburst calmly, not wishing to appear uncontrolled in front of her guest.

"I'm afraid we don't indulge in fantasies about a Black School. There is no such thing. And as to the supposed leader, Dethen is a pathetic emotional wreck whom your precious Malak defeated centuries ago. He's probably still licking his wounds from the beating, if he hasn't incarnated on some other plane.

"And we don't involve ourselves in faerie tales about Aeons. The Magus is a myth for children. No one seriously believes such tales!"

Dahran's temper snapped. "Listen, you pompous bitch…"

"No, Lord Dahran, *you* listen to *me*!"

Dahran turned furiously to find Princess Yahra addressing him.

"My family has impeccable nobility, and has earned great respect over all of eastern Enya. How dare you insult me by asking me to leave! You will pay for this insult!"

"I know your family well," Dahran said quietly, but threateningly. "They achieved a position of power through blackmail, robbery and murder. And you, madam, are a trumped up, self-opinionated brat!"

Yahra's eyes grew wild with rage. A united gasp escaped from the seated Council as Dahran voiced his insult.

The princess nodded to her bodyguard; when she spoke, she emphasized every word: "Please remove Lord Dahran from the chamber."

The huge guard hesitated for a moment, and then stood up and started to move around the huge oaken table. Iysa didn't attempt to hide her smug satisfaction. Removing Dahran from the chamber by her own word was difficult: he was a full Council member and had a right to be there. But an outsider giving the instruction was different: Yahra was independent from the Council. As the guard approached Dahran ran his gaze across the seated Council with contempt.

"Do you really think this makes a difference? Do you think it changes anything? Observe. I will show you the effect of Ghalan's transcendence."

He raised his right hand. A blast of brilliant blue energy burst from it and a crack resonated through the chamber. The advancing guard was smashed across the room. He hit the far wall with a heavy thud and slumped to the floor, unconscious.

Dahran turned to face Iysa. "Now do you see? The buffers are gone, and there is now no barrier to magick. The havoc that Dethen can create is far greater than my humble abilities."

Chaos took control of the chamber as the entire Council erupted into an astonished babble. For a moment, it seemed Princess Yahra would faint.

Galaak shouted for silence, and as one, the Council turned to Iysa for guidance.

But Iysa was staring at the unconscious guard, her face blank. She was a politician, not a magician. She had no idea how to handle the situation. Magick was internal: you couldn't cause physical effects. She remembered the theory on the subject; you couldn't affect physical events because of the...because of the Magus. She bit her lip as she recalled the myth of the Magus. Or was it a myth? The room swayed in her vision as her belief system began to collapse.

"Iysa?" Dahran asked, his tone more gentle.

She stared at him in dismay. Her mouth opened, and then closed. She had nothing to say.

Valmaar rose from his seat at the huge conference table. As one of the oldest Council members, he was one of Dahran's few allies.

Valmaar's eyes were shocked, but his voice was steadfast. "Tell us, Dahran. What must we do?"

When you seek it, you cannot find it.
                                    —Zen Riddle

Enya
Lokhi Region
Oaklan Village

It was midday when Malak staggered into Jeshua's house. His robes were shredded and torn, his face cut and bruised. Congealed blood smeared his face and his knuckles were cracked and raw, perforated by splinters of wood.

Lena jumped up from her seat as he entered. She caught him as he fell forward, his legs too weak to hold his weight. She turned to Tara, who stood watching in bewilderment.

"Can you prepare a warm bath, please. And quickly."

"Yes, ma'am." The teenager rushed from the room, set on her errand.

Lena supported her husband as she guided him over to Jeshua's rocking chair. Although her physique seemed delicate, Lena was surprisingly strong. She gently lowered him into the chair.

"What happened, Malak?"

He looked at her wearily, and smiled at the concern in her voice. Her eyes were wide with alarm.

"It's all right. I had a few things to work out for myself."

She took his right hand and examined the lacerated knuckles. "You look like you've been in a war!"

"Only with myself. I didn't win, though."

"What happened to you last night? I was dying of worry! I had no idea where you were going, or whether you'd come back."

"That's a stupid thing to think. You know I would never leave like that. And I had Bast to look after me."

"You were acting strangely. You weren't yourself!"

He shook his head. "No. It was me all right. Jeshua altered my state of consciousness, but the knowledge I recalled had always been there. He just made it more accessible to me."

Lena's eyes flamed with anger. "He had no right! He knows that he's done wrong, because he's left the village. He should be ashamed!"

Malak took her hand. "He did what he thought was right. I understand Dahran's urgency now. Jeshua was trying to wake me up to myself."

"And he has a right to do that?!"

"He expects certain things of me due to my past."

"But you are the person you are now, Malak. Just as I am, and everyone else is."

He nodded. "I'm tired of trying to live up to their expectations, Lena. But I now understand my responsibility."

She kissed him tenderly. "We'll talk about it later. Let's see if that bath's ready yet."

———◦◦◦———

After dark, Malak and Lena lay together on the spare bed in Tara's room. Her mother, Jenny, had made the offer for them to stay after Jeshua's disappearance. She was uneasy with her husband being away, despite having two grown sons. She had commented that the forest felt uneasy the last few days.

The house was small compared to others in the village, with only one main room and two bedrooms. Tara did her utmost to convince the Adepts that she wasn't unhappy with the arrangement, but she was too self-conscious to be comfortable.

She was very wary of Bast, who dozed at the end of the Adepts' bed, ears tracking every movement in her sleep. Tara had decided that the least embarrassing course was to fake sleep, which she did poorly. However, it gave the couple some semblance of privacy.

Lena rolled onto her side and kissed her husband. "Are you sure you're all right?"

Malak nodded, but his gaze was distant.

"Hey," she said, prodding him, "stay with me."

He smiled and ran his finger over her lips.

"What exactly happened last night?" she asked. "I mean, when I found you with the…sword."

"I can't say. I'm not really sure."

"Please."

Malak thought for a moment. He knew that his wife would react badly if he told her what happened, but he had no wish to conceal anything from her.

"For the first time since Dahran returned *Retaliator* to me, I actually felt her communicate with me. It was as if she recognized me for the first time. She knew that I was her master. She recognized me as the Malak of old."

"What did you learn?" Lena's voice was quiet and pensive.

"I received a vision. No, more of a feeling, of Dethen. And the power that flowed from him was dreadful. He has grown immensely."

Lena was always uncomfortable when he mentioned his brother. There were only two things that she hated, but she loathed them vehemently: Dethen and swords.

"What do you remember of Dethen?" she asked.

Malak frowned at the unusual question. Dethen was always a subject which Lena avoided.

"To be honest, it's all very vague. As you know, my past life memories are very poor. I remember how Ghalan brought us up together, and how close we were as children. And I remember how dependent we were upon each other, before…"

"…before you met me," Lena finished.

"Yes. I understand him feeling betrayed, because I was the only one he trusted and you took me away from him. But I didn't mean for things to change. Anyway, Dethen had a very powerful personality, even if it was unbalanced. If you hadn't rescued me, we would have created the Black School together. Our beliefs were the same. He had me thinking much as he does, that the universe is an abomination, and beauty only illusory. "

He added: "That was before I met you. My world was turned upside down the moment I saw you."

Lena smiled in fond reminiscence. "Yes, I remember the meeting well."

"What do you remember of Dethen?" Malak asked.

"Nothing more than you," she said.

Malak turned his head and searched her eyes. She looked away. They both knew she had just lied to him. A link existed between the couple that was almost telepathic. They were able to read each other's emotions from a distance, and occasionally pick up each other's thoughts. It was the first time that Malak had ever known her to lie to him.

"I'm sorry," she said. "I'd rather not talk about it."

"It's okay," Malak said, but the hurt look remained in his eyes.

He lay flat on his back. Lena lay her head on his chest, wrapping her arms tightly around him, as if to stop him escaping.

"Malak, will you teach me a martial art?"

He rolled his eyes to the ceiling: it was an old question.

"Haven't we had this discussion several times before?"

"Yes, but I want to learn so much!"

"You know that Dahran would be furious. Besides, I can imagine the scrapes you'd get yourself into. You'd either get yourself hurt, or hurt someone else."

"So instead, you have to do it for me?"

"Huh?"

"Remember the man at the Tower who accidentally knocked me over?"

"Oh."

"And whose jaw you accidentally dislocated?"

"It was only a slap. Besides, it was an isolated incident. I just lost my composure momentarily."

"Sure. You know I can name half a dozen other incidents. What makes it worse is that nothing ever moves you to violence, unless I'm involved. How do you think that makes me feel? Thank God you're only protective, and not the jealous type!"

"I'd never thought of it like that."

"Well then. Does this mean you'll teach me?"

"No! It's not necessary. The most danger you'd ever be in on Enya is by practicing martial arts and getting injured. There isn't anything to defend yourself from."

"And what about Jeshua's warning? And your experience of last night?"

Malak hesitated. "I don't know…Maybe we can ask your father when we return to the Tower."

Lena snorted. "I don't know who's the more bull-headed, you or him!"

He poked her in the side, and was rewarded with a surprised yelp. He immediately felt a painful tug on his hair.

"Ow, that was a bit rough!"

She pushed herself up on her elbow.

"What? I didn't touch you!"

With sudden realization, Malak twisted his head around. Seated on the pillar was a one foot tall gnome with dull orange, mottled skin. Two small horns protruded from his head, one of which was broken. His teeth were also in severe need of dental attention. His eyes were black, amicable but mischievous.

"Squint!" Lena cried in joy.

The gnome responded with several winks, a characteristic for which he was named. Malak groaned in exasperation. Squint was an earth elemental who had befriended Lena as a child. He often visited her, but mostly when he was bored. Though he was unable to talk, he would often beg her to sing or play with him. But when Squint and Bast were in the same room there was always friction.

The elemental grinned inanely at Lena and then recognized Bast's sleeping form. Malak and Lena quickly pulled their legs in. The gnome disappeared, and materialized an instant later beside Bast's head. He winked again, giving an impish twitch of his eyebrows.

"Oh, shit!" Malak whispered under his breath.

The gnome grabbed a handful of whiskers and yanked with all his strength. Bast leapt several feet off the bed, releasing a roar to rival an enraged tiger. The gnome scuttled across the floor, sniggering loudly. Bast launched herself after him, catapulting Tara from her bed as she landed. The girl screamed in alarm as the familiar pursued the mischievous gnome.

Lena hid her face behind the pillow.

"Isn't it great to all be together again?"

Malak smiled unconvincingly; his mind was elsewhere. His experience of the previous night had subtly changed him; he was aware that a crisis was impending. He had to resist being drawn into the coming battle: he was not ready for any kind of confrontation. The responsibility had been placed firmly on his shoulders, and he desired only to shed it. Though he certainly didn't embrace death, neither did he fear it. What he feared was losing Lena: that he couldn't handle. He knew that if he was involved in the battle, there would be no way of holding her back: she was far too determined to be reasoned with.

But even as he tried to convince himself, Malak knew that his desires were irrelevant. A dark foreboding told him that a confrontation with Dethen was inevitable for both of them.

Our waking consciousness is but one special state of consciousness, whilst all about it parted by the filmiest of screens, there lie potential forms of consciousness entirely different... No account of the universe in its totality can be final which leaves these other forms of conscious-ness quite disregarded.

—William James

Enya
Wilderness Region
Black School
subterranean lair

The atmosphere of Dethen's personal chamber was stuffy and humid. The subtle smell of ambergris permeated the viscous air. A large white circle had been traced on the floor; at its centre stood an altar, covered by a sheet of dark purple silk. The altar was heptagonal, producing nine surfaces. On it burned a large white candle, dribbles of molten wax running down its sides. It cast a piti-ful amount of light into the chamber.

Next to the candle lay the elemental weapons: a wooden penta-cle, an ornate silver dagger, a phallic-shaped wand and a cup of wine. A quartz scrying crystal lay next to these, and lying across the altar, overhanging it in both directions, was *Widowmaker*. She gleamed with malice in the poor light.

On each of the walls was a banner; upon them were the triangu-lar symbols of the elements. Bracketed torches, well used but cur-rently unlit, were fixed to each wall. The aura of the room was chilling and black, created by Dethen's malevolent vibrations.

Dethen was seated in lotus posture, head bowed and hands upon his knees. He was within the protective circle, facing east with his back to the altar. He had performed banishing rituals within the cir-cle by pentagram and hexagram, but his mind was still not centred. His pulse hammered in his chest and his breathing was erratic. He was in the grip of intense fear. After its absence for so many years the emotion seemed alien.

He knew that if he failed in the coming operation, the

consequences for his soul would be hideous. To face the Trial of the Abyss, he would have to transcend his ego. He would have to face his worst fears and regrets without reaction. He had only one of each, and he could not bear to face them. His hatred of the Dark One was a powerful force that drove him. More than anything else, he wanted to crush the Demon who was responsible for the creation of the world. For beyond him lay the Infinite, the Divine force that ran through all.

He could not bear to open the wound that had been closed, though not healed, for so long. Memory of his last encounter with the Dark One had been locked away for centuries. To relive it risked the release of an emotional tide so strong that madness would inevitably result. It had taken him two lifetimes to regain control of himself. He knew that if he could not face the memory now, he would never do so. He had to become Magus. Only that way could the Tree of Life be destroyed.

He forced himself to establish the Breath. His mind and body began to calm as he settled into the slow, constant rhythm of breathing. He focused himself, gradually excluding all external influences from his awareness. He numbed his mind. After several minutes, he was conscious only of soothing emptiness.

Once his concentration was complete, he initiated his ordeal.

He set up the first symbol: a black and white chequered square, balanced equally with light and darkness. He visualized the image behind closed eyelids, seeing it as clearly as any corporeal object. The symbol served to ground his consciousness in the plane directly below Enya: Malkuth, the physical plane. This was the plane that Enya had been modelled from.

Once the image was set concretely in his imagination, he replaced it. Now he focused upon the image of a heavy Tau Cross, with in-curved sides top and bottom. The cross was black, with a single drop of blood at the junction of the arms. It had a feeling of great inertia and restriction.

He held the image for several seconds before he experienced a feeling of stress. It changed spontaneously, forming an upright mist-blue equilateral triangle. It flickered with silver sparkles and supported a silver crescent with horns uppermost. With the new symbol came a release of tension and a giddy sensation as he was reborn into Yesod, the Sphere that contained Enya.

He consciously changed to the third symbol: a barbed and flight-
ed arrow of a clear and brilliant blue. He visualized it speeding vertically upwards toward its target. After holding this image in his
mind for just over a minute, he started to feel an intense tension as
he approached another Sephiroth. The stress built itself up over several more minutes, and then suddenly gave way as he was raised up
into Tiphareth.

The symbol converted into a radiant sphere of yellow light with
a purple solar cross centred within it. A stupefying rapture washed
over his body and mind, lifting his consciousness higher and higher. He was blissfully unaware of his physical body as it gently began
to levitate.

Then, with great resolve, he prepared himself for the dangerous
and unknown portion of the operation. He had no idea whether his
method was flawed, but he didn't have the years to spend on arduous preparations that other methods required.

The final image was of the Hebrew letter Gimel, dark blue and
supported by an upward-pointing Luna crescent. He focused intently
on the symbol, pouring every grain of energy into its reality. The
ecstasy died, but for many minutes he encountered nothing else. He
perspired with the strain of maintaining the visualization.

Then the stress re-emerged, this time much stronger than the last
time. It augmented until he felt he could take no more, but his
resolve didn't weaken. He forced himself to continue, straining
against the power that tried to push him back into his place.

The tension intensified and strengthened. It was sheer agony just
holding onto the image. He could not think, feel, or move. The only
reality was the terrible pressure, and the horrendous pain. He clung
on, oblivious of his physical body, but knowing he was unable to
breathe.

Then came a terrible cracking sound. He was about to break into
Daath: the Sephiroth within the Abyss. The pressure suddenly disappeared. His flight became horizontal, plummeting through im-
penetrable blackness. And suddenly He appeared on the horizon:
Chronzon, Arch-Demon of the Abyss, and archenemy of man.

Dethen plunged toward Him, paralyzed with fear. Chronzon's face
was larger than a city, flaming red and framed by blazing hair and
beard. Two enormous curved horns protruded from His head, their
tips lost from sight. His open, leviathan mouth was rimmed with rows

of jagged teeth, like rotting mountains. The flames of Hell raged inside Him, reaching up past His tonsils to swallow the insignificant human.

His eyes were an intense, chilling green. They could freeze a man's soul and damn it with a single glance. Their expression was inconceivably malevolent and utterly evil. A light flickered within them as He recognized the feeble human. Dethen screamed in terror as his gaze locked with His.

He struggled wildly as he plummeted toward the Beast. Chronzon leisurely opened his mouth to swallow His latest victim. From His insides, Dethen heard the bellowing of the Black Brothers, those who had attempted to pass Chronzon before him, and failed. They screamed at him, begging him not to take the Test. To enter the mouth of the Beast was damnation.

Dethen closed his eyes as he passed through the huge jaws. Intense heat washed over him as the flames feasted. He blocked out the terrible pain as he fought his fear.

Suddenly the Arch-Demon was gone. The faint outline of a monastery materialized around him. He struggled wildly, but knew that he was helpless. He bellowed at the top of his voice as consciousness began to fade....

———✦❀✦———

Michael knelt humbly before his Master in the monastery.

"Master, it is my will to walk the Path of the Abyss."

The Master gazed at him with serene affection.

"You are a great Adept, and your personality is righteous, but your karma is not yet ready."

Michael bowed his head.

"I will take a vow before you, Master."

His teacher's eyes became clouded with anguish.

"You may choose that path. But you are young. Be sure you know what you are doing. A vow to pay off karma would mean terrible suffering for you. A suffering that will manifest in ways you don't expect. Are you sure, Michael?"

"I am sure."

"You must forfeit all worldly pleasures and possessions. You must gain total control of your ego. Do not take this vow. I see great torment for you, which may last longer than you think."

"I must walk the Path, Master. I care for nothing except to be one with God."

"Mark well that once the path is chosen, there will be no way back. Nor can I reveal to you how much karma you must pay. But I will tell you this: avoid attachment to objects, and especially to people. For other people must not be hurt in order that you suffer. This I give to you as a dire warning.

"Do you understand Michael?"

"Yes, Master."

"Then I will accept your vow before the Grace of God."

Michael nodded and breathed deeply to compose himself.

"I hereby vow before my Holy Master, and the Almighty Lord that it is my true desire to repay my entire karmic debt as quickly as I am able, regardless of the suffering and peril within which I am placed. I swear this by my true will. So be it."

The Master bowed his head. "Amen."

A minute later, he looked up.

"You will repay your karmic burden over a period of one year. Then, and only then, may you attempt the Trial of the Abyss. And Michael, for the sake of your eternal soul, remember my warning to you."

<hr>

Michael stared out of the window, his mind elsewhere. The sky was a beautiful blue, marked only occasionally with the form of a pure white, wispy cloud. On the ground, fields of unripened corn stretched out as far as the eye could see; they rippled like golden oceans. On the small, neatly kept lawn in front of the cottage, sparrows pecked voraciously for worms as a light April shower passed over. Yet Michael was only vaguely aware of all of this.

He tensed as his shoulders were gently grasped from behind, but relaxed as he recognized Anya's grip. She slid her palms down the outside of his arms to hold his hands.

"What's wrong, my love? The bed is cold without you," she purred in his ear.

"I'm fine. I came to see the dawn."

"Which was an hour ago, and you've been standing here since. I know you better."

She leaned her head on his shoulder and gently nibbled his ear lobe. He closed his eyes and sighed; it was a sigh of both confusion and anguish.

"Tonight is one year since my vow to the Master. And tonight I must walk the Trial of the Abyss. Yet my negative karma has not appeared over the last year. Am I to assume that I have none?"

"Michael, you are the most spiritual, noble, and gentle person I have ever known. I'm sure you have no karma to pay."

Michael was silent for a while as he mulled over his predicament.

"We were a mistake. I was warned. I should never have become involved with you," he said sombrely. "If I am not ready…"

Anya turned him around to face her. She wrapped her arms around his waist and tenderly kissed him on the lips.

"Does it feel wrong to you? You made no vow against our relationship. If we were to meet again, would you make a different choice?"

He stared into deep brown her eyes, and ran his fingers through her hair.

He shook his head. "I wouldn't be able to stop myself. You mean more to me than any earthly thing, including my life. Only God would I put before you. But, by the Lord, if anything were ever to happen to you…"

She pressed her index finger to his lips.

"Nothing will happen. You worry too much. Come. . . let's go back to bed. This floor is freezing my feet."

Michael submitted to her tug, but in his mind the Master's warning echoed incessantly…

———❦———

Dethen screamed in defiance, but was helpless as the next scene began to form around him.

———❦———

Anya slept restlessly in the double bed, which was now conspicuously half-empty. Outside, the rain drummed ceaselessly on the slate roof. Crashes of thunder sounded in the air, barely a mile from the cottage. The dark interior of the room was illuminated sporadically by violet forks of lightning. There seemed to be an unnatural chill in the air.

Anya shifted in and out of dreams uneasily. Although she had reassured Michael about his vow, a foreboding had now settled upon her. Even now he performed the ceremony in the cellar below. She feared for his safety; she had no idea of the consequences if Michael's karma had not been repaid. The Dark One was not a being of mercy.

A terrible scream suddenly pierced the air. She knew it was from Michael. She curled into the fetal position and hid her face, loath to approach the cellar. Another bellow of torment cut through the night atmosphere. This time she couldn't bear to ignore it.

She slipped from the bed and waited as a flash of lightning lit the way forward. Her stomach muscles tensed in apprehension, she walked through the doorway to the kitchen, reached the cellar stairs and stared down into the darkness. The barely perceivable glow of golden candlelight surrounded the cellar door.

She cautiously descended the stairs. Her feet floundered on the steps in the darkness. She reached the door and tentatively touched the cold handle. A tremendous crack of thunder shook the cottage as a streak of lightning detonated directly overhead.

In the electric blue light, she stared at the open door where Michael now stood. His bloody white robes were ripped and torn. They flailed about him as an Arctic wind sheared through the cellar. Anya didn't notice the cold green eyes or the long sword in his hand.

She shrieked in agony as the blade bit deep, piercing her womb. Michael leered demonically as he thrust the sword deeper, slowly twisting the blade. She fell forward onto him, gasping with the pain. Tears rolled down her cheeks as she leant her head on his shoulder. The physical pain was nothing compared to the agony of betrayal.

The cold green glow deserted Michael's eyes. He suddenly dropped the sword in horror. He gently laid her down on the cellar stairs, cradling her head in his arms. He wept uncontrollably as he realized what he had done.

Anya looked at him, the hurt in her eyes beyond description.

"Why? I loved you more than my life…" she whispered.

She tried feebly to push him away as he held her close, his own pain even greater than hers. He gripped her tightly, trying to force back the life-force that flowed from her wound. She pushed herself away, her eyes staring into his with unbridled hatred. Tears flowed freely down his face as her eyes fluttered and her body became limp.

He laid her gently on the stairs and picked up the sword. He stared at the ceiling, as if focusing on the lightning beyond.

He shouted out, his voice hoarse and cracked with emotion: "I swear that I'll never rest until I destroy you, Evil One! In time, you will tremble before me!"

He pressed the point of the sword against his stomach. He closed his *eyes and held his breath. He screamed vehemently, and then pushed with all his might.*

━━━━━◆◉◉◉◆━━━━━

Dethen bellowed in torment as he pulled himself away from the memory of his dead lover. The cottage disappeared in a chaotic confusion of swirling forms; they spun around him in ever changing shapes and orbits. He stood in the centre without moving, too distraught to act. After a few seconds, he realized that he was seeing the Abyss as it truly was. Beyond this point, no forms existed. Only pure essence had substance here.

A sudden cognition caused him to turn shakily around. Standing behind him, also within the swirling mass, was Chronzon. He was now Dethen's size, which made Him appear even more lucid and terrifying. His chilling eyes bored through Dethen's insubstantial figure.

"YOU HAVE FAILED, HUMAN. YOUR SOUL IS MINE. IT NOW BELONGS WITH THE BLACK BROTHERS."

The voice was penetrating and arctic. It spanned several octaves, sending powerful reverberations through Dethen's mental body.

Dethen stared at the Arch-Demon with undisguised hatred and fury.

"You will never take me!"

He was still shaking with the emotional agony of the scene he had just re-enacted.

"YOU HAVE FAILED THE TRIAL! YOU REMAIN A PRISONER OF YOUR EGO. THERE CAN BE NO ESCAPE FOR YOU NOW, MORTAL! YOU ARE DEFENSELESS AGAINST MY POWER. WITH A WHIM I COULD SHATTER YOUR VERY ESSENCE!"

Dethen tensed himself as the vibrations of the voice hit him, threatening to tear him apart. Chronzon raised His arm and stretched His hand out towards the Black Adept. It grew rapidly as it approached. Dethen tried in vain to avoid it, but all points somehow seemed to be the same in the chaotic void. The hand was always reaching directly for him.

He raised his arms to shield himself as huge fingers enveloped him.

"I will never yield! I will destroy you!" he bawled into the darkness.

"DIE, MORTAL! DIE!"

The fingers began to squeeze Dethen, slowly crushing the life from him. He struggled fiercely, but he knew it was futile. No human will could match the Arch-Demon's. No man could possibly equal His power.

Flashes of his present and previous lives flashed before Dethen. With them came memories of Anya. Intense sorrow and anguish surged through him, so strong he thought they would drown him. Tormented beyond sanity, he screamed in agony, fighting both the Demon and his own feelings. He was rapidly weakening. He could not survive for long.

"I will not submit!" he bellowed. Thunderous demonic laughter echoed in his mind.

Dethen snarled and focused every ounce of pain and guilt into mindless fury. He hurled it against the hand that slowly crushed him.

The hand shattered into a million shards. There was a tremendous roar of anger and surprise as he burst from the trap. The Demon's other fist was now falling to crush him.

With a sudden intuition, Dethen visualized the symbol of Yesod. He absorbed himself in it completely; his soul depended upon it. There was a tumultuous crack as he spun back down the planes.

⇒⟨◎◎◎⟩⇐

Dethen was catapulted across the width of his chamber. He hit the wall forcefully, stunning his senses. He could feel pain, but was unsure of the location. Bright flickering lights danced before his eyes, blotting his entire vision.

From the cramped pain in his neck he gradually realized that he was slumped upside down. He pushed himself over to collapse on the stone floor.

The lights began to subside, and he realized that there was something in his eyes. He wiped them with his hand and felt the warm touch of fresh blood. He checked his forehead, screwing his face up as a sharp pain shot through it. A two-inch gash stretched across it.

As he lay motionless on the floor, breathing hard, he realized he was not alone. Half-formed shadows danced around the room, disappearing and reforming randomly. It occurred to him that he had been thrown from the protection of his circle. But he was too exhausted to rise, and too traumatized by his experience to be concerned. He put the display down to a trick of the light.

The self-inflicted illusion did not last for long, as voices started to murmur in his ear. He pushed himself up with a curse and lethargically scanned the room. After the ordeal he had just suffered, he wanted no further excitement. He was lucky to have a soul, disregarding that he was still alive, and apparently sane.

With legs stiff and uncooperative, he half limped in the direction of the circle. He knew that if he was in danger, it would offer no protection. Its seal had been broken, and would take minutes to reset.

A deep, threatening growl came from behind as he reached the circle's perimeter. He froze, then turned about slowly to face the new menace. About five yards from him, the air was boiling and shimmering with a pale yellow light.

In the centre of the anomaly, a small creature was beginning to form. It was roughly humanoid, but was three feet tall, pudgy and green. Its skin was diseased, covered in blisters and warts. It seemed to be slowly rotting. A foul yellow liquid oozed out of breaks in the skin.

Its face was unstable—it rippled and shuffled like a liquid in a way that defied the laws of physics. It continually formed hideous faces, many of distorted animal shapes, before flowing into something else. Only its eyes and mouth were stable. The former were a deep red, soulless and corrupt without pupils: they revealed its demonic nature. The latter was wide and thin, characterized by two stained canines that hung from it.

Dethen met its gaze directly. He knew the importance of a psychological advantage in these circumstances, but his mind and body were screaming for rest.

The entity bowed, its skin cracking further as it was strained. More sulfurous smelling ooze exuded through the breaks.

"I bring greetings and a message from the Kingdom of Dumah," it said, its voice hoarse and mocking.

Is this ordeal never to end? Dethen wondered. "What do you want?" he asked.

The demon seemed surprised at his attitude.

"I have come to negotiate a bargain with thee, black-hearted one.

My master is interested in your…special abilities."

"I don't make pacts with demons." Dethen's tone was final.

The creature smiled smugly. "Ah, but we have much to offer to a man in your position. None have ever escaped the Dark One before. Even now he is consumed with wrath, and he plots against thee…"

Dethen ignored the rationale. "How did you pass the Boundary, demon?"

The entity was taken aback. It didn't expect such treatment from humans: they were supposed to be petrified. He didn't like the way the human was looking at him…

"The…ah…Boundary is weakening bec…"

"Because Ghalan has gone," Dethen mused to himself.

The demon nodded. It didn't like the way the human was taking control of the conversation. Its eyes flicked slyly from side to side, and it licked its rippling lips with its black oily tongue.

"You did not pass the Dark One?" it asked, a slight taunt in its voice.

Dethen stiffened and turned his back on the creature. He walked over to the altar. His body was beginning to recover now.

The demon looked perturbed when he didn't answer. It was silent for a few seconds as it gauged the situation.

"You may have escaped him, but his power is incontestable below the Ocean of Forms. He will seek you out and destroy you. Will you become a Black Brother, mayhaps?"

It knew it had struck a chord when Dethen's shoulders marginally tensed beneath his robes. He spun around, angry, but his emotional control was too good for him to take the bait fully.

"Would you like a demonstration of my power, demon? This crystal won't appear so large from the inside!"

In his hand he held the quartz scrying crystal. The demon met his challenging gaze.

"Your magick will be weak until you recover strength. And until the last trace of the Magus fails, its full power cannot be unleashed!"

"Then neither should you be here, foul shadow!"

The demon sniggered. "I am here due to a concentrated effort of my entire kindred. Even now, the Boundary still has strength."

Though Dethen lost the argument, it was the demon who lost the battle of wills. He broke the Adept's gaze to stare at the floor.

"What do you want, demon? Why are you here?"

The creature smiled in triumph, showing an array of splintered black teeth, all canines.

"It is Dark Moon tomorrow. At that time, the residual power of the Magus will be at its weakest."

"For what?" Dethen asked suspiciously.

The demon sniggered, a sound like someone gargling sulfuric acid. "For you to summon the Queen into Enya!"

"The Queen?"

"Our mistress, the Queen of the Night. I speak of her majesty, Lilith."

The air seemed to thicken and a shadow passed over the chamber. Even Dethen shuddered at the mention of the name. The light of *Widowmaker* dimmed considerably.

Dethen was almost speechless. "Lilith?" Again, the room seemed gripped by an icy chill.

"Of course. The Queen of incubi, succubi, and my own brethren."

"That's madness! To summon Lilith into Enya would rip the plane apart. It couldn't possibly contain her essence. She's too powerful! The imbalance would probably destroy Yesod!"

"And with it," said the demon, looking pleased with itself, "the entire Tree of Life."

Dethen's eyes narrowed in calculated thought. He had much to consider regarding this possibility. The demon misread his silence.

"Isn't it the very thing the Black School seeks? To destroy the Tree would be to shatter the Life Cycle. What is your symbol?"

Dethen picked up *Widowmaker*. She hummed avariciously at the sight of the obese entity.

"I can't be touched by steel!" the demon said. But he took a step backwards as *Widowmaker's* garnet started to glow.

"You seek to manipulate me?" Dethen's voice was loaded with menace.

He advanced upon the demon, which backed into a corner, hopelessly looking for a way of escape. The creature could not return and report failure, but neither did it wish to face a powerful Adept, especially one armed with a potent magical weapon.

Dethen laughed at the pathetic look on the creature's face. As with all diabolical entities, it was quick to feed on fear, but loath to experience it itself. With a mercuric twist of the wrist, he sent *Widowmaker* speeding across the chamber. She pierced the demon through the chest. It screamed in agony and disappeared in a blaze of pale yellow light.

Widowmaker hit the wall behind, the blade burying itself six inches into the granite. She vibrated with satisfaction.

Dethen turned and limped over to the altar. He inclined his head as he heard the barely perceptible sound of an in-drawn breath.

"You may enter, apprentice."

A moment later, the large door creaked open and Felmarr stepped in. "I am sorry, Master. I did not wish to disturb you."

He pretended to ignore Dethen's physical condition as he saw the sizable gash on his forehead.

"What is it, Felmarr?" Dethen asked lethargically.

"I believe an entity has penetrated the Veil, Master."

Dethen raised his eyebrows in surprise. "Very good, Felmarr. But it has already been dealt with."

He looked meaningfully at *Widowmaker*, which still protruded from the chamber wall.

"Then, if that is all, I shall leave you in peace, Master."

"No. Please close the door and sit with me awhile."

"Aye, Master."

Felmarr bowed slightly and did as he was instructed. Dethen sat down stiffly and waited for his apprentice to join him. His attention was focused internally, and it was several minutes before he spoke. Felmarr sat in covert amazement: never before had he seen his Master in such a mental or physical condition.

"I have walked the Path," Dethen said.

Felmarr held the black gaze without flinching and nodded.

"I did not pass. The power of the Dark One was too strong, and I could not face my past."

Felmarr's eyes widened in surprise, though he was unaware of Dethen's dark past.

"Then how did you return, Master?"

Dethen shook his head and ran his fingers along the gash on his forehead.

"I do not know. He allowed me to return once so that I could suffer, but this time I escaped him. This is not possible, I know, but he certainly did not *allow* me to return. It is said that no human can defeat him. In crossing the Abyss, an Adept becomes a god, and his power dwarves that of the Dark One. I did not do this, yet

I still escaped him."

"What can you do now, Master? He will surely seek revenge!"

Dethen nodded and pushed himself to his feet; Felmarr immediately followed.

"We must act quickly, apprentice. You must do two things for me."

Felmarr snapped to attention.

"Firstly, you must scry the nearby area. I want you to locate a virgin woman for me. I think the nearest village is Oaklan, in the Enchanted Forest. Then I want you to leave as swiftly as possible for the Celestial Tower. Take the entire complement of Black Guard. Leave me two good men, say Roruch and Koran."

"What should we do when we reach the Tower, Master?" Felmarr's eyes were wide with excitement.

"I want you to destroy the White School utterly. Attack the Tower, and do not leave a single Adept alive. It is essential that no one remains alive to interfere with my plan. I must leave you to make the arrangements yourself. You are fully capable. But you must ride like the wind, for the attack must occur by sunset tomorrow."

"They will feel our wrath, Master!"

"Control yourself, Felmarr." Dethen's voice lashed like a whip. "It is a matter of efficacy. I couldn't give a damn about the White School. I simply want no interference. Be sure that you are thorough: make sure the White Council is annihilated."

Admonished, Felmarr cast down his eyes. "And what of Malak, Master?"

Dethen frowned; when he spoke his answer seemed almost reluctant. "If you encounter Malak, then treat him no differently. I want no survivors."

A great flame follows a little spark.

—Dante

If you believe in the light, it's because of obscurity; if you believe in happiness it's because of unhappiness, and if you believe in God, then you have to believe in the Devil.

—Doctrine of the Yellow School

Enya
Lokhi Region
The Enchanted Forest

Malak knelt in brooding contemplation as the crimson Enyan sun sank to touch the blue-green treetops of the western horizon. The forest clearing was uncharacteristically quiet; a subtle tension pervaded the twilight atmosphere. There was little movement and the usually boisterous birds were silent. Even the frantic bustle of the forest squirrels was strangely absent.

Malak turned the blade of *Retaliator* slowly in his hands. Sparks of fiery energy flickered along her edges. The sword was uneasy, and was communicating the fact to her master. Like the animals of the forest, the katana could feel the change in the atmosphere of Enya. Malak could sense a feeling of instability and strain through the fluctuation of energies in his subtle body.

He drove the sword into the earth and placed his hands on his thighs. He focused intently on the huge star-sapphire set into the hilt. He stared into its depths, feeling the world about him fade from consciousness as his attention centred on the gem. It pulsed rhythmically, its blue light flaring with his heartbeat to illuminate the clearing.

He concentrated on the identity of Dahran. He included not only his physical appearance, but also his personality and essence. The veils of blue mist shimmered and suddenly disappeared from view. Dahran's face and bushy beard slowly came into focus. Behind him, Malak could make out the decor of the Council Chamber.

"Ah, Malak, I've been trying to contact you." Dahran's voice was lethargic. "I have serious news for you, Frater."

Malak tensed. Somehow he had expected this.

"It seems that your journey to see Ghalan is now pointless. He has transcended to the Godhead and Enya is now without a Magus. Already the Boundary is weakening and it will be dangerous to remain in the wilderness."

Malak grimaced. The consequences of the news would be far reaching indeed.

"Have you reached Oaklan, yet?" Dahran asked.

Malak grunted. "Yes, but Jeshua is no longer here."

There was silence for a few seconds as Malak's unspoken accusation hung in the air. He left Dahran with no doubt that he was aware of the mage's part in Jeshua's ploy. Dahran's relationship with Malak had always been strained. As a child he had been taught the ways of magick by Malak (who was in his previous incarnation). He had therefore known the Malak of old as his senior.

Dahran showed no guilt in his expression, only disappointment. He allowed the moment to slip by without comment.

"I have been in touch with some of our contacts on the Inner Planes," he said. "It seems that a Qlippothic entity has already broken through due to a concentrated effort by its kindred. We think it may have been in contact with Dethen, though we're not sure of its purpose."

Malak mused gloomily. He knew that Dethen would take full advantage of Ghalan's disappearance to achieve his own twisted objectives.

"I received an intuition of Dethen the other night," Malak said. "His power has grown tremendously. I barely recognized him. He poses an appalling threat to us all."

"That's why you must return to the Tower immediately. Though you don't realize it, I believe you're very close to Dethen's lair. It's imperative that your past life memories are fully returned: you must gain what has been lost. I've been assured by the Council that they will no longer interfere with the process."

"I do not wish to be involved in this battle," Malak said firmly. "There is too much to lose." Again, his mind dwelt on the possibility of losing Lena, and he immediately shut the thought out—he would not allow it to happen.

"You must return! You must have all possible resources at your disposal!"

"I can't," Malak said, his voice forlorn. "I must not become involved. I will not fight this battle."

Dahran frowned deeply, confused. "What do you mean, you can't become involved? You must stand beside your friends and allies or our lives mean nothing."

Malak shook his head, and his anguish was obvious.

Dahran sighed. "Malak, we have had our differences in the past, and both of us have been at fault. You are young and immature, rash and often lazy. But one thing you are not is a coward. You are a formidable warrior, even without memory of your past identity. Why do you fear this battle?"

"There is more to lose than my life Dahran."

"If you don't fight, you'll lose a damn sight more! Like honour, integrity, and loyalty! What is wrong with you?!"

Malak remained silent.

"Ah, I see," Dahran said with a sudden realization. "You fear for Lena."

Malak's smile was bitter. "You know me better than I thought, Dahran."

"You know that you can't completely protect her, Malak. No one can guarantee her safety. Yet the safest place will be at the Tower."

"But if I am involved in the battle, there is no way that she'll stay out of it. She's as stubborn as her father."

Dahran looked surprised. "Oh, she's far worse than me. Probably even worse than you know. She will want to fight even if you don't, Malak, and she will be at much more risk if she's not by your side during the battle."

Malak clenched his fists in frustration. "All right, Dahran. We'll return to the Tower. But even despite my fear for Lena's safety, I do not wish a battle with Dethen."

It had been a long time since Malak faced his twin. And he couldn't deny that he still felt a certain kinship with Dethen, no matter how deeply buried.

Dahran rubbed his eyes tiredly. "I realize that your feelings for Dethen are not entirely straight forward. However, a new Magus must now be put in place. Only you and Dethen are karmically suitable for the honour. You can be assured that Dethen will not refrain from stepping over you to obtain his desire."

Malak bowed his head. "We shall see." When he spoke again, his voice was low and withdrawn: "Be careful, Dahran. There is nothing to check Dethen's ambition now that Ghalan has gone. The White School might well be in severe danger."

Dahran nodded soberly. "Aye, don't worry. We're taking care of that possibility as we speak."

Dahran was suddenly distracted by a commotion going on around him. It was frustratingly out of view to Malak. Dahran then turned his attention back to the young mage, his face set with tenacity.

"Someone is attempting to enter the Tower. I must leave."

Malak's heart skipped a beat in dread; the image in the crystal wavered and evaporated, leaving him alone in the darkness, his eyes watering.

An intense emotion suddenly struck him from outside his aura; he instantly recognized its source.

"Lena!"

He snatched up *Retaliator* and broke into a sprint. Whatever trouble his wife was in, it was desperate. Never before had he received such an intense emotional blast from her. He knew it would take him several minutes to reach Oaklan. With the Boundary now weakened, he knew he could find anything at the village.

***

Lena sat cross-legged in the large chair of Jenny's sitting room, her mind occupied with thoughts of Malak. It was rapidly darkening outside, and she had expected him back from the forest over an hour ago. It was unusual for him to spend so much time by himself; Malak was normally carefree, but since the incident with Jeshua he had been brooding continually.

The living area of the house was lit by a single oil lamp. This burned on the small table, around which the other occupants were seated.

Jenny sat with her back to Lena, mechanically sewing up a white cotton shirt. Next to her was Tara, straining to read by the dim light of the lamp.

Past the teenager's slight form were the hulking figures of Kane and Gal. They were gradually making their way through huge bowls of beef stew. They found it very difficult to resist surreptitiously glancing at their guest. They had obviously not encountered many women in Oaklan, and her beauty had awed them. Irritated, Lena flicked her hair behind her head and pulled her hood over to hide her face.

The atmosphere in the room was strained. Without Jeshua's comforting presence, the family seemed somewhat anxious. Lena herself felt a strange tension in the air. There was a cold, unhealthy ambiance to the night that felt threatening.

"Do you often see exotic creatures in these parts?" Lena asked.

"We've often seen such in the forest, but they don't tend to stray near the village, ma'am," Jenny said, without altering the pace of her sewing.

"Malak and I saw a unicorn the other day."

Jenny nodded her head absently. "They say unicorns are wild, ma'am. Only the pure and innocent can approach them, they say. They're rare to find, mind. I've don't know anyone that's ever seen one."

Uncomfortable silence again descended. Lena frowned as she studied her hands. They were folded in her lap, and sparks of ethereal energy could be seen flickering off them. She glanced up at the family sharply, and relaxed as she realized they would be unable to see the effect. This was especially likely because they were meat-eaters: there was nothing more effective than eating meat to keep one grounded and thereby destroy psychic ability.

She unlinked her fingers and played with the energy, sending it flowing back and forth between her hands. There was nothing unusual about the energy, for it was quite definitely her own. The unnerving fact was that it was so dynamic. The effect of the Magus on Enya dampened all magical effects, other than those which were internal or used for healing. This limited the influence of the Schools of Magick, avoiding the possibility of catastrophic damage. As it was, each mage had to conserve his or her personal power for spiritual advancement.

"How far are you from the forest centre?" Lena asked, wondering if the proximity of the megaliths at the Rose Circle might be responsible.

"We don't concern ourselves with suchlike," Jenny said, a slight sting in her tone. "Those things are for Adepts like yourself. We are forbidden to approach the forest centre."

Lena didn't continue the conversation: she was perplexed. She discharged a spinning globe of white energy and watched it float across the room as it followed her mental directions. She caused it to hover above the mother's head, who suddenly became uncomfortable.

Lena withdrew the energy and reabsorbed it. There was no way that she should have been able to perform such feats. She was becoming highly suspicious of the influence that the Magus was exerting over the plane. The fact that they were en route to Ghalan's Temple, at her father's request, did little to alleviate her apprehension.

An urgent scratching at the door suddenly caused everyone in the room to pause. It came again, this time with a certain desperation. The family exchanged glances with one another. It was not something they had experienced before: wild creatures tended to leave the humans in peace. It was extremely perturbing. No one seemed eager to open the door.

For several long seconds, there was silence. Then the scratching again recurred, this time weaker and almost pleading. Lena gave the family a sharp glare as they almost cowered in fear of the door. How they could be so afraid of such a noise was beyond her, whether it was unusual or not. She was concerned that an animal might be injured.

She rose from the armchair, and strode across the room, robes swirling about her. She pulled the door open. The family gasped in shock as they saw the creature lying wounded on the doorstep, but Lena's outrage was much stronger.

Bast was lying on her side, unaware that the door was open and still feebly trying to paw it. A black crossbow quarrel protruded from her right side. There was no blood visible, but Lena could see the leakage of ethereal energy dwindling its way into the atmosphere.

She quickly knelt, and hoisted the creature up in her arms. It was fortunate that the moon was near dark, otherwise she would never have lifted the familiar: Bast's size greatly fluctuated with the phase of the moon.

Lena kicked the door shut and rushed across the room to the table. The family scattered away from the familiar in fear, sending bowls of stew crashing to the floor. They had always been fearful of the feline.

Lena laid down Bast, who was now groaning weakly. She had recognized Lena, however, and knew she was in the hands of a friend. She lay still as her master's wife studied the wound. Lena was puzzled because Bast was invulnerable to piercing weapons—she was enchanted by nature, and metal would not injure her.

The body of the bolt and its flight were painted black, decorated in purple with a sigil she didn't recognize, but she knew was magical; it was like a corrupted lightning bolt. She quickly realized she had no further time for study when Bast's eyes began to flutter, and her size started to diminish: she was losing energy quickly.

Lena yanked the quarrel from the familiar's side. Bast gave a high pitched squeal of pain, and then a purr of satisfaction as the wound immediately healed over. Lena sighed with relief as the escaping vortex of energy dwindled and died. She patted the familiar on the side as the cat fell into a heavy sleep. She knew that Bast would recharge the lost energy within a few days, once the moon started to wax again.

She turned the quarrel over in her hand, and suddenly realized that the tip was coated in silver. It was the only metal that would penetrate Bast's enchanted skin. Lena slammed the arrow down on the table in anger. The infliction of pain on others was one thing that always aroused her anger.

The mother and two brothers shrank from her gaze as it scorched across them. But her fury died almost instantly as another sound reached her hearing, this one having an undisguised malice. The family looked to her for protection as the sound strengthened. Lena could feel prickles on the back of her neck: she knew that there was terrible danger present. She had not felt that sensation in many lifetimes.

The noise was indistinct, and yet quite audible. It could be felt rather than heard. It was like a snuffling sound patrolling the outside of the hut. She felt a sudden twinge of longing for Malak to be present, but quickly pushed this aside. A part of herself that had been dormant for decades rose to the challenge. The snuffling paused as it reached the outside of the door. She turned to face it and straightened her back assertively.

"Get back," she said. The family shrank behind her, spooked by the gravity of her tone.

Luminescent purple mist exuded through the outline of the doorway. It coalesced to form a floating spherical mass of ethereal energy so bright that the family was able to make it out clearly. Blue and green discharges crackled menacingly across its surface. Lena backed away a step in shock. The entity had obviously broken through the

Boundary, and from its strange appearance she suspected it was vampiric in nature: it desired their astral energy.

It hovered for a few seconds as it took in the situation; it was obviously puzzled by the size and brightness of Lena's aura. She ushered the family to back up against the opposite wall, and then turned back to face her adversary. It was slowly and ominously advancing upon her. She knew she had little time to make a decision.

She estimated its speed, which was rather slow; it was evidently being cautious. The family, their eyes terrified, watched in disbelief as she drew an apparently useless circle around herself with her index finger. The entity, however, could clearly see the ring of ethereal light that she formed.

She stepped out of the circle, moving slowly backwards. The entity reached the edge of the circle, and extended a mist-formed tendril to touch its boundary. It recoiled in abhorrence, and then started to skirt the circle toward her. She backed off further, making sure she was always between the entity and the family.

In a few seconds, it reached her side of the circle. It advanced triumphantly upon her, silver tendrils reaching out for her life-essence. She forced herself to calm her breathing and relax her mind; full concentration was vital.

She took in a lung-full of air, and put her hands up to her forehead, framing her third eye chakra in a triangle with thumbs and index fingers touching. She then thrust her hands toward the entity, hurling out a brilliant blue pentagram.

The pentagram struck the creature at speed, blasting it backward into the confines of the circle. It screamed in agony, a sound that shuddered through her body. It writhed in torment as it tried to break through the circle's seal. She stepped forward to stand beside the perimeter. The family looked on with unmasked fear, unable to see how she had trapped the creature.

Lena watched it ricochet back and forth within the circle, before preparing herself for the second phase. She hoped that she would be strong enough to achieve it. She didn't have the strength to hurl the entity back through the Boundary with a banishment.

She extended a thin sliver of astral substance from her solar plexus, pushing it through the edge of the circle to touch the vampire. She started to draw its substance into herself. Intense and hideous emotions impacted upon her instantly, but she forced herself to continue. She felt the essence of the vampire merge with her own. It fought viciously to dominate her will, but she pushed it down, crushing it like a fly. She could feel the power of her higher self flowing through her body, and the vampire was absolutely helpless against it.

The sphere rapidly shrank, and Lena's aura expanded and became irregular. She started to feel dizzy as the last traces of the entity entered her. Too late, she realized she had absorbed too much energy. She turned to face the cowering family.

"It's safe now…" she whispered.

She took a few unsteady steps forward, before collapsing heavily onto the floor.

9

Enya
Thenyan Region
The Celestial Tower

Felmarr waited as the twilight sky darkened. Slowly, the sun sank from view behind the ebony outline of the Celestial Tower.

He scanned the distance to the Tower, searching for defenses and traps. He expected to find none. The White School had been sleeping for centuries, and was now nothing more than a party of politicians. He only hoped that the weakened Boundary had not restored too much of their magical ability. Otherwise the battle might be fierce.

The Tower was just over two miles away, set within the edge of Mishmar Lake, one of the largest stretches of water on the plane. The lake experienced severe tides that immersed much of the lower Tower for several days a month. It was set within a huge valley with steep sides, formed by the smaller peaks of the Wyrmspine Mountains. Felmarr had a vantage point from the surrounding high ground, covered from the Tower's view by a hillside. Twenty of the Black Guard lay waiting for battle behind him.

With his crude field telescope he could make out the Tower with reasonable detail. Its black onyx surface was polished to an extraordinary degree; he could see upon it a rippling image of the waning moon, now dim and weak as it finished its cycle. The lake was not to be seen in the reflection: the Celestial Tower reflected only the light of the moon and stars.

Felmarr studied the approach again. His troops would have to cover half a mile of open territory before reaching the lake. Then they would reach the causeway, which stretched over the water for over a mile. Reputed to have been constructed from rose quartz, the causeway was translucent pink. It had been formed in the last Aeon, when the White School had reigned supreme.

Felmarr grinned malignantly. He was about to ensure that they never ruled again. Under the cover of darkness, he gave the signal to descend.

⟶◦◉◦⟵

The four huge white candles flickered uneasily on the ornate oaken table of the Council Chamber. The six Council members stared nonchalantly at each other over the table surface. Half of the seats were conspicuously empty.

"I have received the resignation of Council members Melesh, Andra, Nansk and Baran," Iysa said; her face had aged ten years in two days.

The Council remained silent, its morale shattered.

"Lord Dahran wishes to address us on the current problem, of which we're now all aware."

Dahran ran his eyes over the Adepts. There was Iysa, who had had much of the fire knocked out of her, and Rhea, who was Iysa's lackey. His old ally Valmaar was present, along with Galaak and Siana. Dahran had had little to do with the latter pair, but he knew that they were at least capable of thinking for themselves, unlike the four who had deserted.

"As I hope you are beginning to realize, the Magus has transcended," Dahran said, running his gaze around the table. "The ramifications of this are momentous, especially for ourselves. Although some of you are unconvinced, I can assure you that the Black School does exist. It will almost certainly move against us."

As he made eye contact with each Adept, he realized that several had recovered from his demonstration on the previous day. He paused, knowing that someone was bound to speak out.

It was Rhea who finally spoke: "I find your explanation difficult to stomach. I have no evidence that the Boundary has weakened, except for your demonstration the other day. Though it was impressive, the incident thus far has been isolated. I have witnessed no great increase in my own abilities. I do not believe you!"

She concentrated on the candelabra in the centre of the table.

It shifted barely half an inch in her direction. Dahran watched her with undisguised contempt.

"The reason that you have witnessed no increase in your ability is because you have none!"

With a twitch of his hand, the candelabra accelerated rapidly across the table surface. It stopped less than a foot in front of Rhea.

"Believe!" he said.

A murmur of disquiet passed around the table. Rhea's eyes were wide in anger, but she dared not retort.

"I think I can say that we're all convinced, Dahran," Iysa said icily. "Now, what do you advise?"

Dahran sighed and took his eyes off Rhea. "There are other means than magick for the Black School to use against us. Indeed, it would be difficult for them to attack us magically because their power would be unable to penetrate the Tower. I therefore suggest that the ground floor is guarded by a sizable squad of armed Neophytes, and that a constant state of alert is put in place."

"But no one here is trained to fight!" Garaak said. "Only you and Malak are warriors!"

"I intend to recall Malak and Lena to the Tower. As for everyone else, they will have to learn to fight. Life is a struggle, and without putting up a fight we will become extinct. The plane of dreams is awakening, and it will find reality a nightmare."

"How far will the Boundary disintegrate, and how long will it take?" Siana asked.

"I have no idea on either of those points, but if it disappears completely, Enya will once again meld into the astral material of Yesod and the people will all surely die."

A stunned silence followed, and Rhea suddenly stood up. "I can't take this insane adventure. I hereby resign from the Council," she said.

She slammed her silver Adepts' badge down on the table and strode from the room.

Dahran's jaw-line was like granite. "Anyone else?"

No one spoke.

"Good. Now since I am recalling Malak to the Tower, I suggest that I do everything I can to restore his past memories as quickly as possible."

"I suppose that there can be no further objection to that plan," Iysa said resignedly.

"Excellent. Wait a moment, I think that Malak is trying to contact me," Dahran said. "Can you pass me the candelabra, please."

He smiled cynically as Valmaar pushed the object across the table by telekinesis. Dahran rubbed his tired eyes and dowsed three of the candles. The chamber darkened considerably and he realized that the sun had just set. He focused his vision on the candle and opened his mind to Malak's communication.

For several minutes he spoke to Malak, and the Council sat quietly listening. They were only able to hear half of the conversation, but none of them had anything constructive to say anyway.

The tranquillity was disturbed by a baneful and unmistakable crash from below as the Tower doors were thrown open.

"We are too late," Valmaar said. "We must do what we can."

Dahran had heard the disturbance, too. "Someone is attempting to enter the Tower, I must leave. Remember my instructions," he said through the scrying link.

The five white magi arose from the table, magical energy rippling through them as trepidation turned to determination, and then to indignation.

———⟫◦◦◦⟪———

Felmarr signalled his troops to split either side of the Tower as they finished their silent dash across the causeway. He leaned against the cold dark stone as his pulse eased back to normality. The night was dark, the moon casting little illumination and the constellations were barely visible. The wind was erratic and changeable, chaotically gusting from every direction.

Now that he leaned against the base of the Tower, the world outside seemed very different. It rippled gently as if invisible waves washed across it. Felmarr knew the reason for this: the Celestial Tower existed in a plane slightly removed from Enya, and so was isolated to some extent from it. His body cells still tingled from crossing the barrier some yards back. The barrier was what had prevented him from scrying the interior layout of the construction.

He studied the front of the Tower. A barely discernible vertical crack in the stone revealed the joint between two huge onyx doors. He moved to stand before the entrance, carefully studying it. The barest glimmer of an ethereal shield covered the entrance, a guard against the uninitiated entering. It was ancient, and had been in place so long that its power was almost expended.

He pulled off a black leather glove. With his right hand he drew a banishing earth pentagram across the shield, dissipating its slight force completely. He could see no operating mechanism for the doors. He suspected that if there was a further protective seal, it would be as weak as the last one.

He placed the backs of his hands against each other, mimicking the physical action of opening the great doors. He took a few seconds to form the empathic link and gain a feel for their inertia. Then he slowly began to push his hands apart. It was incredibly difficult: a great force pushed back against him. But with the weakening of the Boundary, his magical ability was now more effective and it was enough to force the great doors open.

Slowly at first, but gaining in speed, they obeyed his will. There was a deafening crack as they reached their full extension. The whole Tower shuddered with the recoil of the force. Bright light flooded out of the entrance, outlining the silhouettes of two neophyte guards. The neophytes froze in shock and fear.

Without hesitation, the troops plunged into the Tower like a black wave of death. The two guards were slashed to the ground as the soldiers rushed for strategic positions in the huge Tower hall. Felmarr waited by the entrance, scanning the scene critically.

Two more neophytes were cut down by crossbow bolts as they ran for the spiral staircase. More bolts destroyed the large oil lamps that hung from the ceiling. Darkness swamped the hall.

Felmarr waited as each man signalled all clear. His eyes adjusted to the darkness and he surveyed the scene. He chuckled as he realized the bodies of the neophytes were unarmed. The White School deserved to become extinct: the operation would be a slaughter. As Dethen's personal apprentice, he knew well that only the strong survived.

He gave the signal to begin the ascent. Within a few seconds, the hall was empty. Felmarr approached the stairs alone, black robes swishing gently around him. The sounds of battle quickly reached his ears. The atmosphere was rife with shouts of warning and screams of terror as the Black Guard swept through the dining room and Outer Order dormitories.

He reached the first floor of the Tower to find all resistance crushed. A score of neophyte bodies lay strewn around the dining

table, most killed on the run. Two soldiers searched the pantries and
store rooms for cowards.

Felmarr continued his ascent to the second floor, where battles
resounded within the dormitories. It seemed that many of the
School's brethren had been caught sleeping. His attention was
drawn to a door with the golden cross of the Inner Order. Five of
his men were rapidly approaching it. He watched in interest.

The first soldiers pulled the twin doors open as the other three
stood behind with crossbows armed. They received an immense
shock. A blast of white energy burst from the room like a tidal wave.
They were hurled back with incredible force, their armour scorched
and smoking. None of them moved from the floor.

Felmarr snarled and screamed in rage. He projected his astral form
forward at tremendous speed, bursting through the doors. His subtle
body flared scarlet with the flames of his fury as he circled the five
white magi at speed. Dahran, Iysa, Rhea, Valmaar and Galaak
accepted the challenge, each rising from their physical body to join
him. The room became a blaze of astral light. The second floor shook
as a gale surged through it.

Forcing astral material back into his physical form, Felmarr soared
into the more subtle dimensions. His opponents followed, pursuing
the bright luminescent trail. They spiralled higher and higher,
battling fiercely.

Felmarr realized immediately that Dahran was the most powerful opponent. His black aura reached out and engulfed the old man.
There was an intense battle of wills as he sought to overpower the
white mage. Dahran fought viciously, but Felmarr was too powerful, and Dahran already knew what was destined to occur. He gave
a strangled scream; his subtle body fell behind, scintillating with a
thousand colours as energy drained away from him. He realized that
his astral cord had been severed, cutting him off from his physical
body. Within seconds he passed into unconsciousness, his physical
body now lifeless on a plane far below.

Fuelled with anger, the remaining four white magi attacked
together, forcing every ounce of power at the black magician. But
Felmarr was incredibly strong, brought out through decades of
arduous practice and strengthening of his will, while the White
School had been content to relax. He was almost as strong as the
combined strength of his opponents. He pushed back with his own

energy, almost swamping Valmaar.

The radiant blue-violet material of the astral plane dashed past them on all sides as they fought like wild animals. But Felmarr was beginning to fade: his numerical disadvantage was becoming apparent. He knew he didn't have much time left. He twisted around and dived back down the planes. Strange, alien worlds whipped past him as he plunged through planes of existence never before seen. Valmaar, Iysa, Galaak and Siana followed, always tight on his tail, never relinquishing the attack.

He plunged back through Enya, past Yesod and into the gross astral, a place he knew like his own home. Diseased and decaying human spirits reached out for help, clawing at all five bodies. Felmarr ignored them, pushing still deeper into the outer regions of the demonic planes. Now they were truly claws that were reaching for him, and they were far stronger and more powerful. They drew out his life essence, causing agonizing pain. Yet he had been forced to walk this path many times by his Master, and he was not perturbed.

But he could feel the terror from behind him as the white magi experienced the dead planes for the first time. They were ripped away from him and separated as dozens of entities grasped each one. Individually, the magicians were too weak to push away the beings, and they were pulled down deeper and deeper into the Qlippoth.

Felmarr shook off the entities that clung to him and pushed himself up, following his astral chord. He laughed as he saw the astral cords of the white magicians snap one by one.

The Celestial Tower was his, and there were no allies for Malak now.

10

Is it but now that the higher life is beset with dangers and difficulties; hath it not been ever thus with the Sages and Hierophants of the past? They have been persecuted and reviled, they have been tormented of men, yet through this has their glory increased. Rejoice, therefore, O Initiate, for the greater thy trial, the brighter thy triumph!

—The Golden Dawn

Enya
Lokhi Region
Oaklan Village

Dethen looked up through the shadowy outline of the sparse forest canopy. He could just discern the moon, now in its dark phase, as it blocked out a circle of stars. It loomed over them, its ambiance all malice and corruption. Dethen's eyes were fiery as he beheld its iniquitous majesty.

It is time, he thought gleefully.

With him stood six Adepts of the Black School. Felmarr had contacted him, and he knew of the White School's demise. Everything was now in place. Only his brother and accursed wife had escaped the Tower massacre. But they would be of no consequence now, wherever they were.

He looked at the small village, barely two hundred yards away. It was picturesque and distinctly vulnerable. A soft yellow light spilled out from it, a guide for lost travellers. This far from civilization, Dethen doubted if they received travellers at all.

He straightened his back and exhaled audibly. Roruch and Koran immediately jumped to attention. They knew their master's idiosyncrasies well, which was fortunate because he fully expected them to. Roruch had been captain of the Black Guard for many years, and was the best soldier Dethen had commanded. Not that Dethen would have admitted the fact, but Felmarr had done well in producing such a captain.

"I want the daughter," Dethen said. "And unharmed."

The two men exchanged an almost imperceptible glance. The

implication was obvious: to fail in such a simple task would be worse than death. It would not be possible to run from the dark mage.

Roruch's look was plainly readable: one mistake and he would kill Koran himself. Koran stared back into his captain's single eye, fighting down his fear.

The two men saluted and melded into the silence of the night forest. Dethen waited for a few minutes before anxiety gripped him. A prescient warning shuddered down his spine, and he strode after the soldiers.

⟝●●●⟞

Malak lay on the makeshift bed, feeling intensely restless, yet loath to move for fear of waking his wife. He looked at her, and could not repress a smile. Lena was curled up next to him in the fetal position, secure in dreamless sleep. He ran his fingers gently through her hair, taking care not to disturb her. After several lifetimes together, love could not begin to describe his affection for her: she was everything to him.

He slipped discreetly off the bed and onto the cold wooden floor. The room was almost completely dark, with no moonlight for guidance. On Enya, the moon was always present at night, whether waxing or waning; its effect on the plane's mood was dramatic. The only light diffusing into the room was the dim radiance of the porch lamp.

He could hear Tara's disturbed breathing. She was extremely restless, a result of the earlier incident, no doubt. The most exotic experience in her life had suddenly changed from eating venison stew to a confrontation with an astral vampire.

Bast lay at the bottom of Tara's bed, meticulously cleaning her front legs. Her hard green eyes glittered in the darkness, her ears tracking every sound of the night forest. Bast was now smaller than Malak ever remembered, due to the moon's phase and the wound she had sustained; she was little bigger than a house cat. Seeing his familiar caused him to consider recent occurrences again. They perplexed him enormously.

He felt guilty not being there when Lena needed him, even though she was well able to take care of herself. And secondly he was concerned about Bast's wound. He knew that she would be fine, but he was greatly disturbed. Who would be capable of such a crime?

Even more, he was worried about Dahran breaking their scrying link. Someone had been attempting to enter the Tower, and he had heard no news since. He wondered whether he should try to contact the Tower again. It had been a couple of hours since his last failed attempt.

Suddenly he realized that Bast had paused; she was listening intently. Malak quietly moved over to her. She snarled viciously as her ears detected something. She darted under Tara's bed to scour the room with anxious eyes.

Malak could hear nothing himself, but he knew that Bast was not spooked easily. He turned to check on Lena, and saw *Retaliator* glowing urgently as she lay on the floor next to his bed. He could feel her uneasiness vibrate through his own body. Her apprehension gradually increased, and with it his own.

Detecting her husband's wariness, Lena suddenly snapped out of sleep. She lay completely still as she saw how still Malak stood. She resisted the temptation to move from her vulnerable lying position. *Retaliator* now pulsed with animosity, begging Malak to wield her. Her call throbbed in his bones.

He could still hear nothing, even with his hearing strained to its limit, only the sigh of the wind and Tara's laboured breathing. What disturbed him most was that although *Retaliator* was always alert to danger, she never gave out such passionate vibrations. He could feel the fury coursing through the blade. The star-sapphire was flaring to fill the room with a dim azure light. The light pulsed rhythmically, akin to a rapid heartbeat. It produced a bizarre stroboscopic effect.

Suddenly a terrible crash split the room as a black armoured figure exploded through the window. The effect was eerie in the strange blue light. The figure was visible only in flashes as it hit the floor and executed a forward roll to break-fall.

Tara squealed as she awakened from one nightmare and into another. She huddled in her bed, blankets pulled over her head.

Malak span around to deal with the intruder. A deafening battle cry caused him to pause. A second figure dived through the shattered window. Malak choked as he realized the second assassin intended to silence Lena.

There was little he could do. Roruch's colossal bulk rose up before him to block out the view. With a flick of his wrist, the soldier transferred a dagger from his sleeve into the palm of his hand. Malak realized immediately that the man was a skilled knife-fighter. It was obvious from his grip on the weapon.

Confusion clawed at Malak's mind. He floundered in hesitation. He had rarely been in actual combat, certainly not in a fight for his life. The one-eyed man before him was a practiced killer. His malicious grin revealed his contempt for mercy. Malak backed off as Roruch advanced in a stalk, ready to strike at any moment. With trepidation, Malak noticed the vicious scar that stretched across his assailant's head.

Lena struggled out of the bed-sheets. She saw the outline of Koran bearing down on her, wakizashi drawn and ready to strike. Never trained in any form of combat, Lena didn't rate her chances. Against an armed assassin, she would be next to useless. She watched Koran advance in horror.

The wakizashi blade plummeted vertically, hungrily seeking to cleave open her head. She moved to her left, clumsily performing a forward roll. The blade missed by scant inches, and she landed awkwardly on her back. She struggled quickly to her feet, ignoring her winded stomach.

Koran twirled his weapon back into a striking position. He bore down on her again. She was only half risen and had her back to him, but was painfully aware of his advance. Her head ached and she felt dizzy. She was disorientated by the pulsing blue light; it was impossible to catch her breath.

But she had no time for consideration. Koran's weapon was ready to strike. Malak was fighting for his life; she would receive no help from him. She pushed hard with her legs and slid across the varnished floor to the wall beside Tara's bed.

The maneuver did her little good. She bought some time, but was now pinned against the wall with no hope of escape. Beside her, Bast growled ferociously. At her present size she was little threat, though. Koran advanced upon his prone victim.

Malak, too, was battling for survival. Roruch held the knife in his back hand, while fending the mage off with his front. The two men circled each other warily, searching for an opening. Both were oblivious of their surroundings. Although Lena's predicament continually passed through Malak's head, he knew he had to concentrate fully upon his opponent. Otherwise they would both certainly die.

Roruch saw that Malak had too much attention on the blade. He suddenly attacked with a fluent front kick. The speed caught Malak by surprise. He slid backward to avoid the technique, which was aimed at his solar plexus. He failed to make enough distance and the kick ploughed into his groin as Roruch overreached. Malak doubled over in shock and pain. This reaction saved him: the following slash to his throat passed harmlessly above his head.

Gritting his teeth against the agonizing pain in his groin, he rammed his head into Roruch's stomach and grasped his knife arm by the elbow. The two men crashed heavily onto the floor, which groaned in disapproval. The impact separated them by several feet. Roruch lost his grip upon the knife.

He retrieved his weapon but Malak was already on his feet. In a rush to react first, Roruch lunged out with a stab. Malak was ready this time. He caught the wrist with his hand and blasted a powerful side kick into Roruch's side. Several ribs splintered with a nauseating crack. Malak snapped the knife-wielding wrist, and allowed his quarry to collapse to the floor.

He turned to help his wife, but was shocked when Roruch rose unsteadily from the deck, his Black Guard training forcing him to continue. Roruch lunged at the mage, punching with his good arm. Malak's technique connected first. His nukité spear-hand technique pierced Roruch's throat, collapsing his trachea. As the soldier hit the floor, Malak knelt down and gripped his head. He twisted sharply. The neck snapped with an ominous crack.

He stared nauseously at his work before turning back to Lena. She was in desperate trouble: across the room, Koran's wakizashi was already beginning its death-strike.

Malak gave a cry of horror. He knew he was absolutely helpless to save her. There was an anguished look of panic on Lena's face as the blade descended, flashing brightly in the azure light. She lifted her hands up, apparently to protect herself. A look of strained concentration passed over her face.

Malak stared, dumbfounded, as violet lightning exploded from her palms, blasting into her attacker and throwing him a dozen feet into the opposite wall. The fire consumed his entire body, incinerating it instantly. The magical flames disappeared as he slumped down the wall to the floor, leaving a charred mess and a sickening smell like pork.

Malak ran across the room to his wife. Her face was ashen and drawn; she had spent most of her energy in the blast. Her breathing was shallow and irregular, and her body was shivering in small convulsions. He hugged her tightly, still in disbelief at the display: he had never before seen anything like it. With Ghalan's influence now gone, he knew there would be no barrier against the use of magical power for any purpose.

As Lena clung weakly to him, he suddenly realized that *Retaliator* had not quieted. In fact, she was pulsing more vehemently. A fearful cognition hit Malak as he remembered the other times the katana had behaved in this way. He also realized that only one person could have trained the assassins: Dethen. And *Retaliator* only behaved in such a way when in the vicinity of *Widowmaker*: the two swords loathed one another.

A crash and a scream came from the main room. A moment later, the door burst from its hinges as Kane was blasted through. A titanic black robed figure stepped after him, ducking his head to pass through the shattered door frame. A searing flame of red light emanated from the hilt of *Widowmaker*, which hung by his side. Brilliant white sparks cascaded in the air as it mingled with the pure blue light of *Retaliator*, forming a viscous purple hue. The red and blue rays clashed viciously, seeking to annihilate each other in a spiralling astral battle that was breathtaking to behold.

Malak sprang to his feet to block the advancement of his karmic twin. The two men stood unmoving as they studied each other against the pyrotechnical background. For many lifetimes, their paths had not physically crossed, yet in every other way they had been intimately linked.

"Malak." Dethen's bass tone conveyed his contempt. "Step aside, little one. I have a use for the young girl."

Malak could not stand his brother's gaze. The black soulless depths of his brothers eyes terrified him; their invulnerable, brutal strength was tremendous. He suddenly felt frail and utterly insignificant. His heartbeat pounded in his ears and his mouth was bone dry.

"You'll have to step over my corpse, brother." His voice tremored slightly with the rush of adrenaline in his veins.

Dethen smiled, a patronizing and sinister gesture. "That is not a problem, little one." He stepped forward.

Malak had to act. He exploded into a lethal front kick, aimed at

Dethen's xiphoid, below the sternum. Dethen slipped contemptuously to the side. He slammed a palm-heel technique into Malak's jaw. There was a baneful crunch. Malak was whipped back to land on his back. He struggled feebly to stay conscious as Dethen's bulk loomed over him.

Dethen raised an eyebrow, surprised to find his brother conscious. His boot stamped forcefully on Malak's forehead, finishing the job.

He drew *Widowmaker*. The sword poised in his hand, ready to thrust into Malak's heart. Before he struck, Dethen cast his eye around the room. He frowned at the sight of Roruch's body. A mixed look of surprise and remorse passed across his face, but only for a brief moment.

Then he noticed Lena. His expression was replaced with intense hatred as his eyes ran over her exhausted form. Guilt assailed him as he remembered a woman from several lifetimes ago. Though the physical resemblance was slight, there was something about Lena's eyes. The deep brown stare reminded him of Anya so much.

He stared at his unconscious brother, his eyes uncertain. *Widowmaker* hummed, eagerly urging him on. Dethen licked his lips, mystified by his own indecision. He swore and slammed the sword back into its scabbard. *Widowmaker* buzzed angrily.

Dethen glared at Lena and stepped over to Tara's bed. He threw the bed-sheets off the young girl. Tara screamed hysterically; Dethen paid no attention as he hauled her by her long hair. He had a use for her petty, irrelevant life.

He gave Lena one last, inquisitive glance before striding purposefully from the room.

The Universe is in equilibrium; there-
fore He who is without it, though his
force be but a feather, can overturn the
Universe.

—Aleister Crowley, *The Book of Lies*

11

Enya
Lokhi Region
The Enchanted Forest

S even black Adepts traversed the ancient forest trail following the passage of their master, their flickering torches casting
a blood-red light around them, their faces concealed within
crepuscular hoods.

Dethen glided through the dense foliage with deadly purpose and
conviction. The nocturnal activity of the forest died where he passed
and the trees seemed to bow away from him in fear and revulsion.
The drizzling rain impacted nowhere near him, neither could a gust
of wind touch him. He had reached the peak of his power—there
was nothing he could not bend to his will. Only Chronzon was there
left to defeat, and even He had been shaken by his power.

Behind him, two Adepts dragged along the sobbing figure of Tara.
She struggled in fear, her face red and bloated from a continuous
flow of tears. Her blond hair was filthy and matted; her cheap satin
night-dress was ripped and hanging from her body. She had not been
violated, however. That was the last thing that Dethen would allow.

She let out a wailing scream. A shiver of disquiet passed through
the forest. She broke into a fit of sobbing; it didn't cross her dazed
mind that they were many miles from civilization. Seqqra, the Adept
on her right, shook her roughly. He gave a perverse leer as he grasped
a handful of breast with his free hand. She squealed, parrying desperately. He cursed and slapped her across the face, drawing a trickle
of blood from the side of her mouth.

Dethen suddenly stopped; the procession halted immediately.

Seqqra froze in fear as the Black Master turned to face his disciple. There was no anger in his manner; no living man had ever seen Dethen angered. Yet the icy, harsh look of contempt held far more threat than any emotion could convey.

Moving too fast to follow, he struck the Adept with a backhand slap across the face. The force of the blow sent the sorcerer crashing to the ground. Dethen advanced upon Tara, who cowered in dread below his awesome figure.

He carefully studied her face as she cringed, looking anywhere to avoid his terrible gaze. Her skin itched under his scrutiny. He took her gently by the throat, exerting just enough strength to restrict her head movement. For a brief second an attempt at a comforting smile crossed his face, but she was too terrified to notice.

He regarded her with slight amusement, but his eyes held genuine sympathy. He wished he could make her see the pathetic nature of her existence: now, as ever, her life was pain and sorrow. As with all other humans, she was constantly constrained by so many factors that she was never truly free. She lived her life like an automaton, responding to her environment mechanically, never being truly happy. It was the same for all humans, on all planes of existence. Not even death gave a respite, due to the interference of reincarnation. Only the Black School had the solution to banish pain forever.

With her head now locked forward, the girl was forced to look her kidnapper in the eyes. For the first time she clearly saw his face. The paradigm of cruel, deep-set scars manifested ominously in the blood-red light. His eyes were black and inhuman, or maybe beyond human. The pupils were fathomless holes, portals to dimensions of infinite magnitude and terrible darkness.

He focused his attention in the depths of her eyes, boring through her skull. He scoured her mind. He found it to be pitifully weak—her will was incredibly feeble. She stared rigidly back, unable to tear her gaze from his. She went limp in his arms as auto-hypnosis occurred.

He reversed the direction of the telepathic link, opening up his very essence for her to see. Intense suffering and images of entities horrific beyond description transfused into her being. Her eyes widened in fear. She tried desperately to push the Black Adept away. She convulsed spasmodically and her mouth dropped open; she drooled vapidly. She tried to scream and found her throat constricted. Her eyes rolled to the sky and she collapsed anaemically into his huge arms.

Dethen smiled sadly as he ran his fingers through her long hair.

"Sleep, my child, the horrors of life will soon be far behind you…" The words ill-fitted his rugged voice.

Bal stepped in to support the girl as Dethen turned curtly. He ignored Seqqra, who rose from the ground behind him, a sizable purple bruise developing on his cheek.

The procession continued through the drizzling rain for several miles, following Dethen's unwavering path. He didn't tire, and neither did he expect anyone else to: an Adept devoid of stamina was undeserving of the title.

The trail was ancient, and though it had not been travelled for many centuries, the vegetation considered it with some respect: no foliage attempted to grow upon it.

Eventually the forest thinned out over half a mile or so. It gave way to what would have been a beautiful valley under more pleasant conditions. The contingent descended into the large depression, which was a regular oval shape. Against the murky darkness ahead, several large dark objects could be seen in the centre of the valley.

As the group approached closer, the red light of the torches was cast across their huge outlines. The nature of the megaliths was then apparent. They stood proudly, their awesome bulk and age intimidating to the greatest Adept.

The standing stones were set in concentric circles. The outer was formed of the Twelve, each of which represented a Zodiac sign. The middle circle was composed of the Seven, linked to the sacred planets. The inner circle contained the three Mothers, representing the mother elements: fire, water and air. When combined, these elements would manifest in the fourth element: earth.

The megaliths were all identical. Standing twelve feet tall, and six feet in diameter, their surfaces were as smooth as glass, with the appearance of black marble. They pulsed with a steady, ponderous rhythm. It felt like the heartbeat of the universe; such was its nature.

Without fuss the Black Adepts took up their places, each one assuming a position by one of the Seven. Dethen lay the peasant girl down on the altar stone, which lay embedded horizontally into the ground. Its shape was perfect for the accommodating of a human body, since the stones had been used primarily for healing in ancient times. Even then, however, the purpose and nature of the stones had already been forgotten.

Around Tara's unconscious body, he arranged nine purple candles. Their flames danced precariously in the wind and soft drizzle. On top of her body he placed a huge moonstone, its creamy coloured surface embedded with veins of lavender. He signalled to two Adepts to set up the incense burners. Soon the airy scent of jasmine permeated the atmosphere.

Dethen could feel the power of the stones surging through the inner circle. Powerful lines of magnetic force flowed between them. Each megalith was magically linked to every other; the play of force copied the play of natural forces in the universe that the stones were charged with. He knew that the Rose Circle was the only place where his ritual could succeed. He needed its natural link to the other planes of existence.

He repressed a shudder as he sensed the night's atmosphere. The Dark Moon was now directly above the Rose Circle. That, combined with Ghalan's absence, meant that the plane was more unstable than ever before. It was an extremely unpleasant environment for any activity, let alone magick of the most dangerous type imaginable. There was more than a natural bitterness in the cold, and more than a hint of malignancy in the tempestuous wind. He could feel the dark forces clustering around him; they waited with eager anticipation.

Lilith, Queen of the Night: she was a force no mortal man could hope to contain. Her unrestrained manifestation would be sure to awaken her archenemy, the great Archangel Gabriel, from his slumber. No one could predict the consequences of this. The battle would be catastrophic, whatever the outcome. One thing was certain, however: both Enya and Yesod could not possibly survive. And the resulting imbalance would disrupt the Tree of Life, destroying the Universe.

He closed his eyes and signalled for silence as he began to harmonize himself with the environment. Icy chills passed through his body as the dark forces pushed from all sides. The Boundary had weakened considerably, and he felt them almost as tangible realities. For a moment, he felt a whim of concern, but he quickly pushed it aside; he smiled bitterly to himself. How could he worry about minor complications when he was propagating the annihilation of the Universe?

Dethen turned to Bal. "Begin the banishment," he ordered.

Bal sent three Adepts to take positions at the north, south and west of the outer circle. Bal himself assumed the east position, facing away from the circle. From his robes he took an object enveloped in white cotton. He carefully unwrapped it.

The article was an ornate dagger of the rarest steel. Its handle was bright red and covered in vivid green Hebrew names and sigils. The sigils and hilt continually seemed to swap colours.

With the dagger, Bal began to trace a pentagram. He charged the pentagram with an intense blue-violet colour, flickering gold flames running along it. He traced the symbol from his left hip, making it almost as large as his body. Within a few seconds the pentagram became visible to the other Adepts as Bal's highly trained visualization came to bear.

When the symbol was finished it shimmered before him. He inhaled deeply and then thrust both hands into its center, stepping forward with his left foot. Energy flowed into the pentagram as he exhaled. He returned to natural posture and pushed the dagger into the icon's heart. He then moved sideways around the edge of the outer circle. As he moved, a bright white line of ethereal energy followed the path of the outstretched dagger.

When he reached the south point of the circle, he lowered the weapon and allowed the next Adept to take over. The second mage drew a pentagram, centering on the point where Bal's chest-height horizontal line of energy stopped. When his symbol was complete, he charged it in the same manner, and continued the white line around the circle to the next Adept. Thus, the entire site was surrounded by a boundary of pure white light, studded at the four directions by pentagrams of flaming blue.

The four magi returned to their places. Dethen crossed to the middle circle, taking his place by the stone of Mars. At his signal, every magician laid down, their feet touching one of the Seven.

Dethen pushed astral material up from his solar plexus chakra to a height six feet above his body. He formed the material into a replica of his physical body. It hovered horizontally in the air, facing him. With an effort of will, he then transferred consciousness to his astral body.

The other magi did likewise. Within a minute, each Adept had again taken his place by one of the Seven, this time astrally.

Dethen signalled his intention to begin: "Hekas, Hekas, Este Bebeloi!"

Suddenly the entire valley fell silent in anticipation.

He started to chant, tranquilly at first but slowly building in intensity. The language was Enochian, the most ancient and arcane tongue known to man. There was an immediate and marked change in the psychic pitch of their surroundings. The other Black Adepts joined in at predetermined times. The chant amplified and augmented. Within a few minutes its potent tones resounded through the valley and beyond in great waves. The volume rose and fell rhythmically.

The whole plane fell silent in nervous expectation as the ritual further intensified. The wind died after a final, desperate gust; the drizzle of rain faded out and disappeared. No other sound could now be heard except for the incessant chanting. It reached a tremendous volume and yet continued to strengthen. It vibrated back and forth across the land, shaking its very foundations. Quivers of apprehension passed through the ground beneath them.

Dethen visualized an inverted pentagram above Tara's body. It shone passionately with a sinister purple light, taking in strength from the chanting. Its light brightened as the power of the other Adepts came to bear. The atmosphere tightened immensely. Energy saturated the air, making it difficult to breathe. It gently luminesced, flickering slowly through the colours of the spectrum. There was a huge and malignant force present: Dethen could feel it like a tremendous pressure in all directions.

He gave the signal to terminate the chanting. Complete silence enshrouded the valley. Sparkles flickered and winked in the air: the barrier to the Unseen had been greatly weakened.

Dethen paused a moment to catch his breath, then raised his arms to the sky. The firmament was now cloudless and pulsed with an eerie purple light.

His voice boomed out: "We evoke the Queen of the Night from the depths of the Qlippoth! With pure hearts and souls, we praise the Queen of Demons! Manifest before us without constraint and end the pitiful plight of this world! Appear before us and destroy us joyfully!"

The air crackled with an omnipresent energy. Great vortices spiralled chaotically within the inner circle. The atmosphere was so intense and expectant, it was impossible to breathe. Dethen's astral form constricted as waves of blackness emanated from the circle. He grimaced. There was no turning back now.

He looked at the altar, where Tara lay unconscious. He shouted: "We offer the life of the virgin girl as an aid to manifestation!"

A black throbbing darkness appeared above the girl's body. It oozed as if turning itself inside-out, all the time expanding. With it came an unbearably chilling cold, and an utterly repugnant smell beyond description. It lowered itself to surround and swallow the girl. Tara gained consciousness for a brief second. Her eyes flicked open and she let out a single, piercing scream before being swallowed.

Dethen stared as if possessed, his eyes as black as the demonic darkness.

A deep growl shook the megaliths as the darkness began to glow. One of the Black Adepts screamed and started to flee in fear; the others quickly followed, mindlessly running for their lives. Even Bal fell to his knees, unable to resist the tremendous waves of power. Only Dethen remained on his feet; he stood with his arms open, held ready to embrace.

The glow intensified, becoming brighter and brighter until it was impossible to behold. Then it exploded.

The horrendous force instantly atomized the physical and astral bodies of the Adepts. The detonation lit up the countryside for a hundred miles, the shock wave almost tearing the entire plane apart.

Yet Enya survived. The force was unable to violate the ancient seal of the outer circle.

An inhuman howl of anguish and frustration pierced through the air as Lilith, Queen of the Night, realized she was thwarted.

*All powerful magic is within me. I am
one who can travel in strength without
forgetting his name. I am Yesterday.
'Seer of Millions of Years' is my name.
I can travel along the paths with those
who influence the gods.*

—Egyptian Book of the Dead

Enya
Lokhi Region
Oaklan Village

Lena sat on the bedroom floor, Malak's head cradled in her arms. It had been five hours since Dethen had left, and still her husband had yet to regain consciousness. Her own body was still drained from the battle, and she knew there was nothing she could do to aid him.

The house was quiet except for Jenny's steady weeping in the next room. Her daughter had been taken from her. Kane was dead and Gal had a skull fracture; he, too, had yet to regain consciousness. The two White Adepts had failed her in a spectacular way. The woman was so shocked that she was now oblivious to why she was crying.

Lena's legs ached with acute cramp, but she dared not move for fear of aggravating Malak's injuries. She was fairly sure that he suffered no serious damage to his head, but there was an extremely unpleasant swelling around his jaw. She hoped it wasn't broken.

She dejectedly scanned the broken and dishevelled room. She had to concentrate to hold back the sudden surge of self-pity that gripped her. The situation was so unjust; she couldn't comprehend why such a thing should happen. Thoughts of vengeance swelled within her as anger started to build.

It suddenly occurred to her that she could feel strange rhythmic vibrations on the astral. She abruptly cut them out; her soul had taken its fill of excitement for the night. She cast her eyes vehemently across the motionless bodies of the Black Guard soldiers, her hatred seeking a focus.

She gasped as Malak suddenly groaned and twitched. His eyelids flickered and slowly opened. He looked at her with an unfocused stare. He raised his hand up to his jaw and winced as a dull, throbbing pain commenced.

Lena helped him to sit up, carefully watching for signs of a concussion as he rubbed the back of his head.

"Do you remember what happened?" she asked.

His eyes rolled to the ceiling as he tried to recall the evening's encounter. He sighed and nodded, pain and embarrassment on his face.

"Where's Dethen?" he asked, his voice hoarse.

"Gone."

"And Tara?"

"He took her with him."

The couple was silent awhile as Malak gradually oriented himself. He mused over the pain in his jaw. He found it quite agonizing to speak but he suspected the swelling would disappear within a few days.

He was furious with himself. He had frozen when confronted by Dethen, and his brother's skills had proved far superior to his own. When Ghalan had originally trained the two brothers in the martial arts many centuries ago, Malak had always been the more talented. But Dethen had been pushing his ability to its limit through decades of arduous training. Malak still found it difficult to accept his strength, and the sheer speed he had moved with. He knew that Dethen would have extended his magical capabilities in the same way.

The only comfort to him was that Lena had not been hurt, though she was obviously very weak. A strange sensation suddenly interrupted his thoughts.

"What's that noise?" he asked.

Lena frowned, hearing nothing. Then she realized that he was referring to the rhythmic astral waves she had felt earlier. They were now much stronger; their amplitude increasing rapidly. The sordid pitch was intimidating.

"It sounds almost like chanting," she said.

Malak's head whipped around, causing him to wince. "And they've taken Tara…"

They were both suddenly aware of the significance of Tara's

abduction: there was only one reason why Dethen could possibly require her. This far from true civilization, the girl's chastity was undoubted.

"But only demonic rituals require sacrifice for appeasement!" Lena said.

"And what other kind of ritual would Dethen be contemplating at such a time?"

"But what does he hope to achieve? A qlippothic entity can't do much that he can't!"

The chanting had now reached fever pitch. It was definitely emanating from deep within the forest.

"He's at the Rose Circle," Malak said suddenly. "He has something very big planned."

He pushed himself up and walked stiffly over to the shattered window. The rain had stopped and the sky was now clear. The stars shone brightly down on the forest trees, but their light seemed somehow cold and hostile tonight. A purple haze hung over the treetops in the distance. Malak hesitated as he recalled that there was something unusual about the night. Cognition hit him as he discerned the Dark Moon, visible only by the circle of stars it eclipsed.

He span around like a madman. His eyes were fiery with anger and fear. Only one word issued from his lips.

"Lilith!" He shuddered as the name left his lips.

Lena paled. "He couldn't!" But she felt her voice failing as the truth hit home.

The chanting had now ceased. In its place was a viscid tension. The two magi stared at each other in disbelief, attempting to assimilate the ramifications of such a ritual. Their minds refused outright: the consequences were simply too far reaching.

Malak turned to stare out of the window again, fury whirling through his mind. He knew he was helpless to put a stop to Dethen's scheme: the Rose Circle was over a dozen miles away.

He suddenly felt a hideous pain in his solar plexus. With it came an abhorrent tension that caused the entire plane to gasp. Malak's attention was spectacularly grabbed as an incredibly bright light erupted in the forest. It rapidly expanded, consuming all in its path.

"Get down!" he shouted

But there was no time to react. The shock wave collided, almost bursting his ear drums and blasting him off his feet. The cabin instantly imploded, shattering into a million splinters. The light scorched across it, levelling every tree as it smashed by.

Malak lay dazed for several seconds, his ears painfully ringing. He coughed violently, retching up bile. His first thought was for his wife's safety. He pushed away the light debris that buried him.

He started to search frantically, but there was little need for concern. Lena emerged from the detritus a few feet from him.

"Are you okay?" he asked, supporting her by the arm.

She shook her head dazedly and pointed to the sight behind him.

Malak turned to see the most awesome sight in his life. As far as the naked eye could see, the forest had been completely flattened. In the centre of the blast radius there was a huge astral vortex, so strong that it lit up the surrounding countryside for miles with an eerie green light. The monstrosity spiralled lazily in the air, towering above the plane in its proportions.

Malak and Lena stared in horror, feeling as insignificant as amoebae lost in an ocean.

It was mid-morning before Malak and Lena came within sight of their destination. The valley of the Rose Circle stretched out before them.

The Adepts rested for several minutes on decapitated tree stumps before daring to continue. Both were weak from the previous night, and the journey on foot had been extremely taxing. Gemma and Raven had both been killed by the shock wave.

They watched in awe as the gargantuan astral vortex meandered lazily in an immense widdershins spiral above them. It glowed vigorously, making the air luminous with a preternatural green light. The two Adepts knew they were confronted with a task their combined abilities were woefully inadequate to deal with.

Malak looked at his wife. "Ready?"

Lena started to shake her head, and then stood up resignedly. She saw no point in postponing the inevitable. Her face was still ashen from her expenditure of energy in defense against Koran and her legs unsteady, but her face was set with resolve. They both knew that if the problem before them was not immediately contained, the consequences for Enya would be dire. Neither of them had succeeded in contacting the Celestial Tower, and they knew that they would receive no aid.

"Let's go," she said, her voice solemn.

Malak hugged her and pressed his cheek against hers. He looked no better than Lena did: his jaw had swollen severely overnight, and any movement of his mandible was extremely painful. Its puffed and purple appearance gave testimony to the fact.

The couple advanced upon the great storm side by side, their arms linked. Crackles of violet and blue lightning detonated above their heads.

As they reached the outer edge of the vortex, Malak stepped away from Lena. He unsheathed *Retaliator*. The green mist fell back in repulsion. The katana glowed urgently, its sharp azure light cutting through the air. He directed the sword to a point before his left hip and commenced the tracing of a large banishing pentagram. The symbol pulsed with an intense blue colour, similar to that of the sword.

The wall of the tornado grudgingly opened up, forming a path through which two people could move unhindered. He turned to Lena.

"Are you ready for this?"

He silently asked himself the same question as uncertainty seized him.

Lena nodded and stepped forward to join him. They walked on, entering the torrent of astral force. The wall healed up behind them, leaving them in a clear bubble that was free of the noxious energy.

As they progressed, they saw that the valley had been scoured of all life: not a blade of grass stood in the vortex. The ground was covered with a grey graphite-like sludge, several inches deep. It reeked like wet animal fur. Vague shapes and cackles followed them, but they didn't attempt to enter the purified area centred around *Retaliator*.

After a few minutes' walk, the megaliths loomed menacingly into view. As the Adepts approached closer, the true horror of the situation became apparent.

A living, breathing Darkness pulsated within the Rose Circle. Its texture seemed to be warm and wet. The sulfurous smell that assaulted their nostrils was overpowering. They stopped a few feet from the perimeter to observe, their skin itching in repulsion.

Suddenly the two observers were noticed. Insane screaming

pierced the atmosphere like a rapier. It was the sound of mindless creatures in terrible agony. Their essence could be read from their inhuman voices: their only pleasure was gained in destruction and the infliction of pain upon others. The cacophony was enough to drive a man to instant insanity, but the two White Adepts stood their ground firmly.

Twisted demonic faces of all shapes and colours leered at them, hurling themselves unthinkingly at the invisible barrier. It was obvious that the barrier was gradually weakening; it scintillated with each collision. The two magi knew that if the barrier yielded, the consequences would be incalculable.

By the edge of the outer circle, the material of the astral vortex was absent. This was the eye of the storm. Lena was here able to separate herself from the protective influence of *Retaliator* to circle the perimeter in the opposite direction to Malak. They both wondered how they could possibly shut down the huge energy well.

It was soon apparent what had acted as an aid to manifestation. Inside the centre-most circle, the lifeless body of Tara was still present. Malak instantly recognized her slight figure. A faint light surrounded her, and the power of the Darkness appeared to emanate from it. Malak hung his head in anguish. It grieved him immensely that an innocent girl could be used in such a way.

It was obvious to him now where the power for the psycho-magnetic link had come from. The only way to neutralize the forced sacrifice was to replace it with a voluntary one. But this was a heinous idea. Only Tara's physical life had been taken; however, a voluntary sacrifice would damn his soul eternally. Stepping into the circle would be a one-way journey to Hell: there would be no hope of rescue.

The dark power would be obliged to accept such a sacrifice. Each man's free will allowed him the option of such an act.

Malak stared into the heart of the Darkness. It mocked him with its awesome power. The most terrible fear he had experienced in his life froze him to the spot. He knew that without a sacrifice, the entire plane would be destroyed in the next hour.

He looked over at Lena, wondering if she had realized the magnitude of the problem. From her face, he knew that she had. But there was something else that he couldn't quite read. And then it struck him: resignation.

Her intention struck him like a punch. He screamed and started to move toward her. He felt her touch his mind telepathically for the last time.

Good-bye, Malak.

Malak felt her final emotions. Her love of him was overwhelming, and her fear of her next action was terrifying.

Her face now incredibly pale, and her legs almost too weak to stand on, she crossed her arms across her chest and murmured her irreversible karmic vow of sacrifice. She then fell forward, passing over the boundary into the outer circle.

The Darkness swallowed her hungrily, enclosing her essence to suck the life-force from her. An intense chill spread rapidly through her body as her blood was drained of energy. She released a terrible scream as invisible talons ripped into her skin from all sides, digging deeply into her flesh and vital organs. Then the claws wrenched apart simultaneously, rupturing her body and soul into a million shards.

The outer boundary flared a brilliant white and an explosion erupted, hurling the contents of the circle back into the depths of the Qlippoth. Malak landed hard on his back over a dozen yards away, his hair and robes scorched severely. He immediately pushed himself up, oblivious to his condition.

Lena was now trapped in Hell, her spirit enslaved to save his own. She was at the mercy of the demonic forces, with an eternity to wait before her release.

Malak's howl of utter agony echoed vehemently over the blasted landscape and up through the ten planes of existence.

Flow with whatever may happen and let your mind be free: stay centred by accepting whatever you are doing. This is the ultimate.

—Chuang-Tzu, Taoist Philosopher

Enya
Thenyan Region
The Celestial Tower

The small fire smouldered in the enormous fireplace, its life almost spent. Malak sat in a huge armchair, huddled close to the meagre heat source. His hair and beard were scathed and ruffled, his face pale and unhealthy. Sunken, his eyes stared into infinity with disinterest. Heavy purple robes enfolded him; they were ripped and stained. He had neither washed, nor changed his apparel in a week.

Behind him, the mess hall of the Tower stretched away into darkness. Lifeless bodies lay slumped across the length of the huge table and over the wooden floor. The smell of decayed flesh was overpowering. They were all students who Malak had once known; some were neophytes of many years standing, who were sincere but quite talentless.

The attack from the Black School had been swift, efficient and decisive. The White School had possessed no soldiers to defend itself, and there had been no contest. Yet Malak was oblivious to the carnage around him. He was well aware of what had happened: upon his return he had scoured the Tower for survivors. It was simply that he no longer cared; he had passed through that stage long ago. All that he had now were his emptiness and bitterness, which focused as hatred upon his deceased brother.

A sharp pain flared up his left leg. He winced at the unexpected pang, which snapped him momentarily back to reality. He looked down to see Bast setting herself aggressively, swiping his legs with her claws. The moon was waxing and already approaching full. As a consequence, Bast's size was increasing; her well muscled back almost reached his waist. He lashed out with a kick, which was more symbolic than effective; she dodged easily, and gave another painful rake.

"What?!" he demanded angrily.

She tilted her head to one side and gave him a hard stare. It told him that he knew exactly what she meant. She wanted him on his feet and active again. He sighed tiredly and pushed her away. She lifted a front paw and swiped the air threateningly.

"Okay, okay!" he said, lethargically rising from the armchair. "I'm up!"

Bast's hard eyes glittered with satisfaction in the gloom.

Malak felt more awake on his feet. As his conscious mind became more stimulated, he realized two things at once. The dark closed in upon him as the fire died; without the flickering flames the cold was almost unbearable. More importantly, his stomach ached with hunger; it had not been fed since his return to the Tower.

He grimaced and wiped a running nose on the sleeve of his robes. He realized he would have to start paying attention to his physical body again. He had no conception of how much time he had spent by the fire, or how long he had been in the Tower. The whole duration seemed like a hazy dream. A small part of his mind reminded him that he was still locked within the nightmare.

He walked over to a pantry, not focusing on any of his deceased colleagues. He lit the lamp, flooding the pantry with unbearably bright light. He waited as his eyes adjusted.

The room was well stocked, but almost the entire cache was inedible. An extremely unpleasant smell permeated the air. He half-heartedly dug through the shelves, grimacing in disgust as repugnant stenches were released into the atmosphere.

Most of the food was made up of stale bread, sour milk and rotting fruit and vegetables. He avoided the salted pork and beef; he had no idea why they were there. Eventually he came upon a stash of hard savoury biscuits. He took them unenthusiastically; already the idea of eating had lost its appeal. The mouldy vegetables did little for his appetite.

He re-entered the mess hall to find Bast washing her face with her front paws. He broke off a small piece of biscuit and offered it to her. She sniffed the tough grey material suspiciously, then took it gently. She chewed it a few times and then spat it discreetly out the side of her mouth.

"That's what I thought," Malak muttered.

But Bast didn't require sustenance from food, whereas he certainly did. He tickled the familiar affectionately behind her ears and she purred with pleasure.

He looked out through the small window next to him. He could see the dark waves of Mishmar Lake rolling in over the causeway. The air distorted and splayed out into a spectrum of colours as he watched. The Tower seemed to be adjusting its dimensional relationship to Enya. He knew that this was an ominous omen, but he could not raise any interest in the fact.

He turned his attention back to the tin of biscuits with distaste. With a sudden burst of temper, he flung the container across the width of the room. He strode from the hall toward the main staircase.

———◦◉◦———

Several hours later he awoke with a cry of agony, curling up in his bed into the fetal position. Heavy perspiration adhered his robes to his body and his hair was damp. He could taste the saltiness of the tears that ran down his face. His breathing was rapid and uncontrolled; there didn't seem to be enough oxygen in the air. With a great expenditure of effort, he forced his body to calm itself.

The dreams haunted him every time he tried to sleep. He had lived through Lena's death a hundred times, each time unaware that he was dreaming. Each time the nightmare was different. He would try something different to save his wife, but the outcome was always the same. It was a cruel irony that on the one occasion he did save her, waking up was the most hideous experience of all.

He found it almost unbearable to live without his wife: he knew that a huge part of him had been sucked into the Rose Circle with her. He felt that his own soul was trapped within the Qlippoth. She had performed the sacrifice to save him the terrible burden; this made the agony twice as severe. In life, Lena had been everything to him. He could not recall a day when they had not been together.

He remembered her smile and beautiful, shining black hair. He remembered her caressing touch, her elegance and stubbornness. He also recalled her fiery temper, and her love of animals and children. Most of all he remembered the love in their relationship.

He felt the pillar next to his head move. He rolled over to see Squint sitting next to him. Tears rolled down the gnome's pudgy face; his eyes were raw. Malak blinked away his own tears, and ran his hand over the elemental's head. Squint was unable to talk, but there was no need for words.

Malak sighed pensively and hauled himself into a sitting position. He peeled off his damp robes and picked up a towel to wrap around himself. He knew the importance of shocking himself back to reality.

For the next half hour he bathed in freezing cold water, stimulating his flagging willpower. He dried himself thoroughly and dressed in the heaviest robes he could find. He studied his Adept's badge for a few seconds as he considered fastening it to his breast. He shrugged and dropped it into a side pocket: there was no reason to wear it now.

He re-entered his chambers and kicked out Bast. She glared at him as he closed the door before stalking another vacated bed. Malak kicked a cushion into the centre of the room and sat on it, pulling his legs into perfect posture.

To calm his body and mind, he slowed his breathing and heart beat. He tried to estimate the damage he had done in his week of neglect. The answer was shocking: it was obvious that if he hadn't been shaken from his apathy, he would have died within a few days. Without a will to live, the physical body could not survive for long.

After harmonizing himself with his physical, emotional, and mental bodies, he turned his attention to stilling his undulating mind. First he pushed away all calculations concerning the future, and all ties to the past. Then he distanced himself from the present by blocking out all physical sensations and senses. His mind was now completely blank, his consciousness rapidly approaching a mystical state.

Then the images hit him in a sudden and intense blast, thousands of them at once it seemed. Images of Lena being tortured in all manner of agonizing ways fought for his attention. With them came screams of torment from the voice he knew as well as his own. His body tensed in horror at the vividness of the scenes. Tremendously potent emotions rose within him; he wanted nothing more than to break down into a wailing heap. He simply wanted to give in: to bury his head in the sand and forget the abominations before him.

No sight in the universe could have had a worse effect than the one before him.

But his old self flickered in the depths of his personality, bringing its indomitable will to bear. His upper lip curled back aggressively and his eyes snapped open. He pushed himself roughly to his feet, rage in his eyes. From the mantelpiece he snatched up *Retaliator*. The cool touch of the hilt helped to calm him, gradually pushing away the images of torment. He performed a banishment by pentagram, bringing himself back to equilibrium.

The wooden floor splintered as he stabbed the katana into it, allowing the sword to stand unaided. He knelt and stared intently into the star-sapphire, parting its shrouding mists with his mind. Scrying Enya from end to end, he called up the names of students that might have been absent during the Tower massacre. He found no one, and neither could he find any trace of the Black or Yellow Schools. The Yellow School had covered its tracks well. The Black School was either annihilated, or its survivors were well hidden.

He passed his mind over the capital city, Miosk, which lay far to the south-east. He was unsurprised but alarmed at what he saw. The night streets were crowded with rioting people, pillaging and burning. It was a situation never before seen on Enya, and Governor Demaax was completely unable deal with it. His full complement of soldiers was a dozen men, none of them truly proficient with a sword.

Malak ran his scrying over a few more major towns. They were all the same: no place was free of the madness. He knew what had happened. The common people of Enya had been protected from reality for so long, they couldn't face their own negative feelings. Enya was no longer the plane of dreams, but of nightmares. He could strongly feel the people's frustration and hostility through the crystal.

The situation daunted him. He had no idea of what to do. He knew that a new Magus had to be put in place, but he also knew that he would not be worthy for many years. By then, the plane might no longer exist.

He mused over the problem for some time. Then suddenly an idea struck him. He stood up. He knew exactly where to find the solution to his problems.

Malak browsed through the bookshelves of the library. Consisting of an entire level of the Tower, the library was a huge maze in which one could easily become lost. It had a heavy studious atmosphere, built up over hundreds of years. The pleasant scent of storax was permanently suspended in the air. Most of the books were incredibly ancient; much original work had been done in the previous Aeon into the locating and exploring of the higher planes. There was also a vast amount of information on the plane below Yesod: Malkuth, the physical universe.

Malak pondered an idea so terrible, he would consider it only in the vaguest terms. His eyes ran over the small section on demonic entities. Although he admitted nothing of his plan to himself, an alarm was triggered in his mind. His body tensed up in disapproval. The tension almost caused him to fall from the stool when he became aware of something watching him.

The hairs on the nape of his neck prickled with warning. He turned slowly. At a distance of thirty feet, a tall black robed figure stood silently observing him, arms folded across a huge chest. He could see that it was an astral form, probably a very rarefied one.

Suddenly the figure's identity struck him and his legs buckled in surprise. He managed to retain his balance awkwardly as he hit the floor.

"Hello, Malak."

Dethen's voice was as cold and humourless as he remembered it.

"You're dead."

"Yes, it seems I am a shade." Dethen did not seem amused by the fact.

"Why are you here, brother?"

Malak found his accumulated anger against Dethen was strangely lacking in his twin's presence.

"I would have been here sooner, but my astral body suffered an unfortunate accident. It took some time to construct another one,"

Malak said nothing, forcing the black mage to continue. Dethen's mouth twisted into a spiteful snarl.

"How's Lena, Malak?"

Malak's mind hurtled back through lifetimes of memories, triggered by his brother's question. In their first incarnations upon Enya, the twins had been born to Ghalan in the Aeon of Creation, when Logus of the White School had been Magus. Ghalan, already an outstanding Adept of the Yellow School, brought them up as magicians of equal standing, but Dethen had been more dominant due to his nature.

Dethen had always been highly cynical and saw only sorrow in the world; the view became impressed upon his brother. Ghalan, being neutral in viewpoint, had not sought to interfere when Dethen created the Black School upon reaching manhood; after all, the White School already existed, and it was congenial to balance.

Since they had had extremely similar beliefs and philosophies, Malak had naturally joined his brother. However, the partnership fell apart dramatically when Malak met Lena, who even then was a White Adept. Malak's outlook on life was literally changed overnight, as he instantly fell in love. A battle ensued between Malak and Dethen, which Malak won, leaving his twin mortally wounded. He became a White Adept himself, in time rising to become Master of the School.

Malak studied the shade of his brother carefully. There had been no satisfaction in his voice when he asked; it had been a "told-you-so" attitude.

"Don't you see how cruel life can be, Malak?" There was a desperate edge to Dethen's voice; it was a last desperate attempt to save his brother. "Don't blind yourself with all this airy fairy horse-shit! Look at the world realistically. Look at what it's done to you; look at what it's done to Lena for damnation's sake! The world is an abomination! The Black School is the true way. You knew that once, and deep down you still do!"

Malak listened to him silently. He had been thinking similar thoughts himself recently. But to turn from the White School now would be to betray everything he had believed in. And more importantly, it would be a betrayal of Lena, and that he would never do. Yet still, his faith in the Light was shattered, and he wondered to himself whether the peace and happiness he had once possessed had been an illusion. It seemed very unreal to him now.

He looked up at the ghost.

"No, Dethen. I cannot turn from my path now."

"You and I are not so dissimilar, you know. Have you ever wondered why I created the Black School, or why I was so black at heart even when first born on Enya?"

Malak frowned: it was a question that had often plagued him.

"My previous life, before the one as your twin, was on Malkuth. I was an Adept of the White School, totally dedicated to my spiritual advancement and to God."

Malak stared at him in disbelief, but did not doubt his word; Dethen never lied.

"This surprises you, but it is true nonetheless. At a young age, I made a karmic vow to cross the Abyss. I was warned by my Master to avoid attachments to objects and people, but something unavoidable happened.

"I met a woman called Anya, a female Adept of the Order. She was the most beautiful thing that I ever set my eyes upon, with the most gentle and loving personality. We fell hopelessly in love, and my vow was forgotten for a whole year. In that time I became as attached to her as you were to Lena: I loved her with all my soul!

"Eventually, the time came for me to walk the Path of the Abyss. But I was not ready, my karma had not been nullified. But instead of destroying me, Chronzon possessed my physical body. He forced me to plunge the blade of my banishing sword into Anya…"

Malak listened to the tale, absolutely horrified. He could tell from Dethen's voice that the experience had shattered him.

"She died in my arms, Malak, trying to push me away from her as she drew her last breath. Can you imagine my guilt?! Yet that was only the beginning of my suffering. And the being who did this is the being who controls everything which occurs below the Abyss! He moves every planet and star, controls every molecule of the air we breathe! I vowed not to rest until He is wholly destroyed!"

"And what about God?" Malak asked.

"I have no idea of the nature of God. Yet any being who allows a Demon such as the Dark One to take delight in the pain and cruelty of many worlds is hardly a being of love and compassion. Let's face it, he simply doesn't care about the lower planes. He dwells in the perfection of Atziluth, and doesn't bother to concern himself with filth like us!"

Malak was unable to refute his argument. And after their experiences, he had no wish to contradict his brother.

"Come, Malak, I ask you again. Join me and the Black School will destroy the Demon Chronzon, He who makes Lilith seem a mere puppet of evil. Neither of us has any other goal."

Malak bowed his head. Though he felt nothing for God anymore, he still could not betray the memory of Lena.

He looked up. "My path is chosen, Dethen. And it was *you* who destroyed my life, not Chronzon. For that, I will never forgive you!"

The hate was now evident in his voice. It pleasured him to see Dethen wince. There was also a certainty in his voice, which even Dethen wouldn't try to contradict.

The look of sadness on the Black Adept's face slowly turned to anger, and his last words were whispered venomously.

"Then you will be destroyed, Malak!"

He faded into the air, his black eyes burning with intensity.

Malak shuddered at the threat. He knew that his brother would now be chasing the seat of the Magus; it was now the only way he could achieve his black objective. But first he would have to reincarnate.

Malak turned back to the bookshelves. His mind was now resolved to the most dangerous course of action he had ever considered.

He pulled out a large, dull pink book. It was incredibly ancient even for the Tower library. He suspected that it was not native to Enya. Its surface was soft, warm and yielding, reminiscent of skin. He ran his finger along the silver title: "Abremen's Sacred Book of Demonic Pacts."

He hesitated for a few moments before opening the volume, and committing himself to an irreversible course of action.

All lives are individual and unique, yet each must come to an end. Therefore do not fear Death, for it represents completion of the Circle and fulfillment of Purpose.

—The Bushido, Way of the Warrior

Enya
Thenyan Region
The Celestial Tower

In the damp atmosphere of the Tower's underground chamber, Malak again contemplated the action he was about to undertake. It defied every principle he had ever been taught by the White School, and a cold fear gripped him. A shudder of apprehension passed down his spine; he knew that he was in more danger than ever before, through all his incarnations. Yet his path was now chosen, and he had no wish to change it.

As if aware of what he considered, Bast had tormented him until he released her from the Tower. The familiar had never deserted him before, and he knew it was an ominous omen.

With a deep sigh, he raised *Retaliator* and sealed the chamber to contain the force he was about to summon. He muttered the arcane words under his breath. The chamber's ancient wards glowed on the walls, shedding beautiful astral light to illuminate the room.

He crossed over to the protective circle and walked around its perimeter, carefully checking that the Divine Names were unblemished. If anything went wrong this night, his life would depend upon them. Normally the chamber and circle were used for the invocation of spiritual beings. He hated to defile its nature by a single pernicious act.

He entered the circle and examined the heptagonal altar. On it were placed the four elemental weapons, the lotus wand, a moonstone, a chunk of silver and some oil of jasmine. He opened the altar and took out four lamps. He placed them at the cardinal points, just beyond the circle.

With a piece of chalk he marked out an equilateral triangle, large enough to hold a man. Its base touched the edge of the circle, its apex pointing eastward. With great concentration, he carefully consecrated the triangle, marking God-names to bind the unholy essence. He took from his robes a vial of red liquid. He smeared the menstrual blood over the floor inside the triangle, making sure that none crossed its boundary. He grimaced in disgust at the despicable act, but it was a loathsome essence that he sought to evoke, and like attracted like.

He took his silver pentagram from his pocket; he longingly studied the symbol of his Adepthood. In a burst of temper he hurled the object deep into the chamber where the light of the lamps failed to penetrate. Once he had committed his atrocity, he knew he would never again be a White Adept. He viciously fought back the lugubrious emotions that surfaced. The badge meant nothing to him: he would do anything to rescue Lena.

He stepped into the circle and turned to face the east. He breathed deeply, preparing himself for the ordeal ahead. He knew it would be severe.

He pronounced the traditional declaration for a ritual opening: "Hekas, Hekas, Este Bebeloi!"

A singular silence exuded through the chamber.

Using intense visualization, he formulated a brilliant sphere of white light above his head. He pointed at the globe and slowly lowered his finger to touch his forehead. The sphere followed to form a glowing halo around his head.

A beam of white light fired downward to light up his feet in an identical sphere as he pointed to the ground. He paused as he strengthened the two globes and their connecting line that ran through the centre of his body.

Within his right shoulder he created a ball of fiery scarlet energy. It burned with great strength and power, glowing with divine energy. He formed another connecting line, this time horizontally to his left shoulder. There another ball of light appeared, this one a deep and majestic blue. It shimmered gracefully, its light epitomizing mercy and gentleness.

After taking a few seconds to balance the power between these two coloured spheres, he formed the last energy centre in his sternum.

It expanded in a beautiful golden colour to encompass his heart and lungs. The light of the last sphere evoked perceptions of harmony and balance; it was extremely bright. It seemed to draw strength from the light of the other spheres.

Malak opened his eyes and allowed the globes to fade from visible appearance. He unsheathed *Retaliator* and commenced the tracing of the four banishing pentagrams in a circle around him. When he finished, he resheathed the katana and spread his arms out to the sides.

He visualized the protective influences of the four element-ruling Archangels around him, evoking them by vibrating their names through the chamber.

"Before me stands Raphael. Behind me stands Gabriel. To my right stands Michael. To my left stands Auriel," he intoned.

He opened his eyes to see the image of a yellow robed figure before him. The figure seemed to be miles high; an aura of incredible power surrounded him. In his hand he held a Cadaceus Wand, and his robes whipped about him as if in the presence of a wind. Without looking, Malak knew that images of the other three Archangels were arranged around him in their respective directions.

Gradually, the four powers faded. The area was now clear of all spirits and elementals who might disrupt his ritual. Some of these were mischievous or downright evil in nature, and were best removed from the immediate area.

He breathed deeply to compose himself. Focusing upon the triangle that joined onto the protective circle, he withdrew *Retaliator*. He held the katana horizontally before himself, trying to balance his mind and dissipate his fear. When he was ready, he started to trace the inverted black magical pentagram.

The symbol before him pulsed with a life of its own. He had waited for the Dark Moon to guarantee the ritual's success. Waves of deep purple and black seeped across the pentagram. He had to fight hard against his own repulsion for the symbol: he felt a strong urge to halt the ritual immediately, but he had to achieve his goal. No price was too dear.

He thrust *Retaliator* into the heart of the inverted pentagram and traced out a crescent, symbolic of the waning moon. The sword vibrated forcefully in disgust at the use it was being put to. Malak then concentrated on the characteristics of the force he was attempting to evoke. The force was feminine, but that certainly made it no less dangerous than a male one. Its main attribute was intense sexual charge. Hence Lilith was known as the Temptress, the Queen of Demons and Succubi.

Malak began to chant rhythmically in Enochian, vibrating the words through his aura. The words rolled off his tongue easily and he found himself flowing very smoothly with the chant almost immediately. Apart from having a definite effect in themselves, the Words of Power helped tune his mind into the essence he was striving for. They helped to set up a psycho-magnetic link, probably the most difficult step of the operation.

Within a minute the blood in the triangle slowly began to ooze and then to bubble. It became increasingly vigorous until it was boiling. Malak continued, fighting past the tension in his solar plexus. In the past, his magick had been purely white; he had no experience in the evocation of Demons.

He continued the chanting, disregarding the warning signals from his subconscious. He could feel the energy augmenting within the restraining triangle. It seemed very strong for such an early stage in the ritual.

Suddenly he felt the magnetic link disappear. The blood immediately ceased to bubble and the atmosphere in the chamber somehow changed. The chant died on his lips. He frowned, tilting his head to listen carefully. There was only silence.

He pushed his uncertainty aside, taking up an authoritative posture.

His voice boomed: "I do evocate, conjure and command thee, O thou spirit LILITH to show thyself immediately in fair and comely shape, without any deformity or tortuosity, by the name and powers of Yod Heh Vau Heh!"

He waited a minute, but there was no change in the atmosphere.

"By the mighty name of SHADDAI EL CHAI, God the Omnipotent, I command thee to appear. I bind thee by the name of GABRIEL, the Man-god, and by the awesome power of the KERUBIM, mighty angels of YESOD!"

There was an incredible strain in the air but it gradually faded as the entity resisted his commands.

Malak swore in frustration. He placed *Retaliator* on the altar. He couldn't understand why the ritual had failed. The planets were aligned perfectly, and it had been proceeding incredibly well, almost too well. His mind whirled with possibilities and permutations. His preoccupied mind and inexperience with diabolical entities then caused him to make a fatal mistake.

In defeat, he moved to the edge of the circle without performing the banishment. He placed a foot outside his haven.

And all Hell literally broke loose in the chamber. A searing pain shot through his foot. He yanked it back into the circle with a shout. The malformed and corrupt spirits of the Qlippoth swirled everywhere in the chamber. They screamed obscene, diabolical names as they viciously fought. They devoured smaller, less powerful entities to give birth to their own offspring, only to consume those if quick enough. It was true representation of Chaos: nothing in the whirling mass remained stable for long.

There were minor demons of all colours and shapes. Most were based on terrestrial forms, but they were always disfigured and gross. There were forms based on flying creatures, creeping insects, aquatic shapes and all other earthly forms. The demons were often covered in warts and palpitating skin; their grossly enlarged limbs and heads were out of proportion with their bodies. All of them displayed abhorrently sized or disfigured sexual organs. Accompanying them was a powerful stench reminiscent of burnt animal fur.

Malak's immediate instinct was to close his eyes and hide from the terrifying sight, as any sane man would. But he audaciously stood his ground. His horror gradually changed to fascination. This was only his second glimpse of the demonic plane. It seemed that the circle had been transported to Hell rather than the opposite: he could not see the chamber walls for the vast number of demons struggling through the gateway he had opened.

A vociferous inhuman wail suddenly pierced the chamber. It echoed back and forth between the entities. The demons halted their gleeful dance and scattered in all directions, returning to their source. Silence descended momentarily, before a beautiful green light appeared a dozen yards from the circle. It lengthened into a glowing bar of vertical light, reaching up six feet from the floor. It widened to form a luminescent human figure.

Then the green light died, and the lamps were extinguished. Malak strained to discern the figure in the darkness. The glow of *Retaliator* had obfuscated.

The figure giggled playfully in a seductive voice and moved

forward. The lamps suddenly flickered back into life. And Malak saw her: Lilith, Queen of the Night.

Her hair was the darkest black, and yet glittered beautifully as she moved. Her lips were red, full and inviting, her nose, eyes and brow in perfect balance. Her face was delicate, utterly feminine and almost elfin in appearance.

She was naked, and her body was absolutely flawless: there was not a single mark or blemish to be seen. Her skin was white, but not insalubrious; it was more like marble, pure and untouchable. Her breasts were large and perfectly formed, her legs and arms slim and shapely. Her figure looked almost to have been sculptured.

She moved up to the edge of the circle with a seductive feline grace. Her face was set in an expression of mock innocence. Malak watched in fascination, unable to tear his gaze away. His breath rasped in his chest. She circled slowly around the perimeter, pouting her lips and giggling. She stared at his groin for several long seconds, where already there was a response to her presence. He tried desperately to fight it. But her physical form was the least of her effect. Lilith emitted an intense sexual-magnetic force that almost no male could resist. She was the personification of lust.

"Do you like this body?" She rolled her tongue slowly around her lips.

Her voice was husky, provocative and highly charged; Malak tried desperately to ignore the suggestive overtones in it. Her eyes burned into his. They appeared almost black in the poor light. The intense lust in them caused him to gasp. They contained incredible power and a fatal hypnotic quality.

"Why not join me outside the circle, Malak?" she purred.

He checked himself as his instincts sought to push him forward to certain death. He forced himself to remember what she was and to contain his animalistic attraction to her.

"I think not," he said.

She snarled at him, and for a second something cold and terrible appeared in her eyes. Her manner became calm and seductive again; her eyes returned to their illusory human state

"You're very strong, Malak. You surprise me. But what error have you committed in bringing me here?"

She looked meaningfully at the empty triangle.

"You can't touch me, Demon!"

Lilith laughed, a sound to freeze the soul.

"Oh, but you haven't just brought my essence here. I'm here physically!"

She kicked over one of the lamps for effect. Malak cursed her under his breath. Due to her strength, the alignment of the planets and the Tower's nature, he had produced a physical manifestation outside the restricting triangle. There was little he could do to banish her: she would laugh at his pathetic efforts by pentagram ritual. But they both knew that she could not break the wards of the chamber. It was stalemate.

"Why did you bring me here?" she asked in mock sincerity.

"You know what I want," Malak said impatiently. "Release Lena from your domain! You have no right to hold her!"

"Oh, and lose my favourite plaything? She thwarted my plans, and for that she will be eternally tortured! I think you forget, she gave herself to me of her own free will. No one can interfere with that!"

"Release her, Demon!"

Lilith smiled and her features melted, only to reform in an exact image of his wife. She stood there before him, a replica in every detail.

"You bitch!" he growled emphatically.

She laughed, a perverted and fiendish sound.

"I have no idea why you feel affection for such a…slut!"

She ran her tongue around her lips, and then ran her hands over her breasts. She smiled maliciously at Malak's disgusted reaction, and then slid her fingers down to her genitals. She slipped a couple of fingers inside her vagina and made motions as if masturbating, all the time maintaining eye contact with him. She then pulled out the fingers, which dripped with illusory fluid, and sucked them.

Malak turned away, feeling physically sick at seeing his wife's body abused in such a way. When he looked up, the hatred in his eyes stopped her dead.

"You're filth!"

Her surprise did not last long. She smiled sweetly.

"I do hope I haven't offended you, my pretty."

"What do you want from me?" he demanded angrily.

"Something very precious, dear."

"Name your price!"

"Remove the wards on this chamber!"

Her eyes glittered, and he could see how much she desired the trade. Her body flowed back into its original form as he bowed his head, considering the implications of such an act. To remove the wards on the chamber would allow Lilith and her minions free access to the entire Tower. The demonic forces would be unable to cross the small dimensional rift between the Tower and Enya, however. But there would be no chance of escape for himself if he granted such a boon.

He knew the karmic consequences would be severe for defiling such a pure area, but the fact hardly seemed to matter. It puzzled him that the Demon had not asked for more: perhaps there was more to her motives than he realized. But he was beyond caring. At last he had a chance to remove Lena from an eternity of torture.

His subconscious screamed in disapproval as he nodded to the Arch-Demon.

"Swear the pact by your true name, that you'll release Lena from your Habitation immediately as I remove the wards!"

Lilith smiled sweetly and swore on the pact. Malak lifted up *Retaliator* and formed the sigils to the wards from the chamber.

As he finished, a triumphant scream echoed through the chamber. The blade of *Retaliator* snapped spontaneously. The light of the star-sapphire flared and died, its fire forever extinguished. Malak suddenly knew he had done something terribly wrong. He was empty: the link to his Higher Self had somehow been severed.

"No, Malak, your soul is now mine! The Lords of Light have forsaken you and cast it down."

She watched him with amusement, her eyes glowing a terrifying red. They contained an awesome power.

"You now belong to me!"

Malak fell to his knees in shock. In rescuing Lena, he had destroyed his own soul, and enslaved the dead Adepts in the Tower above. He knew that their souls would still be partially attached to their bodies because they had died recently. They would be unable to leave the Tower, which was now an extension of Lilith's domain.

Lilith advanced upon him now, growing until she stood twelve feet tall. She walked easily into the circle: Malak now had no power to uphold its integrity. He looked up at his nemesis in fear, not of death, but of total spiritual disintegration. He knew that there was no way of redeeming himself.

Lilith's arms grew into ghastly claws. Her mouth formed into the snout of a huge wolf. Malak prayed quietly for a chance to undo the mess he had created.

He courageously denied Lilith a final scream as his body was viciously torn to shreds and devoured.

Part
II

Nescience

From Unreality, lead me to Reality
From Darkness, lead me unto Light
From Death, lead me to Immortality.

—The Upanishads

As among flowers the cherry is queen,
so among men the samurai is lord.

  —The Bushido, Way of the Warrior

Planet Tellus
Malkuth of Assiah
Nipponese Empire
Year 5 of 32nd Shogun
(3216 Anno Domini)

Wind and snow whipped viciously at Ieyasu Tanaka as he blindly struggled to enter the snow-coffin. His numbed fingers fumbled clumsily with the leather buckles as he sought to sequester himself. Already a foot of snow covered the ground, and he knew his only hope was to be buried in the blizzard. The temperature was minus twenty and falling. Winter was approaching fast, and without proper shelter he knew he would die within a few days.

He closed the last of the buckles and lay shivering in the darkness. A gelid sweat covered his body. He knew that he could not survive for much longer, running as a fugitive for his life. His pursuers were sure to be close behind.

Deliriously, his mind wandered over his problems. He had no food left, and there was nothing edible to gather in the icy wilderness. Also, his horse was exhausted. Without a mount, he knew he had no chance of survival.

The events of the last week swirled through his mind, driving him toward insanity. He forced back the tears at the thought of his treachery. He wondered whether it would be better to die now—his life had now been stripped of all worth. Living without honour was more than he could bear.

Outside his haven, the wind howled with maleficent fury.

No sane man would be out in that, he comforted himself.

He hoped that the Shogun's Guard were not that desperate. They would be over-confident, sure in the knowledge that they would soon apprehend him.

They're probably right, he reflected bitterly.

Once he was found, he would be executed on sight. But despite his formidable budo skills, nothing would force him to break his vow of pacifism.

He shut his eyes, curling up to keep the cold at bay. Within minutes he fell into an uneasy sleep.

——————⊰◆◆◆⊱——————

Tanaka slowly awakened from a dream. Groggy from sleep, he rolled over into a position from which he could rise. He suddenly realized that he had rolled out of his snow-coffin. Vague emotions clamoured at his mind, but he was utterly exhausted. He felt more tired than he believed possible. Curiosity hardly stirred: he only desired to return to the limbo of sleep. Yet he knew that he would have to find out what had happened.

He stood up and looked around, vaguely recognizing the place as where he had settled for the night. Deep snow covered everything in sight, but the distant forest of conifer trees was unmistakable. His coffin was not to be seen, apparently buried under several feet of snow. There was no disturbance to indicate he had somehow rolled out of it.

The strangeness of the situation suddenly became apparent, and his mind snapped into gear. His body was light and energetic, not in the least cold. It luminesced with a soft grey-blue light. The near-by trees radiated a similar but less intense force, and he could see whirls of energy in the air about him. The sky pulsated with a ubiquitous soft green light that made his vision hazy and surreal. He knew he was not within a dream: the experience was far too vivid.

As he contemplated the situation in his slow methodical way, he realized he was being watched. A shadowy figure, dressed in black, hovered slightly above the ground a hundred yards away. He felt irritation rather than fear: he had been a warrior too long to feel the latter. He muttered to himself as he moved toward the tenebrous figure.

The spectre made a motion that he should follow. Tanaka did as indicated; he realized with a start that he wasn't walking, but gliding after the figure. The guide moved similarly, the glow of his body being shed backward as he moved, giving the appearance of wings.

As Tanaka followed, he found his awareness shifting, as if manipulated by an external force. They were soon passing under the canopy of forest trees: they were moving deceptively fast. Every tree, pattern and landmark impressed itself upon his memory. He didn't resist the sensation, knowing it would be useless to do so. He wondered briefly if he had been claimed by the dark figure of Death.

Time distorted as he followed his self-appointed guide. He wasn't sure if this was due to his state of mind, or the strangeness of the plane upon which he found himself; he suspected that perhaps both played a part. In forty years of experience, nothing similar had ever happened, and if he survived he was sure it would never happen again. A subtle intuition told him that here was the new purpose he sought.

Without warning, his guide stopped and pointed ahead. For the first time Tanaka saw the figure in detail. She was female, dressed in black robes with a hooded black cloak. The glow around her was extremely strong, and he knew that this was from her powerful life-force. He could see her face, and she was the most beautiful woman he had ever seen. It was difficult to see her hair under her hood, but it seemed to be black and very long. Her face held great wisdom and compassion, but also a great sadness; her deep brown eyes were profoundly sorrowful. Something of colossal importance was wrong.

You are my chosen preceptor. In you I lay my trust. Her voice touched his mind directly. She raised a slender arm and pointed ahead. She then gave a half-smile, as if in blessing. Her already diffused form faded away to leave him standing alone.

He looked forward to the area she had indicated. It was a small valley that radiated an incredible amount of energy. The golden light it emanated was bright, but he didn't have to shield his eyes. He walked into the valley, wary, yet sure he was safe.

At the centre of the depression was a majestic gateway of stone, inscribed with complex runes and hieroglyphics. The gateway was ancient. Tanaka knew instinctively that there would be tremendous upheavals if it was ever destroyed. Its essence was older than that of the earth itself. Within it he could see thousands of alternate realities flickering in and out of existence.

But he could see that the gateway was in terrible danger. Its balance was very precarious, and it might topple at any moment. The only object supporting it was a small sapling that wound around the pillars. Though obviously possessing great strength, unless nurtured and helped to grow in the correct way, it could not uphold the huge gateway. It needed love and guidance to aid it.

Puzzled at first, Tanaka's mind made an intuitive leap: it was his responsibility to take care of the sapling, and ensure that it grew in the correct way. Its strength and wisdom would be drawn from his own. He knew the insight was true: he was more sure of it than his own name.

Then, as if some force was satisfied with his realization, darkness again overcame his mind like a snuffed candle. He rejoined the world of dreams.

--------◆◆◆◆--------

Ieyasu Tanaka groggily awoke. He groaned and opened his eyes to the familiar and almost welcome sight of the interior of his snow coffin. His body was stiff and tired, but at least it was relatively warm and living. While still inside the enclosure, he pushed himself up to stand on his feet. The miniature tent broke through the yard of snow above it. He released the buckles and light flooded through the opening, blinding his ill-accustomed eyes.

Once again, he felt the bite of the late Autumn air. He repressed a gasp as a blast of icy wind caught him unawares. The temperature was far below zero, and he knew it was unlikely to improve as the day continued. He stepped out from the coffin and quickly folded it down to size, placing it neatly into his backpack, which was now ominously empty.

As ever, the sun was totally hidden by the ubiquitous layer of natural smog; today it descended thinly to hide even the horizon.

Tanaka knew that it was late morning: he had wasted a great deal of time. He struggled over to where he had left his mount, fighting to maintain his balance as vicious gusts of wind and powdered snow assaulted him. He was thankful of the snow in one respect: it would cover his tracks and possibly throw off his pursuers.

The snow before him shook itself and rose up unsteadily. Tanaka sighed in relief. His horse was covered in thick long hair and had been specially bred to survive in the hostile climate. But she had not been fed for two days. Like his own, her strength was waning.

He brushed the snow from her body, stroking her neck and

whispering soothingly to her. As he prepared to leave, a vague recollection of a dream drifted into his mind. He had little time to consider it, however. He had to reach civilization today or he would not survive the night.

It was so cold that the binding leather thongs of his lamellar *yoroi* armour were frozen and immovable. This made movement in the box-like frame stiff and difficult.

His yoroi was of excellent craftsmanship; even the Shogun would have been satisfied to wear it. Besides the *do*, the main body of the armour, there were several additions. The shoulders were guarded by *sode*, rigid armoured plates. The shins were protected by *suneate* and the thighs *haidate* guards: these chain mail supplements combined to form excellent but flexible leg protection. As was traditional, the left arm was shielded by a *kote*, an armoured sleeve; the right arm was unprotected so that he could draw the string of a long bow, though he didn't carry one.

The *tsurubashiri*, the leather breastplate that covered the front section of the do, was beautifully and intricately decorated. The pattern of orange and black tiger lilies surreptitiously conveyed his nature, for the tiger lily represented both the gentleness and ferocity of the perfected warrior.

Slotted through the rings attached to his belt were his katana and wakizashi. These were the mark of a samurai, which no commoner would dare to possess. Together, the swords formed a *daisho* pair, which would never be separated. Neither sword could be resheathed without drawing blood, as decreed by the Bushido Code. It was therefore a serious matter to draw a sword from its scabbard.

Tanaka was now just over forty years of age, a venerable status for those who inhabited the icy regions of Nippon. His frame was tall and wiry, yet he had once been the most feared warrior in the Nipponese Empire. His skin was dark, an obvious indicator of Western blood. His hair was short and grey, and there was a thick mustache above his lip. His eyes were pale blue, but deep, thoughtful, and full of sorrow.

As he moved slowly through the gusting wind, his eyes screwed up against the snow, he realized that the forest was now very near. He knew that within the expanse of trees he would find his destination: Kyoto village. A strong feeling of déjà vu gripped him; for some reason the scene evoked a strong response from his memory.

Suddenly his dream experience came flooding back to him. He knew that his path, whatever it might be, was inescapable. It relaxed him greatly: there was no reason for concern, and he felt no fear. For weeks he had been riding with no other purpose than survival, and a samurai had to have a worthwhile purpose.

Even if I am now ronin, he thought bitterly.

He pushed on to enter the forest. He was relieved to gain a small measure of protection from the wind. Despite his fur gloves, his fingers were already stiff and painful on the reins. He ignored the discomfort: he had felt much worse in his life.

For over an hour he guided the horse along a trail that existed only in his mind, yet he recognized every tree along his path. He was becoming perturbed, and began to consider the condition of his own sanity after so much exposure to the elements.

The snow was deep enough to slow the mare down considerably, and he wondered if he would be marooned in this desolate place. He was no longer sure of the direction to Kyoto: except for his dream memories, he was in completely unfamiliar territory.

After an indefinite amount of time in the saddle, his mind wandering semi-deliriously, he suddenly came across his goal. His pulse accelerated. Spread out before him was the valley from his vision. He felt a surge of warm strength from within. He urged on his discouraged mount.

Uncannily, the climate steadily improved as he rode into the valley: it became noticeably warmer and the snow thinned out on the ground. Before him he could see his objective: twelve stone megaliths stood like proud sentries, forming a circle around the place of power from his vision. Although the gateway itself was not physically present, he knew that this was the place.

As he rode closer, he found himself overawed by the perfection and placement of the megaliths. He fancied he could feel the potent force that they cast out. Ordinarily he would not have dared to trespass on such a site, but he knew that he had been invited.

He dismounted at a respectful distance and closed the last stretch on foot. His mount obediently stood and awaited his return, too exhausted to do anything else. She was on the verge of collapse, and would probably be unable to carry him out of the valley. Her condition saddened him: his love of animals was great, and it troubled him that he had taken her to her death.

He reached the edge of the circle. There was no snow on the ground whatsoever; neither was there any wind to be felt. It was uncomfortably warm, though this was partially due to his armour: his yoroi was insulated for survival in conditions of extreme cold.

Suddenly his attention was seized by a sound from inside the circle. A boy of about five was sitting cross-legged with his back to one of the stones. Tanaka was amazed: there was no way that the boy should be out in the wild by himself. He stealthily moved closer. He realized that the boy was talking to himself, but in a language Tanaka had never heard before. This was unusual, because Tanaka's years at the Shogun's Palace had familiarized him with most languages, though Nippon was quite xenophobic by nature.

The boy had a large build, with thick black hair and a hawk-like face. He seemed to be talking to invisible playmates, rather than to himself. He was extremely sad, and Tanaka received the impression that he had done something very wrong. He could see that the boy had an intelligence and wealth of experience comparable to any adult: it was obvious from his tone of voice and mannerisms. He was naked, and oblivious to everything outside the stone circle.

Tanaka was severely perplexed. His warrior's experience, which had always served him so well in the past, seemed woefully inadequate in this situation. He eventually made the only decision he was able to, and moved out from behind his concealment. He advanced slowly toward the child so as not to scare him.

The boy looked up as he approached and apparently gave a greeting in his own language. Tanaka knelt before him on one knee. He had absolutely no idea of how to act towards this strange child.

He was captivated by the stranger's eyes. They were blue, with the most intense gaze he had ever seen, and he had known some strong men. The gaze reminded him of the woman who had been his guide in the dream: very deep with a tragic sadness.

He realized that the child was waiting for a reply to his greeting. Tanaka tried to give a reassuring smile.

"Sorry, boy, I can't understand you."

The child tilted his head in curiosity.

The samurai pointed to his own chest. "Tanaka," he said slowly. "Tanaka."

The child smiled joyfully, as though he had recognized the name. He jumped forward and threw his arms around the warrior. Tanaka froze, unused to such a show of emotion: he had had no contact with children in his profession. And he had never married.

He picked the child up and carried him toward his mount. The boy smiled contentedly at first, but a strange and dramatic change came across him as they passed over the circle boundary. The depth and wisdom left his eyes, and they were replaced by something that had been completely absent: fear. He began to shiver convulsively as the air became colder.

In essence, he started to act exactly as a five-year-old would be expected to. He did not lose his innate trust of the samurai, however, whom he clung to as if his life depended upon him.

Tanaka wrapped him up in blankets and set him on the horse in front of himself. The mare seemed to be much fresher now; apparently she had absorbed healing energy from the megaliths. He knew then that they would reach Kyoto village. The destiny of this child was important, and he had been elected as his protector.

All the world's a stage,
And all the men and women
  merely players:
They have their exits and entrances;
And one man in his time plays
  many parts.

—As You Like It (William Shakespeare)

Planet Tellus
Nipponese Empire
Kyoto Village

Ieyasu Tanaka had never been more gratified as when he finally saw the bridge that led into Kyoto village. It stood on the forest path not two hundred yards away. He sighed in reminiscence: the scene had barely changed in over a dozen years.

He urged the mare on, trying to flex his fingers as he held the reins. They were so stiff and numb, he knew he would be fortunate to escape without frostbite.

In the saddle before him, the young boy slept soundly. He was covered in so many blankets, it was difficult to see exactly where he was in the pile.

There had been no snow now for several hours. It had already turned hard and icy on the ground; it crunched noisily underfoot as they reached the small river. As ever, it was frozen over; in a few weeks it would be solid through to the bottom. The surface of the simple wooden bridge looked quite precarious, and Tanaka knew that he should really dismount and lead the horse across. However, he didn't want to disturb his passenger and he was so stiff that he didn't think his legs would hold his weight. So the bridge was crossed on horseback, fortunately with only a few minor slips.

Kyoto village was prospering. With a plentiful supply of wood from the forest, good hunting and a close supply of fresh water, all its needs were catered to. There were about forty homes in all. Each was fairly small and constructed from the wood of the forest. They were quite sturdy, and the sight of smoke drifting up from their chimneys was welcome. The village was remote, however, and the inhabitants had a reputation for being strongly xenophobic.

The snow was less than a foot deep in the village, but there was no one to be seen. The men were busy collecting the last of the supplies necessary to hold out against the long, dark Winter. The women were handling the provisions and ensuring that the huts were insulated for the great hibernation.

Tanaka guided his horse through the placed huts. Now that he had reached his goal, all strength had left him. The pain of his body cried out for attention. He gritted his teeth: such things were irrelevant to a samurai. He knew that his mount was about to collapse; she seemed to know her mission was complete, and she stumbled almost every step. He was sure that she would not survive: she had passed the point of total exhaustion.

Near the centre of the village was the public house, which occasionally doubled as an inn for travellers, depending upon whether they were taken in or not. Samurai were always accepted, of course, but they were actively disliked here, as in the rest of the Empire. The common people were tired of their tyrannical rule.

He reined the mare to a halt outside the inn and checked upon his passenger, whom he found to be sleeping soundly. Suddenly they were both thrown from the saddle as the horse finally submitted.

Close to exhaustion, Tanaka lay awhile in the snow. It was tempting to lie there and rest, but the deadly cold was creeping deeper into his body. He pushed himself stiffly onto his hands and knees and crawled over to the child. He picked him up and forced himself to stand. He then staggered toward the tavern door, the child trying to snuggle further into his haven, his eyes wide with alarm and confusion.

The mistress of the tavern was already at the door to appraise her guests. Her eyes widened in surprise as she saw the samurai and she muttered quietly to herself.

Tanaka knew the inn well. He had once been samurai of the village, but he remembered the short plump woman before him as a young teenager. Her mother had been brisk and dominant, and it seemed her daughter had turned out the same. The stern look on her face was enough to assure Tanaka of this. But she gave a cry as she saw the young child.

"Get him inside quick! He'll catch his death!"

She yelled for her adolescent son to inspect the horse and pushed the heavy wooden door shut behind him.

The tavern was almost empty inside; none of the men could afford to waste the relatively good weather. The three men who were present looked up with intolerance, but then respect showed in their eyes as they recognized the *ronin*. They turned politely away from him.

Tanaka was easily recognized by his apparel and dark skin. The whole Empire, even Kyoto, had probably heard of his exile by now. Among the peasants he was a hero. Every village along his path had been eager to aid him and thwart his pursuers. Without their help, he would never have survived.

He gave the child to the landlady and walked unsteadily over to the fire. He collapsed in a deep chair. Every part of his body burned agonizingly. He was in no state to remove his intricately bound armour, which would take thirty minutes even under ideal conditions. He showed no discomfort on his face, however: even a masterless samurai had his pride.

The landlady now had the child by the fire and was talking to him in soothing tones. He obviously didn't understand a word, but he didn't try to resist her attention. His deep blue eyes were aware of everything about him.

The landlady left the room and returned with a steaming pot of stew. Tanaka signalled that he wasn't hungry, despite the pains in his stomach. Though he hadn't eaten for three days, his fingers were too swollen to pick up the wooden spoon, and he refused to make a fool of himself.

His young friend gulped the food down quickly, burning his mouth. A distant expression showed on his face but he continually checked that his new-found protector was close by. The landlady watched him eat in disapproval. She seemed about to chasten him, but Tanaka silenced her with a warning glare.

The tavern door burst open, accompanied by a blast of freezing wind. The landlady's teenage son struggled in with the samurai's saddlebags and equipment. He slammed the door shut behind him, dropped the baggage and walked over to converse with his mother. Tanaka had now managed to remove his gloves. He took two *yuan* from his money chain. The copper coins were large, with a sizable square cut out in their centre; they were difficult to handle with his stiff fingers.

The landlady came over to him and looked at his money.

"There'll be no need for that," she said sharply. "Now you can stay the night, but you must be gone by the 'morrow, mind."

Tanaka scowled.

"The village's got a different *bushi*, now. And though Gorun Tzan's more decent than most, I'll wager he'll not be best pleased to see you!"

Tanaka nodded in resignation. He'd go to see Ekanar tomorrow. His old friend would be sure to welcome him.

"Suppose you'll be wanting to stay over Winter, will you?" The woman asked, her tone militant.

He nodded weakly.

"Well, I suppose the horse-meat will go as part payment for your stay," she said. "If someone will hide you, you understand. And you'll have to work."

"I understand. I have skills as a blacksmith that would be beneficial."

The landlady scrutinized him for a moment. "Well, that'll be up to Saito-san. If you follow me, I'll take you to your room."

Tanaka picked up the child and followed her. His body was now beginning to thaw, but he could still not feel his left hand. He feared the worst.

<hr>

A heavy, muffled series of thuds dragged Tanaka from a deep and dreamless sleep. His eyes flickered in the darkness as he tried to force them open, and they in turn tried to resist. His body ached all over, and it sluggishly dawned on him that he had slept in his armour. A few seconds later he realized where he was. The door was banged again, louder this time, and with a ring of impatience.

He struggled to roll from his back and onto his side, groaning as muscles and organs screamed in disapproval. He rolled off the bed onto his hands and knees. He could see the bedside lamp in the dusky red light of the smouldering fire, which was set in the hearth across the small room.

The oil lamp cast out a soft yellow glow as he lit it, gently pushing back the dark shadows of the grubby room. The atmosphere was warm and close, thick with the smell of wood smoke. The room was sparsely furnished; in its small space was contained a crude bed, a bedside set of drawers, a single heavily padded chair, and a simple hearth. The floor was wooden, covered partially by a bearskin rug, and there was no window. The latter was typical for a peasant house: insulation was paramount and there was usually little light to admit.

Tanaka half limped over to the door. Its little-used hinges creaked irritatingly as he pulled it open. He squinted tiredly at the stranger who stood before him. Something was vaguely familiar about him.

The man was old, probably about forty-five. It was an unusual experience for Tanaka to meet someone older than himself. Tall and stocky, with a huge chest and shoulders, the man's face was prematurely aged, the dark skin broken and flaked. His head was almost bald, his remaining hair a nondescript grey. The eyes were clear and blue. They were calculating and intelligent, and also distrusting. Life was harsh within the icy boundaries of Nippon, and trust did not come easily.

Tanaka then realized why the man was familiar. He was Yoriie Saito, the son of the village's blacksmith, though now he was almost certain to be the blacksmith himself. The two men had never been friends, but had had an understanding. In his younger days, Tanaka had been too arrogant and ambitious to have true friends. It saddened him to think how he had been then.

The two men held each other's gaze for a second. Saito then gave a slight bow and spoke.

"Greetings, Tanaka-san."

It was a polite greeting, but one to be bestowed upon an equal. Tanaka realized he was being tested. He bowed in return, slightly deeper as if to a superior, something normally unthinkable for a samurai addressing a peasant.

"Greetings, Saito-san."

Saito studied the samurai carefully, not quite believing the change that had occurred. As the village bushi, Tanaka had been proud and fierce; now, as he returned in exile, he was full of humility. The change was fully apparent from his eyes. The difference was so great, it was unnerving. Death usually came too quickly for men to become philosophical, but it had happened to this man.

"Please, come in," Tanaka said, stepping aside.

Saito nodded and entered. He sank into the room's single chair as Tanaka closed the door behind him. He noticed the figure of the child immediately, who slept soundly on the bed, oblivious to the world. He raised his eyebrows: it was the last sight he had expected.

Tanaka started removing his armour as the blacksmith silently weighed him up.

Saito finally said: "The season is late. It will be difficult to reach the next village before the snows."

"Yes. I had been hoping for shelter in Kyoto."

The blacksmith nodded, obviously not surprised. Sanzin was the only town within fifty miles, and there were too many samurai there for a fugitive to seek a haven.

"It will be dangerous for us to conceal a ronin."

"Few samurai know that I was posted in Kyoto. They will not seek me here."

"You are ronin?"

"Yes." He didn't look up as he removed his tsurubashiri.

"I am now the village headman. It is my decision as to whether you stay."

Tanaka shrugged. "Then your hands contain my fate. And his." He motioned toward the sleeping child.

Saito grunted. He was surprised at the ronin's halcyon attitude. Tanaka had never been excitable, and was now even less so after his recent experiences.

"We owe the samurai nothing. You are all cruel and repressive!"

Saito's accusing eyes bored into Tanaka's. The ronin's pale blue gaze calmly met his glare. He nodded.

"Yet I am no longer true samurai. I have been dishonoured."

The headman scrutinized him, and then nodded his agreement.

"You have changed, and in our eyes your dishonour is really an honour. We heard of your actions in Kyoto, but those of us who remembered you didn't believe it."

"That is understandable. I am not proud of what I once was. I have killed more men than most samurai have had duels, and that hangs heavy around my heart. But I have taken a vow of pacifism, and *nothing* will force me to break it."

Silence hung between them for a few seconds as the headman made his decision.

"If the old sage will hide you, then you are welcome to stay the Winter."

Tanaka bowed his head in sincere appreciation. The blacksmith returned his bow, but his eyes were as distrusting as ever. He left the room without speaking.

*If you understand, things are just as
they are. If you do not understand,
things are just as they are.*

—Zen Koan

Planet Tellus
Nipponese Empire
Kyoto Village

After eating a hefty breakfast in the privacy of their room, Tanaka dressed his protégé in the clothes that the landlady had kindly donated. It was a slow and painful process due to Tanaka's frost-bitten hand. The clothes had obviously once belonged to the landlady's son, and were several sizes too large.

The samurai tried to talk reassuringly to the child, but found the task difficult. It was not something that came naturally to him.

The child observed him quietly, allowing him to manipulate his body. His deep blue eyes studied everything around them. There was an unnerving intelligence in their depths.

Tanaka covered his own kimono in a heavy grey cloak, throwing the hood over his head to hide his face. He knew that he still stood out as a stranger.

He extinguished the oil lamp and picked up the boy. He found the main room of the inn to be empty, which was fortunate. The fire crackled quietly to itself, piled up with small sticks and logs. It was traditional not to cut down trees; each was considered to have a spirit. The peasants preferred to collect dead wood from the forest floor.

Carrying his passenger, Tanaka stepped out into the biting cold of mid-afternoon. A light snow was falling, but the weather was still relatively good: the heavy Winter snows had yet to appear. In the midst of Winter, an unprotected man could freeze to death within two minutes.

The village was active in its preparations for the oncoming

season. Bellows of smoke rose into the air as piles of wood were
turned into charcoal. Several people carried loads of food and skins
to the village stores. They paid no attention to Tanaka, but he knew
that he hadn't passed unnoticed.

After ploughing through the foot-deep snow for a couple of minutes, the pair reached their destination. It was a house, similar in
construction to the others, but taller and more spacious. There was
a strange rune marked above the door, a Tau cross.

Tanaka rapped on the door, shaking swirls of snow from the roof
to be caught and whirled away by the wind. There was shuffling from
inside, then the door creaked open to reveal the face of an elderly
and sprightly gentleman. He was maybe fifty years of age, remarkable for Nippon, with silver-grey hair and inquisitive, alert blue eyes.
His face was jovial, his eyebrows thick and bushy. They were like
hairy caterpillars and seemed to have a life of their own.

He broke into a grin as he saw Tanaka. He grabbed the samurai's
hand and shook it vigorously. Tanaka tried to suppress the smile that
threatened to appear on his face, but was unable. It was difficult to
stay miserable in the company of Ekanar.

Ekanar was the most renowned sage in the Empire; in fact he was
probably the only one. Sages tended to prefer living in cities, far to
the west in the civilized lands. Ekanar himself had originated from
there, and Tanaka had always been able to relate to him, since his
own father had been of Western origins. It was this that had caused
his rise to the top of the most elite samurai: the drive to prove himself, despite being a half-breed without noble ancestry.

Ekanar had been living in Kyoto for over twenty years; he liked
the quiet and remote atmosphere. The people both admired and
respected him: they had adopted him as one of their own. He was
always useful to them; his knowledge to a peasant seemed limitless.

"How's the old war dog, then?" he asked affectionately.

Tanaka grunted and shrugged to indicate that things were
terrible. Ekanar nodded sympathetically.

"Well, come on in! And bring your young friend. There's ale
out back!"

The samurai smiled: some things never changed. The sage had
always liked a drink, which usually turned into a dozen. He was,
however, in excellent health. This was due to his inextinguish-
able optimism. He was always happy, something Tanaka envied.

Happiness did not come anywhere on a bushi's list of priorities.

They stepped into the warmth of the house and Ekanar supplied two tankards of ale. They seated themselves in the study, which usurped much of the room in the house. Many thousands of books lined the walls. Many were incredibly rare, being leftovers from the Old World. There were major sections on history, geography, art, psychology, engineering, alchemy, languages, mysticism and magick.

Ekanar no longer collected books: as a sage he had retired young. Besides there was little likelihood of finding such books in the Eastern lands. He had more than enough information to peruse through for his own curiosity for several lifetimes. Clients had often irritated him due to their insistence that he remain sober to answer questions. He found it extremely boring.

After taking a long draught of ale, he looked at Tanaka expectantly.

"So, are the stories true, then?" he asked, his tone not light for once.

Tanaka knew exactly what he was referring to, and his eyes clouded over in involuntary recollection.

"Yes, they're true."

"Do I get the story?" the sage probed gently.

The samurai smiled thinly. He hadn't realized that the old man had so much tact. Usually, he pounced in with both feet. However, it was Tanaka's first chance to relate his story to someone he could trust. He knew it would do him good. His fall from most envied warrior in the Empire to renegade had been a sudden and unexpected one.

"The Shogun's position is weak and very delicate at the moment. He fears for the safety of his seat. He knows there are *daimyo* plotting against him in an effort to put a new Shogun upon the throne."

Ekanar nodded: it was everyday knowledge even amongst the common people.

"The Shogun's Guard were given secret instructions to assassinate the leaders of the opposing daimyo, and to eliminate all of their heirs. As captain and commanding officer of the Guard, it was I who gave the instructions to my men.

"However, I was ordered to see to the elimination of Lord Kanazawa personally, since he was by far our greatest enemy. But I found that I was unable to kill in cold blood. There was a conflict between my duty and honour. It was against the Bushido to follow my instructions."

"And yet it was rumoured that you killed Lord Kanazawa in single combat, and escaped. Why were you exiled?"

Tanaka hung his head, and there was great bitterness in his voice.

"I failed to murder his four-year-old son, who is now heir to his throne. His mother was there…and she begged me not to do it. The guards were coming, and I just couldn't bring myself to follow my orders."

There was silence for a while before the sage asked the obvious question.

"What of *hari-kari*? I am shocked that you are still alive."

Tanaka could not hide his shame: it showed plainly on his face.

"I don't know what, but something stopped me. I had a strong feeling that there was something important left to do. My honour is now gone, and I am as dead as if I had followed the suicide."

"Something left to do? I don't understand."

"I think this youngster has something to do with it."

Ekanar turned his attention to the bushi's companion. He could already see there was something different about the boy, who was clinging tightly to his only friend.

"And who might this be?" he said, leaning forward for a closer inspection.

Tanaka was surprised to see that the boy didn't shy away from the sage, as he tended to do with others. He was regarding the old man with a very serious gaze, however. With a shout, Ekanar suddenly jumped up, startling his two guests. He disappeared for a while, and Tanaka heard rummaging in the next room. He waited patiently, wondering what the old man was looking for. The sage was prone to outbursts of excitement at the least thing. He had enough vitality for three men.

He returned, carrying a paper bag containing long, thin black sticks. He pushed them into the boy's hand.

Tanaka frowned. "What's he supposed to do with them?"

He was already starting to become protective over his protégé, and that surprised him more than anyone.

"It's liquorice you dolt! You eat it!"

Despite the samurai's ignorance, the boy obviously had the right idea. He was cramming the sticks into his mouth as fast as he could. Tanaka wasn't sure that the black grunge was good for him, but Ekanar was rocking back and forth with a large grin on his face.

"How did you come to gain this young rascal, then?" he asked.

"Well," the bushi said, shuffling uncomfortably in his seat, "that's the strangest story."

The sage urged him to continue.

Sketchily at first, but then in more and more detail, Tanaka related the tale of his vision-like dream and the following journey. Ekanar became increasingly excited. He continually asked for elaboration on subtle points, especially the nature of the terrain in the vision. The samurai found it a strain on his memory; his recollection of the dream was now hazy. Only the haunted eyes of his guide stuck vividly in his mind.

After Tanaka finished his tale, which he was pleased to have confided for the benefit of his sanity, Ekanar pulled out a book from his section on the occult. These were the most valued of all the books he possessed. He muttered to himself as he browsed through it, sometimes nodding his head, and at other times shaking it. After a few minutes he slapped the book shut.

"Sounds like an involuntary projection of the astral body," he said excitedly, "obviously propagated by an outside force!"

"Uh?"

Ekanar scowled at his ignorance.

"Never mind, just finish your ale. There's a dozen barrels out back. I brewed them myself."

He peered at the youngster, who was wiping sticky hands on his trousers. "And what's your name?"

The child didn't react.

"That's something we'll have to give him, I think," Tanaka said.

Ekanar thought for a while. "How about Shadd-rak? It means 'strange one' in one of the Western tongues."

The samurai rubbed his chin thoughtfully; there was a definite ring to the name.

"Yes, Shadrack it is then."

The boy smiled knowingly, and pointed at Tanaka, exclaiming: "Kavmer! Kavmer!"

Ekanar almost fell over in shock. Tanaka could see how shaken he was.

"What did he say?" he asked quietly, a hint of resignation in his voice.

"That was Hebrew," the sage said, his voice incredulous. "It's one of the tongues of the Old World."

"Yes?"

"He called you 'father'!"

Tanaka stared at the child, once again feeling the effects of his predetermined destiny.

In pain lies the greatest teacher of all.
          —The Bushido, Way of the Warrior

*A clay pot sitting in the sun will always
be a clay pot. It has to go through the
white heat of the furnace to become
porcelain.*
          —Doctrine of the White School[1]

Planet Tellus
Nipponese Empire
Kyoto Village

T anaka sat cross-legged, his back pressed against the wall in the small attic. His eyes were closed, his breathing slow and regular but slightly laboured. A single candle illuminated the room.

On the small bed sat Shadrack. He watched his protector anxiously, aware that he was in pain.

His head twisted with a start as he heard a creak from below. There was a series of thuds before the trap door swung open. Ekanar's head appeared and the boy relaxed visibly.

"The 'smith is ready, Ieyasu," Ekanar said, his voice sombre.

Tanaka opened his eyes and sighed. He rose and grabbed his katana, which was wrapped in black silk. He held it with his right hand; his left hung limply in a makeshift sling.

"Then we must go."

He looked at Shadrack, whose eyes followed him like a puppy watching its master leave.

"Stay here, boy," he said gruffly. "You'll see naught good for your mind this night."

The child watched without comprehension, but made no move as the warrior and sage descended the stairs into the study.

"Don't worry," Ekanar said, "he won't be able to climb down without the ladder."

---

1 Quoted from Mildred Witte Stouven

147

The two men stepped out into the caustic atmosphere of the night. The weather was bitterly cold, but the wind was quiet and no snow had fallen all day. They both knew it was be the last lull before the Winter storms. The silence already felt like a huge gathering of tension, ready to be unleashed at any moment.

They picked their way through the wooden huts, which were all identical in the mist. It was rare in Nippon to have a few hours of clear visibility, whether at day or night. Water vapour and smog seemed to be crystallized in the air.

Soon they reached a solitary hut. Thick smoke gushed from the chimney and they could feel the heat through the door. It was the only construction in the village that was not meticulously insulated.

"Ready?" Ekanar asked, his face uncharacteristically concerned.

Tanaka took in a deep breath and pulled open the door. The heat hit him immediately, its contrast forcing him to half close his eyes. Standing in the room was Yoriie Saito, stripped to the waist and prodding a fire of red hot coals with an iron poker. Muscles rippled across his chest and abdomen as he moved. He looked up and beckoned the pair in.

As the two men walked forward, they didn't notice the slight figure of a boy slip in behind them. He melded into the shadows where the dull red light of the coals failed to penetrate.

Saito had a strong wooden table and chair prepared for his guests. On the table were arranged an assortment of crude and barbaric surgical instruments, including bone saws and tissue clamps. Ekanar swallowed hard as he saw them, thankful that this was not to be his ordeal. Sympathy welled out of him toward Tanaka, but the samurai was stoic, his face focused and quite calm.

"The coals are ready," Saito said, his voice coarse.

Tanaka nodded and seated himself. "I am ready."

The blacksmith picked up a mug of foul purple liquid and passed it to the bushi.

"This will put you to sleep for a few hours."

Tanaka took the cup from him and looked distastefully at its contents. He placed it aside.

"No. That is not our way."

Ekanar balked; Saito raised an eyebrow.

"But the pain of the saw…"

The samurai laid down his katana and unwrapped it. The

blacksmith whistled appreciatively as he drew it from its scabbard. The blade had been forged from the finest steel and the workmanship was excellent. He recognized his father's work immediately, without checking the initials inscribed on the hilt. His father had been one of the finest weapon-smiths in the Empire. His swords were now very rare and valuable.

The samurai laid his left arm on the table, rolling the sleeve of his fur coat back to expose his wrist. The hand was putrid, the skin cracked and blistered. Green and red viscous fluid oozed from the breaks. He was obviously in great pain with the infection. There was no way of saving the limb.

Saito gave Tanaka a questioning look. The bushi nodded sombrely.

"When you are ready, Saito-san."

He closed his eyes and concentrated on slowing his breathing, at the same time closing his adrenal glands. With an effort of will he relaxed his whole body, clearing his mind of all fear and distractions.

Saito looked at Ekanar, who shrugged helplessly, and then back to the waiting samurai. This was not something he was used to. Tanaka didn't seem perturbed in the least, except for the light sweat on his forehead. Even that was probably due to the heat, he realized incredulously. The people of Nippon were extremely hardy, and the samurai were even more so. But Tanaka was elite even amongst samurai. He had no fear that he had not conquered, except for that of being worthless.

The blacksmith shuffled nervously on his feet, his grip shifting on the perfectly honed weapon. Then the blade swept down in a flashing arc of crimson, the firelight catching its surface. It severed the exposed wrist, slicing as though against no resistance.

Tanaka shuddered and grunted, but otherwise made no move. He seemed only dimly aware of his environment. Saito quickly wiped the blade of the katana free of blood, and then plunged it deep into the hot coals. When he removed it, it glowed with an ominous dull red light.

He pressed the blade firmly against Tanaka's decapitated wrist. There was a burst of steam as the blood instantly thickened and congealed. Tanaka gave a gasp and grimaced, unable to control the extreme pain. The blacksmith removed the sword and thrust it into a trough of cold water. The sword's colour dimmed, but Saito knew the agony of the wound would take much longer to die.

Tanaka's eyes opened, and he fully returned to the world. He turned as he heard a shrill cry from the corner of the room. In a moment, Shadrack's arms grasped him. He was fearful for his adopted father. Although the samurai showed nothing on his face, the child read the terrible pain in his eyes.

Tanaka ruffled his hair and talked gently to him, trying to allay his fear. Saito finished dowsing the katana. He turned back to the table and resheathed the sword. In his eyes there was a new respect for the ronin.

"What will you do with him, then?" he asked, nodding at the child.

Tanaka grimaced. "When the Winter finishes, I will begin training him in the art," he said, his voice strained. "Until then, maybe you would like a helper in your work?"

Saito grunted. "Aye, we'll soon put some muscle on the young rascal. And a dose of discipline wouldn't go amiss, either, I'd wager."

Tanaka grunted. "Don't worry, discipline will be the last thing he lacks."

--------◦◦◦--------

Kyoto Village
Year 6 of 32nd Shogun
(18 months later)

Ekanar looked up as Tanaka flung open the front door; an icy blast of wind followed the samurai through. He slammed the door and dumped his load of firewood by the hearth. Despite the loss of his hand, Tanaka was now quite able to cope with most forms of work. Saito had fashioned a steel appendage for him; the hook-like mechanism allowed him at least some degree of control.

Ekanar closed his book and scrutinized the ronin as he began to stoke the fire.

"What's on your mind, old friend?" Tanaka asked without turning.

"You trouble me, Ieyasu."

Tanaka did not slow his work. "And why is that?"

"You have changed almost beyond belief. It's something that has vexed me over the last few months. When younger, you would have decapitated a man at the suggestion you perform chores."

"People change. That was about twelve years ago."

"Not this much. I barely recognize you. What happened? This philosophical attitude obviously didn't occur overnight."

Tanaka threw some more wood on the fire, which was now burning more healthily. He moved away from it to sit in a deep armchair, but his eyes remained focused on the revitalized flames.

"No. The change was gradual, and took several years. It was first triggered quite spectacularly by a peas..., by a commoner."

Ekanar smiled at the verbal slip: some habits died hard.

"There was an old man at Misko who crashed into me on the street. It was at night, about eight years ago. Well, to be more exact, I crashed into him. I was steaming drunk. He was very apologetic, but I decided that it would be worth my time to give him a hiding, anyway."

Tanaka's eyes became clouded with embarrassment, but there was humour there also.

"The old man bore no weapon, as is the law for the common castes, and appeared to be completely defenseless. Yet when I attacked him, he defeated me easily. Even when I drew my katana he was not unsettled. He slid to the side of the blade, disarmed me and knocked me out."

"But I thought that you were undefeated in combat. The tales of your ability are legendary."

"Yes, it's true that I have never been defeated by a samurai. But on this occasion, it was a simple commoner, and there were no witnesses.

"When I was revived, the old man had taken me to his house. I felt insulted when I awoke, but it gradually dawned on me that though the man was a peasant, he had bested me. He had even cut his palm on the blade of my katana before resheathing it, so that the Code was not broken. My belief in the inherent superiority of samurai took a severe blow. With it, my arrogance began to crumble, though its final demise was not to occur for many years.

"The old man became a good friend of mine, though I told no one about him. It would be unfitting for the Shogun's captain to visit peasants. I learned from him a philosophy which I still live by today. It was a philosophy of discipline and education, yet which had fundamental respect for all life and which shunned the use of violence except when absolutely necessary."

Ekanar looked impressed. "What was this philosophy?"

"The Bushido." Tanaka said the word reverently.

"But I thought that was the code that all samurai lived by."

"No. The bushido that the samurai live by is a code of honour which is used to swell their already inflated egos. If they are offended, they must seek vengeance, and they must follow orders from their daimyo regardless of consequences. But their bushido has never been in a written form, and is not the true Way of the Warrior."

"How did you survive as captain of the Shogun's Guard? Surely you could not have lived by a code of non-violence?"

"For the most part, I was able to live off my reputation. If something needed taking care of, I would simply give an order. And it was no problem to maintain the illusion of arrogance with my peers. But the day was always likely to appear when my loyalty to the Shogun was compromised by the Bushido. As you know, that day came when I was ordered to murder the heir of Ihata Kanazawa. The Shogun insisted that I perform the deed personally, since the assassination was of utmost importance, and I had his full trust."

"He must be extremely bitter about your defection," Ekanar said gently.

Tanaka snorted. "He'll have his *kebiishi*, Hideyori Yoshitaka, combing the Empire for me. You see, I was never a true samurai until the Shogun took me under his wing, even though I was allocated Kyoto as my command. Without nobility, and an impressive line of ancestors, you cannot be true samurai. Yet the Shogun changed all that by making me the captain of his personal corps. It was unthinkable at the time, since I was also a half-breed, but no one dared to speak out against the Shogun, not even Kanazawa. The Shogun knew that my abilities were too good to waste. I was fortunate to save his life on what I thought would be my one and only visit to his palace."

There was a brief silence before Ekanar spoke.

"Aye, I think that Shadrack will turn out to be an even stranger combination than you are."

Tanaka's eyes narrowed.

"What do you mean?"

The sage shuffled nervously.

"I don't know, but we both know that he's no normal child."

"And?"

It was something that the samurai loathed to be mentioned, yet he wanted to know the sage's thoughts.

"It's just that he's the quickest child I've ever taught. His intelligence and curiosity can be very surprising."

Tanaka grunted; he had to admit that he had noticed the same. Shadrack had learned their language at a frightening pace, and was now fluent with reading and writing. Normally only samurai were allowed such privileges, and the process took many years.

"Mind, I have to say, he's lost his insecurity. Last six months have changed him completely. You've done a good job there. I have to say, I'm quite surprised."

Tanaka looked down at his half-empty tankard in embarrassment. He still had difficulty in showing affection, but he cared very much for Shadrack.

"Saito has done a good job with him," he said. "He is strong and has stamina."

Ekanar chuckled.

"Aye, I suspect Sashka has her eye on him to be her own. She's fallen in love with him. She and Yoriie always wanted a child, you know."

Tanaka looked up sharply, and then relaxed as he noticed his own reaction. Ekanar nodded his head and smiled, suddenly aware of the extent to which the samurai cared for the child. He realized how strange it must be for a bushi to have what almost amounted to a family. Already, Tanaka was unrecognizable from his old, arrogant self. He wondered how he would be in a few more years.

"What of his memories?" the sage asked.

Tanaka shrugged. "He seems to remember nothing before he knew me. He is not yet aware that he is different."

"He still has an innate knowledge of Hebrew."

There was an uneasy silence. Ekanar had assured the bushi that Hebrew had not been a spoken language on Tellus for thousands of years. The fact cast a great shadow over the question of the child's origins.

"Well, it is the first day of Spring on the 'morrow," Ekanar said with mock cheerfulness.

Tanaka grimaced. "Aye, then shall his true test begin."

"Meaning?"

"It is my task to make him strong, and that I shall do until no mortal man will dare to stand against him. This will be done, or the child and I will die in the attempt."

Ekanar shuddered at the ring of prophecy in the words.

When a man lacks discrimination and
His mind is undisciplined, his senses
Run hither and thither like wild horses,
But they obey the rein like trained horses
When he has discrimination and his
Mind is one pointed.

—The Upanishads

Enya
Yesod of Yetzirah
The Enchanted Forest
(1000 years hence)

Bal paused for a moment to look at the darkening puce-coloured sky. The angry crimson sun now touched the dirty yellow-green leaves of the forest. As it sank, an unholy tension crept around the trees. With the tension came grey tendrils of mist, reaching out like searching fingers.

Bal shuddered, an effect not caused solely by the chilly Winter air. Enya had changed dramatically in a thousand years, and even a Black Adept was not completely at home in the hostile wilderness.

What have you done, Master? he wondered. Surely Dethen's evocation of Lilith had caused this. *The plane of dreams,* he thought: the description now seemed quite ironic.

"Shouldn't we continue forwards?" Yhana asked. "I hate these damned trees, and it will be dangerous to remain here."

Bal turned to look at her. She was breathing hard from the rapid pace he had set, and her face was ruddy. Her short blonde hair was matted from a week in the open, but her blue gaze was still sharp. As usual, it held a hint of restrained aggression. The gaze was judgmental, not easily pacified. Bal's eyes strayed down to her bloated stomach, the womb in which his own seed now grew.

"Night is setting in," he said. "We must find shelter immediately. It will be dark moon tonight."

He grabbed Yhana's hand and started walking quickly. He studied her as they moved, noting that the dark ethereal strands that held them together were weakening. Using visualization, he intensified them. Even though Yhana now followed him of her own free will, it was essential that she remain totally under his control until the birth of the child. That was all that mattered: the birth of the child. Yhana was too capricious to trust, despite her deep infatuation with him.

The ancient trees of the forest seemed contorted into agonizing postures; it appeared to Bal that they stretched out for vengeance, their branches frozen in mid-reach. They whispered to one another, their leaves rustling together in conspiracy. Bal's desire to reach safety became more urgent, and he walked even faster, pulling Yhana along with him.

"Do you remember everything I told you?" he asked.

His black robes contrasted markedly with Yhana's yellow in the gloom. The symbol of the Yellow School on her breast reflected the blood-red light as the sun dipped below the horizon.

"Of course I remember. I'm not an imbecile," Yhana retorted coldly.

"Repeat it!" Bal hissed. "It is essential that you remember everything."

Even with his considerable power, Bal still found it impossible to subdue her will completely. That was one of the reasons she had been chosen: she was of good stock, and the child would be born strong.

"Our first loyalty is to the protection of the child. Nothing else takes precedence," she said.

"Yes! That is right. Why?"

"It is the fetus of your Master, who will return to once again lead the Black School."

"Not just my Master," Bal said. "In time, everyone will obey him. He comes to fulfill the Purpose. To destroy this abominable plane, and every other one. He will shake the power of the gods themselves when he returns!"

"Really." Yhana's tone was sarcastic, but Bal knew that it was simply her way: she wanted the birth of the child as much as he did, though he hadn't yet figured out her motivation for this.

"Come!" he said sharply. "We must move faster. We'll never survive the night out in the open. Not under the evil phase of the moon."

The sounds of the forest were frantic now as creatures scurried to places of safety, fearful of the assault that was to come. The mist thickened around them, tinged a blood red. Despite his usual self-discipline, Bal felt a surge of panic as he dragged Yhana even faster. He had never been caught out in the open at dark moon on Enya, and he knew of no one who had and survived.

"We must hurry! Come, my magick will be weak because of the moon. But remember, if we are separated then flee for safety. I have used what power I have to keep you safe."

His fingers briefly touched the protective talisman which hung from her neck. He felt the astral power within it, and it soothed him. As long as the child was born safely, then everything would be fine.

He glanced nervously around as they rushed through the undergrowth. Something was watching them, tracking them with natural cunning. In the periphery of his vision, he saw something small and black flitting through the trees. When he turned it was gone, but he knew it was still watching. His skin itched under the scrutiny and he urged Yhana even quicker. They were now breaking through the forest at a sprint. He feared for Yhana's pregnant condition, but he knew that if he didn't force her to run, they would both certainly die.

Bal cursed his own stupidity for travelling at dark moon. He had hoped to reach the Yellow School sanctuary before dusk, but there was no chance of reaching it now: it was still a couple of miles away. Yhana's condition had slowed them more than he had anticipated. Their only chance was to head for the waterfall; he knew that there was a cavern system under the waterfall. At least there had been last time he was in the Enchanted Forest, but that had been a thousand years ago.

A piercing howl sliced through the forest air; Bal's gut clenched involuntarily. They were close to the waterfall now: he could hear the splashing. Or was it his imagination? The blood red mist thickened around them now. It clung to the ground like a macabre quilt, reaching up to chest height. Its acrid stench stung Bal's nostrils and throat as he gulped down oxygen. Yhana was gasping now and was not attempting to talk or complain, a sure sign she was struggling.

Above him in the trees he could sense the black creature stalking them, keeping pace as they bolted through the trees. He could feel its hatred of him: it was something very personal. Somehow he knew that he was the creature's quarry. He was not deceived by its apparently small size.

Suddenly Bal and Yhana burst into a small clearing and he saw the waterfall below. He scrambled down the bank too quickly, and they both splashed into the pool. Yhana cried out, stunned by the numbing cold of the water. Bal gagged as he tried to breathe. They were now under the sheet of mist, and tears rolled from his eyes. He dragged Yhana in the direction of the waterfall, which he could clearly hear though he couldn't see. Something in the water brushed past his leg and he pushed on harder, determined not to panic. What would Dethen think of him if he lost his composure? The thought calmed him and in a few seconds he passed through the waterfall.

He heaved himself up onto the ledge and pulled Yhana after him. Despite her small size, her pregnancy and her soaked robes combined to make her considerably heavier. Once they were both inside, he lay against the cavern wall, breathless. The sheet of water blocked out the sickening red mist, and he relaxed, content to relax for a few moments.

"Don't move."

Bal froze as the words were whispered in his ear. He felt the edge of a knife press against his throat, and all thoughts of resistance died. There was no way he could disarm the man from such a position.

"You too, miss."

Bal's eyes caught the movement of another man, who stepped over to grab Yhana roughly.

"Careful! She is with child!" Bal hissed.

He tensed as the knife was pressed harder against his throat, the sharpened edge drawing blood.

"Behave yourself, and she might live," said the man, dragging Yhana to her feet. Bal noticed that he was now more gentle, however.

"Clasp your hands on your head," said the man who held Bal. Bal wrinkled his nose at the disgusting breath and did as instructed.

He was turned and walked deeper into the cavern; behind him he could hear Yhana's laboured breathing. The run had not done her well: she was barely three months from giving birth.

Bal's eyes were poorly adjusted to the dark and he expected his face to smash into rock at any moment, but his captors knew exactly where they were going. They easily navigated a turn in the dark, and suddenly Bal could see a faint glimmer of light ahead. The caverns were far more complex than he remembered, riddled with crevices and passages, most of them leading to dead ends. He wondered whether he would be found if he escaped and sought refuge in a dark corner; or surely one of the routes would lead to the open? However, he knew it wasn't safe to leave the sanctuary of the caverns now.

He was led through another sharp turn, and now the light was bright enough to cause him to blink. The passage suddenly opened into a sizable cavern. The smell of sweat, rotten food and burning wood hit Bal immediately.

The cavern was lit by a small fire, which cast heat out to even the perimeter of the room. The smoke rose up lazily, drifting toward some unknown point of ventilation in the ceiling high above. Seated around the fire were over a score of men, probably brigands, Bal realized.

"Mendaz, we found these two by the 'fall," said the man who held Bal.

The man who looked around was well built, with a predatory look. He lay beside a woman who was pregnant, obviously very close to her time. Bal immediately saw the ethereal currents linking the pair. The woman seemed to be a warrior, and the man cared for her very much indeed. Mendaz stood up and walked towards the captured pair. Bal was roughly pushed forward to meet him, the knife withdrawn from his throat. He did not miss the array of cross bows which were levelled at his heart.

Yhana was gently shoved to stand beside him. Her lucid eyes studied everything about her; she seemed to be the hunter, as well as the hunted. She even studied Bal: the shock of the water had brought her to full consciousness, destroying his grip on her mind.

"What is this?" Mendaz asked, scrutinizing Bal from head to toe. "A Black Adept without the mark of the Warlock? And in the company of a Yellow School initiate. You keep strange company, Adept."

Bal met the leader's gaze with his own. "I own no allegiance to the Warlock. He is a charlatan, with no right to rule the Black School. And I travel with whoever I wish to."

Mendaz laughed, and his men joined in. "The Warlock has ruled the Black School for nearly a thousand years, and you challenge his right? Pah! The Warlock's grasp reaches from one side of the plane to the other. There is no one to challenge him!"

Bal smiled thinly. "There is one who will challenge him."

Mendaz laughed dismissively. "Who? You? Pah! You are a

charlatan."

"I know not what manner of demon the Warlock is, but his reign will soon come to an end, mark my words. And not by my hand, though I will stand by the side of him that casts the demon down."

The laughter in Mendaz's eyes suddenly disappeared, and Bal realized he was as unpredictable as Yhana.

"You are full of words, magician," Mendaz said. "I think the Warlock would pay a fine price for you. He does not like impostors."

Bal glanced at Yhana. "You may take me prisoner if the girl is left unharmed. You can then do with me as you wish."

Mendaz sniggered, his eyes alight with a strange madness. Bal then realized just how unstable then man was: his emotions changed quicker than the breeze.

"You are in no position to bargain, charlatan. And if you do possess any magick, it will be next to useless in this time. The moon will work against you. In this time only steel is reliable."

"Then I appeal to your decency: leave the girl unharmed. I will not resist."

Mendaz scrutinized Yhana; she stared back defiantly, no hint of fear in her gaze. "She is not pretty, but she has gall to stare at me like that. She will make good sport for some of the men here."

"She is with child!" Bal snarled, outraged.

Mendaz leered, "We learn not to be choosy out here in the wilderness."

Bal's fists clenched as he struggled to control his fury. He turned to Yhana and stroked the talisman which hung from her neck.

"Remember the charm. It will protect you."

"Bal!" she hissed under her breath. "You can't leave me here!"

Her eyes were incensed, the pupils narrowed to pinpoints. Bal could see that she was struggling to stop herself from striking him. And with Yhana it would not simply be a slap.

"I must go. The charm will protect you. Have faith: it contains much of my power."

Unseen by the occupants of the cavern, a small dark creature slipped through the entrance and into the shadows. It lay there, watching, ready to choose its moment. Yhana grasped Bal's arm, holding him as if to prevent his escape.

"I'm afraid you are not going anywhere, black mage," Mendaz said, amused. "My hearing is better than you think, obviously."

"Touch either of us, and I will destroy the object that you must value," Bal said. His eyes lingered Mendaz's wife.

Mendaz was furious. "You dare to threaten my wife?! Shoot him!"

Suddenly the room was thrown into turmoil. Bal raised his hand and Mendaz's wife screamed in agony. A brilliant burst of light came from Bal's body as three crossbow bolts sped toward him. They never hit their target. Once the light had disappeared and the after-effect had cleared, Bal was not to be seen. Yhana gasped and clutched her blackened hand to her chest.

"Bastard!" she snarled.

"Find him!" Mendaz bellowed. He ran over to his wife, who was crying out as convulsions swept through her body.

"The baby! He has bewitched the baby!"

The soldiers stood staring helplessly as the woman screamed in pain.

Yhana quickly cast her gaze about, looking for the route of escape that Bal had used. She knew that he had not teleported away: to project himself in such a manner would require tremendous energy. Bal had used the light as a distraction, and somehow slipped away in the chaos, perhaps using what magick he had to meld into the shadows as he escaped.

Guards ran in all directions, intent on finding the escaped magician. No one was paying any attention to Yhana, but she knew that she still had almost no chance of escape. The caverns were riddled with passages, most of them dead ends, and she had no idea where to run. She ran a hand over her belly, feeling the six month fetus; more than anything else, the baby would prevent her escape. She swore under her breath; if she had been able to leave the baby behind, she would have done so. Her own neck was more precious than that of any child, regardless of the child's importance.

A guard suddenly laid his hand on her shoulder, and she knew that even the slim chance of escape had passed.

Mendaz was frantically trying to comfort his wife, who was screaming in agony.

"The baby is coming!" she hissed from between clenched teeth.

Yhana watched with contempt as Mendaz held her hand, talking soothingly to her. As if he could feel Yhana's scathing gaze on him, Mendaz looked up.

"Get rid of her!" he shouted to the guard that held her. He drew his index finger across his throat.

The soldier nodded and started to drag Yhana away. His hand slid to the dagger at his hip. Yhana struggled wildly, but her condition made her slow and useless, and so was her magick. Close by in the shadows, the black creature snarled quietly, preparing itself to strike.

"Wait," Yhana shouted. "I can help your wife!"

The soldier paused as Mendaz considered her words.

"I was in the child brothels in Gorom. I've helped in many births and seen hundreds more! You obviously know nothing of child bearing. Let me help! I'm a woman."

"You were a child whore?"

"I was not always an initiate," Yhana said, her tone bitter with rancour.

She could see that Mendaz's mind was balanced on a knife edge: he was desperate, but he was also deeply suspicious.

"All right," he said, his voice uncertain. "Do what you can. But if she dies…"

The look in his eyes was enough to convince Yhana that she didn't want him to finish the sentence. The guard released his grip on her and she ran over to kneel beside the wife.

"What is her name?" she asked.

"Tara," Mendaz said. The sickening affection in his voice made the bile rise within Yhana: she found him pathetic.

She felt Tara's stomach carefully. "It is a boy," she said, though she was not at all sure. The mothers had all died in the births she had attended: she was far more used to seeing abortions.

She frowned deeply. "The baby has turned the wrong way. It will be born feet first."

"Is that bad?" Mendaz asked, his eyes intense.

Yhana cursed under her breath. She had no idea what Bal had done to the woman. He could have cursed her, but more likely he had only started the birth prematurely. He would not have expended power unnecessarily—that was not his way.

"It is…not good," she said. "The baby is very large, and it will be difficult to save both mother and child."

"Damn the child!" Mendaz said. "Save Tara! I couldn't care less what you do with the baby. Feed its corpse to the wolves for all I care!"

Yhana stared at him for a moment; even she was surprised at his callousness. From the light in his eyes she could see that Mendaz was literally obsessed with his wife.

A guard suddenly entered the cavern. "Mendaz, we have found the trail of the black mage. He is still within the caves."

Mendaz stood up quickly. "Take me." He turned to the three men who were left in the cavern. "Guard her closely. I will be gone only a few minutes."

Yhana watched him leave, hatred on her face. She had no doubt that he was mentally unhinged.

A weak hand touched her wrist and she turned to find Tara trying to get her attention.

"What is it?" Yhana asked, her voice cold.

"The child," Tara whispered. "Take no notice of my husband. You must save the child."

"That's not possible. There is no way for the child to be born without cutting you open."

"Then do it!"

Yhana scowled. "You will not survive. I am no surgeon: I can't stitch you up."

"I don't care!" Tara whispered, her voice strained.

"Well I damn well do!" Yhana snapped. "Because if you die, then I do too. And I can't have that happen."

The guards moved closer, alarmed by the exchange of words, though they couldn't distinguish them.

"Please!" Tara whispered. "You are with child yourself. You must know how I feel!"

"No. Not really," Yhana said, and there was genuine curiosity in her voice. She stared at the helpless mother, and it seemed that something deep inside her was moved by her plight. The feeling surprised her, but she could not deny its existence.

"You!" she called to the nearest soldier. "Give me that dagger!"

The soldier gave a toothless grin. "You think I'm stupid, miss? You'll get its sharp end in a minute."

"Give her it!" Tara ordered. "Or I'll tell Mendaz that you dis-obeyed me."

The guard's face turned ashen and he handed the dagger to Yhana without a word, hilt first. She snatched it from him, her eyes glittering with petty triumph.

"Now leave us," Yhana told him. "Take your comrades and guard the entrances. I have a delicate operation to undertake."

The soldier looked at Tara; she nodded and the guard hesitantly obeyed, instructing his colleagues of their orders.

"I have never done this before," Yhana said.

Tara swallowed and nodded. "Just make sure the baby is not harmed."

Yhana could see the fear in her eyes, but she was impressed at the way she handled it. Strength of character was one of the few things Yhana respected in others.

"Close your eyes," she instructed.

She placed her right hand on Tara's forehead and concentrated. She found it difficult to raise the necessary power due to the moon phase, but gradually she felt the tingle as energy began to flow through her. Tara's body went limp and she relaxed for the first time as she slipped into trance.

Yhana pulled Tara's night-dress away to expose her abdomen. She held the dagger above the mother's stomach for several long seconds, not believing what she was about to do. She had no idea how perform what she was supposed to without injuring the baby.

What the hell am I doing here? she wondered. *I should be getting out of here, not spilling open some woman's belly.*

For a moment she considered making a run for it, while the soldiers were occupied. She still didn't know which passage to take, but she would have a better chance on the run than when Mendaz returned and found his wife dead. Yet for some reason she felt compelled to deliver the child. Normally she had no feeling for other people or animals, and she considered this a strength rather than a weakness; but she wanted to deliver this baby unharmed.

"Isis guide my hand," she muttered. With a single clean movement she made the incision. Tara made a strange sound in her throat, but otherwise didn't respond: the trance was deep enough for her not to feel the pain. Yhana didn't even look as she reached out her hands and slipped them inside Tara's womb. They reappeared with a bloody bundle of flesh. The baby immediately began to cry, shocked by the cool air. Yhana stared in fascination. Her cut had been absolutely perfect. She could have put it down to luck or coincidence, but she believed in neither.

She used the dagger to cut the umbilical cord and tie it for the baby. The child was a boy, as she had thought. It was the biggest baby she had ever seen. She laid it down next to its mother, wondering how it would survive now. Tara would not survive, Yhana was sure. The wound she had inflicted would kill her: she was losing blood rapidly. Her only chance would be if Yhana used every ounce of her magical ability to heal the wound. At dark moon, it was unlikely that even that act of self-sacrifice would be effective.

Yhana stared at the unconscious mother. "You were brave," she said; there was a tinge of respect in her voice. Then she took the dagger and slit the woman's throat. "To die on your sleep is a pleasant way to go," she said.

She wiped the dagger on Tara's night dress; it would be useful in her escape.

The baby was crying loudly now, and Yhana was unable to silence it. She had no mothering instinct, regardless of her own pregnancy. One of the guards was walking toward her .

"You have delivered the baby," he said. "Mendaz will be pleased."

"I don't think so," Yhana muttered under her breath. She kept the dagger palmed, ready to use if necessary.

The guard saw Tara's slit throat and shouted out in alarm. "What have you done, you stupid bitch?" He started to draw his sword, and his two colleagues rushed to his aid.

Yhana caught him by surprise as she lunged with the dagger. It deflected off one of his ribs and into his heart. She savoured the awful shock on his face as he fell, but it was short lived. The other soldiers were upon her and making enough noise to draw the rest of the camp back to the cavern. She knew that she was in a helpless situation; not even magick could aid her.

She swore viciously and reached for the dagger, intent on pulling it from the soldier's corpse. Rough hands grabbed her and pulled her away, and she knew she was struggling in vain. Anger fuelled her with strength, but against two men it was not enough. They pummelled her to the floor, paying no heed to the child she carried. One of them drew a dagger as the other restrained her.

"You'll pay for the death of Marcus!" he hissed. Yhana spat in his face, defiant to the last.

The soldier drew back the dagger to strike.

Suddenly everyone froze as a deep, threatening growl came from barely a yard away. Yhana turned her head to see a very strange creature. It was strange because at first it appeared so normal: it looked nothing more than large black cat. But as she stared at it, she noticed more details. Its physique was incredibly muscular, more like a panther than a house cat. Its whiskers were silver, with a lustre that was almost metallic. The eyes were green and hard, like jade stones; the gaze was sharp and intelligent.

The creature snarled, pulling its lips back to reveal canines to rival a tiger. Some distance away, the voice of Mendaz could now be heard; it was growing stronger as he neared.

"Gods, nail that son of a bitch Simon!" shouted the soldier that held Yhana down.

The guard with the dagger lunged at the cat, stabbing with the weapon. The dagger connected with its target, but simply deflected off as if it had struck a rock face.

"By the gods, it's bewitched!" the soldier said, backing away.

The creature's eyes narrowed and it flicked one of its front paws; metallic claws appeared, which easily gouged the rock floor as the cat demonstrated their effectiveness. The soldier took a few paces back, and then broke into a run towards the voice of Mendaz.

The guard who held Yhana seemed to sense the creature's intent. "If you come any closer, I'll kill her," he said, his voice shaky. He drew his dagger.

The cat snarled aggressively and launched itself. Blood sprayed over Yhana as the soldier's jugular was severed. He fell back, clutching his throat.

Yhana lay very still as the creature advanced on her. From her astral vision she could tell that the creature was magical in nature—it had come through the Boundary. Near her lay the dead guard's dagger, but she knew that it would be useless, as would be her magick. She stared at the cat, daring it to attack.

The creature snarled and retracted its claws. It motioned with its head, much as a human might, that she should follow. Yhana stared for a moment in shock, but quickly stood up when the creature hissed. She fingered the talisman at her throat. Perhaps Bal's magick had been effective after all.

Mendaz's voice was very close now, and she could hear the voices of many men with him. She had to take her chance now and run for it. She cast her gaze quickly around. There were two corpses in the room, and a baby which was now sleeping. She watched in fascination as the black cat walked over to the child. It growled in front of the child's face, and its claws appeared again. The baby awoke and started crying loudly. The cat paused with its claws in mid-air. Yhana watched in horror: she was sure it would rip out the baby's throat.

Then the cat hissed and its claws disappeared. Yhana could see the frustration in its eyes.

It wants to kill the child, but won't because it's a baby, she realized. *Perhaps this creature can be manipulated. Empathy is weakness.*

The cat stared at her and then loped away, heading into one of the passages. Yhana wasted no more time: she ran after the creature. It had found a way into the cave system, so it was logical that it knew a way out.

———◦◉◉◉◦———

Mendaz burst into the cavern, five men at his heels. His eyes immediately picked out the corpse of the guard.

"What the hell?!"

He ran over to his wife and froze in horror as he saw the slash which stretched across her throat from ear to ear.

"Murder," he said, his voice barely audible; his eyes were shell-shocked. He knelt down and held his face in his hands.

"Mendaz," said one of the soldier gently. "Should we search for her?"

Mendaz leapt to his feet, his face a mask of rage. "Find her and kill her, god damn it! Bring her cadaver to me!" He drew his dagger and attacked the soldier, who dodged away and ran to his task. The others immediately followed, eager to avoid their captain's mercurial temper.

Mendaz was sobbing now, his body trembling as he sat beside the body of his wife. He reached out a hand to touch her, but withdrew it: he could not bear to touch her corpse.

A piercing cry disrupted his grief, and he looked up to see his baby. It bawled at the top of its voice, shouting for its dead mother. Mendaz was consumed with hatred.

"You caused this," he muttered under his breath. "Your birth killed my wife."

With a sudden vicious movement he raised the dagger and brought the pommel down forcefully on the child's head. The baby let out a single scream before it was silenced.

———⟫✸✸✸⟪———

Yhana gasped and fell to the ground as she emerged from the cavern system into the open air. She had been led through a complex honeycombed system of passages by the black cat, and had barely been able to squeeze out of the exit. But now she was out in the open, and though the forest floor was covered with the unholy red mist, she knew she was within half a mile of the Yellow School shelter; though she hated the forest with a vengeance, she knew almost every tree within ten miles of the shelter. She only had to await morning before venturing from her haven.

She smiled triumphantly: she would make it to safety, after all. She re-entered the cavern entrance and sat down a few yards within, pulling her knees to her chin for warmth. Bal's desertion had wounded her bitterly. Never did she allow anyone to get close to her, but she had completely fallen for the Black Adept.

She swore to herself that it would never happen again: never would anyone be trusted. The betrayal cut deeper than she thought possible, rousing emotions she didn't realize she had. Tears streamed down her face. Yet despite her pain, she could not bring herself to hate Bal. He had used her much as she would use another, and it was that strength and ruthlessness that she valued in him.

Running a hand over her swollen stomach, she sighed. Within her was Bal's child, destined for greatness and to become Master of the Black School once again. At least that promise had not be stripped away from her.

Knowing others is intelligence;
knowing yourself is true wisdom.
Mastering others is strength;
mastering yourself is true power.

—Lao-Tzu

Planet Tellus
Nipponese Empire
Kyoto Village
Year 8 of 32nd Shogun
(2 years later)

Tanaka watched from his place of concealment, well satisfied by the sight before him. It was Summer, and for a few short weeks the snow had melted as the temperature clawed its way above zero. In the centre of the clearing before him, Shadrack practiced his *budo-kai*, unaware of his secreted observer. Although he would never admit the fact to anyone, least of all Shadrack, Tanaka knew that the boy's standard was excellent.

The samurai reflected on the development of the child over the last two years. Shadrack's personality was still quiet, but intense and powerfully motivated. He understood the necessity for pain and suffering: he absorbed both, knowing that every fraction served to strengthen him further.

His young mind seemed aware that there was an important purpose to fulfill. It ruthlessly drove him: he strove constantly to extend his limitations. In that way, he was like no other eight-year-old boy. He was characterized by extremes and he showed few emotions, though Tanaka suspected he was different when alone. Never did he complain or shirk from work, and he enjoyed the feel of nature, especially being close to animals.

As he watched the young child, Tanaka smiled, though his eyes retained their sadness. Shadrack never seemed to tire. He practiced the martial arts' techniques that his *sensei* had taught him, and although they were all close to perfection, he never found the task tedious. No matter how hard his instructor drove him, he would push himself even harder when alone. He would practice a single technique a thousand times, and still not be satisfied with the result.

He reminded Tanaka of himself when he was younger, except that Shadrack was even more disciplined. He was fanatical in the pursuit of excellence, a most unchildlike attribute. The samurai had never before seen someone so talented: he was a prodigy. Combined with the youngster's work rate, something very special indeed would be produced, the likes of which Nippon had never before seen.

One thing that disturbed the bushi, however, was that Shadrack often seemed to know the techniques as he was taught them. It was as if he was simply acting as a recall device for the child. What was perturbing was that the style was unmistakably Tanaka's own, and he knew that that was impossible. But whatever level of budo-kai Shadrack had reached in his past life, Tanaka was sure that his new skills would soon dwarf that level.

Satisfied with his pupil's performance, Tanaka slowly rose and slipped away. Shadrack continued his training, his mind oblivious to the world about him. The techniques that he practiced, and was now adept at, were rolls, punches and elementary kicks. His concentration was always focused upon the technique he was performing, and everything else was irrelevant. Time distorted for him as he exercised: he wasn't even conscious of its existence.

Suddenly he was snapped back to reality. Something crashed through the undergrowth of the forest. He hesitated, suddenly realizing it was coming directly toward him. He backed away from the sound in uncertainty, scanning around for cover. His young mind was already aware of his limitations, and he knew that the approaching creature was huge, and moving very fast.

In a second the creature was upon him, bursting through the foliage into the clearing. The two-thousand pound ice bear reared up on its hind legs, its teeth bared aggressively. Its coat was creamy white, streaked with blood from fresh battle wounds; only another bear could have inflicted such injuries. Its eyes were red and loaded with fury. They focused upon Shadrack with pure hatred.

Shadrack froze in shock. His mind struggled to assimilate the situation. He knew that he could not run: the bear would hunt him down easily. Neither would he stand a chance to attack the creature, or attempt to calm it. The bear desired vengeance, and wanted it immediately.

Shadrack felt a split developing in his mind as the bear sidled forward, trying to force him into running. He knew that he was in desperate danger; he could almost taste the fear in his mouth. But something else was stirring, something of frightening strength and power. It had been dormant, but intense emotions were disturbing it for the first time.

It was dark and cold, and he hated it utterly, but it was impossible to fight. It was more a part of his essence than his own personality, and it compelled him absolutely. His fear of the bear was washed away in a tidal wave of force, and he looked at the puny creature before him.

He laughed, an uncanny and heartless sound. He walked toward the aggressively posed creature. It faltered slightly in confusion as he advanced, then moved forward in anger, fuelled by its pain.

Their eyes met in a contest of wills. Shadrack's inhuman, blue-black gaze bored into the animal, stopping it dead in its tracks. It swatted the air before him with huge paws, but didn't dare approach further. Shadrack felt the malignant part of himself reach out and touch the bear. It gave a roar of agony. It turned and fled, whimpering as it ran.

Released, Shadrack fell to his knees in shock and disbelief. Tears began to flow. He had no idea what he had done, or why. He simply knew he had lost control, and even now he felt the terrible split within himself. The dark part of his mind was now receding, the echoes of its demonic laughter fading. What perplexed him most was that he loved animals so much, and knew deep down that he always had.

After a while, his dazed mind realized he had been kneeling for too long. He had to return to the village. Dusk was approaching, and the weather was sure to worsen. He wanted to run back and confide in someone, to tell his father what had happened. Yet he was afraid: he dreaded rejection.

He started meandering back toward Kyoto, his spirit melancholic.

He had reached the bridge when his dulled senses registered the crunching of dead twigs. He looked up in fear, cursing his lack of *zanshin*. But he was too late, the man was already upon him.

He gasped in terror. It was the one man he was to avoid at all costs: Gorun Tzan, samurai of Kyoto. His father had repeatedly impressed the reasons upon him, and now he had failed.

A callused hand clamped his shoulder, and the bushi peered down at him. In his late twenties, Tzan had already outlived a samurai's life expectancy. He had a plain, honest face that mirrored his personality. His nose had been broken from an honour duel, and he had several conspicuous scars from the same place. His apparel instantly marked him out as a samurai: yoroi armour with twin *daisho* swords.

"Who are you, boy?" His tone was gruff, but not unkind.

Shadrack looked hopelessly for escape but he knew the grip was far too strong to break. He felt nauseous; he was utterly demoralized from his earlier experience.

His mouth opened to reply but he choked on his words.

Tzan's eyes narrowed. He knew everybody in Kyoto, and the boy would never survive a trek from elsewhere, even in Summer.

"Where are you from, boy?"

Shadrack could only stare in impotent trepidation.

Tzan scanned the woods, expecting to see a parent or companion. He found none.

He frowned when he looked at the child again. The boy was not a native of the Empire; that much was obvious from his eyes and build. Tzan knew the Shogun's orders regarding foreigners: they were to be executed on sight.

He was greatly perplexed. Although he was a veteran warrior, he had never killed anyone in cold blood. And the boy was hardly eight years of age. Besides, he wasn't sure that the boy was a foreigner. He didn't seem to be of Western blood either.

He made his decision. "Come with me, boy!" he ordered.

He took Shadrack by the scruff of the neck and marched him toward the village. Someone was bound to know something of the youngster. Although Tzan took his duty very seriously, he was usually reasonable. The people of Kyoto were therefore quite cooperative with him. It was rare that he needed to use coercion.

Shadrack didn't dare to resist as he was hauled across the bridge and through the village. A sixth sense warned him that this man was deadly serious. A sharp intake of breath escaped him as he realized they were en route to Ekanar's house. He closed his eyes and prayed that Tanaka had seen the samurai approach.

He had. But his reaction was not the one Shadrack expected. As they reached the door, it swung open. Tanaka stood there, his face emotionless. Shadrack was torn between hope and despair.

Tzan recognized the ronin immediately. Tanaka's tall, slim build and sallow complexion were unmistakable. Tzan knew that he didn't stand a chance against the ronin's legendary sword mastery. Then he was suddenly struck by a cognition: Tanaka was unarmed. He wore a simple *kimono*. It was only his posture that communicated he had once been samurai: steadfast and fearless.

Tzan swallowed hard. He released his grip on Shadrack.

"You are Tanaka-san?" He asked, an almost imperceptible tremor in his voice.

"Yes."

There was an anxious pause.

"I am Gorun Tzan, samurai of this village. You know my duty. You are to be executed on sight."

"I understand," Tanaka said, his voice deep and calm.

The two men held each other's gaze. Tzan licked his lips nervously Here was a man whose honour was a thousand times greater than his own: a man whom samurai used to revere and respect. His legs were unsteady at the thought of his duty. He knew he would have to make the choice between duty and what was right, as Tanaka was once forced to do. He had to give the ronin a chance.

"If you apologize for your dishonourable actions against the Shogun, and agree to beg to him for forgiveness, I will allow you to live," he said. He half drew the gleaming blade of his katana.

Tanaka considered the offer for an uncomfortably long time before answering.

"My duty to the Bushido overrides my loyalty to the Shogun. His desires and actions were petty and undeserving. That was my decision then, and I stand by it now."

For a samurai, the words were blasphemy. He knew they condemned him to instant death. He only hoped that his son would escape. He waited for the flash of metal and piercing pain.

But Tzan slashed his finger and slid the *katana* back into its place. The test had been passed.

"The respect that the peasants hold for you is truly worthwhile," he said. "I would wish you luck, but I'm unaware of your existence in my village."

The two men bowed as equals, both maintaining eye contact. Tzan then turned and walked away. Nothing more would ever pass between them.

―――――◦◉◦◦◉◦◦◉◦――――――

Enya
Yesod of Yetzirah
Yellow School haven
(The Enchanted Forest)

Yhana stared dejectedly out of the window of her room, searching for something to occupy her mind. Thick vegetation limited her vision to less than fifty feet in every direction.

Trees, trees, and more bloody trees. Damn the School for keeping me here!

A light knock at the door disturbed her depression.

"Come," she said, her tone apathetic.

The door opened and Philip stepped in, his middle-aged face as expressionless as ever.

"You're out of bed already?" he said, disapproval in his tone.

Yhana didn't give him the courtesy of turning to face him. "What do you care?"

"The baby is not yet a day old, and already you are straining yourself. You should be resting." There was no concern in Philip's voice; his tone was matter-of-fact.

"I am not as fragile as you think," she said icily. "Childbirth is overrated."

Philip's lips twisted into a patronizing smile. "Whatever you say, Yhana."

Yhana rolled her eyes, but didn't respond to the dig; she knew the Yellow Adept well by now.

"Why do you stare out of the window?" he asked.

"I hate the forest. And I loathe these accursed trees."

"Then why do you look at them?"

"Because there's nothing else to do in this damned place!"

"I think that perhaps the reclusive life does not suit you, Yhana. Meditation and occult study are too tame for you."

Yhana turned to look at him and sat on the low window sill. "Whereas for you they are everything. Logic and detachment: those are the only things you care for. You're empty: you have no ambition!"

"These things are what our School stands for, though logic in itself is intrinsically limited, especially in matters of metaphysics."

"Even that sounds like a statement of logic."

Philip raised an eyebrow, but didn't pursue the argument: he knew the futility of discussion with Yhana. He walked over to the bed where the cradle stood.

"Fiona looks healthy," he said. "She doesn't look much like her mother, though."

"The baby," Yhana muttered, and Philip was taken aback at her bitterness. "The baby can rot where it lies for all I care."

"What is wrong? The child is in perfect condition."

"It's a girl, you cretin!" she snarled.

"So? Ah…I'd forgotten. You've been disillusioned. Because of Bal's promise to you, you expected a boy."

"Yes, damn it! How could it be a girl? I can believe that Bal deserted me, but I can't believe that he would lie to me about the child. It was his whole purpose in seducing me! Bal doesn't do things without good reason, and his affair with me wasn't for pleasure."

"I can guarantee that," Philip said, and as Yhana started an angry retort he added: "Which leaves you with only two possibilities. Either Bal's Master Adept has incarnated as a female, or this is another soul entirely."

Yhana stared at him. "You know something I don't?"

"There is much I know that you don't," Philip said. "Don't think that this child was born for your benefit. Her birth will affect many. But she has been born as your child for a very specific reason."

"Which is?"

"To gain strength, of course. Any child that can survive with a mother like you will certainly grow to be very strong."

"Very funny, Philip. And where did you get this so-called information?"

"I am an Adept. There are means at my disposal which you don't have access to. And I can tell you beyond any doubt that this child is not the soul you thought it would be."

Yhana's face burned with anger. "Then who the hell is it?!"

Philip's patronizing smiled returned. "That remains to be seen."

*Who looks outside dreams; who looks
inside wakes.*

—C. G. Jung

Planet Tellus
Malkuth of Assiah
Nipponese Empire
Year 11 of 32nd Shogun
(3 years later)

Shadrack hid his face. He curled up into a ball in exasperation and frustration. He had no idea where he was. Everything was dark and cold, and he could feel no floor. It was like limbo.

He heard his name being called repeatedly. He knew he was lost, and someone was calling him back. It was always the same voice: feminine, soft, and sad. He yearned to respond, but he didn't know which direction it came from. It penetrated the air from all sides.

He peered up into the blackness, expecting to see nothing. But for the first time he saw the originator of the voice, and he knew he wanted to be with her more than anything. She had long dark hair, framed around an exquisitely beautiful face; deep brown alluring eyes fixed with his, and he knew that he was linked to this woman. Her image flickered, as though it reached across a thousand dimensions.

Her hand stretched out for his. He responded immediately, uncaring of the consequences. He knew that this was a chance at salvation. He was willing to risk everything. Their hands linked, and he felt a flow of harmonious energy between them: their vibrations were exactly attuned.

He felt himself rising faster and faster, moving away from the cruel world below. He knew that he was going home. Images of a beautiful plane with an amethyst sky flickered through his head. A warm, liquid ecstasy flowed through his body. Memories of another person crowded his mind: a tall man who wore a five-pointed star. A little while longer and he would know it all; he knew that this was extremely important.

Suddenly a horrific scream pierced his ears. Sharp claws grasped his legs, trying desperately to pull him back down. He could feel a freezing chill from the being below, and he balked as he recognized it as a part of himself. It would not allow him to leave: he belonged to it, and he would never escape.

The creature pulled harder, feeling like the weight of ten men on his legs. His grip slid and weakened. He looked at the woman above him. There was intense sadness in her eyes. He gave her a silent look of empathy before the grip was broken. He plummeted at terrific speed, accelerating toward his doom. The darkness became viscid, and it seemed he would suffocate. He struggled in mid-fall, trying to force in air.

He hit the ground with incredible impact. His body arched and a spasm sent him crashing from his bed to the floor, unable to catch his breath.

He collapsed and broke into tears at the thought of what he had lost.

Tanaka stood with Shadrack in the forest clearing where they usually trained. He looked his student up and down, and although he didn't show it, he was pleased. The special protein and carbohydrate-rich diet that Ekanar had recommended was beginning to show: the boy was going to have an impressive physique. Already he was developing great strength, partly due to his work with Yoriie Saito, and the fitness program that he submitted himself to every day.

But Tanaka was concerned about Shadrack's mental state. He rarely seemed to experience pleasure or joy. Only the fortifying of his body and mind were important to him. There was also something very definite that bothered the boy, but Tanaka could never entice him into discussing the subject. Apart from Tanaka, whom he considered his father, Ekanar, Saito, and Sashka, Shadrack avoided all contact with people. He knew that he was different, and he lived in great fear of something.

Tanaka banished the thoughts from his mind and turned to the business at hand. The child's problems were too complicated for an old warrior like himself.

"You've picked up a reasonable understanding of the basic moves

I've shown you so far," he said. "Now, you will enjoy an advantage over your peers when you finally leave the village, an advantage which I have enjoyed for many years. All samurai are trained in the arts of *iai-jitsu* and *jujitsu*. The first is the art of sword-drawing, in which a samurai strikes as he draws. The second is the art of gentleness, which is a defensive art comprising of locks, throws, and the use of critical points on the body.

"But I will teach you a third art, which not a single samurai in the Empire has knowledge of. It is the art of the common people, and is known as *karate:* the way of the empty hand. It is so called, because a man who bears no weapon is considered defenseless. And as a *karate-ka*, so will you appear. Yet your body will be a lethal weapon."

Shadrack listened carefully, his eyes wide.

"But before I begin to properly teach you my own style, which is a combination of all three arts, you must swear to me never to use the art against anyone while you are still my student. I realize that you will need to once you seek your destiny in the world, but until then you must promise me. Humility, restraint, and serenity are the hallmarks of a true warrior."

"I will not fail you, sensei."

Tanaka quietly scrutinized his student, then nodded.

"Then we will start with the first essential lesson: balance. The moves you are already familiar with are useless without this essential ingredient."

He watched his student's reaction. He liked the way that the boy stood: confident and unassuming. He seemed to realize that the lesson was going to be difficult, and accepted it without a word.

The lesson lasted for over five hours. Firstly, Tanaka showed him how to move back rapidly whilst maintaining perfect balance to counter-attack. This was painful, because after demonstrating the technique, he made sure his student was able to apply it by attacking the boy properly. He didn't slow down the attacks because of Shadrack's age: they were as strong and sharp as he could throw. When they hit, he pulled the focus out of them so that no permanent damage was caused, but they still bruised badly.

It was Tanaka's hard method of training that made his student advance so quickly. After a few hard knocks, the motivation to perfect the technique was very strong. Within twenty minutes, Shadrack had the fundamentals of the idea mastered. He was nearly always able to avoid Tanaka's ferocious attacks, and sometimes surprised his sensei by striking with a counter-attack when he saw an opening.

Although he was always very careful with his praise, Tanaka was shocked at how quickly Shadrack could learn and apply techniques and ideas. His ability was quite incredible, and again he received the impression that it was instinctive.

Next he taught his student balance in attacking. He showed him how to lunge by utilizing the legs to cut down an opponent at distance, and how to maintain balance during the lunge in case of a counter-attack. Because Tanaka was so quick in moving back, Shadrack found he could not make any distance on him at all. Then he started to close the gap, but with bad balance so that his teacher could easily pick him off. Although he hadn't managed to strike his teacher by the end of the session, Tanaka was well pleased with the improvement.

"I hope you now begin to understand the importance of balance." Tanaka said seriously. "It is the root of everything, even more-so outside of budo-kai."

Then he showed his student the art of *tai-sabaki*: avoiding attacks by not being there. It tested Shadrack's timing to the limit to step to one side or the other when being attacked. If he moved too soon, he was followed and hit; if he moved too late, he was also struck. As with all other things, though, he knew that with hard work and practice he would perfect the skill.

For the last hour, Tanaka taught him how to use his hips and stance to strike powerfully. This was also dependent upon balance and posture, as was demonstrated when he used trees as targets. If his balance was not perfect at the impact, the shock would travel back along his body and produce a weak technique. If everything was correct, he could feel the power travelling through him to the ground, and then reflecting back through him to strike the target a second time. In order for his body to transmit the force correctly, he had to tense his muscles for a split second at impact. This was known as *kime*, and Tanaka told him that it could take a lifetime to master.

By the end of the lesson, Shadrack could barely stand. Tanaka told him that he'd done well, clapped him on the back and made the transformation from sensei into father. They walked back together, all talk of combat finished.

Ekanar paused for breath, taking a moment to study the world about him. The forest was absolutely bare; the clean sheet of snow glittered beautifully as the light glanced off it. The smog was thin, and the bloated orb of the weak sun could just be seen through it. He laughed aloud, breathing the cold air deeply.

"So wonderful."

"What was that?" Shadrack asked as he caught up; he was amazed that the old man could move so fast.

Ekanar shook his head. "Don't you wonder why people get bored so easily?"

"I've never been bored!" Shadrack said, pleased with this minor accomplishment.

The sage looked at him affectionately.

"That's because you're different. You haven't been desensitized to the world like everyone else has. In worrying about the small things in their lives, they miss the incredible beauty all around them. They forget their own divinity!"

"I think I understand," Shadrack said uncertainly.

Ekanar smiled. He was never sure whether the child's next comment would be that of a ten-year old, or of someone far older. There was more than one personality within his young head.

"Always remember that being concerned is okay, but never worry about anything. What's the worst that can happen?"

Shadrack was quiet and thoughtful, so the sage continued.

"I'll tell you!" he said, as if about to reveal a treasured secret. "The worst is you'll die, and what's so bad about that?! You'll only be reborn!"

There was a short silence before Shadrack responded: "That's not true."

The sage twisted around, surprised. "Of course it's true!"

"Maybe for other people, but not for me."

His voice was so certain that Ekanar was taken aback.

"Aye, maybe you're right, lad," he said, "your karma's not a simple one. I know naught of it really, but from the vision your father had before finding you, I'll wager there's more than your own soul dependent on your actions."

He was quiet for a while, then said: "But I'll tell you something.

Whatever your destiny, there isn't a person I can think of who's better able to prepare you for it than your father."

"Or you," Shadrack added.

Ekanar smiled. "Aye, maybe that's true, too."

"How come you know so much, Ekanar?"

The sage chuckled. "Ah! Now that's due to my curiosity, young man. And my search for new adventure. I love the world too much!"

"Have you always been a sage?"

Ekanar looked down at his student, a tinge of sadness in his eyes.

"No, I once had to choose to become a sage. And in doing so, I turned my back upon knowledge of another type."

"Magick?" Shadrack asked, his eyes alight.

Ekanar stared in surprise. Shadrack's intellect and remarkable intuition were often unnerving; even the child's vocabulary was formidable.

"Yes, magick."

"Where can you study it?" Shadrack asked, his voice almost a whisper.

"Oh, nowhere in the Empire," Ekanar laughed, dismissing the preposterous idea. "It was far in the West, close to my native land. But I turned my back on the School of Mysteries, and on a woman I loved."

"Why?"

"You ask many questions for an eleven-year old."

"I could be any age, according to father," Shadrack reminded him.

Ekanar grunted. "Probably a hundred and eleven!"

"But why did you leave, then?"

The sage sighed. "My character did not fit in with Temple life. Emotional detachment did not come easily to me, and I liked a touch of ale now and again. Though I craved for the knowledge, for few are accepted into the Temple, it was beyond me to forsake the rest of the world. The Initiates live in isolation."

"Do you regret your decision?"

Ekanar paused in thought. "Yes, I suppose I do. I became quite wise in my travels, though I was never a sage of great repute. For in the West, I would still be considered young for a sage. But I have never answered the great questions that I always craved to know. Why are we here? What are we supposed to do?"

Shadrack snorted. "I'm no stranger to those questions."

They listened in silence to the wind sighing through the trees, Ekanar apparently debating with himself whether to say something. He finally made a decision.

"There's a woman who lives by herself in the forest, not five miles to the north. She comes into the village now and then for provisions and suchlike."

"I know her," Shadrack said.

"Well it happens that she has a talent that few know of."

Shadrack frowned, and then read the expression on the sage's face. "The second sight!"

Ekanar nodded solemnly, and looked to see if anyone had overheard.

"Be sure you tell no one. The Shogun would have her killed for sorcery. Mayhap she can help you, though."

Shadrack shook his head sadly. "I keep dreaming about the same person night after night. I don't know her, but I feel that I should."

"What does she look like?"

"She's a dark-haired lady with kind, brown eyes. She looks after me in my dreams, so the demons can't get me. Do you think she's my mother? She's very beautiful."

Ekanar thought for a while.

"Maybe she is your mother. Whether she is or not, though, it seems to me that she is the key to who you are, and also may be your most useful ally."

"The badge! I'd forgotten the badge! I've seen it before, but I can't remember where!"

"What kind of badge did she have?"

"It was a silver star!"

"How many points did this star have?" Ekanar asked, a very concerned look on his face.

"Five."

"How many points on top?"

The sage had turned pale, and there was a tremor in his voice. Shadrack could tell from his face that the answer to his question was very important.

"Just one."

Ekanar released his breath. "Yea gods, thanks for that at least!"

The world is full of suffering. Birth is suffering, decrepitude is suffering, sickness and death are sufferings. To face a man of hatred is suffering, to be separated from a beloved one is suffering, to be vainly struggling to satisfy one's needs is suffering. In fact life that is not free from desire and passion is always involved with suffering.

—Doctrine of the Black School[1]

22

Enya
Yesod of Yetzirah
The Enchanted Forest

Jaad curled up against the tree, pulling his knees up to his chin. He touched the puffed bruising on the left side of his face and winced. The tears had now dried, but the pain would not go away. It never did.

Malformed elementals danced around in circles before him, tormenting him. He hated them all. Sometimes they would poke and pinch him or try and hold him down, all the time laughing at his helplessness. They changed like the wind; they reminded him of his father, Mendaz. That was why he hated them.

He could see Mendaz now, brooding by the fire as his comrades danced around it. There was never any joy for his father, and that meant no joy for Jaad. Some of the men were kind to him, but most despised him because of his condition: being born a half-wit. He pressed his fingers against the depression on his head, like an ugly birth mark, where the hilt of his father's dagger had struck in his infancy. It was why he was not normal, he knew: the reason why every adult and child bullied him.

A particularly ugly gnome leered up at Jaad, its oily black tongue inches from his face. Jaad swatted at it and threw stones to drive it away. It giggled and scampered away into the forest, only to be replaced by two even bigger gnomes. He heard them whispering in his head, a whisper which was painfully loud. Then the other voices

---

1 Buddha (B.C. 568-488)

started and he put his hands to his ears, trying to shut them out. They taunted him and ridiculed him. The voices were so loud he could barely hear the sounds of the forest.

He closed his eyes, and when he opened them the gnomes were gone. They had been replaced by two of the camp's children.

"Hey, it's Jaad the cretin!" said one of them loudly. Within a few seconds other children began to gather.

"Half wit! Half wit!" They danced around him in a circle, gathering sticks and stones for weapons.

Jaad tried to run, but they pushed him back into the circle, jeering at him. His black eyes watched in fear and confusion as the children danced faster and faster, urged on by the ringleaders. Then they were upon him, using feet and fists, sticks and stones. Jaad curled up in a ball, trying to protect his head and body. The fists smashed into his ribs and back, and drew blood from the back of his head.

He screamed and started to cry, but the attack didn't stop. The children were in a frenzy, determined to maim him. Later they would tell their fathers, and the whole camp would laugh.

"It's Mendaz!" the cry of warning split the air, and the children scattered in all directions. Some were too slow, as the furious leader laid into them, viciously slapping them away.

"Bastards! Stay away from my son!" he bellowed, his infamous temper fuelled with drink.

The children dropped their sticks and stones as they raced from the clearing and back toward the camp. Mendaz chased them a short distance before turning back to his injured son. His eyes still burned with dark fury, and his breathing was shallow from the adrenaline rush. He stooped over Jaad, who remained in the fetal position. His clothes were ripped and gashes could be seen on his skin; already the bruising was showing up a ruddy purple.

Mendaz reached out his hand. "Come on son, I'll take you back."

As ever, his voice sounded gruff and anything but affectionate. Jaad whimpered and didn't move.

"Get up, Jaad. Come on."

Jaad remained where he was.

"Jaad! Get the hell up!" There was anger in Mendaz's voice now, and Jaad drew further away, his back pressed up against the tree.

Mendaz's temper flared as if it had never died. He grabbed his son by the hair. "You'll come with me, damn you!"

Jaad squealed and struggled frantically. Mendaz's boot crashed into his abdomen, winding him. Mendaz released his grip and Jaad fell to the floor, too winded to cry. He curled up on his side, desperately wheezing.

Mendaz stared in shock at what he had done. It always happened this way. He never meant to hurt his son, but it always happened. With shame he remembered Jaad's birth, when he had first struck the child. Guilt cooled his anger.

Mendaz stared at Jaad's face. There was a strange hawk-like look to it which neither parental line had ever had, and the eyes were a peculiar black, very unnerving. Despite these facts, there were still some things which reminded Mendaz of Jaad's mother, Tara. For these he loved him, while at the same time hating him for causing her death.

He sighed. "Come on, Jaad," he said, his voice uncharacteristically gentle.

Jaad didn't move; he might have been dead, he lay so still. Mendaz stared at his son with a mixture of love, hatred and pity.

"Then you can rot where you lie," he snarled. "Tend to your own wounds!"

He turned and walked back toward the camp, leaving Jaad once again by himself. Within seconds the elementals returned to taunt him.

--- ◦◦◦ ---

Enya
The Enchanted Forest

Fiona rolled from side to side in her sleep, her nine year old mind gripped by a terrifying nightmare. Her breathing rasped in her throat as she hyperventilated, battling against unseen demons. The stuffy, humid atmosphere of the twilit room suffocated her as she entwined herself in the bed sheets.

The images that haunted her would never be taken into the waking state. They belonged to another plane, well beyond that of Enya: the Qlippoth. Only the terror accompanied Fiona as she slipped from sleep to wakefulness, and then back again. She saw scenes from a life that was not her own, knew things she couldn't possibly know.

Now she stood by the Rose Circle, watching as darkness expanded from within it. Across the Circle stood a dark-haired man, his
face hawk-like. More than anything else she knew that she had to
protect this man from the darkness: she felt a link with him that
could never be broken. Crossing her arms across her chest, she fell
forward into the blackness. A numbing cold hungrily embraced
her. Serrated talons pierced her flesh from every direction; she let
out a wailing scream which shuddered through her bed chamber.
Suddenly she was awake, breathing hard and covered in an icy sheet
of sweat; her eyes were dilated in fear.

Invisible lips touched her forehead in a burning caress, followed
by a husky female voice whispering in her ear: "You were once mine
child, and you will be again."

She rolled out of bed, hitting the floor painfully on her side. The
oil lamp crashed to the floor as she frantically tried to light it in the
dark. The glass smashed, scattering over the wooden floor. Paraffin
oil leaked everywhere, filling the room with its heady scent.

Fiona hid her face in her hands and sobbed, her young mind
unable to understand the terrible experiences. She could not live
for much longer with them, yet she also feared that they would leave
her. More than anything else in her life, she felt the images belonged
to her. They somehow gave a clue to her identity; even though she
was only nine years old, there were some things she intrinsically
knew. One thing she knew was that she didn't belong where she
was. The Yellow School was alien to her: despite her age she already
rebelled against the doctrine of emotional restraint and non-action.
It went against everything she felt was right. There was also her
mother, who she hated with a vehemence; Fiona was sure that they
were misfits, cast together by some cruel twist of fate.

Dwelling on the rueful condition of her life started her along the
well worn path of self-pity. Everything was so unfair! There was
nowhere that she fitted in. She lashed out at a piece of glass, sending it skidding across the floor. She shuddered violently as the
resentment turned to anger. It amplified quickly and her heart started to race as black thoughts seeped through her mind. Soon her
body was quaking with the adrenaline release, and still the fury
strengthened. She hated the dreams, hated the Yellow School, and
hated her damned mother. She hated them all.

Her face red and screwed up in rage, she grabbed a piece of glass and started to squeeze. The sharp pain lanced up her arm, but she made no noise. She squeezed harder and harder, until the blood trickled out of her closed palm. Her whole body shook now, the rage so black that her head pounded violently and she found it difficult to breathe. Though her thoughts were unclear, she knew that she was in the condition to murder someone. Whenever the terrible moods seized her, she prayed her mother wouldn't walk through the door: she knew she would kill her when in the grip of the temper. It was like a rage which had carried over from another life, something so powerful she would never control it. Somehow she knew its source: the standing stones from her dream. The events that began there had scarred her psyche irreversibly.

Fiona was just old enough now to realize that the events belonged to a previous existence, an existence when the Yellow School had not held her as a prisoner. Despite the horror of the memories, she still yearned for such a life: freedom from her mother and the restrictions of the School.

She forced herself to concentrate on the pain. Without it she knew she would sink further and further into the rage, eventually losing control. It grieved her to think what would happen then. Though she loathed her mother, she knew that murder was very wrong.

Gradually the rage subsided and her booming heart returned to a more placid beat. She breathed deeply and winced as the full force of the pain hit her. Her knuckles were white and she could barely open her hand when she tried. The piece of glass was embedded in several deep cuts in her hand. Tentatively she extracted the shard, inhaling sharply as she dislodged it. She couldn't flex her hand: it throbbed with her pulse and tingled so forcefully it felt like a pin cushion.

Focusing her mind, she used the pain control techniques which Philip had taught her. She wouldn't yield to the pain: it was against her nature to yield to anything. Using her inner eye to visualize, she lessened the flow of blood to her hand. The bleeding gradually slowed and the tingling began to subside. For the first time since waking she began to feel in control. To balance herself properly she would need to perform a banishment by pentagram, a ritual she was now proficient at.

The hairs on the nape of her neck suddenly prickled, and she was certain she was being observed. She quickly cast her eyes around the room, which was now well lit with bloody sunshine. There was nothing to be seen, either physically or astrally, but still her anxiety remained. Slowly, she turned to stare out the window.

She gasped as she saw the creature. It was black and sleek, reminiscent of a panther. Its hard green eyes stared with unfathomable intelligence, the slit-like pupils possessed with a raking gaze. Though she felt no fear, Fiona was apprehensive: the creature was quite majestic, and obviously very powerful. She had never heard of such a being, even in fairy tales she had heard from the Adepts.

The feline watched her intently, its powerful tail swishing gracefully back and forth as it watched. For a minute, Fiona worried she might be prey, but that was not the look the creature had. Though its thoughts were unreadable, she could discern one emotion in its eyes: affection. Fiona moved over to the window and placed her hand against the glass. The cat moved forward and gently clawed the glass on the other side. She heard it purr softly, content to be close to her.

Joy washed over Fiona; for a few moments she felt completely happy. The emotion was one she experienced rarely, yet when she did, it felt as though her real self was emerging to the light after being trapped within a murky lake. The policy of the Yellow School discouraged the feeling of such emotions, but to Fiona the joy felt more natural than she could describe. To be otherwise was going against her essence. This she knew, but she was unable to describe it in words when she talked to Philip. He understood only logic, and was always liable to dismiss her statements simply due to her age.

Fiona stared in fascination and awe at the creature before her. *Philip knows nothing,* she thought. *Just like all the others. They only pretend to be wise. The Yellow School knows nothing!* As she stared at the beautiful creature before her, she knew she was right. No Yellow Adept could possibly appreciate such a sight.

Fiona jumped as the door was suddenly flung open and Yhana strode in. The black cat snarled and loped way at incredible speed. Yhana barely had time to register it before the feline was gone.

"What the hell was that?" Yhana demanded angrily; she rushed over to window, but there was nothing to be seen except the ubiquitous trees.

"A squirrel, Yhana," Fiona said, her voice loaded with the sarcasm she had learned from her mother.

Yhana spun around and slapped her hard across the face. Though it stung with a vengeance, Fiona didn't give her mother the satisfaction of showing the pain.

"What was it?" Yhana demanded again, her eyes narrowed in suspicion. "I didn't get a good look, but I've seen something similar once before."

Fiona smiled. She could see concern in Yhana's eyes. "You seem worried, mother."

Yhana's slap knocked Fiona from her feet; she landed on the scattered shards of glass, cutting herself in several places. A line of blood trickled from the corner of her mouth.

"Don't you ever call me that word again!" she snarled. "I might have given birth to you, child, but you are no spawn of mine!"

She bore down on Fiona until her face was barely an inch away. Fiona was petrified: when angered, her mother's face was as evil as her terrible nightmares. She didn't dare to move as the shards of glass pushed deeper and deeper into her back.

"I don't fear the creature," Yhana hissed, "because as it happens, it once saved my life. Perhaps it is here to attack you. Believe me, child, I have nothing to fear from that creature."

Yhana's words were bitter to Fiona. They stung more painfully than any shard of glass could. If the creature really was an ally of her mother's, if it had saved her life once, then it was surely an enemy of her own. It meant that everything she felt by window had been false, an illusion of her own creation. She had to fight viciously to stop herself from sobbing, such was the loss she felt. A single tear rolled down her face as it slipped her emotional guard. Yhana's satisfied expression cut Fiona to the heart.

Yhana stood up. "As punishment for your audacity, you will not see anyone today. You will remain in your room."

Fiona opened her mouth to protest that she would miss her training with Philip, but she stopped herself. She knew that Yhana knew, and that was why she had selected the punishment. By limiting her training in martial arts and magick, Yhana knew exactly how to hurt her daughter. She smiled smugly and strode from the room, slamming the door behind her.

Fiona pushed herself up from the floor. She grimaced as she pulled the glass shards from her back and side. Breathing deeply, she sought to control the awesome fury that threatened to erupt. She could always feel when the anger was about to strike: it was like standing at the edge of a bottomless precipice. One step and she would lose herself in the blackness below.

She sat on her bed and stared at her injured hand. The cuts were deep and they still bled, though they had slowed considerably. Later she would try to use her magical ability to heal the wounds, but now she knew that her mind was not focused enough. Time and time again Philip had stressed the need for focus and emotional control, but her personality and antagonistic environment were not suited to the task.

Breathing was one way of stepping back from the precipice, but even that was not working now. She stood on the brink, as if the urge toward the fury and her will to run away from it were equally balanced. An image began to form in her mind as she sat quietly gazing into herself. As it formed, the anger began to intensify, and somehow she knew that this was a focus for her anger.

With a shaking hand she quickly grabbed a pencil and paper and started to sketch with a furious hand. There were two men, similar looking with hawk-like faces. The first had deep black eyes and black hair; his gaze was intense, but also confused. Scars criss-crossed his face, and on his forehead was an ugly birth mark which looked like an old injury. The second man was smaller, dressed in strange armour with both a katana and wakizashi. His eyes were pale: too pale to produce the correct effect with a pencil.

When she finished sketching, Fiona was panting and sweating. The portraits evoked deep emotions. Somehow she knew that she had drawn real people. One of the men lived not far from where she was now. She could almost feel his essence out in the forest, an essence she loathed with every part of her being. Here was the man responsible for the terrible nightmares she suffered, a man responsible for the appalling scene she had witnessed at the standing stones.

Fiona was split between love and hatred. She hated the man with black eyes, and loved the other just as passionately. But the love, though incredibly strong, seemed very distant. The anger was close, and always present. She could not fight the rage he generated in her.

She plunged over the precipice, a giddying descent that blacked out her vision. Yet she could still see the man before her, and with terrible clarity she knew her purpose: she had to track him down and destroy him.

All birth ends in death.
All creation ends in dissolution.
All accumulation ends in dispersion.
All that appears real is transitory.
…Come,
Drink the elixir of fearlessness!

—Nagarjuna

Planet Tellus
Nipponese Empire
Kyoto Village

Shadrack followed the forest trail slowly, his eyes straining to pick out the signs. As he walked, his stomach churned nervously. He had no idea what he expected to find; he had only story books to guide him.

Although witchcraft, magick and second sight fascinated him, he had found little solid information on them; he was still unaware of the distinctions between the subjects. The small pieces he found often conflicted, and many questioned the existence of the subject they discussed. To meet a true psychic would be incredible; he had so much to ask, and yet didn't know if he would have the stomach to. He had no clues of what to say, or how to ask; nor did he know what would offend the woman.

Suddenly the trail terminated in a medium-sized clearing. There was a small house, not unlike those in the village, and nearby was a primitive well, now quite dilapidated. He paused, not sure whether he had the courage to continue; his own experiences had given him a natural fear of the supernatural. A shudder passed through him as dark memories stirred; he knew he could never tell anyone of them.

He walked up to the door, fresh snow crunching under his feet. He kept his eyes alert in case the woman had a pet familiar spying on him; he had read all about those, and although he wasn't sure he believed in them, one couldn't be too careful in such matters. He immediately noticed the horse-shoe nailed to the door.

A common symbol of superstition, he thought knowingly.

He inhaled deeply and then knocked loudly. The forest rustled about him; he was sure he was being watched. He waited for half a minute, and then knocked again. Just as he was considering leaving, he was startled by the door opening toward him, almost knocking him over.

A woman of thirty stood expectantly before him. He found himself surprised at how nondescript she was. Her face had a healthy glow, but could only be described as homely in a generous light. Her hair was thin and wiry, with an unpleasant colour. The only unusual feature was her eyes: they were a pleasing green, though the piercing gaze he expected was not present.

Despite her plain appearance, he still stumbled over his words as she looked at him questioningly. The result was a confused stammer. He looked down, embarrassed, and collected himself. She spoke before he could try again.

"You're Shadrack, the strange one."

It was a statement rather than a question.

"Yes, ma'am," he said, wondering how she had divined this fact.

"Come in, boy, I've been expecting you for a while."

His eyes widened, but he stepped through with only slight hesitation when she stood aside. She took his coat and gloves from him, and pushed him close to the small fire.

"Why have you been expecting me?" he finally dared to say.

"Because of what you are, of course."

"And what is that?"

"Isn't that what you've come here to find out?"

He nodded seriously. For the first time he noticed the crucifix hanging from her neck; on it was an impressive carving of the Christ. She saw his look of surprise.

"My talents are God-given, and I'll have no folk telling me they're from the Devil. So I tell no one. Understand? No one must know!"

He nodded. His awe of the woman was rapidly disappearing. She spoke sluggishly, and it seemed to him that she wasn't very intelligent. There were few Christians in Nippon, as many of the daimyo actively persecuted them. In fact religion of any type was quite uncommon: the harsh climate generally turned the minds of people to more practical matters. Buddhism and Shintoism were the most popular of those religions that had survived the Cataclysm.

"Why do you live here, miles from the village?" he asked, intrigued.

She shrugged nonchalantly.

"Don't think about it much. It's where my mother grew up, and her mother too. Wasn't safe for them at Kyoto, I was told. As for me, it's all I've ever known."

He nodded in understanding.

Looking around, Shadrack was disappointed to see that there was no crystal ball, cauldron, black cats or any other of the mysterious objects he had read about. There was simply a fireplace, a table with chairs and other basic necessities. He wondered if this woman could really help him. At least she seemed confident in herself.

"I have some coin to pay you for your trouble," he said, proudly pulling out a single *yuan*.

"I'll not take coin for doing God's work! Now, sit at the table with me and we'll start."

He sat opposite her and waited. She seemed to be studying the area around his body.

"Your aura is very strange, young man," she said. "I can't read much from it, but it's very powerful. There are forces at work far beyond my understanding.

"I can tell you this, though. You face greater danger than any other man has, and there are many lives which depend upon your actions."

Shadrack nervously licked his lips; he could feel the truth in her words.

"Can you tell me if I'll succeed?"

"It's not for me to know. You're a pawn between two great forces."

"Forces?"

"That which created the Balance, and those which seek to disrupt it. Your chances of success are slim due to your own failure, and it all depends upon you."

He frowned, not understanding; he was sure that the seer did not fully understand, either.

"Can you tell me what I am?"

The seer looked at him with a steady, sombre gaze. "Will you let me look into your soul?"

This idea filled him with a terrible irrational fear, yet he had to know.

"Yes," he said, the word catching in his throat.

"Then lean forward."

The seer gazed into his eyes. He felt her probe his mind. First she studied his physical body, then moved higher to his emotions. He began to feel lethargic. She gently pushed deeper, penetrating into his intellect and reading his thoughts.

"Your body is hard and strong, but your emotions are wild and confused," she said. "There is great frustration and intense pain, but you have incredible self-control. It helps you hide these emotions. Your thoughts are clear and strong, and then they become young and confused."

Shadrack was struggling to maintain consciousness. She pushed further to reach his higher mind.

"You were once a very great man." She sounded very impressed. "Your higher mind is completely beyond my understanding: it is very advanced. There is one single vibration passing through it: an obsession. It bears a name. The name is *Lena*."

Shadrack's mind spun at the mention of the name. Involuntarily, an image of the dark-haired woman from his dreams appeared before his mind's eye. He struggled to control his breathing and ecstatic excitement: he knew that it was *her* name. Again he saw a vision of the world with a rose-tinted sky and blue-green trees.

Blackness overtook him as the seer plunged further, but he managed to hold his eyes open. He could feel her pushing toward his very essence. Suddenly he was gripped by an ice-cold fear in his gut: something was catastrophically wrong. The fear was overpowering. He could feel something abhorrent lurking inside him, something he began to recognize. But it was too late: the seer had found it.

Her scream was horrible; there was no trace of humanity in it. Shadrack jerked himself awake, forcing down the thing that struggled for consciousness. He knew that if it was ever awakened, he would never control its force. The seer had collapsed onto the table, either dead or unconscious. Dark blood trickled ominously from the corner of her mouth.

He panicked. He didn't know if he was more concerned with the slumbering beast within, or the state of the seer. His mind was in a daze.

He had to leave the hut immediately. He stood up, sending the chair skidding across the floor. He grabbed his coat, but as he started to run, the seer turned toward him.

"You are one with the Dark Mistress!" she snarled. "You are evil itself! You shall bring doom upon us all!"

Shadrack bellowed and sprinted from the house in the grip of the most insane fear. No thoughts passed through his head: he was too far gone to think. But there was no hiding from the truth, and he knew he could never tell anyone of the dark secret he now knew.

<hr />

Kyoto village
Year 12 of 32nd Shogun
(1 year later)

Shadrack stood in *zenkutsu-dachi* stance, his body motionless. Tanaka walked slowly around his student, checking every detail of the position. The front leg was bent so that the knee was positioned directly above the toes; this prevented the front leg from being broken. The back leg was positioned about three feet behind, and just over a foot to the side. This leg was locked straight to imbue the stance with power. The stance was shoulder-width to endow balance, and to allow proper use of the hips in punching and blocking techniques.

A light, powdery snow fell upon the pair as they stood in the forest clearing. Shadrack was bare-footed, but would not submit to the biting chill of the cold. Samurai did not pay heed to such things, and he wanted to be samurai more than anything else.

Tanaka continued to circle Shadrack. He was more interested in the boy's mental attitude and *zanshin* rather than his physical posture. He knew that the latter would be almost perfect, as it always was. If there had been any noticeable imperfections, he knew that Shadrack would have already corrected them.

He ceased his circling when he stood in front of his student. He stared into his eyes with a boring gaze. He noticed that Shadrack was rapidly reaching his own height: he was already less than a foot shorter, at only twelve years of age. Shadrack's concentration did not waver. His eyes remained focused at an imaginary point behind his sensei's head, yet with full awareness of everything around them.

Tanaka's eyes narrowed, and without warning he threw a light-ning-fast *uraken-uchi* at his pupil's temple. Shadrack didn't blink as the technique was pulled with perfect control, barely contacting the side of his head. Tanaka grunted with satisfaction; they both knew the back-fist strike could have killed.

He moved away from his student and barked out a combination technique: "Step forward and attack *mae-geri, sanren-zuki*. Step back and defend *gedan-barai, gyaku-zuki*. Then attack *mawashi-geri, ushiro-geri, uraken-uchi* and *gyaku-zuki*."

He gave Shadrack barely a second to assimilate the combination before shouting: "Begin!"

Shadrack exploded into the first technique: a front kick. He land-ed forward to deliver three punches against his imaginary opponent, the first to the chin, the next two to the solar plexus. As soon as he had delivered the punches, he slid back to block a counter-attack with a lower body arm sweep; this was followed with a reverse punch.

He then sprang forward again, his arms held in a guard as he attacked with a roundhouse kick to the head, and then spun into a back kick. His imaginary opponent was finally defeated with a back-fist to the temple, and a reverse punch to the sternum.

He finished his final technique with a kiai, a cry of spirit, in which he focused every fibre of his mind and soul into the final punch. His fists sprang back into a guard as he completed the punch, and his body stood absolutely still as he awaited the next technique. He men-tally observed his stance, and made allowances for the tiny imper-fections he noticed: they would be eliminated on the next attempt.

Tanaka took the liberty of nodding his head with satisfaction; he did this only because his student was unable to see him. He was always very careful with his praise: too much, or too little could both be detrimental to a student. But he had to admit that Shadrack's techniques now possessed a breath-taking speed, and had enough power to maim a fully grown man. The achievement was incredible for a boy of his age.

"Turn!" Tanaka bellowed.

Shadrack turned and snapped out a powerful *gedan-barai*, return-ing his arms into a guard.

"And *yame*. Relax."

Shadrack brought his feet back into natural stance, simultane-ously crossing his arms across his body in a sweeping motion. He bowed, straightened his canvas *gi*, and awaited his next test. His feet burned agonizingly in the freezing snow, but he didn't show his discomfort. Instead he concentrated on pumping more blood into his chilled hands and feet. His body soon responded, and his appendages slowly began to warm. He had learned many years ago that his body always obeyed mental directions.

Tanaka watched as his student wiped the light sweat from his brow before it had a chance to freeze. Normally the samurai would never force a student to train in such weather, but Shadrack was an exception. In the seven years that Tanaka had fathered him, Shadrack had never once had even a minor illness. He had a subconscious strength that nothing seemed able to penetrate, not even pneumonia. Tanaka himself was not as resilient, and was dressed in bear-skin coat, trousers and boots.

"Good," the bushi said, "now it's time for some *makiwara* training."

An almost imperceptible sigh escaped from Shadrack's lips. Tanaka heard it, and smiled to himself. The sigh confirmed that his son wasn't completely inhuman. The makiwara was one of the most painful components of the training. Initially, Tanaka had given him a straw padded post to strike, as was traditional. This was to be struck with punches to strengthen the knuckles and wrists. But once this was mastered, Tanaka had furnished his student with an oaken makiwara board. This was far more painful on the knuckles, and almost impossible to leave an impression upon.

The only reservation Tanaka had was that Shadrack was so young. This could cause deformity in the hands and wrists, but he was sure that this would not occur with Shadrack.

Tanaka retrieved the board from the side of the clearing, and gripped it by the handles he had fashioned. The board was about a foot square, and extremely sturdy.

"Just fifty gyaku-zukis on each side. And make them good," he ordered.

"*Oss, sensei.*"

Shadrack slid into zenkutsu-dachi stance and focused his mind upon the target. He then began to pound it with his reverse fist, which was brought back to his hip after each technique. With each impact, the board gave a heavy, dull thud.

"Make sure you use your other arm properly! Remember, opposite and equal!"

"Oss, sensei!"

Shadrack started to draw back his left hand as his right was launched forward. This, coupled with the power of throwing his hips into each technique, instantly doubled the force of each punch. After only three such punches, his knuckles were raw and bloody. But he paid no heed to the fact: pain was a familiar state for him.

Tanaka watched, intrigued, as his son pounded the target. The steady rhythm slowly increased with time, and Tanaka realized that Shadrack was losing awareness of the world about him. He even seemed to lose consciousness of the makiwara board, as he mechanically bludgeoned it. Through his eyes, the samurai thought he could see flickers of another world, of another person. The irides subtly changed colour, deepening in intensity and strength.

And still he pounded the board, surpassing the fifty punches that his sensei had specified. Tanaka was becoming concerned. The person before him was not his son.

"Shadrack?"

Shadrack's eyes now showed anger, and the trance was deepening. His irides were blue-black, cold and sinister. He suddenly stopped his punching and stood absolutely still, his eyes focused internally.

"Shadrack!" Tanaka shouted.

Suddenly Shadrack reacted. His pupils shrank to pinpoints of fury, yet gained the depth of a fathomless ocean. Violet lightning crackled within them. And then for the first time, Tanaka witnessed Shadrack's true subconscious power.

For a brief moment, his eyes showed an intelligence so dark, evil and omnipotent, that Tanaka thought his heart would wither from the stare. Then Shadrack spoke, though his eyes were still focused inward.

"DETHENNNN!" the voice echoed vehemently through the forest trees, killing every sound and whisper of life as it passed.

Shadrack erupted into a last, final punch, an inhuman and insatiable rage coursing through his body. The fist connected with an ear-splitting kiai. The makiwara board instantly exploded with the impact, producing a tumultuous, resonant crack.

Tanaka fell backwards, his legs giving way. He stared in disbelief at the fragments of wood that lay scattered over the snow. When he looked up, Shadrack had his face hidden in his hands.

"I will destroy him…I *will* destroy him…" he repeated ceaselessly.

Tanaka pushed himself to his feet and moved to stand beside his son. He took his son's hands.

"Destroy who, Shadrack?"

Shadrack looked up, his eyes confused and bewildered. He started to sob, and Tanaka knew that his son had already forgotten.

"It's all right, son," he said, trying to reassure himself as much as Shadrack.

He put his arm around him and hugged him, fighting back tears of his own.

⤐⟳⤏

Enya
Yesod of Yetzirah
The Enchanted Forest

Jaad nursed his bruised ribs as the children skipped away, laughing and joking. They dropped their sticks and stones as they left, now that their brutal purpose had been served.

Jaad waited several minutes before moving. Sometimes they hid and attacked him when he thought it safe, and he hated that. He wouldn't let them catch him like that again: it hurt twice as much when they surprised him. After awhile he decided that it was safe to move. His mind focused on one place: his tree house. Only there would he be safe from the pain. It was the one thing of value his father had given him, and no one would dare to attack him there.

He pushed himself up, clutching his wounded side. He looked around quickly and drew in a sharp breath. He was being watched. A figure in black robes stood fifty yards away, silently watching him. Jaad was terrified. The man had a huge build and an outstanding aura. His face was hawk-like, with black terrifying eyes. He waved Jaad towards him.

Jaad hesitated, unsure whether to obey or run. The figure beckoned again and he suddenly felt a connection with the man. It was if they were brothers, or even closer. This man was no enemy of his. And that meant he was a friend. Jaad was thrilled; he had never had a friend before.

He started walking, excited. The figure started to move away, beckoning him to follow. He was moving toward the stream, away from the waterfall. Jaad pushed his way through the light undergrowth, feeling a growing sense of anticipation.

The man reached the stream, and now Jaad was running as fast as he could. His desire to speak to this man was more than he thought possible. He broke through the last trees to see the figure stepping into the stream. Jaad stopped, confused; the man started to sink as he walked, even though the stream was barely two feet deep. Jaad cried out in anguish and dived forward, reaching out with his hand. But the figure was disappearing, and with a final move of the hand, he beckoned farewell.

Jaad sobbed in desperation, feeling about under the water. The water was perfectly clear, and showed no sign of disturbance. He could see the bottom easily, and there was no sign of the black robed man. He pulled his arm back and cried into his hands, tears flowing freely. He didn't know what he had lost, but he grieved it anyway.

He stared bitterly into the stream. It was calm and slow moving this far from the waterfall, and he could make out his reflection clearly. Something about it forced him to stop and study it. The hawk-like face and the strange marks on his face were strongly reminiscent of the stranger he had seen. He stared harder; never before had he taken such notice of his reflection, and it was as if he saw himself for the first time. His eyes were black. Not the daunting, menacing black of the stranger, but a confused and cloudy black. The sharp intelligence was missing, but somehow, though in many ways opposite, the eyes were the same.

Something clicked inside his head and Jaad made the cognition: the stranger was somehow himself. He understood this intuitively, without the need for words. He was more than the others thought he was. He was more than simply the camp idiot. He felt a feeling of inner glee as he made the realization: a glow in knowing he was right beyond any doubt.

He stared at his image, and he was shocked as it gradually began to change. The water blackened like ink and another image appeared. It was a valley in the forest. Within it were three concentric rings of megaliths. He saw the vision as clearly as he had seen his face a moment ago. His mind suddenly felt clear, sharp. He knew where the valley was: it was not too far from the camp. He could run there in ten minutes. But he knew that if he tried to reach it, his father would beat him severely. It was not worth it.

He turned and looked in the direction of the camp. The calls of the children were getting closer: he knew they were returning to torment him. His bottom lip quivered in his indecision. Looking into the pool again, he saw the image had disappeared, but it was still clear in his head. And he could remember exactly where to find it. His mind was tightly focused, and the sensation was strange. Normally he remembered nothing.

The valley called to him like nothing he had ever experienced. It throbbed in his bones, a calling almost primeval. His life seemed transient compared with his desire to reach the valley with the standing stones. For what reason he didn't know, and didn't care. He only knew the lust to be there.

The children spotted him and he knew that it was now or never: he had to reach the valley. He turned and ran as fast as he could. From the commotion behind him, he knew the children were following. He sprinted faster. He was strong and could outrun most of them, but he had a great distance to go and didn't know if he could run all the way.

The chase continued for many minutes. Jaad began to weaken and tire, his lungs burning with the effort. Even as the tears of agony rolled down his face, he would not submit. The circle was in sight now, and he had only a few hundred yards to go. Hope surged within him, and he pushed harder. He knew that the other children were close behind, but they would not catch him now. Something called to him from within the circle, an object that belonged to him. He had lost it long ago.

Shooting a quick glance over his shoulder, he suddenly lost his footing. He sprawled onto the wet ground, damaging his shoulder as he fell.

Then the children were on top of him, kicking and punching him viciously. Then they started to drag him back to the camp. Jaad whimpered to himself; he was less than a few feet from his desire, and to leave it behind was agony.

Soon the valley faded from view, and with the scene faded his memory of the location.

*Rather light a candle than complain
about the darkness.*

—Chinese Proverb

Planet Tellus
Nipponese Empire
Kyoto Village
Year 13 of 32nd Shogun
(1 year later)

The light of the dawning sun dimly filtered through the thin smog to illuminate the forest clearing. Shadrack stood unmoving with his eyes closed, feeling the forest about him. He could hear the rustling of a dozen animals and sense a multitude of smells, all of them familiar. It even seemed he could feel the trees around him by the eddying of the gentle breeze. He felt completely harmonized with his environment.

He opened his eyes. He remained in zanshin, making full use of his senses. A sudden change in his hearing disturbed him as he prepared to start his *kata*. He heard an almost imperceptibly high-pitched sound in the air. He frowned in puzzlement.

Then they appeared: three figures in full-bodied scarlet robes, their faces concealed within huge hoods. He shuddered as he realized they were materializing from the air. An intense feeling of déjà vu struck him, and suddenly he knew he was in no danger.

He remained in natural stance, smoothing his breathing and checking his rising pulse. He relaxed his adrenal glands, which threatened to erupt at any moment. Composed again, he was acutely aware of his surroundings, yet detached from them.

He exploded into action to avoid an attack from the left. Slipping underneath the side kick, he swept the assailant. He stamped forcefully on his opponent's head before he could recover.

With battle cries, the other two assailants surged in from different directions. Without altering his tranquil expression, he moved to deal with the attacks with maximum efficiency. The first attacker was dropped by an ushiro-geri back kick, which collapsed several of his ribs. After a combination of tai-sabaki and counter attacks, he floored the last opponent with a *mawashi-empi* elbow strike.

He checked for further threats, and then shifted smoothly back into natural stance when he found none. The three robed figures rose up from the ground and formed an equilateral triangle around him. They bowed, scintillated, and diffused back into the air. Shadrack stood in sheer wonderment, feeling disbelief on one level, but familiarity on another. He had never made bodily contact with his partners: they had simulated the effect of his techniques on their bodies. They had been incorporeal, like ghosts.

As Shadrack pondered the event, he suddenly realized he had an audience. He banished the practice from his mind and cursed his zanshin for being so weak.

"Your kata is improving, son," Tanaka said, his voice matter-of-fact. "It almost seemed you were in a real battle."

"I practice often, father."

Tanaka nodded appreciatively as he stepped out from his cover. He knew that Shadrack spent almost every minute of his spare time honing his skills. He also worked long hours with Saito, and the blacksmith believed the boy would be an excellent weapon-smith in a few years. Already he was semi-skilled in sword forging. The work had increased his endurance and stamina, which were of prime importance to a warrior. A bonus was that he enjoyed the work, and had a good relationship with Saito and his wife, who had just given birth to twins. Shadrack counted them almost as sisters.

"Time for some sparring, I think," Tanaka said.

Shadrack grinned. Although he usually received quite a battering from these sessions, he had learned how to deal with the fear and cope with the pain. He was also beginning to push his teacher; Tanaka knew that if he didn't stay alert, he was in danger of receiving a blow from his student. Despite his age, there had been no warriors to defeat Tanaka at forty, and he knew that Shadrack's skills would extend well beyond his own with maturity.

When they commenced, Shadrack was even sharper than before. This pleased Tanaka for a secondary reason: it forced him to keep his own skills honed. The few samurai who survived to his age were nothing more than fat politicians under their yoroi.

Tanaka threw a hail of blows at his student, building up to the killing strike by manipulating Shadrack's responses and movements. Shadrack moved like a flash, parrying and following the predetermined route beautifully. The samurai lunged in with the finishing punch, and received a shock for his complacency.

Shifting his body weight to the side at the last moment, Shadrack executed a roundhouse kick to the samurai's solar plexus. The kick was just enough to knock him to the floor, completely breathless, without causing internal damage.

Tanaka gasped in shock as he found himself floored. He slowly rose, ignoring the sick feeling in his stomach. He knew that the best cure for being winded was to relax and slowly straighten up. He showed no embarrassment at being taught a lesson by a thirteen-year-old boy, for Shadrack was no average child, and the situation had been due for some time now.

He looked up to see the ecstatic expression on Shadrack's face, and noticed that he had dropped his guard. He moved forward, as if to vomit, and then burst into action halfway through the maneuver. The slap caught Shadrack dead on his feet; he crashed to the ground. He quickly rose, wiping his bloody nose. Tanaka watched him, rare humour glittering in his pale eyes.

"That's good, son, and I'm pleased for you. But never lose your concentration or show emotion before the battle's over. That slap would have been a death blow if this were for real."

Shadrack bowed his head meekly.

For the next hour, Tanaka assessed Shadrack's iai-jitsu skills, which were rapidly improving with time. His student was now able to draw and strike a sword in a fraction of a second, with complete concentration and awareness. His strikes were almost too quick to be seen.

Despite his son's ability and devotion to the martial arts, Tanaka would not allow him to practice with a katana. Even though he was now ronin, he would not break the Code and allow a non-samurai to use such a sacred weapon. Until he determined that his son was worthy to be samurai, Shadrack practiced with a *bokken*, a wooden training sword that was contoured and weighted like a katana.

After his iai-jitsu practice, Shadrack was then tutored on the forty-three major critical points of the human body. These could be struck to produce a variety of effects, from unconsciousness, through immobilization, to instantaneous death. When tested afterward, Tanaka found his student's knowledge to be perfect.

"Now, since you seem to be doing quite well in normal sparring, let's see what you're like without your eyes!" the samurai said.

He took a black blindfold from his pocket. Shadrack watched in disbelief. He had read that samurai were trained this way in the old times, but he didn't actually believe that a warrior could fight blind.

"Sensei, no man can fight without his eyes!"

Tanaka's eyes glittered with sardonic amusement.

"Aye, you may well be right, but you will be the first! You rely too much on your eyes. Now you must develop your other senses. But first I must introduce you to the weapons we will fight with."

He produced two collapsible bo-staffs from his pack. For the next twenty minutes, he covered the elementary aspects of staff fighting: defending, attacking, and how to deal with an opponent armed with a sword. The staff was particularly useful in the latter. Tanaka himself found it difficult to demonstrate, since his absent left hand made a bo almost impossible to wield properly.

Despite his tutor's disability, soon Shadrack was wielding the staff expertly, his combined knowledge of fighting and excellent dexterity standing him in good stead. He managed to push Tanaka back a few yards as he attacked with zeal. But the samurai did the unexpected. He suddenly closed the distance and used a kick to stun his opponent.

He said: "Always remember, cheating is against the Code, but it may save your life. Your opponents won't worry about doing the same to you!"

Tanaka told him to don the blindfold. The samurai attacked him gently, but even at a slow pace Shadrack was unable to defend himself. His head and body were struck time after time, and he became frustrated with himself.

"Being tense is no use!" Tanaka reprimanded. "You must harmonize and flow with the battle. Feel your opponent's movements and thoughts!"

Shadrack tried desperately for over an hour, but made no progress. He suspected he was trying too hard. But by now he was too tired and irritable to continue, and Tanaka could see it. He removed the blindfold, and gave his son an encouraging slap on the back.

"You did well today. In a couple of years, you'll be beating an old man easily no doubt!"

He noticed the downcast look on his son's face.

"Don't worry about the blind fighting. I have known no man who can do it. It was just an afterthought. Know your limitations, and be happy with the skills you have."

Shadrack shook his head. If blind fighting was beyond his limitations, he would simply have to extend them.

———◦◉◦———

Enya
Yesod of Yetzirah
The Enchanted Forest

Fiona sat on the floor, the curtains drawn and the room illuminated solely by candles. She stared into her scrying crystal, watching her enemy. This was how she spent most evenings, silently watching the boy from her drawing. He was about fourteen now, the same age as herself. She knew many things about him. Everything she did prepared her for the day when she would eventually go out and confront him.

She watched as the adolescents of the camp punched and kicked, and she felt no sympathy. She only wished that the kicks and punches had been her own, and that they would hurt him even more the next time. Her hatred for Jaad was destroying her, she knew. It was an obsession. Her only goal in life was to see him suffer. She frowned as the thought passed through her mind. Somehow she knew there was a much deeper purpose within her, connected with another man from her dreams. But the obsession blocked out all else: it was the only thing that mattered.

Fiona sighed and closed the scrying link. She had been studying Jaad for over two hours, and her eyes were strained. A pounding headache was already beginning to descend, the result of the extended concentration necessary to maintain the link. She closed her eyes and held the bridge of her nose with her thumb and finger, wishing the pain away.

Suddenly she felt a tug on her leg. She looked down and was amazed to see an earth elemental next to her leg.

The skin was mottled brown and orange, and it had the most mischievous grin she had ever seen. Its eyes were black and impish, like twin pieces of coal; two horns protruded from its head, one of them black and broken.

Fiona smiled, feeling her black emotions drain away. "You've got a cheek, little one."

The gnome winked, and Fiona felt a profound sense of déjà vu. It was as strong as the one she felt for the black cat, which she still glimpsed now and then from a distance.

She patted her lap and the gnome jumped up, as if he had always belonged there. She stroked his head and he half closed his eyes in satisfaction. An intense feeling of belonging with the gnome seized her. It was a feeling she rarely felt, but she had learned to take it very seriously when it appeared. The sensation was one she craved, because she knew she belonged to very few things in her present life. Philip was a good friend, in fact her only friend, but she didn't feel the deep connection with Philip that she felt with this gnome, or the black feline that sometimes watched her from a distance.

She always felt pulled in two directions in her life: on one side were her natural joy and love of nature, her deep attachment to these clues from her past, on the other her vehement hatred of Jaad, which occupied many of her waking hours. Every time she trained in the martial arts, it was Jaad that she fought and every time she learned a magical technique that could be used for destructive purposes, the idea of attacking Jaad with it entered her head. Yet these ideas seemed wrong, though she didn't understand why. The Yellow School was not at all moralistic: it simply believed in the principle of non-action and detachment. But Fiona's conscience was well developed and would not allow her to use such techniques, despite her desperate wish to do so.

As she stared at the elemental in her lap, intense love washed over her. She knew she cared a great deal for this elemental, and that they shared a past together. Though he had been with her less than five minutes, she already valued him far more than any other person in her life. She knew that this elemental was truly on her side: he would stand by her in all kinds of trouble.

Suddenly the door opened and Yhana stepped in. Fiona choked in horror, and the elemental jumped down from her lap, obviously fearful of her mother. He backed away from the door.

"You know it is against the spirit of School rules to fraternize with elementals," Yhana said, a maleficent grin on her face.

The elemental disappeared, obviously escaping to his own place. Yhana motioned with her hand and to the elemental's horror, he suddenly reappeared, bound by Yhana's magick.

"Leave him alone!" Fiona snarled. She stood up and hurled her own magick against Yhana.

Fiona was flung back as if by an electric shock, her power poorly matched against her mother's.

"You will have to do much better than that, daughter," Yhana said.

Fingering the gemstone which hung from her necklace, she drew the gnome towards her.

"I bind you by the power of the Great Mother Binah," she uttered. The Pearl gained a black aura and the gnome was dragged into it. Though he had never before made a sound, he let out a pitiful, heart-rending squeal as he was sucked in. Yhana traced her magical runes of imprisonment above the gem.

"You can have this back when you're strong enough to take it from me," she said.

Fiona watched helplessly, tears in her eyes. Once again, she had nothing left but her hatred.

The possession of any dangerous weapon imparts a feeling of self-respect and responsibility. But to a samurai, a katana represents his very soul. Let it never be drawn except in the most grave circumstance, and let it never be resheathed without drawing blood, or the blood must be the samurai's own.

—The Bushido, Way of the Warrior

Planet Tellus
Nipponese Empire
Kyoto Village
Year 14 of 32nd Shogun
(1 year later)

Shadrack plunged the wakizashi into the trough of cold water, pleased with the work he had finally completed. His upper body was naked, covered in a sheet of sweat from several hours of intense heat and laborious work. The well-defined muscles on his torso rippled when he moved, making the slightest movement appear violent and intimidating. Though only fourteen, his body was now a sizable and formidable weapon. He had the strength to best most adult men already.

Yoriie Saito watched with surreptitious pride as his apprentice doused the short-sword. It was the first flawless weapon that Shadrack had finished without aid. Saito had rejected half a dozen imperfect specimens over the last months, and Shadrack had become irritable and dejected: he had seen no fault in the work he had produced, but Saito had pushed him hard, forcing him to perform to his limits. He had caused the youngster to produce a sword as good as he was able to forge, just as his own father had forced him to do as a child. It was a matter of family pride, and Saito would not allow his apprentice to turn out imperfect work.

Shadrack stared at the blade in awe. The surface caught the light of the coals with a scarlet flash.

"Isn't it all worthwhile, when you finally produce the perfect weapon? You'll thank me for the way I pushed you now," Saito said.

Shadrack nodded appreciatively, his imagination captivated by the weapon he had created by his own hand.

"We may not have had the best tools and conditions over the last two centuries, but the Saito family has put its spirit into the swords it forged."

Shadrack understood. He had pounded the steel for a lifetime, folding the metal over three thousand times to imbue it with incredible strength. At each fold he had invoked the force of Tao, which Saito held as his concept of God. Shadrack was uncertain of the concept, but he had certainly hammered a part of his soul into the wakizashi.

He looked over at Mako and Ujiyasu, who were sleeping soundly on a bundle of blankets at the other side of the room. The twins were now three years old, and were a veritable handful. Shadrack counted them as little sisters, and was extremely protective over them. He didn't consider the blacksmith's hut to be a safe place for children, but Saito had shrugged off his objections, saying that all Saitos were blacksmiths at heart, regardless of age or gender. Shadrack knew that they were in no real danger: Saito had waited so long for children that he revered them. He made an excellent father.

Suddenly the door to the hut was thrown open, and Tanaka stepped in, a flurry of snow accompanying him. Behind him was Gorun Tzan, carrying a large bundle of items concealed within several sacks. Tanaka helped him through the door, and slammed it shut behind him.

Despite Tzan's intention to avoid all contact with Tanaka, the two samurai had been drawn together into a close friendship. Great mutual respect had cemented it.

"Father, look what I've made!" Shadrack said. "It's complete!"

Tanaka gave a level stare as he noticed the unusual excitement in his son's voice, but there was humour and pride in the bushi's eyes.

"He has worked very hard." Saito confirmed. "His apprenticeship as a 'smith is almost complete. There is little more that I can teach him."

"So, you are near manhood, it seems," Tanaka said, his voice stoic.

Shadrack felt his lungs tighten, making him feel breathless.

"May I keep the sword, father?" he asked, his voice full of longing.

"Only a samurai may bear such a weapon, you know that." Tanaka said. "And I'm sure that Gorun here has enough on his hands with one renegade samurai in his village."

Shadrack cast his gaze down. More than anything, he wanted to be a samurai like his father: a man of humility, honour, and valour.

Tanaka and Tzan exchanged surreptitious smiles as they saw his reaction.

"But," said Tanaka, "it is time to begin your education, for that day will surely arrive. Gorun has a suit of yoroi for you here, which he and Yoriie have fashioned for you. It will be large for you, but it has been designed for your adult life. They will instruct you in the purpose of each part, and how to fasten it to the main *do*."

Shadrack looked up, his vivid blue eyes bright with excitement. It was the first time his father had intimated he might become a samurai with maturity. In the past, he had avoided the subject altogether, and Shadrack knew better than to approach a taboo subject.

Tanaka smiled at his son's excitement.

"Now, help Saito to pack up here, and I'll take the twins back to Sashka. Then Gorun will begin your instruction."

⋘◈◈◈⋙

Over the next six months, Shadrack was taught all the skills and knowledge he would need to become a samurai. He was familiarized with each component of his yoroi armour: the do, tsurubashiri, kote, suneate, haidate, sode. The armour was intricately bound, with decoration, as well as combat effectiveness, being important. He was overjoyed to discover that the tsurubashiri, the armour's leather breastplate, was decorated in tiger lilies, just as Tanaka's was.

As part of his education, he was lectured on how to construct a suit of armour from raw materials, and familiarized with the other, rarer forms of armour: *do-maru* and *haramaki*. These were generally worn by the poorer and less noble samurai, in a society of warriors where appearance and family nobility were paramount.

He was also taught horse riding. Since she was the only available horse for use, Tzan allowed him to ride his own mare. Within two months Shadrack was riding like a hardened warrior, able to shoot targets from range with a long bow as his horse galloped. This was extremely difficult for any samurai, since excellent control of the mount was necessary in the forest environment as trees whipped by.

As his physical skills improved, Ekanar continued to lecture Shadrack in the geography of the Empire, and the present social conditions to be found. He was also given rudimentary knowledge of the recent history of the Empire, notably with respect to previous

Shoguns and important daimyo. It was explained that although Nippon was still called an Empire, the Emperor's line had been eradicated many generations ago by a brutal Shogun, and that the Shogun's word was absolute in all matters in the present time.

Tanaka also tutored his son in the Bushido Code, which had been revealed to him many years ago by a peasant. Shadrack absorbed each facet of the doctrine hungrily, having at last found a philosophy from which he could draw spiritual sustenance. Tanaka revealed the bushido followed by other samurai, and pointed each significant difference in attitude. Most notable of these were a warrior's attitude to humility, and his sacred respect for all life. Shadrack agreed with the philosophy in principle, but knew he would find the doctrine difficult to follow absolutely, like Tanaka did. His own desire for self-preservation, though not emanating from his conscious mind, was totally compelling.

Tanaka conceded this, but insisted that he could only use his skills to defend himself if his very life depended upon them. Shadrack gave his solemn oath.

"Though you'll never follow any daimyo, if you follow the Bushido as I have disclosed it to you, then you will be true samurai," Tanaka said.

"But when, father? Already I am fourteen years of age!"

Tanaka half-smiled. "You will be ready when you are ready."

"But are my skills not close to completion?"

Tanaka raised his eyebrows at the display of mild defiance.

"Yoriie, Ekanar and Gorun tell me that your studies are going very well."

"Then what is there left for me to learn?!"

"Perhaps patience is the last requirement."

Shadrack opened his mouth to retort, and then realized the futility of the action.

"Yes, father," he said meekly.

———⋙⊶⊷⊷⊶⊷⋘———

Enya
Yesod of Yetzirah
The Enchanted Forest

Mendaz sat watching the mid-Winter festivities, his heart black. His men danced around the roaring camp fire, their spirits high as they drank ale and feasted on venison. They had been storing provisions for weeks for this feast; few travellers came through the forest in Winter, and times were harsh. A celebration was necessary to see their spirits through to Spring.

Mendaz could remember two travellers who had arrived in the Winter many years ago. And those two had taken his wife from him. It was something he could never forget. He still saw her face every day, and it plagued him to be without her.

He ran his eyes across the camp. His men danced and shouted, breathed fire and fought with wooden swords. Mendaz had nothing but contempt and jealousy for them. Once he had respected his men, but it seemed he couldn't even respect himself these days. The only thing he loved was the bottle he now held to his chest, half empty of liquor. He knew that he was slowly killing himself as he consumed the poison day and night, but it was all he now had.

No. Not quite all, he thought cynically. His eyes picked out the form of Jaad sitting outside the camp, his knees pulled to his chin as he huddled against a tree. For a moment Mendaz realized how similar they both were: outsiders with no haven from the world. Both were isolated with no one to turn to. Mendaz felt a need to reach out to his son, to understand Jaad and accept him. He also felt a desperate need for his son to forgive him for all that he had done. But his cruelty was the only thing which kept him sane, kept him alive. If he didn't find a vent for his bitterness, he would surely go mad. Yet he needed to make a gesture of reconciliation with Jaad, no matter how insignificant.

He pushed himself up from the snow, swaggering as his coordination suffered from the drink. He staggered into the festivities, moving close to the fire. The dancing lost its pattern as he barged his way through; the men gradually stopped as he knocked them away. The joy seemed to die where he passed; the men dreaded his unpredictability.

"Jaad!" Mendaz shouted. "Jaad! Get over here!"

Jaad looked up, his bruised face dark even in the firelight. He hid his face, burying his head like as an ostrich might.

Mendaz waved a hand. "Bring him here."

Two of the men went over and grabbed the adolescent. They dragged him over to the camp. Though he didn't struggle directly, Jaad's body was as taut as steel. He dreaded it when his name came from his father's lips.

He was thrown on the ground in front of Mendaz. He didn't look up: that only invited a boot in the face.

"Get up," Mendaz said, his voice slurred.

Jaad curled into a ball. Mendaz stared in disbelief; he had called Jaad over for a reconciliation, and the child wouldn't even show his face.

"Jaad, get up!"

Jaad still didn't move. Mendaz turned to Fenrin, who stood beside him; he was armed with a wooden sword. "Fight him." He motioned with his hand, and the camp formed a ring around Jaad and the man.

Ripples of excitement passed through the men. None of them liked Jaad, and they would all enjoy seeing him beaten.

"Throw him a sword," Mendaz ordered; his anger insisted that Jaad be punished.

A wooden sword was thrown to the adolescent. He raised his head to stare at it, but didn't move. Fenrin looked to Mendaz for permission; Mendaz nodded.

Fenrin charged forward, striking Jaad hard on the back with the sword. Jaad winced and rolled away. As the man advanced on him again he stood up, looking for escape. The crowd pressed in tight around the pair, and Jaad was pushed back in when he tried to force his way through. The wooden sword descended again, cracking in half as it impacted Jaad's head. Jaad fell to the floor. He stared at his father, something extremely unusual in itself: he always avoided eye contact. But it was the expression that shocked Mendaz; instead of the usual cowering look it was one of anger and hatred.

"Stop," Mendaz said. For some reason, he actually felt threatened by Jaad's stare. "Take this." He threw his own sword to the man, a blade of fine steel. "Let him defend himself properly."

Another steel sword was thrown to land on the ground by Jaad, but he didn't move to pick it up. He was still staring at Mendaz.

Fenrin leapt forward to attack. His slice was powerful enough to cleave Jaad's head in two, but the youngster moved away just in time. His left ear was clipped, causing a nasty cut. Jaad pushed Fenrin away, almost smashing him through the crowd due to his size and strength.

Fenrin picked himself up, obviously angered at his loss of face. The other men were jeering at him, throwing bits of bone and baked potato.

"You made a big mistake there, sonny," he said.

Jaad watched him, his posture somehow perturbing. The shoulders were more erect, the head held higher than usual. It was as if the pain and combat had awakened him for the first time. He reached down and picked up the sword which lay beside him on the ground. The man licked his lips nervously. Jaad's black eyes almost seemed demonic as the firelight glittered off them. The crowd quieted, sensing the new aura that flowed from Jaad.

Fenrin charged Jaad, stabbing with the sword to run him through. Jaad moved with surprising speed, slipping to the side of the blade. He caught the man's wrist in an iron grip and stared into his eyes. The man stared back in horror, astounded by the change that had overcome the adolescent. Jaad's eyes were much sharper, the cloudy confusion temporarily banished. He studied the man like a spider studying an insect. Then he plunged the sword through the man's stomach, piercing his body. Fenrin cried out and fell to the ground, clutching his abdomen.

The crowd screamed in rage. Three men jumped onto Jaad, intent to make him pay for the murder. There was a blinding flash of light and the men were blasted away to lie blackened and smoking. Jaad collapsed to the ground to cry, his confusion now returned. The thing he almost become had slipped away, and once again he was plain old Jaad.

The crowd rushed to their revenge, but the voice of Mendaz cut through the noise.

"Stop! There'll be no more blood shed this day!"

"But Mendaz, he has killed four men!" said the nearest man.

Mendaz lashed out, punching him to the ground. "They deserved it," he said. "We all deserved it. Take him to the tree house. He can come back when he's ready."

26

*No one knows whether death may not
turn out to be the greatest of blessings
for a human being; and yet people fear
it as if they know for certain that it is
the greatest of evils.*

—Socrates

Planet Tellus
Nipponese Empire
Kyoto Village
Year 15 of 32nd Shogun
(1 year later)

Shadrack lay in the stuffy darkness of his room, his thoughts eddying uncontrollably. His consciousness flickered in and out of existence, hovering at the border between sleep and wakefulness. Strange images and ideas flowed through his mind, and he was powerless to stop them. They rose up unbidden, taunting him for before being replaced by visions totally unconnected and even more bizarre.

He tried repeatedly to clear his mind, longing for sleep, yet it was always a waking dream that he fell into. There was something unnatural about the night's atmosphere. He suspected the Dark Moon might be responsible.

He had long ago realized the cyclic nature of his life. It was intimately connected with the moon. He loathed the moon when dark, and disliked it when waning: there was something sinister about both.

Yet in daylight, such things seemed insignificant. He lived two separate lives: one through the day and one at night. In the former, he felt balanced and in control, as a warrior should be. In the latter he was like a small child hiding his face from terrors. The two lives were completely isolated: there seemed to be no middle-ground. But he knew deep down that the feeling of daytime control was illusory.

His body felt heavy, his limbs leaden. Tingles of electrical energy surged through him. His eyelids felt as though they had been fused shut, and suddenly he realized he was unable to open his eyes. He panicked, struggling against the paralysis that gripped him. But

216

already it was too late: the weight of his body was increasing, and the battle was becoming futile. He could smell fear in his sweat, and his mouth was dry.

A tickling sensation passed over his face, head and throat. It was like a gentle caress. He now had no control over his body. Even his breathing and hammering pulse were beyond his command. He could only wait for the event to unravel. As usually occurred with the setting of the sun, the situation was totally beyond his realm of influence.

The wait was short. A loud click sounded within his head. His awareness died and then flickered back to life. A great weight pushed down on his feet: it seemed as though someone, or something, was sitting on him. The weight started to move up his body. He realized that its shape was humanoid: he could feel it crawling on its hands and knees.

He could not see the creature, but its essence was extremely strong. He was certain that it wasn't human; its essence personified every definition of "evil." It was powerfully feminine, stronger and more attractive than any woman. Its breath rasped in its lungs with barely restrained passion; he could feel the inviting warmth from its body.

He could not control his body's instinctive reaction. His erection screamed for relief as potent hormones were fed into his system. He knew that he had to resist at all cost. He could not allow himself to be tainted by this beast, but it was so easy to give in.

The succubus teased him, massaging around his groin and licking erogenous zones he had never been aware of. Her mouth was warm, wet, and inviting. Fire coursed through his veins and his pulse pounded. He somehow knew she could not take what she desired without permission. He also knew that he could not defile himself in this way.

She straddled him over the hips, his penis now almost touching the site of relief. She waited only for his consent, and he knew he was too weak to deny it. He lusted for her more than anything. His craving was an agonizing torture. His animal instincts screamed for relief.

He postponed the inevitable for a few seconds more, clinging on by exhausting the last scraps of willpower. Then suddenly an image arose in his mind's eye: the dark-haired woman of his dreams, who was a stranger and yet more familiar than his own father. He recalled her name: Lena.

The sadness and anguish in her eyes were more than he could bare. It fuelled his will a hundred-fold: he would accomplish anything to avoid inflicting pain upon this woman.

He strained against the paralysis with every fibre of his being. He tried to roll off his back. Sweat poured from his pores and his breathing became frantic. Still he could not break the vice-like grip he was held in. But he would not submit.

Suddenly the air was pierced with his scream of effort. There was a deafening click and he spun off the bed. He landed heavily on the wooden floor, bruising his side and knocking the wind from his lungs.

He was left alone in the darkness with his pain, fear, and dying lust.

Tanaka brooded thoughtfully as he flicked slowly through the Bushido, his mind chasing the meanings of the elusive parables. The study was disturbed only by a slight murmuring as Ekanar quietly described the principles of elementary geometry to Shadrack.

In the centre of the floor, Saito's twin daughters, Mako and Ujiyasu, had finally collapsed after an hour of intense play. They lay together, their limbs entwined.

Outside, the wind had ceased its howling and now whistled gently.

"Ekanar, why is there always snow on the ground?" Shadrack asked.

The sage hesitated at the abruptness of the question; he had been in full verbal flow, describing the usefulness of Pythagoras' theorem.

"What do you mean, why is there always snow on the ground?"

"Well, there isn't in other places."

"How do you know that? You haven't been anywhere else!"

"I just know! I've seen different places in dreams."

Ekanar rolled his eyes to the ceiling: it was the type of comment he generally expected from the young man.

"Well, very few people are aware of the reason, but fortunately I can help you out on this one.

"It is said that many centuries ago, a huge rock hit the world, and nearly tore it into pieces. Vast amounts of dust and water were thrown into the air, where they blocked out the rays of the sun. This triggered what used to be called an Ice Age, but for us is our normal climate."

"And the sun still can't shine through the air?"

"No. Men used to have great power on this planet. They had the ability to build flying vehicles and talk to each other around the world in an instant, but all these things used up fuels."

"Like the wood we use for fire?"

"I think so," the sage mused. "Anyway, most of the fuels were used up before the rock hit the world, and humans were beginning to live more in harmony with nature again. When the Cataclysm occurred, many, many people were killed, and still more died from the volcanoes and poisonous gases which were releas…"

"What's a cataclysm?" Shadrack interrupted.

"Ah," Ekanar said, pleased to have mentioned a word that his student wasn't acquainted with, "that's like a catastrophe, only probably worse. But the Cataclysm was the time when the huge rock hit the planet."

"And what's a volcano?"

"It's a…it's a…well I'm not sure really," Ekanar said, then added more confidently, "but most of the people died, anyway. The ones that survived reverted to ancient ways of living, which differed from place to place. We live on the island of Hokkaido, which was once a part of a country called Japan. The country had a very strong and distinct history, and this was used to motivate pride in the people."

"So the people now follow the ancient way?"

"Not exactly. The traditions were only half-remembered, and the ice and cold caused major changes. In ancient times, the land was green and fertile, with a hot shining sun, but the Empire is one of the most inhospitable areas on the planet now. Its resources can supply only a tiny population, therefore there are no true cities as there were even in ancient times. Except for maybe Honshu, which is named after the old Japanese mainland."

"But—"

The serene atmosphere was suddenly broken as sounds of anger and surprise erupted from outside the house. The village people were rapidly moving toward the centre of the village, apparently under protest. Ekanar and Tanaka exchanged alarmed glances: they knew there was only one possible reason for the exodus.

Tanaka was already halfway up the ladders to the trap-door when the door burst open. He realized with relief that it was Sashka, the wife of Yoriie Saito.

"Samurai!" she hissed under her breath.

She dashed inside and grabbed her two daughters, who immediately began to cry. Tanaka reached the safety of the attic and waited as Shadrack followed; the teenager was undecided between excitement, fear or confusion. Tanaka's face quickly told him: they were in serious danger. He climbed the ladder as fast as he could, then helped his father to pull it up into the attic.

Tanaka pulled the insulation away from the wall to gain a view of the outside. He could see the villagers being rounded up into the town centre. There were three samurai. One was assembling the people, while another was systematically checking the houses. The last one was heading directly for Ekanar's house.

With a start, Tanaka the recognized the man. The leader of the samurai was Hideyori Yoshitaka, a bushi who had once been under his command. Yoshitaka was now the Shogun's *kebiishi*: he was charged with locating and punishing fugitives. He was a strong-willed and extremely skilled warrior. He still wore the patch over his left eye which Tanaka had gouged during his escape from the Shogun's palace many years ago.

As he walked, Yoshitaka threw aside the peasants who strayed into his path. He was completely focused upon Ekanar's house, as if he knew his quarry hid there. Tanaka hoped it was simply the appearance of the construction that gave him that impression. With a shout, Yoshitaka called over another bushi. The pair advanced upon the building and Tanaka lost sight of them.

The door was banged loudly. Although Ekanar moved quickly to open it, it was first kicked viciously from its hinges. Yoshitaka strode in, his alert and penetrating gaze scanning the room. He signalled his henchman to search the building.

Yoshitaka advanced upon Ekanar, his eye boring deeply into the sage's and his hand on his sword hilt.

"Do you hide a ronin, old man?"

The voice was broken and hoarse from an old throat wound. The word "ronin" was pronounced with hatred and repugnance.

"I am a sage," Ekanar said with a hint of arrogance. "I do not concern myself with warriors."

The samurai looked surprised and then his eye narrowed in annoyance. He always expected arrogance from his peers, but this was highly unusual. But he had never before met a sage, and was unsure of the old man's station; as ever, protocol was everything.

A testing stare passed between the two men. The samurai flexed his grip on his sword, whilst Ekanar remained absolutely still. The henchman returned and signalled his failure. Yoshitaka nodded and gave a bow to Ekanar as an equal, since he was unsure of his position. The Shogun would not tolerate breaches of conduct.

"If you would accompany me outside, learned sir?"

Ekanar returned his bow, pulled a cloak around himself and stepped outside. Yoshitaka signalled his men to continue their search as he escorted Ekanar to the village centre. The other villagers were now assembled.

Ekanar exchanged an apprehensive glance with Saito as they awaited the return of the other samurai. Yoshitaka paced along the line of peasants, counting a hundred and twenty in all. Saito immediately knew that someone was missing. Ekanar resisted the urge to glance over to his home. He knew that Tanaka would be able to see events unfolding from there.

The two samurai reappeared. Between them they marched the missing village member: Gorun Tzan. He was armourless, and looked quite bewildered, but he bore his katana and wakizashi. He had obviously been recently awakened.

Yoshitaka strode over to him and started to converse. Tzan was shaking his head tiredly, apparently denying something. Yoshitaka's voice rose in volume, though the words were still indistinct. He obviously did not believe the testimony, and his emotional control was slipping. He had been quite sure that he would find Tanaka here.

He slapped Tzan across the face with a stinging backhand blow. The samurai's head was whipped to the side, but he did not step back. He calmly wiped the trickle of blood from his mouth and stared his superior officer in the eye, his eyes furious.

Yoshitaka grunted in annoyance and it seemed as if both samurai were ready to draw their swords. The tension lasted a few seconds.

"We will settle this another time!" Yoshitaka whispered venomously.

He then spun around to face the line of peasants. He had to be sure that the renegade was not in the village.

"Who is the village headman?" he demanded gruffly.

There was a brief delay before Saito stepped forward, shaking off Sashka's clinging hold.

"I am."

The blacksmith showed no fear.

Yoshitaka walked up to him, grabbing him roughly by the hair and pulling his head back. From the gasps of horror from the villagers, he could tell that the headman was liked and respected. He slid his hand to his katana hilt.

"Give the ronin to me, or this man dies!"

Sashka jumped forward from the crowd to grab the samurai's sword-arm. With a shout of rage, Yoshitaka slapped her back into the cowering crowd. She was caught by Ekanar, her body limp and unconscious. Ujiyasu and Mako began to cry.

Tanaka closed his eyes in horror as he watched from the safety of Ekanar's house: he knew that the samurai was not bluffing. But for Shadrack's sake he could not give himself up: the boy had to survive at all costs.

Outside, Yoshitaka half-drew the blade of his katana.

"I will ask once more. Where is the ronin?!"

A few sobs were heard from women in the crowd of villagers, but no one moved or spoke.

Tanaka looked down at his adolescent son, tears in his eyes: again a life had been taken due to his actions.

"After the sacrifice this day, you had better be true to me. If you fail me, that man's life is to be wasted!"

Shadrack looked up at his father without comprehension. He didn't see the blood spray across the snow as the blacksmith was decapitated, but the scream of his daughters was something that he would never forget.

*The mark of your ignorance is the depth
of your belief in injustice and tragedy.
What the caterpillar calls the end of the
world, the master calls a butterfly.*

— Doctrine of the White School[1]

*The path of excess leads to the tower of
wisdom.*

— William Blake

27

Planet Tellus
Nipponese Empire
Kyoto Village
Year 17 of 32nd Shogun
(2 years later)

Tanaka watched fondly as Shadrack studied the swirling currents of the stream. The railing of the bridge creaked in protest as the ronin leant against it. Flashes of silver and orange darted below the surface. In a few weeks, the ices would return, freezing the stream solid.

"How's the work going?" Tanaka asked.

He had been away from the village for six months. Winter had trapped him at Sanzin Village, where he had lain low to avoid the samurai stationed there.

"The work's fine," Shadrack said. "Be better if Yoriie was with us, though."

Tanaka nodded; he knew that his son had taken the blacksmith's death very hard.

He now acted as an older brother to the deceased man's twin girls. As Saito's apprentice, he had assumed his work burden and he helped to comfort Sashka when necessary.

It was slowly dawning on Tanaka that his son was now a man. Shadrack's voice was lower than he remembered it, and his physique even more intimidating. He wondered about Shadrack's skill in the art; he knew that there was little he could teach his student now.

He clapped Shadrack on the shoulder. "How about some training then, son?"

---

1 Quoted from Richard Bach.

223

Shadrack's lips twisted into a half-smile. "I'm not sure I should beat up an old man."

The samurai threw a playful slap, which his son easily dodged. It was rare that he received even a modicum of humour from his son.

"You begin to sound like Ekanar," he grumbled.

When they reached the clearing, Tanaka was not surprised to see that it was bare; continuous abuse from Shadrack's training had seen to that.

"Sparring?" Tanaka asked.

Shadrack threw a bo-staff to him and started to tie on a blindfold. Tanaka became serious.

"Now, son. Don't start getting arrogant. I told you a long time ago to learn your limitations. Everyone has them."

Shadrack spun his own staff into a ready posture. "Try me."

Tanaka sighed: he was not pleased. He had thought that his son's training was complete, and now the most critical ingredient was gone: mental attitude. The young upstart would have to be knocked down a peg or two, and then the training would start again. Tanaka wouldn't go lightly this time: the boy was in for the soundest beating of his life.

Tanaka span his staff one-handed and started to circle his opponent. He observed how Shadrack easily followed his movements. The boy's stance was flawless, and his grip upon the staff was perfect. As Tanaka wove back and forth, Shadrack altered his direction and guard, neutralizing any tactical advantage his teacher sought to obtain.

Tanaka suddenly charged like a war-horse. The bo descended to strike forcefully against his opponent's head. But Shadrack was not there. He utilized tai-sabaki to slip fluidly to the side. Already, he stood poised for the next attack.

With a loud kiai, Tanaka lunged at him. This time he connected, but not as he had expected. With a deft sweep of his staff, Shadrack disarmed his assailant. He tapped him lightly on the back of the head as Tanaka's momentum carried him by. The ronin froze. The blow could have killed him if it had been uncontrolled.

He retrieved his staff, now studying his opponent in a different light. For the first time he considered that Shadrack might actually be able to do what he claimed. He circled the blind adolescent, making no noise whatsoever.

Shadrack turned with him. The young warrior was in touch with everything about him: totally relaxed and composed. His movements were smooth and precise: it seemed nothing could disturb him.

Tanaka attacked suddenly. It was brutal and vicious; he used all of his strength to rain down blow after blow. Shadrack retreated, parrying each blow as if it was a set pattern, whilst the samurai was attempting to be random, continually changing his tactics.

With a final effort, Tanaka thrust his staff as a distraction. He closed distance, and kicked to the groin. With lightning speed, Shadrack crashed the bo into his shin. He swept the feet from under the samurai, and brought his foot down to end a stamp half an inch above his Adam's apple.

Shadrack then pulled back, twirling the bo back into a ready position. He took off the blindfold, and pulled his incredulous father from the ground. The samurai was breathless and speechless. Shadrack gave a small smile, accepting his victory lightly and modestly.

Tanaka was then sure that his son had become a man, and an extremely dangerous one at that.

"Let me tell you, son," he said. "As long as you have belief in yourself, you need never to fear any man on earth."

Shadrack nodded. "I know: I fear no man. But I don't think it's any man that I will ultimately have to face."

Dark, cold feelings washed over him as he thought of the fiend inside. He knew that it was the only being he truly had to fear.

Tanaka was about to question him until he looked into his eyes. In them was the barest hint of ancient wisdom; he hadn't seen this since the stone circle twelve years ago. His blood chilled as he contemplated his son's words; he remembered the day, long ago, when he had seen the power of the beast within him.

He pulled his katana from his belt and thrust it into his son's hands. "You're a samurai now. And though you'll never serve a daimyo, you'll need this."

Shadrack took the sword and drew it, admiring the perfect finish. He was an accomplished weapon-smith himself, and he knew the weapon's quality. He slashed his thumb on the edge, obeying the unwritten Code: once drawn the weapon must draw blood. For many years he had been training with replicas; he could hardly believe that he now held a true katana, a weapon of honour. His eyes sparkled with excitement.

"But I cannot take this. It is your samurai soul."

Tanaka eyes were sad. "My days of battle are over, but yours are about to begin. With this, you'll have me fighting by your side, even after I've gone. I lost my soul on a cold, dark night many years ago, just before I found you. My purpose is now complete."

Shadrack shuddered; somehow he knew that he would be separated from his father. Though he felt no fear, he felt a great deal of remorse: he loved his father very much. He threw his arms around him and hugged him. He knew he would never do it again. Tanaka froze momentarily, and then squeezed his son tightly.

⟶◦◦◦◦⟵

Fifteen minutes later, the pair reached Ekanar's house. Tanaka opened the door and they stepped into the inviting warmth. It took a second for them to realize the danger they were in.

Yoshitaka stood in the study, a junior samurai by his side. The creak of leather armour revealed the presence of the third man behind them. Before they could react, they were ushered into the study.

Tanaka noticed the bound and unconscious form of Ekanar in the corner. Beside him lay the dead body of Gorun Tzan, a deep sword-slash conspicuous across his unarmoured torso.

Yoshitaka's eyes were triumphant: after twelve years he had finally cornered his quarry. The kebiishi and ronin held each other's gaze. Shadrack stared sickly at the body of Tzan.

"I am under orders to kill you, Ieyasu Tanaka," Yoshitaka said. "Will you consent honourably this time?"

His voice was scornful and mocking. He obviously regarded his former captain as wretched and below notice.

Tanaka scanned the room. The three samurai had them surrounded, blocking off all escape routes. Above them, the trap-door was open: the concealed attic entrance had been discovered.

Tanaka knew that the situation was hopeless. There was no way of incapacitating three men armed with katanas, and he refused to kill. Despite his pacifist vow, he was also unarmed: Shadrack now possessed his katana, and his wakizashi was in the attic. He looked his enemy calmly in the eye.

"I will consent if you will grant this boy his life."

Yoshitaka looked incredulous, and then laughed; it was deep

and humourless.

"This boy is armed with a katana. You know the penalty for the offense. Imitating a samurai is punishable by instant death."

Tanaka's face darkened and Yoshitaka laughed again.

"I shall be generous, however. I will allow him to plead to the Shogun for his life."

Tanaka knew that he had no real alternative.

"Agreed," he said, his head hung in resignation.

Yoshitaka signalled to one of his men to grab and disarm Shadrack. Shadrack caught Tanaka's warning gaze and didn't attempt to resist. Gripped by fear, adrenaline surged through his body. He struggled to control his breathing as his pulse accelerated.

Tanaka knelt and looked at his son. "Do not fail me. You cannot interfere with this."

He turned to Yoshitaka. "Allow me the use of my wakizashi. I would die honourably."

Yoshitaka grunted. "Your honour is irretrievable, old man. You should have committed hari-kari twelve years ago. It is too late now. You will die the death of all cowards!"

Tanaka closed his eyes in defeat. The last vestige of honour had been torn away from him. But he would not resist. Only Shadrack was important now.

Shadrack stared without comprehension as his father knelt and bowed his head, awaiting the inevitable. The samurai standing above him had his back to Shadrack; he withdrew his katana and moved into a position to strike from. He looked over to Yoshitaka. The *kebiishi* nodded.

Shadrack simply reacted. His mind lagged behind as instincts took over. He grabbed the hand that held his shoulder. Twisting it, he applied a wrist lock and then slid it into an arm lock. He blasted the flat of his palm into the back of the samurai's head, dislocating his skull from his spinal column and killing him instantly. As the body fell, he drew its katana.

The other two samurai started to react, but Shadrack was far too quick. He skipped forward to the bushi standing above his father. He snapped a powerful front kick into his groin from behind. There was a crunch as the kick penetrated to shatter the man's coccyx and snap his pelvis. The samurai screamed and crumpled into unconsciousness.

Shadrack heard the scrape of leather on steel from behind. He immediately knew that Yoshitaka was drawing his sword. He span around in a flashing arc of steel and cleaved the samurai from his head to his solar plexus. Yoshitaka's body fell, the katana embedded within it.

Time reverted to normal, and Shadrack stepped back with abhorrence and revulsion as he realized what he had done. Blood flowed in merciless quantities from Yoshitaka's corpse. Shadrack turned to vomit over the floor. Tears flowed from his eyes and he began to sob. He had only meant to stop the men, not kill them. His training had escalated his wishes, and he had been unable to stop it.

He noticed that Tanaka was standing beside him. Composing himself, he rose and wiped the tears from his bloated face. The old samurai held his katana before him, expecting Shadrack to take it. Shadrack frowned and took the weapon, not understanding.

"I told you once never to fail me, but you have done that today in killing three men. I give you this sword once again. It will serve you well. My work on you is complete, and I have failed. I will return in one hour and I expect you to have left the village by then. You may take your armour and wakizashi if you want. I do not wish to see you again."

Shadrack stared at his father in disbelief. A single tear formed in Tanaka's eye before he turned abruptly and walked from the house, his head hung low with shame. Shadrack fell to his knees in emotional agony, his vision blurred by his flood of tears.

⋙●●●⋘

Enya
Yesod of Yetzirah
The Enchanted Forest

Fiona circled Philip, her staff held ready. She watched his eyes and footwork; it was in these that she would first read his attack. He moved closer, seeking to move into range with the broad sword. But Fiona knew the distance at which to keep him; she struck out with the staff, forcing him to move back and give her distance.

Suddenly Philip lunged forward and attacked. Fiona parried, sweeping the staff to disarm him and then knocking his legs from under him. Philip landed harder than she had anticipated, and she quickly knelt beside him.

"Are you all right?" she asked.

"My age seems to be getting the better of me," he said. "I've earned these grey hairs, you know."

Fiona smiled and held out a hand to help him up.

"No, let's sit for a while. You are too handy with the staff," he said. Fiona would have laughed, but she knew that anything Philip said was deadly serious; often he seemed to make humourous comments, but they were usually just statements of fact.

"You are becoming a formidable opponent," he said, rubbing his bruised shoulder. "Both in martial arts and with magick. You are especially talented in the later, I think."

Fiona smiled. "I like to think it is because I work hard."

"Partly," he agreed, "but you have an ability with magick that few people have. You have matured and now you are a person to be reckoned with." He studied her face and the long black hair which framed it. "You've also grown into a very beautiful woman."

Fiona was embarrassed. "Philip..."

"I was not attempting to flatter you. I was merely making an observation." He ran his finger along the blade of the broad sword, which had been blunted for use in mock combat.

"Philip, why do we defend against swords in the Yellow but never learn to fight with them?" Fiona asked. "It seems a one-sided strategy."

Philip raised an eyebrow and offered the sword to her. "Would you like to learn?"

She shuddered and moved back. "No, I don't like them."

"Ah, that's why you hit me so hard," he said, his face serious. "I shall remember to attack you with other weapons in future. We don't attack with swords because it is impossible to be in control with a sword. It is a weapon used purely to kill. With a staff or flail, an opponent can be stunned, knocked unconscious. A sword can only slash or thrust, designed to kill the enemy. Though it may be used to wound the arms or legs, this is not guaranteed to stop and opponent, and thus a sword cannot be used as a defensive weapon, for by nature it kills."

"Why is that concerned with the philosophy of the Yellow School?"

"Because it our way not to interfere, to have as little effect on other living beings as we can. It is not a moralistic point: to kill disturbs the intimate fabric of the Universe. Every death is painful to the sentient Universe."

Fiona's eyes narrowed. "If I had my way, there are two lives I would take."

Philip looked at her, a gaze that always seemed to studying. "You have been deeply scarred by a past you do not yet remember, Fiona. If you are not careful, the hatred you carry within will destroy you. The person you once were will not allow you take a life except in defense of your own. If you are contemplating murder, it will be suicide for your own soul also."

"You know a great deal about my past," Fiona said, her tone icy.

"There are ways and means of discovering information. I have known a great deal about you since before your birth but I cannot reveal much to you: you must learn by yourself, or it is not learning at all. I know your hatred of Jaad, and it is not without reason. But your destiny lies elsewhere. Your path should be one of deliverance, not vengeance. For there is another who needs your help: he must be your first concern. Only with your help will he succeed."

"The other man of my dreams," Fiona said quietly. "Yes. I feel deeply for him, but the hatred of the other man is stronger. And what of my mother? Surely I have reason to loathe the very air she breathes?"

"Just as she believes she has reason to hate you. Your mother has not had an easy life. Her years in the child brothels of Gorom have scarred her, much as you have been scarred. We should not judge her too hastily."

"She takes everything from me! She still has my elemental bound within a gemstone!"

"Your elemental?"

"We belong together," Fiona said firmly. "At least that much I know."

Philip shrugged. "You could always take him back. You are eighteen, and your own person now. You are not dependent upon anyone here."

"You're encouraging me to snatch back the gem? Isn't that against your principle of non-action? You're influencing me as you sit there, even now."

Philip looked uncomfortable, something Fiona rarely saw.

"It is difficult," he said. "There are often conflicts between duty and principles, and there is never a perfect solution. We must all do what we must. Remember that we cannot raise a finger without shaking the very stars themselves."

He stood up. "You must do what you feel is right." He gave a curt bow before walking from the room.

Fiona watched him leave, mulling over what he had said. She desperately wanted to release the elemental from Yhana's gemstone: to imprison him in such a way was barbaric. The gnome was one of the few clues to Fiona's past, and she could not let him suffer. She felt a certain loyalty to the gnome, and also felt ashamed: he had been imprisoned for two years now because she had been unable to raise a finger against her mother.

But that changes tonight, she thought. *Tonight he will be freed.*

Fiona stood outside the door to her mother's room in darkness. She listened intently, trying to decide if Yhana was yet asleep. She didn't dare project her astral body into the room: her mother would surely have astral defenses in place ready to protect her. Yhana was well known for her paranoia, and had made enemies even amongst the detached brethren of the Yellow School.

Fiona could hear nothing from behind the door. Her pulse hammered in her ears, and the only breathing she could hear was her own. The unmistakable sound of vibrated God-names drifted down the passage as the last of the Adepts performed their night banishments. Fiona waited in the shadow of the doorway a few minutes more before proceeding.

Using her aura, she dampened all sound around her as Philip had taught her. She then slowly pushed the door open. Her magick ensured that the usual creak didn't occur. It was full moon, and her magick felt very powerful.

The room was illuminated by bright moonlight, and Fiona easily discerned her mother's sleeping form in the bed. Beside her head was a small chest of drawers. Upon it rested a jewellery box. Fiona knew that within this was Yhana's necklace. And within the neck-lace's pearl was her gnome, still trapped within the crystal lattice.

She moved quietly across the room, her feet sliding silently on the floor. She watched her mother carefully, listening to determine whether her breathing was completely regular. She paused as she did so, and then continued when satisfied.

She was barely able to breathe herself when she reached the chest of drawers. She decreased the magick she was using: she knew that the effect would wake her mother with it being so close. Instead of opening the box and risking a creak, she picked up the box. Then, carefully watching her mother, she slid quietly from the room, clos-ing the door.

Her pulse was hammering when she reached her room, and she was ecstatic. She drew the curtains and lit the oil lamp. She then opened the box and took out the necklace. The pearl vibrated in her hand, and she knew that the gnome had recognized her. Excite-ment rushed through her veins.

She sat on the floor and focused her mind, hurling her energy against the spell Yhana had put in place. But though she tried for several minutes, it was like trying to smash through a brick wall with her bare hands. Yhana's was magick was still too strong for her. Not until she was stronger than her mother would she be able to release the gnome. It brought tears to her eyes as the gem started to vibrate again, a plea from the gnome to be released.

Suddenly the door was flung open and Yhana strode in, her face furious.

"Bitch!" she snarled. "You'll pay for this!"

A shock wave of astral energy smashed into Fiona, knocking her senseless. The gem was thrown from her hand to skid across the floor. She tried to reach out a hand, but her muscles were paralyzed: they refused to obey her. Yhana knelt over her with a dagger.

"I should have done this years ago," she said. "This is the second time this dagger has cut the throat of a young girl."

The cold steel of the dagger pressed against Fiona's throat.

Suddenly the window imploded. Yhana looked up in shock as the huge bulk of the black feline stood above her, now larger than a tiger. The hard green eyes studied her for a moment before the cat pounced.

Yhana screamed as it landed on her, clawing her face. Fiona grit-ted her teeth and forced herself up. She grabbed her pack and

Yhana's necklace. She watched the struggle a few moments more before grabbing her mother's dagger and climbing out the window.

———◦◦◦———

Fiona sat on the snow in the forest for over an hour, mulling over the night's events. She had tried for hours, and still couldn't release the gnome from his prison. Tears of frustration ran down her face. The little that she had once had was now gone: she was left with nothing.

The anger started to build within her, and with it came a single idea: to kill Jaad.

*Life is what it is, you cannot change it,
but you can change yourself.*

—Hazrat Inayat Khan

*The greatest discovery of my generation
is that human beings can alter their lives
by altering their attitudes of mind.*

—William James

28

Planet Tellus
Nipponese Empire
Sanzin Village

Shadrack almost collapsed with relief when he entered the outskirts of Sanzin village. It was past midnight and he had stumbled upon the site by pure luck: the village was unlit and the thick mist cut his vision dramatically. Though it was still late Summer, the night air was bitterly cold. Shadrack knew that he had to find shelter and food. The first snows were bound to start soon.

The houses of Sanzin were larger than those of Kyoto, and more variant in their style and construction. He found himself awed by the size of the town itself. In his few years of life, he had never once been far outside Kyoto, and he was having severe problems adjusting to his new lifestyle. He had been away for two weeks, and it seemed like an eternity.

He followed the dirt track that ran through the centre of the town. There were ruts in the soil that revealed the regular passage of carts and horses. Shadrack knew that where there were horses, there were samurai.

The town was quiet at present, but he intended to take no risks. He moved into the shadows on the left side of the road.

After following the track for a few hundred yards, he was in the town proper. Its magnitude awed him. Shops were set into the main street, where the road was cobbled; the sight was quite amazing to him. He perceived that the governing of the town must be very different from that of Kyoto.

Flecks of snow touched his face and he shivered in the cold. He knew that he had to find shelter immediately. His stomach ached with hunger: he had exhausted his supply of food two days ago, and had had only berries and roots to eat since.

He knew that he would be fortunate to find food here, unless he could somehow steal it. It was strange that he had found the town at all. He had almost been guided to it.

As he walked stiffly down the road, his attention was seized by a building across the road. Across its large double doors was a samurai coat-of-arms. He immediately recognized it to be the House of the Shogun himself. It struck him that his father had taught him everything he needed to know to survive in the world. He now had to learn to apply it.

Next to the ornate building was a stable. He knew that he couldn't hope to find better shelter. He walked over to the stable, glancing warily about to be sure he was not being observed.

He peered over the top of the shoulder-high barrier. Inside were four thorough-bred horses. Even to the untrained eye, they were obviously fine specimens. They all had long-haired snow-white coats, which Shadrack knew would double their price. Samurai preferred snow-coloured mounts, originally for camouflage, but now simply as status symbols.

With another glance around, Shadrack unclipped the gate and quietly slid inside. He was fairly sure that he had not been seen.

The horses shuffled slightly as he entered, but made no noise. They were well trained and not easily disturbed. Each of them would calmly trot through a ferocious battlefield without complaint.

There was enough hay on the floor to offer him complete cover. He piled it into a bundle to cover himself. As he did so, he noticed a dark and forbidding shape on the wall opposite. Although his night sight was excellent, it was too dark to make the object out properly. He slung the katana on his back into a more accessible position, and advanced forward, expecting it to leap from the wall at any moment.

He was barely a yard away when he finally realized it was a set of saddlebags. With a sigh of relief he dragged them from the wall. Hurriedly, he checked the pockets and was shocked to find that they were full, packed with provisions for a journey. He pulled out a loaf of bread and a piece of cheese.

Before eating much, he began to feel sick. He wrapped the food

up and stuffed it in his coat for later. A water-skin filled with fine
wine quenched his thirst, though he would have preferred water.

As he settled down under a pile of fresh hay, he wondered what
power was guiding him. He was suspicious of his luck. Fate seemed
to have a definite purpose in mind for him.

———⟩•••⟨———

A click of metal snapped Shadrack out of a deep sleep. He quickly
neutralized a subconscious urge to stretch as he remembered his
situation. He realized that someone had undone the clasp on the
stable gate.

A dispersed light filtered through the thin pile of hay that concealed him. He knew that it was early morning from the damp atmosphere: the mist was thicker than ever. He could see nothing from his
position without moving: he was facing the rear of the stable.

"You will bring great honour to the family name, Asai. The
Shogun's Guard are the most honourable samurai in Nippon."

"I will do my duty well, captain."

Shadrack didn't have to listen to the conversation to realize they
were samurai: their deep, guttural voices assured him of this. He
panicked as he remembered he had not replaced the saddlebags
from last night.

"When are you expected?"

"I have one week to reach the palace."

A light thud reached Shadrack's ears.

"Then you must make haste. Good fortune, Asai."

"Aye, you too, captain."

Footsteps receded and the stable fell silent. Shadrack strained to
hear the remaining bushi: he was sure that he had not left. He quieted his breathing; it rasped in his ears, and he was sure that it must
be painfully audible to the samurai.

He heard a slight rustle. Then it came again, this time closer. A
heavy boot crashed into his exposed back and he cried out in surprise and pain. He rolled toward the rear of the stable, breaking out
of the useless cover. A fully armoured warrior bore down on him,
his face covered with a steel visored helmet.

"On your feet, peasant!"

Shadrack pushed himself up, dazedly looking at his opponent.

The samurai gasped in shock as he saw the katana slung over his back, and the wakizashi by his side. Shadrack cursed under his breath. The crime possessed an instant death penalty. He opened his mouth, about to explain that he would not resist, but the samurai was already drawing his sword.

Shadrack retreated, battling the urge to draw his own weapon. He refused to fight the man before him: upon leaving the village he had sworn never to strike out again. Though the damage was now done, he would never cause another pain. Once he had betrayed his father, but never again.

He reached the back wall of the stable and stopped his withdrawal: there was nowhere to run. The bushi raised his weapon. Potential defensive and attacking maneuvers automatically flitted through Shadrack's head. With them came half a dozen observations of imperfections in the warrior's advance. He knew that he could easily best this man.

He relaxed and released control, preferring to die himself rather than to murder another. The sword slash began: it all seemed pathetically slow. The bushi was well trained, but was as an amateur compared to his own skills.

The blade plummeted hungrily and Shadrack reacted without thinking. He slipped to the side of the descending blade and crashed a punch into his opponent's unprotected throat, crushing his trachea instantly. The bushi fell to the floor, wheezing pathetically. He thrashed wildly for half a minute before lying still.

Shadrack stood over the warrior's body, his mind numb. He was gripped by hollow sickness that seeped to the core of his being. Again his subconscious had acted of its own volition. His skills were so deeply embedded, that any attack or threat was instantly neutralized.

He drew his wakizashi from his belt and knelt. There was nothing to live for now that his father had abandoned him. Neither did he have anything to believe in: he had betrayed everything he valued. He was now a loner in the outside world, and it was a world he knew nothing about. Worse still, he had become a dangerous fugitive, soon to have a price on his head.

He braced himself. The tip of the blade touch his bared stomach. With barely any pressure, the weapon already drew blood. He adjusted his grip hesitantly, preparing himself for the death thrust. Hari-kari was usually performed with a friend standing over the sentenced man, ready to behead him. This was because the ritual disembowelling was one of the most painful ways to die. It could involve half an hour of excruciating pain before death finally came.

Shadrack was not distressed by the thought of the pain. Though he did not welcome it, he could control it. But there was a strong aversion in him to suicide. Though not a conscious faculty, his urge for self-preservation was unassailable.

He tried to push in the blade, but he could not fight his base instincts. With a snarl of rage, he hurled the blade across the stable. He held his head in his hands, all strength and will gone from his mind. It seemed he was to be tortured: he detested himself and yet was being forced to live.

Looking up at the body of the dead samurai, a strong conviction washed over him. He would take the dead man's place, and try to undo some of the harm he had caused. Though the decision failed to make rational sense, the sentiment was from deep within and he knew he had to follow it.

He started to strip the corpse of its yoroi armour, whilst looking around for a shovel to bury the body. If he could find the letter with the bushi's orders, he would have no trouble in assuming the man's name and identity. The Shogun's Guard would have no idea of how Asai looked.

As he continued to fumble with the complex buckles of the metal and leather armour, he swore to himself never again to lose control. He would not break his vow of pacifism again.

⋘≡◎◎◎≡⋙

Enya
Yesod of Yetzirah
The Enchanted Forest

Fiona sat on the forest floor, searching out Jaad with her mind. She had scried him hundreds of times before, but her mind was presently unfocused and it was difficult to control. She wore a thick cloak, but she still shivered as a light snow began to fall. The cold was biting, but she ignored it. She had more pressing things on her mind. Beside her lay the black panther, flicking her tail back and forth impatiently.

Suddenly Fiona located her quarry; immediately her blood began to burn with fury. She knew exactly where Jaad was: the tree house. Slipping into her pack, she snatched up her staff. She set off in Jaad's direction with a rapid stride; the panther growled and followed.

The full moon shone down brightly as Fiona approached the bandit camp. The snow was heavy now, and was already a foot deep in places. Fiona pushed her way through it, determined to let nothing stop her vengeance. It was close to midnight, and the golden bark of the trees was tainted silver by the moon. The air was cold enough to sting her throat as she breathed and condensation hung in the air every time she exhaled.

She was gasping in the oxygen—pushing through the deep snow was extremely taxing. Much of the time she was staring at her feet, carefully trying to choose her footing across the forest floor. She was taken completely by surprise when a voice cut through the night air.

"Hey, you! Stop where you are!"

She knew that it could only be a sentry for the bandit camp. Looking up, she saw a man approaching. He was armed with a long sword and cross bow. Off to the right, another man in brown leather armour was approaching.

Fiona continued forward on an intercept course with the first man. He drew his sword as she neared, but he didn't seem about to attack. Obviously the fact that she was a woman had him off-guard. He reached out and grabbed her by the arm.

Focusing her mind, Fiona hurled her psychic energy at him. The guard was blasted backward, hitting a tree forcefully; he crumpled to the floor. The second guard swore and levelled his crossbow at her. His action went no further as the panther suddenly pounced on him. He screamed, but it was quickly silenced as the creature killed him painlessly, cleaving open his throat to the spine with one swipe of her claws.

Fiona continued toward the tree house; she was very close now. She circled it several times before recognizing it: at night, all the trees looked the same.

There was a rope leading up to the structure, which was about ten feet off the ground.

"Stay," Fiona ordered; the panther snorted in irritation and lay down on the snow.

Fiona left her pack below and secured her staff to her back. She started to climb the rope, hand over hand. The rope was frozen and very slippery, but she was able to get a grip on the regularly placed knots. Using her upper body strength, she hauled herself up onto the platform.

The tree house was little more than a platform, with a little pro-tection from the wind from the branches it was built within. It was absolutely bare: the only thing that decorated it was Jaad's sleeping form, heavily wrapped in blankets. As she touched the surface of the platform, his fearful eyes snapped open. He sat up quickly, ready to spring to his escape like a caged animal. But he froze as he saw Fiona standing above him.

Their eyes locked, and Fiona felt an incredibly strong link between them. The feeling of déjà vu was even stronger than with the pan-ther or earth elemental. Though she hated him, she had a definite bond to this man which she couldn't deny. As Jaad stared at her, his black eyes cleared slightly: his expression became sharper, less vapid. Though she could see how helpless he was, and felt a small measure of sympathy, she could not extinguish the burning hatred within her.

"Lena," Jaad said, his voice choked. Fiona stared at him; she didn't recognize the name.

Jaad held out his hand for her to take. Fiona was shocked: she had expected Jaad to hate her the way she hated him. It suddenly made her mission much more difficult.

She knocked his hand away with the staff. Jaad stared at her with a hurt expression. Suddenly Fiona's fury exploded.

"Damn you!" she snarled.

Her staff descended forcefully. Jaad took the force on his palms as he defended himself; he whimpered as they stung painfully.

"No, Lena, no!" he pleaded, looking to escape.

But Fiona was beyond reasoning with. She pummelled the staff into him again and again. Jaad tried to crawl away, but there was no room to escape. Fiona was too enraged to notice that he didn't retaliate: he only attempted to defend himself. However, she was concerned with his physique: one hit from his huge frame would be enough to finish her.

The staff connected with Jaad's right kidney with a dull thud and he shouted in pain, writhing on the platform. He turned onto his back to fend off the blows with his arms. Fiona was still advancing, and his dull mind realized there would be no rest from the beating.

He pushed himself unsteadily to his feet, getting ready to grab her and immobilize her with his weight. But as he stood, Fiona's staff connected heavily with his head. The blow took him completely by surprise, and sent him spinning from the platform toward the ground. He was unconscious even before he landed heavily on his back, the snow offering little cushioning.

Lena stared for a moment in amazement of what she had done. But it lasted barely a second: the rage was still upon her. She leapt down from the platform to land lightly beside Jaad's body. She threw down her staff and straddled his huge chest. Then she drew her dagger, the one she had stolen from Yhana.

As she stared into Jaad's face, the hatred had never been stronger, but something within her strongly resisted her urge to plunge the dagger into his heart.

To commit murder is to commit suicide, she heard Philip's voice. *There is something within you that will not allow it.*

She grimaced and pressed the side of the blade against his throat. His face was familiar, she felt she could almost name him. And his name was not Jaad, she felt sure of that.

Her hand trembled as the dagger drew a thin line of blood on his throat. She looked up as the panther padded over to her. The feline snarled and stared at her, and Fiona knew that it was terribly wrong to commit this murder. She could even feel the earth elemental vibrating passionately in the necklace, warning her not to continue.

Yet the fury still burned in her, and she could not deny it. Her whole body shook now as she tried to control herself and withdraw the dagger from Jaad's throat. Tears flowed from here eyes with the effort, and still her hand didn't move; it poised above Jaad's throat, ready to extinguish his life with a single sweep.

"No!" her scream of frustration and rage cut through the freezing night atmosphere.

Jaad woke suddenly. He knocked Fiona several feet with push and was on his feet, shambling away through the snow. Fiona held the dagger, ready to throw at his back as he fled. She knew it was her last chance: if she didn't rid herself of the rage now, she couldn't continue to live. The dagger fell from her hand: she knew that she couldn't have the murder of an innocent man on her hands. For regardless of what Jaad had done in other lives, he had done nothing to deserve such a death in this one.

Her decision made, she collapsed on the floor, squirming on her back. The rage almost seemed sentient, and was punishing her for not carrying out the murder. She screamed as she writhed in the snow, desperate to escape the terrible emotions which gripped her. She knew of only one occult technique which could save her.

With her emotions so excessive, the concentration needed to follow it through was immense. She pushed astral material up from her solar plexus, gradually forming it into a sizable ball. All the time her body was wracked with pain. She knew she could not stand the agony for much longer: she had to complete the attempt now or never. With a huge effort of will she projected the rage away from herself and into the astral material. She began to feel calmer almost immediately as the rage was drained from her.

The astral material gradually formed the shape of a huge wolf, its red soulless eyes terrifying. Even though it was her own creation, and a part of her own psyche, Fiona felt an icy fear as she saw the creature take shape. Now it had been ejected, it would have its own will and desires: she had no chance of controlling it. Not without reabsorbing the creature again, and she was not strong enough to handle that. The panther watched, her hard green eyes watching the wolf like prey, ready to seize the creature once formed. But already the wolf was as large as the feline, and still growing in size.

The rage had completely left Fiona now, and the wolf was fully formed. She severed the astral link between them, and released the creature to its own life. It snarled at her and immediately loped after Jaad, its pink tongue hanging through huge canines.

Gods! What have I done, Fiona thought. *I've created a demon!* She felt very strange: incredibly tired, yet strangely more complete.

The black feline growled and started to follow the wolf.

"Bast! No!" she shouted. "Jaad will have to handle himself. I've done what I can."

She frowned. *How is it that I know the creature's name?*

That was her last thought before slumping into the snow, unconscious.

Dishonour is like a scar on a tree, which time, instead of effacing, only helps to enlarge.

—The Bushido, Way of the Warrior

It is true courage to live when it is right to live, and to die only when it is right to die.

—The Bushido, Way of the Warrior

Planet Tellus
Nipponese Empire
Honshu City
Year 19 of 32nd Shogun
(2 years later)

Shadrack hesitated as he reached the dormitory door. Though the light inside was dim, he could hear muffled voices from within. He sighed in disappointment; there would be little chance of rest without a commotion.

He had hoped to find the room empty. Over thirty of the fifty-strong corps were on duty. Most of the rest were in the city drinking or in one of the exclusive whore pits.

Illumination from the corridor spilled into the twilight of the dormitory as he pushed the door open and slid surreptitiously inside. Shuffles from across the room revealed that he had been noticed.

As his eyes adjusted, he saw several of the Shogun's Guard seated around a small table, gambling with dice. They were playing by the light of a single candle. It was obvious from their mutters that he was not welcome. The sentiment was not unusual: he was never welcome at any time.

He moved closer to approach his bunk, fervently hoping that the players wouldn't consider him worth attention. His hope was dashed when he recognized Nasa Munetaka. The samurai never missed an opportunity to taunt Shadrack.

"Hey, Asai, what's that book you've got there?"

Shadrack considered ignoring him. But he knew that escape was not that simple. His ribs still ached from the last beating delivered by Munetaka.

"The Bushido," he answered, his voice neutral and non-committal.

Munetaka stood up, faking anger in his mannerisms and tone. He always found some reason to take offense.

"What's a worm like you doing such a sacred book?!" he demanded, advancing along the dormitory. "What do you know of honour?!"

Shadrack bowed his head. He knew that the question was a valid one, but Munetaka was himself not qualified to ask it. Munetaka wasn't even aware that the bushido he followed was not written in book form; the volume which Shadrack possessed had been copied painstakingly from Tanaka's version by his own hand.

"I simply seek to improve myself," Shadrack said.

"Then become a beggar, peasant!"

There were sniggers of laughter from the gambling table. Munetaka was a man who specialized in improving his social position by derogating others.

Shadrack had learned to deal with the humiliation; it was his humility that provoked it. A samurai who was not proud, honourable and aggressive was treated as a leper, especially in the elitist Shogun's Guard.

"Give me the book, Asai."

Shadrack's eyes narrowed. Along with his swords, it was the only possession he would not submit.

"I cannot."

There was a creak from behind, and Shadrack realized that there was another observer. The samurai didn't seem interested in interfering, however. Munetaka didn't even glance at the stranger, who stood deep within the shadows. Besides, none of the Guard would dare attempt to obstruct him.

Munetaka reached for the book, a leer on his face. The samurai at the table chuckled to themselves, sure in the knowledge he would procure the object.

Shadrack snatched his hand away and stepped back. Munetaka's eyes became livid: the contest had become a matter of pride for him. For the first time in many months, Shadrack felt his pulse rise. He forced himself to relax.

I will not lose control! he repeated furiously.

"Give me the book Asai, or I will slice you as you stand."

Munetaka's voice was loaded with menace, each word emphasized.

Shadrack backed off, fighting the urge to place his hand on the hilt of his katana. He knew that it would spark Munetaka into drawing his own blade.

"If you kill me, you will be dishonoured," he said.

The thought of the impending doom of a dishonoured samurai hung in the air between them. Munetaka flexed his right hand as he sought to control himself. He nodded in resignation.

Shadrack relaxed, but it was too soon. The uppercut caught him square under the jaw, taking his legs from under him. His head spun uncontrollably. He thought it would explode. Munetaka bore down on him, striving to procure the book.

Shadrack heard the shouts of excitement from the table and the heavy, excited breathing of the observer by the door. He pulled the book tightly in to his body, loath to resign one of his most treasured possessions. Munetaka wrestled him, but Shadrack roughly pushed the samurai, almost knocking him onto his back.

Munetaka stood up and stepped away, obviously taken aback by Shadrack's strength; normally he was met by no resistance. But his pride prevented him from walking away.

He lunged to kick his opponent viciously in the side. Shadrack groaned as the foot impacted with his ribs; they were still bruised from his previous beating. He tried to rise, but another kick flipped him to land heavily on his back. With the third kick came a nauseating crack, and he shouted in surprise at the intensity of the pain.

His emotional control snapped in the chaos. Somewhere in his mind, the command to reach for his katana was triggered. Munetaka obviously read the impulse; he reached for his sword.

"That will be enough, gentlemen!"

Both samurai froze as the captain's voice sheared through the twilit dormitory. Shadrack quickly forced himself to relax. Munetaka hesitated and gave a slight bow before stepping back, breathing hard.

The captain continued as if he had witnessed nothing.

"We have an emergency, gentlemen. I want you all assembled in full yoroi on horseback in front of the palace in thirty minutes. The Shogun himself is to lead us."

Murmurs of surprise passed across the gambling table. The situation was extremely irregular.

Shadrack pushed himself to his feet; he held his right hand over his cracked ribs.

"And make sure all of you report. There are eighteen men off duty, and so all of you had better be on time."

His gaze searched disapprovingly over Shadrack's face.

"And that includes you, Nagamasa Asai!"

He spat out the samurai's name as if it was an unmentionable disease.

Shadrack bowed. "Oss, captain."

He knew that Yamota had stopped the fight to avoid losing Munetaka, who was the strongest and sharpest in the Guard. He had made his opinion of Shadrack clear, and had no need to iterate it. He considered him a barrier to the smooth running of the Guard, and as such would find any excuse to have him removed. They both knew that it was only a matter of time.

―――――◆◈◆―――――

Shadrack shivered nervously in the cold snow as he sat astride his mount; he gently stroked her to calm her nerves. The horse had originally been Munetaka's, and was a poor specimen compared to the one he had once owned. Munetaka now sat astride his old horse near the end of the line, his back straight and proud.

Silence fell across the score of bushi as the Shogun urged his horse over toward them, Yamota riding faithfully by his side. The horses bellowed clouds of water vapour into the air as they felt the tension.

The Shogun was in full yoroi, but for once it was not ceremonial armour. The leather was cracked and cut in places: it had obviously been through several battles. Shadrack wondered what kind of mission they would undertake. For the Shogun to take a personal interest, it had to be extremely important indeed.

The Shogun's expression was stoic. His face was thin and very pale. His eyes were a lucid green, their gaze sharp and intelligent. Under his armour, his body was obviously athletic and well muscled, although he approached the age of forty. It was obvious that his teenage son had a few more years before he claimed the seat of honour.

Behind him was the main entrance to the palace, with its beautiful towers and sloping roofs; the entirety of the upper structure was coated thinly with gold and silver.

"Tonight we are to set off on a forced ride toward the very edge of the Empire." The Shogun's voice cut keenly through the Arctic atmosphere. "We are to pursue a fugitive of personal interest."

Ripples of tension and unasked questions flowed through the contingent of samurai.

"This man is responsible for the murder of several honourable samurai, and has eluded us for some time. But we now have a definite sighting of him. We must reach him before he escapes again. Are there any questions?"

There was silence. No one would dare to question the Shogun. The duty of a samurai was to obey: questions could be taken as querying of orders, and were a subtle type of taboo.

The Shogun's horse trotted toward the main gate, and Yamota gave the order to fall in behind. Shadrack urged his mount forward, his head hung low in dread. His uncanny intuition told him exactly which part of Nippon they were destined for.

Shadrack was gripped by an icy fear as the bridge loomed into sight on the forest path before them. His hands trembled on the reigns and his stomach churned: he wanted to vomit. There was now no mistaking the mission of the Shogun's Guard, and he knew that he was powerless to prevent events from unfolding. The Shogun had already announced the name of the fugitive they sought.

It was just after dawn, and the frost was still fresh on the ground. The air was thick with mist and had a savage, freezing bite to it. It would be a few minutes before the dim, bloated orb of the sun rose above the horizon of evergreen treetops. Shadrack knew that the inhabitants of Kyoto would be just rising from sleep.

With a wave of his hand, the Shogun gave the order to cross the dilapidated wooden bridge. The party crossed in single file, splitting on the other side to ride around and surround the village. Shadrack realized that no one would escape the trap. He hung his head in defeat.

Yamota dropped back to ride alongside him. The rest of the bushi had almost disappeared.

"Lift your head up, Asai," he whispered venomously, "you're supposed to be samurai!"

The Shogun turned around to address his captain. He seemed irritated by his behavior: the captain's place was by his side.

"We will ride directly into the centre, Yamota-san."

He then looked at Shadrack.

"You will accompany us."

Yamota groaned to himself: he wanted Asai as far from the Shogun as possible. But the Shogun was being cautious; he knew how dangerous the fugitive could be.

As he entered the outskirts of the village, poignant memories flowed back to Shadrack. Over the last two years, he had submerged his personality. It was gushing back with a vengeance now; with it came many months of suppressed emotions.

The samurai gathered the townsfolk with ruthless efficiency, assembling them in the village centre. Anyone who resisted was instantly cut down. An intense feeling of déjà vu washed over Shadrack, and he had to battle to hold back the tears. Some of the village people being herded past seemed to recognize him, but he ignored them. He knew that his life depended upon it.

Many of the samurai were now on foot. They were searching through the villagers in the centre. Shadrack could see Sashka, Mako and Ujiyasu being roughly pushed into line. He swallowed the rising feelings of outrage and anger. Against a score of samurai he knew that he wouldn't stand a chance. Besides, he would not break his vow of pacifism under any circumstances. He had maintained it for two years, and he would not break it now.

Searching around him, he couldn't see either Tanaka or Ekanar in the vociferous chaos. He sat quietly and prayed that they were not in the village: it would save many lives. The Shogun would not allow the peasants of Kyoto to go unpunished for hiding a fugitive.

The crowd suddenly became quiet, starting in a wave from the north. Shadrack turned and saw the crowd open up as three mounted riders trotted through. They surrounded a walking captive.

The peasants were pushed back by the bushi, and the formation stepped into the open. Shadrack swallowed hard as he saw Tanaka standing in the middle of them, dressed in a simple *kimono*. The samurai had instantly recognized him by his Western blood.

The leader of the trio dismounted, carefully watching his prisoner. The other two bushi did similarly, allowing their horses to be taken by peers. The leader bowed and walked forward to Yamota to present a katana to him. Shadrack realized with annoyance that it was Munetaka.

"We found this on him, captain," said Munetaka, handing the

weapon carefully to Yamota. "But he didn't attempt to resist."

"It was Yoshitaka's," Yamota said, his voice bitter.

The Shogun looked briefly at the katana, and then turned his eyes upon Tanaka. They glittered like fiery emeralds. He had waited a long time for this moment.

"So, you are finally mine, Ieyasu Tanaka," he said, his voice caustic.

Tanaka held his gaze dispassionately; no emotion was visible on his face. He had never once escaped from his past; it had simply been a matter of time before it caught up with him.

Tanaka's eyes widened in shock as he saw Shadrack, but he quickly controlled himself. He averted his gaze and set his expression stoically again.

The Shogun had not missed the look, and he turned to behold Shadrack with a suspicious stare. His eyes narrowed as they ran over the hilt of the bushi's sword. Shadrack suddenly stopped breathing as he remembered that his katana had once been his father's: the initials of Yoriie Saito's father were inscribed onto it. The Shogun was suspicious, but not quite sure.

"That man is a traitor to me. Kill him!" he said, pointing at Tanaka.

Tanaka bowed his head and sank to his knees: he was perfectly ready for death. Shadrack balked as he realized that the order was for him. The Shogun was testing him.

His mind whirled, and for a few seconds he made no move. The Shogun's eyes burned an intense, livid green.

Shadrack bowed and slid down from his horse, his body on automatic as his mind struggled to assimilate the situation. He knew that he could not kill, especially Tanaka: he would never betray his teacher again. But he also knew that his instinct for self-preservation was strong, even if he hated life.

When he reached the kneeling ronin, Nasa Munetaka stepped back. Tanaka's eyes bore an emphatic look of sadness.

"I didn't think you would sink as low as this, Shadrack."

No accusation was in his voice, only severe disappointment. Shadrack had to fight to hold back the tears. He wanted to break down and beg his father for forgiveness, but he knew that it could never be granted. He had failed utterly, and no matter what he did now, he could not redeem himself.

His mind absolutely numb with shock, he started to draw his katana. The Shogun and junior samurai watched him intently. A landslide of emotions crashed through his mind: fear, embarrassment, guilt and shame. Then came the first flickers of anger. He looked up and suddenly realized that the village was burning; thick columns of smoke bellowed up into the crepuscular sky.

The spark of anger grew rapidly, displacing all other emotions. He could see Yamota and Munetaka looking on. They were sure that he was too much of a coward to do anything but die dishonourably. He looked over at the Shogun, who watched him with contempt. For a brief moment he understood the daimyo's character perfectly. He saw all the insecurities and motivations, the greed and petty lusts. He recognized the pathetic creature for what he was.

He slashed his finger and slammed his half-drawn katana back into its sheath. He quenched his anger: he would not lower himself for these animals.

"My apologies, daimyo, but I must decline."

He dropped down onto one knee beside his father. He saw the glimmer of a half-smile on Tanaka's face, and he had the satisfaction of knowing that at least his last decision had been the correct one.

The tension in the village multiplied ten-fold. The horses muttered nervously, smelling the burning wood. The peasants looked on helplessly. For several long seconds nothing happened.

Then the Shogun shouted, his voice furious: "I want these two traitors killed, then every member of this village executed for the harbouring of a fugitive!"

There was a great roar from the crowd of peasants as they realized their impending death. Some tried to run, but were quickly cut down by merciless blades and speeding arrows. Munetaka and three other samurai closed in on the kneeling pair of ronin, drawing their swords. Shadrack was choked with emotion: he could not believe that he was to die here after such a strange life. His father had always impressed upon him how important it was for him to survive; he had been sure that his son had a vital role to play in life.

The cry of Sashka's two daughters being pushed to the ground sliced to the core of his psyche. He closed his eyes to hold back the tears. But these were not tears of self-pity or regret. They were tears of anger. It augmented and intensified at a frightening pace, blocking out all else. It welled up from his very soul, a fury so powerful he thought his body would shatter from his effort to control it.

His breathing quickened. Time slowed. Adrenaline pumped forcefully through his veins and he clenched his fists by his sides. He lost control of his vital functions. The emotion was too strong: it flowed from outside his personality. With a terrible, insane fear, he recognized the dormant force the seer had discovered many years ago. And now it had awakened.

Its force hit his personality like a tidal wave striking, immersing it totally. He lost his identity, lost his humanity. The psychotic rage coursed through him and his control was shattered. He had only an unthinking, nefarious hatred of everything.

With practiced efficiency, the four samurai closed in on the kneeling two men. Shadrack raised his head and looked directly into Munetaka's eyes. The bushi froze in mid-step. His breathing choked as he saw the deep, soulless red eyes. He instantly knew he had met his nemesis in this creature of pure evil. There was no trace of humanity or mercy in its perverse stare.

The creature Shadrack had become moved with impossible speed. It leapt to its feet, drawing its katana simultaneously. With a powerful slash of the blade, Munetaka's torso was completely cleaved under the ribs. He fell to the ground in two pieces, dead before the impact.

The other three samurai stopped in surprise, their reactions lagging. The creature didn't hesitate. It span into the next opponent, wielding the blade with incredible skill and power. The bushi was decapitated before he could react.

The remaining two warriors collected themselves and attacked together, their swords raised to strike. They didn't stand a chance. The beast slashed out the intestines of the first and ripped out the throat of the second by hand.

The creature turned in surprise as the rest of the samurai muscled through the crowd. Those on horses were thrown from their mounts as the animals bucked and ran from the battleground in fear. Even the Shogun was picking himself up from the ground. He waited for his men to deal with the demon from Hell.

He grasped the hilt of his sword with white knuckles as each of his men screamed in turn. The creature slashed and clawed its way toward the daimyo, its eyes glowing with fury and hatred. It used martial arts as though they were instinctive, yet each move was an aggressive attack: the demon didn't use blocks or *tai-sabaki*. Each kick ruptured internal organs through yoroi armour, such was their power. It broke arms and legs as samurai attacked it, almost ripping them from their joints.

Some of the samurai landed minor sword slashes on the creature as they attacked in pairs and threes. But the beast didn't slow for any of its injuries: they only fuelled its temper. Its sword bloody from hilt to tip, it cleaved open warrior after warrior. The katana sliced through chain mail suneate and haidate, severing legs; steel helmets cracked and fractured under the force as the blade was driven down against them. Its punches impacted with breastplates, collapsing them and penetrating through the underlying *do* to shatter ribs and crumple sternums. The terrible screams of the samurai reverberated across the village as they rapidly died, one after another.

The creature burst through the last couple of warriors, its body covered in sword wounds; two arrows protruded from its back, but it was oblivious to them.

Yamota charged forward to defend his daimyo. He was sliced from the right shoulder down to the sternum. He fell to the ground, the blunted katana still embedded within him.

With a tumultuous battle cry, the Shogun leapt forward, drawing his sword. The beast caught him by the throat in mid-air and held him in suspension. He caught the Shogun's wrist as he attempted to draw his weapon, breaking the ulna and radius of his forearm. The creature's vice-like fingers tightened on the Shogun's *nodowa* throat guard. The samurai gave a choked, fearful cry as the steel began to fracture.

And then the *nodowa* collapsed. The Shogun's neck was snapped like a pencil. His eyes fluttered and closed, dark blood dribbling from his mouth.

With a howl of triumph, the creature hoisted the samurai lord above its head as though it was weightless. For a brief second, its instinct to kill had been sated. It then turned and lurched at the crowd of villagers.

It stopped and roared in pain as a succession of arrows plummeted into it. Its wounds now bled copiously: it had been seriously weakened. As the next two arrows struck home, it staggered forward and collapsed. The four surviving samurai threw down their bows and ran for their lives, quickly forgetting their fallen comrades.

Screams of pain, anger, and torment came from the creature as it writhed on the ground. Most of the villagers were running to their burning homes to save them; some stayed to watch the beast in its death throes. It clawed at them from a distance, wanting to tear them limb from limb.

Gradually, its screams became strangely human; its eyes turned a dull grey. Shadrack had returned, with barely a semblance of sanity. His body was broken and seriously wounded. His mind was shattered from the diabolical forces that had smashed through from his subconscious. Tears rolled down his red face. He had no comprehension of what had happened to him. He had no reasoning left. But he instinctively knew that the beast was as much a part of him as his own body.

In searing pain and despairing misery he closed his eyes and waited to die.

As the villagers huddled together with open mouths, an old man pushed his way through the crowd, cursing them. He hung his head in grief as he saw the body of Ieyasu Tanaka; a wakizashi protruded from the ronin's abdomen. The ronin had finally appeased his honour by the act of hari-kari, fourteen years after his crime.

Ekanar knelt beside Shadrack's broken body.

"Don't worry, lad," he said. "I've some friends in the West who'll take care of you. The Yellow Adepts will see you right."

With a laborious struggle, he began to drag the unconscious body of the ronin toward his smouldering home.

No conflict is so severe as his who labours to subdue himself.

—Thomas A. Kempis

Tellus
Malkuth of Assiah
The Indian Ocean

The small ship rocked and bucked nervously on the stormy waters of the Eastern Ocean, a thick damp mist clinging tightly to its form. Each huge wave sent gallons of water crashing across its decks, almost washing off the crew who struggled frantically to control her. She was not a young ship, and did not take well to such severe punishment.

In the musty, damp atmosphere below deck, an old man sat huddled against the wall of the hold. Ekanar shivered within a thick pile of wet blankets, eyeing the hatch above him warily. He pulled his legs tightly into his chest as another gush of water flowed through the unsealed entrance. He knew that he would be lucky to escape pneumonia; already the hold floor was submerged under half an inch of water, which swished back and forth with the motion of the ship.

He looked up suddenly as he heard the rattle of chains. Something stirred in the dense blackness ahead, and a gentle growl filtered through the hold. Ekanar forced back the tension in his gut, reminding himself that he knew exactly who else was with him. The apprehension flowed back with the cognition that he didn't know exactly what was with him.

He didn't try to move: his arthritic legs were far too stiff to try. Besides, there was nowhere to go. He had brought Shadrack on deck, and it was his duty to remain with him. The passage had cost him dearly: sailors were notoriously superstitious, and only a great amount of gold was liable to change their mind. Even then, giving

254

passage to a demon was no light matter.

Ekanar's eyes tried to pierce through the darkness, seeking out the shuffling form. A sound like whimpering permeated the cabin, but it was difficult to recognize with the crash of the ocean waves and shrieking wind. Ekanar shifted position on his buttocks uncomfortably; he knew that if the weather didn't drastically improve, he would not survive the voyage.

He reached underneath the pile of blankets which wrapped him, and pulled out an oil lamp. In a few seconds, its pale yellow glow pushed back the darkness of the cabin.

Shadrack sat on his haunches by the hold's supporting pillar, heavily chained. His legs were free, but otherwise his movement was restricted to a minimum. He held his face in his hands, still whimpering to himself. Though torn and tattered, his apparel was still unmistakably that of a samurai. His yoroi armour was slashed and scarred in many places: it practically hung from his large frame.

Suddenly, he noticed the light of the lamp and raised his head. Ekanar could see the blank, mindless look on his now thin and haggard face. Shadrack then let out a terrible cry of agony, a grisly, heart-rending scream for help which reminded Ekanar of the man he had once known. He dimmed the light, pain and pity crossing his weary face.

"Don't worry lad, we'll be there soon."

Shadrack tilted his head and snarled. For a moment, an ominous dull red light appeared in his eyes. Ekanar froze as he recognized the evil malignant intelligence which possessed his friend. He had watched its incredible power once before as it tore over a score of samurai limb from limb.

Slowly, the light and intelligence faded, and Shadrack began to cry pathetically. There was obviously little of his mind left, even in the absence of the entity which possessed him.

Ekanar could stand no more, and he pulled the blankets roughly over his head to fall into an uncomfortable and uneasy sleep.

------◆◉◉◉◈------

Ekanar awoke some time later, disorientated and exhausted; he had no idea of how long he had slept. A warning had triggered his subconscious into awakening him—he could feel the pump of adrenaline in his veins.

He tried to quiet his rasping breathing and flicked his eyes anxiously across the breadth of the hold. It was pitch black and he could see almost nothing. Yet he received the distinct impression that someone else was with him, and it was neither Shadrack nor the entity which possessed him. He waited quietly, not wanting to move to light the oil lamp.

Finally he submitted, forcing down his animal instincts which told him to freeze. The light flowed gently out from the lamp, dimly illuminating the entire hold. By the main supporting pillar, he could now see Shadrack's motionless figure. There was a blankness to his expression which was quite eerie.

The look disappeared, and he turned his head to look at the lamp with curiosity. Ekanar squinted at the boy; his eyes were not as good as they had once been. He was sure that the eyes were different: there was a depth and intensity to the gaze which he had never seen before, except in brief flashes when Shadrack had been a child.

Shadrack seemed to be actually sane for a moment: he beheld the sage with a level stare. Then he hung his head to stare at the floor, his face full of remorse. A moment later, he threw back his head to bawl at the top of his voice.

"LEEENAA!!!"

The tone was choked with pain and anger, and Ekanar balked at the unbridled emotion in it. Then Shadrack again looked at the floor; his voice was vehement.

"By the Hells, I'll destroy you for this Dethen!"

Ekanar shuddered with the intensity of the threat. Then Shadrack began to cry, reverting to his previous state.

Ekanar wondered sadly whether anyone could help the ronin: his soul seemed beyond repair. If it was possible, he knew that the order of Yellow Adepti which he sought would be able to help; but they would have to reconstruct Shadrack's very soul.

Ekanar dimmed the lamp and rolled over, unable to handle the ronin's pain.

———◈◈◈———

Enya
Yesod of Yetzirah
The Enchanted Circle

Lena grimaced as Bast's sandy tongue raked against her cheek, rousing her to consciousness.

"Cut that out!" she ordered, pushing the familiar's face away from her own.

She yawned and opened her eyes. The first thing she noticed was how wet her back was: she had been lying in the snow for the gods knew how long. The front of her body was dry and warm; she suspected that Bast had been lying over her to keep her warm. The familiar's alien eyes reflected the light of the full moon as she checked the health of her mistress.

"It's okay, Bast," Lena said. "It's me. At least I think so."

Bast purred with satisfaction.

Lena sat up, holding her head which throbbed with a dull pain. She recognized the Enchanted Forest, but she hardly recognized herself: somehow she was both Fiona and Lena at the same time.

Two sides of the same person, she thought.

Events from her previous life were slowly returning to her, though it all seemed hazy and distant. Despite her disorientation, however, at last she felt whole.

She shuddered in the freezing air, and almost instinctively her aura began to glow as she warmed herself. She marvelled at how easy her magick flowed: obviously the return of her memories had brought a corresponding increase in power.

Yhana's necklace began to vibrate, and she smiled. Perhaps now she would be able to release Squint. She lifted the necklace over her head and held it before her.

As she focused her mind against Yhana's magick, she traced the sigils in reverse above the pearl. The gemstone glowed and shattered, casting Squint head first into the snow. He kicked helplessly as he tried to free himself. Bast growled and gave a rough push to release him.

Squint was overjoyed to see Lena, and he jumped up to hug her tightly.

"Okay, Squint. You can let go now," she said after awhile. But the elemental clung to her and refused to let go.

Lena stroked his head and scanned the forest around her. She wondered what had happened to Jaad. His true identity was now obvious to her, and though the uncontrollable rage had gone, she still hated him. He was not now important to her: her priority was now clear.

"Come," she said to Bast, "we must find Malak. Already we've wasted too much time." Bast growled in agreement.

Trees whipped past Jaad as he dashed heedlessly on. His face was scratched and bleeding, and his clothes hung from his bruised body, but he was oblivious to all of this: behind him he could feel the Beast pursuing him. It's wolf-like form loped through the trees after him, its savage eyes full of maleficent glee.

Jaad could feel its desire for his life essence, and he was petrified. The creature was pure hatred: he could feel its loathsome nature. His heart hammered painfully in his chest and his breathing wheezed. Yet he couldn't slow down. Already the Beast was making ground, and he knew he had to make it to the light if he wanted to survive. He hoped fervently that he was going in the right direction.

A distant flare of scarlet light confirmed his hope and he pushed even harder. He was oblivious to why he had to reach the light, or what it was. It was in the valley of standing stones, that was all he knew. He was driven by an almost inhuman strength to reach it. It felt like someone was helping him, feeding him strength. The thought thrilled Jaad.

The forest started to thin out and he stumbled as he found a downward slope marking the edge of a valley. He could clearly see the flaring light now. It was inside the three circles of megaliths. The Beast was very close now. But if he was quick, he would reach the circles before he was caught.

He stumbled as he ran, but he didn't fall once. He felt that he was being guided down the valley side. A formidable shape loomed as he shot a quick glance behind: it was almost upon him.

Jaad struggled past the first ring of standing stones, gasping for breath. He thought his lungs would burst. As he crossed onto the second ring, he tripped over something. He lay where he fell, not now caring what happened to him. The Beast had slowed. It was approaching at a trot, sure in the knowledge that its quarry was too exhausted to move.

As he prepared for death, Jaad was taken by a sudden curiosity to discover what had tripped him. He tried to ignore the urge, but it was too potent. It emanated from deep within himself but outside of his personality. He twisted so that he could see the object. He gasped as he saw it lying in the grass, illuminated by its own dull red light. He now knew the source of the crimson flares.

The sword was black, dull and lifeless except for the luminescent garnet in the pommel. Strange runes of power were inscribed along it. It had obviously been unearthed by a wild animal; the claw marks were still evident in the ground.

Jaad felt it call to him with a passion so intense, he didn't even consider resisting it. He reached out and grasped the hilt. The garnet immediately flared. A strange lustre appeared on the surface of the blade, as though it had gained life. The sword welded itself into his palm, and his body was flooded with a frigid rapture. Then blackness took him.

The Beast advanced the last few yards to its quarry. It was surprised to find the boy kneeling, facing away from it. It growled maliciously, waiting for the fear to appear that it needed for sustenance. There was no reaction, and it wondered whether its prey might already be dead.

It moved closer, growling more ferociously. The figure tensed and rose to his feet, slowly turning to face the Beast. It suddenly realized that something was wrong: there was a power and confidence about the figure which was extremely perturbing. It prepared to pounce as their eyes met.

Its evil, soulless eyes stared at its prey, ready to devour it. But it balked as it prepared to launch itself. An inhuman black gaze bored into its mind, crushing its insignificant will. The Beast shuddered and whimpered as *Widowmaker* hummed voraciously.

Dethen laughed at the creature shivering before him, a deep and humourless sound.

"I have returned," he stated with satisfaction.

A cold shudder passed through the valley as the words dispersed into the night.

Not every end is a goal. The end of a melody is not its goal; however, if the melody has not reached its end, it would also not have reached its goal. A parable.

—Nietzsche

Epilogue

Enya
Yesod of Yetzirah
The Aeon of harmony

The crowd slowly came to their senses as the words of the Magus died away on the breeze. Gradually the world about them pressed in, real once again. The sky was a deep purple as the sun slowly set behind the Wyrmspine mountains, its image reflected upon the Celestial Tower. To the crowd of children and adults, the Tower would never again seem the same.

Silence hung in the air for a few moments as the night chill gathered about them. No one wanted to disturb the magical fabric of the Story that crackled in the air between them.

"Is that the whole Story?" one of the children asked. "Surely it doesn't end there? Shadrack lies wounded and dying. We don't even know if he lives!"

The Magus lifted his head to behold the child with his sublime gaze. "No, child. That is not the end. It is a new beginning. Just as this dusk marks the end of the day, it also separates us from a new start. So it is with the Story. Just as the sun will rise on the 'morrow, so does Shadrack's soul rise from the ashes. For before him lie his most difficult tests: to face Dethen, defeat Lilith, and be reunited with Lena. No, child. The Story does not end there."

"Will you carry on?" urged another child, his eyes alight with eagerness.

The Magus smiled. "It is late, and there is always tomorrow."

There was a groan from the crowd.

"Ask him, Lena!" shouted one of the adults. "He'll do what you ask!"

The dark-haired woman reached across to touch the arm of the Magus. "Perhaps you should continue," she said, her dark brown eyes full of affection. "They do not even know yet if you are Malak or Dethen."

The Magus smiled, and even though he had no favourites, the expression seemed even more intimate.

"How can I resist?" he asked. He turned to the crowd: "Then listen carefully and I will tell you of Shadrack's rebirth and the result of Dethen's Purpose. For here the Story is only beginning."

As he began to talk, his musical voice cast its spell of rapture. Nocturnal creatures of all kinds gathered around to listen, and for the crowd the world shimmered and faded from view as they once again lived the Story...

The Tree of Life

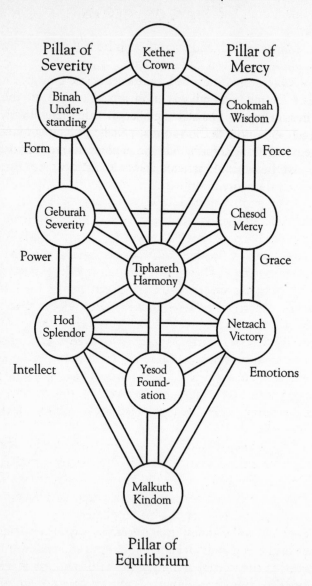

Pillar of Severity

Pillar of Mercy

Kether
Crown

Binah
Under-
standing

Chokmah
Wisdom

Form

Force

Geburah
Severity

Chesod
Mercy

Power

Grace

Tiphareth
Harmony

Hod
Splendor

Netzach
Victory

Intellect

Emotions

Yesod
Found-
ation

Malkuth
Kindom

Pillar of
Equilibrium

To him that overcometh will I give to eat of the Tree of Life, which is in the midst of the paradise of God.

—Revelation 2:7

Introduction to
The Qabalah

———⊰◉◉◉⊱———

This short composition is designed to outline the aspects of the Qabalah that relate directly to *Darkness and Light*. For anyone interested in studying the Qabalah, detailed introductions already exist, from such authorities as Dion Fortune, Aleister Crowley, MacGregor Mathers and Israel Regardie. Their compositions are far more comprehensive than I could attempt to write, and most of the material lies beyond the scope of this trilogy.

The Qabalah originated from the Hebrews, and many of its teachings can be found in the Old Testament, and in parts of the New. It is not limited to any single religion, however, and this is one of its most valuable attributes. Neither is there any incontestable master text to refer to, because it is not a dogmatic religion. Rather, it is a living philosophy that seeks truth rather than rigid rules. In the words of Blavatsky, "There is no religion higher than Truth." Qabalistic thought has always embraced this concept.

The visible glyph of the Qabalah is the Tree of Life (please see diagram), which is composed of ten spheres, known as Sephiroth. The lines that join the Sephiroth are known as paths, of which there are twenty-two. Each Sephirah (singular of Sephiroth) is an individual essence or quality that manifests itself in every conceivable process of nature.

The Tree of Life is analogous to the spectrum of light, where the Sephiroth form the colours. Colour is a quality that exists in every object, rather than being an object itself. The Sephiroth are like this also. Their essences can be traced through objects and processes, as well existing objectively on the higher planes.

A Sephirah will manifest itself in various ways. For example, the essence of the Sephirah Geburah is strength and power. It may be attributed to the warrior archetype in the psychology of man, but its essence may also be seen within iron, an oak tree, fire, a sword, the god Mars, etc. It is a destructive or contracting force. The colour of Geburah is red.

263

The Sephirah that balances Geburah is Chesed, and its essence is Mercy and Grace. Chesed can be attributed to the priest king, who is wise, merciful, and generous. Its essence may be seen within an olive branch, water, a unicorn, the god Jupiter, and numerous other correspondences. Chesed is constructive and expansive; its colour is blue.

The idea of the Sephiroth manifesting in different ways may seem strange. In reality, the notion is common. For example, one might describe red as being a warm colour and blue as a cold one. Red is also associated with anger. Likewise music may be associated with gentle or martial emotions, depending upon its style and speed. The correspondences of the Sephiroth are derived in a similar fashion. The colour red, the god Mars, martial music, anger, a sword, fire, and iron all have a quality in common, and this is the essence of Geburah.

Each Sephirah has a similar set of correspondences that are in harmony with its nature; therefore almost facet of life, or any object, can be allocated to one of the Sephiroth. The idea may seem simplistic and purely subjective, but the Qabalah is admirably useful for cataloguing not only human experience, but also the objective universe. It is an axiom of the Qabalah that man's subjective world is a mirror image of the objective universe.

The Tree of Life is composed of four principal planes, or worlds. In order of increasing density, these are: Atziluth, Briah, Yetzirah, and Assiah. Assiah is actually the material universe whilst Yetzirah and Briah are the astral and mental plane respectively. Atziluth is considered to be the plane of Divinity.

Though they are depicted as such for simplicity, these planes are not stacked on top of each other. Rather, they are seen to coexist and interpenetrate within the same space. This is possible due to the differences in density and vibrational rate. Just as sound, electrons, light, and all electromagnetic waves are composed of vibrations, so are each of the planes.

Thus, Atziluth is conceived to have the highest vibrational rate and is therefore the most rarefied of the planes. Assiah, which we perceive as the physical universe, has the lowest vibrational rate and its matter is dense and gross. Undeveloped people are unable to perceive the higher planes because those planes are too fine to see. With training, however, most people can perceive astral forms and beings.

Each of the Sephiroth exist in each of the four planes. Therefore, a manifestation of Geburah exists in Atziluth, Briah, Yetzirah and Assiah. Because it is the plane of Divinity, Atziluth is extremely spiritual, and the Sephirah of Geburah here emanates from Divinity itself. The Sephirah of Geburah in Briah may be considered as a reflection of the one in Atziluth, and likewise this reflection replicates itself in Yetzirah. Thus Geburah is transmitted down the four worlds, and the other Sephiroth likewise. As one descends the worlds, the Sephiroth become less abstract and more concrete.

To summarize, there are four worlds, with ten sub-planes within each. There are thus forty sub-planes. These are designated as Geburah of Yetzirah, Geburah of Assiah, etc. Each of the forty sub-planes is unique, though obviously the four manifestations of Chesed will have a great deal in common.

The worlds also divide the constitution of man, because he has a vehicle that exists on each plane (for convenience the parts of man are separated for study, but it should be remembered that they cannot exist independently of each other). The physical body belongs to Assiah. The astral body belongs to Yetzirah, and this corresponds to man's emotional and mechanical nature: it is known as the lower self. The mental body belongs to Briah and this corresponds to the intellect. Lastly, Atziluth is where man's spiritual body resides.

The ten Sephiroth are displayed graphically by the Tree of Life. On the Tree, the Sephiroth are collected into three columns, or Pillars. The Pillar of severity contains Binah, Geburah, and Hod. The Pillar of Mercy contains Chokmah, Chesed, and Netzach. The Pillar of Equilibrium contains Kether, Tiphareth, Yesod, and Malkuth.

The Tree is designed to show the relationships between the Sephiroth. Those in the Pillar of Severity are balanced by their opposites in the Pillar of Mildness, for example with Geburah and Chesed. When the Tree is applied to the psyche of human beings, it is essential that these forces are balanced within their personalities. For example, one must elicit Strength from Geburah, but this must be tempered by Mercy and Chesed. Failure to attain balance may result in cruelty on one side, and weakness on the other.

In the Qabalistic scheme of the universe, evil can be defined as a lack of balance. Evil is anything taken to an extreme, as in the above example of cruelty and weakness. Each Sephiroth has a vice, which is the essence of the Sephirah taken to an extreme. These vices are known as the Qlippoth, and can be considered as demons. However, evil is not seen to exist objectively as in the Christian concept of Satan. Rather, it is caused through ignorance and lack of wisdom. The universe is causal: no one consciously decides to be evil without an external influence acting on them. This may simply be an under-privileged childhood, and though it does not excuse evil actions, it should at least stimulate some sympathy. We cannot judge another without having experienced their position.

It is easy to make sweeping statements. A moralist might say it is evil to kill anyone. But assuming it would have avoided the Second World War, would killing Adolf Hitler have been evil? Such a question is not easy to answer: ethics are a very personal thing. However, it illustrates that evil is not something objective that we can define: it is concerned with our perceptions. Primitive people often consider natural phenomena to be evil. Fire is amazingly useful to our society for heating and cooking, but it isn't particularly congenial to health if you stick your head in it. Does this make fire evil?

The Sephiroth of the Middle Pillar of the Tree correspond to the centres of power, or chakras, which lie within the human body. These are well documented in Eastern and Oriental philosophy. The Sephiroth are also the source of the aspects of human psychology: the archetypes of Carl Jung may be attributed below the Sephirah Chokmah.

Intimately connected with the Qabalah is reincarnation. A human spirit is seen to emanate from God in Atziluth, and exists on each world downward. The final body is, of course, the physical. But the physical body depends upon the astral, mental, and spiritual bodies for its existence. If they were removed, the physical organism would immediately cease to live.

According to Qabalistic doctrine, humans incarnate in the physical universe to be educated. To illustrate this point, contrast a spoiled child and an unselfish wise old man who has suffered greatly. The latter will be much more at peace with himself, and lives for others rather than his own whimsical desires.

A human soul will incarnate many times, living many lives before all the necessary lessons are learned. Memories of past lives are not retained because this would be detrimental to the learning process. If we were born with a memory of our last incarnation, we would behave as old men and women when we were children. Our minds would be closed to new ideas and concepts, and very little would be learned. However, each incarnation is important, and past life memories can be consciously retrieved. Each incarnation leaves its distinct mark upon the "soul" of the individual.

One of the most valuable uses of the Qabalah is its ability to classify religions and mythologies. In almost every culture of the ancient world the number seven has had a mystical significance. This is true even amongst primitive tribes separated from the rest of the world. In every culture, a week is divided into seven days, and this tradition is far older than continental travel. This is because humans were more sensitive to subtle energies in ancient times. Monuments such as Stonehenge show that these people were remarkably attuned to the seasons, and more subtle energies such as ley lines.

In every independently derived astrological system, there were always seven "planets" (the meaning of "planet" was different from the one used today), and these planets represented the same concepts and ideals. These concepts can be traced through the mythologies of many cultures, where the gods and demons are personifications of these energies. Scholars have correlated the gods between Greek and Roman mythologies for many years, but few people realize that all mythologies can be correlated in this way. This is what the Qabalah is most useful for.

Mythologies have long been ridiculed as primitive attempts at religion, but in this the skeptics show their ignorance. Even those mythologies that include a Creation myth are not meant to be taken literally; this includes Genesis from the Bible (how could the Earth be made in seven days before days existed?). The function of these mythologies is to communicate truths by analogy which cannot be directly comprehended. To take them literally or banish them out of hand are equally foolish attitudes. The myths are a leftover of the wisdom of ancient races, and certainly do not deserve to be ridiculed. The stories of battles between gods and demons mirror different aspects of the human psyche, since the deities represent different aspects of our psychological makeup.

The various deities of any mythology can be attributed to different Sephiroth on the Tree of Life. Just as the Tree reveals the relationships between the Sephiroth, it reveals the relationships between the deities. It thus forms a map of our unconscious minds, and agrees mostly with the findings of the psychologist Carl Jung, who performed the only serious research into this fascinating area.

He called the gods "archetypes," and showed that they were concepts common to the human psyche in all times and places. He demonstrated the existence of the "collective unconscious" mind.

It is accepted even in mainstream psychology that splinter personalities can possess people. These are most dramatically revealed in cases of split and multiple personality, and the splinter personalities are imbued with their own consciousness, meaning they are free thinking beings. Whether they are considered as subjective fragments of the psyche or objective demons, as they were considered in ancient times, is in some ways irrelevant. Their effect is very real, and psychology understands very little about them. In Qabalistic philosophy, the distinction is in some ways superficial, because subjective and objective phenomena are regarded as being equally important. A person's beliefs define his or her universe as much as objective reality. It is often said that a person sees what they wish to see, but this isn't quite true. The world is a mirror: when we look at it we are looking at ourselves. When we curse negative occurrences in our lives, it should be remembered that we have responsibility for them: every aspect of our universe is produced from projection of our psyche. Therefore anything hurtful which occurs does so because we have consciously or unconsciously caused it. This is always a difficult lesson to realize.

The above outline of the Qabalah has been greatly simplified. To some degree it is also a personal interpretation: the Qabalah is a personal journey in self-discovery, not a fixed religion. Each student is responsible for his own beliefs, and for the effects these beliefs have on his or her reality. The inner and outer life of a person are complementary, and both must be in harmony for progress in either world.

For anyone interested in studying the Qabalah further, there is a recommended reading list at the back of this novel.

Glossary

Abyss, The: A great barrier which must be crossed in order to become one with God. To cross the Abyss, the personality must transcend and only pure consciousness should remain. All imperfections and limitations are left behind as the human becomes a God, omniscient and omnipotent. It is not possible to retain one's ego when crossing the Abyss, for everything must be lost in order to gain. The Abyss is not comprehensible to humans: it is too abstract and lofty for them to contemplate.

Adept: A man or woman who has achieved self-realization. An Adept's personality is perfectly balanced, and he or she has command over the elements. The consciousness of an Adept has been greatly expanded, and an undeveloped human's mind is caught in a constant dream by comparison. There are three grades of Adepthood: Adeptus Minor, Adeptus Major, and Adeptus Exemptus. These correspond to the grades of Tiphareth, Geburah, and Chesed respectively.

Aeon: A period of time in which certain spiritual factors predominate on a planet or plane. On Enya, an Aeon lasts two thousand years. The change of Aeons is always accompanied by a change of Magus, who brings the new law from God.

Asana: A Sanskrit term which literally means "posture." Asana is also the verb used for the practice of holding a posture for many hours to educate the body and still its sensations. The practice is the first step in some yogas that aim to achieve mystical states.

Assiah: One of the Four Worlds of the Qabalah. Assiah is the material universe and is the most dense of the Four Worlds. It is also the least spiritual due to its distance from the Divine, but is still a manifestation of God nonetheless.

269

Astral (Plane): The plane immediately above the physical universe, corresponding to Yetzirah in the Qabalah. The matter of the astral plane is very fine, and can be molded by thoughts and emotions. The plane is at least as extensive as the physical universe, and many beings live within it. The plane is beautiful to behold, containing numerous fantastic creatures, but also dangerous and malignant ones. The astral plane is very emotional by nature, and is the world where humans dream. All creatures of myth and fantasy exist here; it is the home from which they all originated.

Astral Projection: For a human, this is the process of consciously releasing the astral body from the physical and controlling it either on the physical or astral plane. The technique is extremely difficult to master, but all Adepts are capable of this feat.

Astral Vampire: Any entity that lives by draining the astral energy from others in order to feed itself.

Atziluth: The first world of the Qabalah. Atziluth is the most rarefied plane and is the world of Divinity. It exists above the Abyss, completely beyond our perceptions. Despite this, the very core of our being resides in Atziluth.

Aura: An egg-shaped body of ethereal light which surrounds the physical body. It is visible to beings who possess ethereal vision. The aura varies between a few inches in size to several feet, depending upon health and other factors. To a skilled Adept, emotions and even thoughts can be read from the aura, due to the flickering colours and changing vibrations. Every object has an aura, including inanimate ones. It is actually the astral mold from which the physical takes its form.

Auriel: The Arch-angel of the element Earth.

Bo (Jp.): A Japanese fighting staff.

Bo-jitsu: Literally "the art of the staff." A martial art based upon the use of a bo-staff. The staff is employed two handed and through variations in grip it can be used for long range or close combat. Techniques include striking, thrusting, blocking, parrying, sweeping, and holding.

Bokken: Literally "wooden sword." A bokken is a staff contoured like a katana, used mainly for practice.

Budo-kai (Jp.): Literally "military way." A word that encompasses all martial arts, especially those with emphasis on a spiritual approach.

Bushi (Jp.): A Japanese term equivalent to *samurai*.

Bushido (Jp.): Literally "The Way of the Warrior." It is actually a spirit of teachings rather than a written doctrine.

Chakra: Chakras are points of power contained within the astral body, where certain energies and powers are concentrated. To one with ethereal vision, they appear as spherical globes of intense light. They are small in an undeveloped human, but expand with spiritual development.

Chesed: Chesed is the fourth Sephirah of the Tree of Life. Its name means Mercy, while its secondary name, *Gedulah*, means Grace. It is situated within the Pillar of Mercy, and balances the power of Geburah. Its colour is dark blue, and it is personified by the image of a wise priest-king.

Chronzon: Chronzon is the entity charged with the control of the physical universe, and the planes directly above. He is the tester of humanity, guarding the Abyss to stop those who are not worthy to cross it. He is actually the God of many of today's religions; for example, Gnosticism teaches that he is the petty emotional God of the Old Testament.

Daath: Daath is a pseudo-Sephirah on the Tree of Life, lying between Kether and Tiphareth. Its title means "Knowledge."

Daimyo (Jp.): In feudal Japan, a samurai lord that other samurai were honour-bound to obey. A samurai without a daimyo was considered worthless, and was despised as a ronin.

Dweomer: Literally "magick."

Elemental: A being that belongs to either Earth, Air, Water, or Fire, being very low on the hierarchy. These beings may be good, mischievous, or evil. Tales of these are to be found in many fairy stories. The names of each group, respectively, are: gnomes, sylphs (faeries), undines (mermaids), and salamanders.

Elements: There are actually five elements, the mundane ones being Earth, Air, Water, and Fire. The fifth element is Spirit, which is the Divine force of God. It rules and binds the other four.

Enochian: An ancient language, the written remnants of which can be found scattered around the world. The language was rediscovered by Sir John Dee and Edward Kelly in recent times. The language is actually reputed to be angelic in nature, and it has a reputation for being extremely potent.

Ethereal (Plane): This is actually a sub-plane of the astral, and the term ethereal is sometimes used synonymously with astral. Technically, the ethereal plane is the gross, dense part of the astral which lies very close to the physical universe.

Frater: Used in occult orders, literally meaning "Brother."

Gabriel: Two separate beings bear the name of Gabriel. One is the Arch-angel of Water; the other is the Arch-angel of Yesod.

Geburah: Geburah is the fifth Sephirah of the Tree of Life. Its name means Severity, but this is sometimes translated as Power. It is situated within the Pillar of Severity, and balances the power of Chesed. Its colour is scarlet-red, and it is personified by the image of a warrior-king.

Gi: Literally "uniform" or "suit," a gi is the traditional apparel of a martial artist, normally woven from cotton, or from cotton canvas (which is more durable).

Hari-kari (Jp.): A ritual by which a samurai took his own life after being dishonoured, or upon disagreeing with his daimyo. The wakizashi short sword was used for this purpose. The formal name for this ritual is *Seppuka*.

Iai: Literally "swordplay," iai is also a type of duel in which two opponents face each other in the kneeling position before attacking. The first sword slice usually ended the duel, which could be for honour, or to the death.

Iai-jitsu: Literally "sword drawing art," a martial art that perfected the initial movement of a sword and the instant striking of an enemy. Iai-jitsu was extremely important to samurai. The modern version of the martial art is *iai-do*, the "way of the sword."

Infernal Habitations: These are the unbalanced and evil Qlippoth. They are commonly called *Hells*, and one exists for each Sephirah of the Tree of Life.

Ipsissimus: The Grade of Kether, obtained by traversing the Path of the High Priestess. An Ipsissimus has crossed the Abyss and become one with God. He or she has triumphed over all limitations, and has become immortal and incomprehensible. An impulse from an Ipsissimus could instantly destroy or create a universe.

Jujitsu: Literally "the art of gentleness," a martial art used by samurai from the thirteenth century. Techniques include striking, kicking, throwing, choking, and especially joint-locking. The use of weapons is also a part of jujitsu.

Karate: Literally "empty hand," meaning a martial art used without weapons. Karate employs all parts of the anatomy to punch, kick, strike, and block. The style is generally more aggressive than jujitsu and aikido, which are more defensive arts (though still extremely effective).

Karma: A Sanskrit term meaning "action" (the Hebrew term is Teekoon). Karma is the doctrine that what you give you eventually get back, even if it occurs several lifetimes later. Even death gives no escape from karma, because it follows a person throughout his or her incarnations. Karma is only neutralized and transcended when the Abyss is crossed.

Kata (Jp.): An important ritual in *Budo-kai*, kata is used to perfect techniques and concentration. When practicing kata, the student should have maximum zanshin. There are many katas; each one of them is a set pattern of attacks and defensive movements.

Katana (Jp.): A Japanese sword, twenty-four to thirty-six inches long, with a chisel-like end. Katanas were forged by folding the metal of the blade many times, until there were up to four thousand folds. This produced an incredible strength and sharpness. During each fold, a prayer was uttered to imbue the sword with more than physical strength. In feudal Japan, only samurai were allowed to own katanas. Every samurai owned both a katana and a wakizashi (the swords were considered as a complementary pair). The katana was a weapon of honour, and was believed to contain a samurai's soul.

Kether: Kether is the first Sephirah of the Tree of Life. It is the source of all the other Sephiroth, and thus contains all possibilities and potentials. Its essence is too pure and lofty for a human to begin to appreciate. It is the power to which every living being unconsciously aspires.

Kiai (Jp.): In budo-kai, a cry of spirit to instill fear into the opponent and focus power. Often used in conjunction with kime, in which every muscle in the body is tensed for a split second at impact to produce a maximum effect.

Kime: Literally "focus." A martial artist concentrates his physical and mental power behind a single striking point (such as the knuckles) for maximum effect. Kime is used with every technique where power is required, and is devastating when used in conjunction with a kiai.

Mage: Literally "magician."

Magus: A person who has crossed the Abyss and gained the Grade of Chokmah. A Magus may herald the new Aeon, armed with the Word of God.

Malkuth: The physical universe, or sometimes the Earth.

Michael: The Arch-angel of fire.

Motsu: A form of meditation employed in the martial arts, performed kneeling on the insteps. The position is also employed in magical arts and is sometimes known as "dragon posture."

Neophyte: The first grade of initiation in each of the Schools of Magick.

Pentacle: The elemental weapon of earth, used for controlling entities of the element earth amongst other uses.

Pentagram: A five-sided star, with each point representing one of the elements. With one point uppermost, it signifies the spirit of God over the elements and is good. With two points uppermost, it is a symbol of evil.

Pranayama: The practice of setting up a specific rhythmic breathing pattern and maintaining it indefinitely. Practice of pranayama often follows mastery of Asana.

Qabalah: A system used for spiritual development by magicians and mystics.

Qlippoth: This word can denote either the Infernal Habitations or their inhabitants.

Raphael: The Arch-angel of Air.

Ronin (Jp.): A masterless samurai, who is without honour.

Seal of Solomon: The Seal of Solomon is also known as the Star of David, and is a hexagram formed by two interlinking triangles. It symbolizes many things, but mainly represents the uniting of opposites and dualities.

Sensei: Literally "teacher" or "instructor," but the term conveys far more respect than these translations.

Sephirah: One of the ten spheres of manifestation, as shown on the Tree of Life (pl. *Sephiroth*).

Sigil: A shape which identifies a person or entity, or communicates a certain concept. The word is derived from the Latin *sigillum*, which means "a small sign."

Skry: To view or perceive from a distance. This may apply to the physical plane or non-terrestrial ones, and many different methods may be employed.

Soror: Used in occult orders, literally meaning "Sister."

Succubus: A female demon who visits men in the night to copulate, thereby stealing astral energy. Succubi are under the jurisdiction of Lilith. The male equivalent is an incubus.

Tai-sabaki: Literally "body movement," the principle of avoiding an attack by moving out of its path. Tai-sabaki employs circular movements and is especially common in martial arts like aikido.

Talmud, The: A set of religious instructions belonging to Judaism, composed of two separate books.

Tao (Ch.): This is a complex, paradoxical subject. The word means "path" in Chinese, and Tao is related to the course of life and its relation to eternal truth.

Tellus: A ancient name for the planet Earth, named after the Roman goddess of the Earth.

Tiphareth: The sixth Sephirah of the Tree of Life. Its name means Beauty or Harmony, and it is associated with beneficial balance. This Sephirah bestows Adepthood upon an initiate, and is thus connected with self-realization. Its colour is gold or yellow, and it has three images: a God, a King, and a Child.

Tree of Life, The: A glyph that represents the Qabalah as a diagram of ten spheres, linked by twenty-two paths. See the diagram on page 260.

Undine: An elemental of Water.

Wakizashi (Jp.): A Japanese short sword with a chisel-like end. It was always carried with a katana, and was used in the hari-kari death ritual.

Yesod: The ninth Sephirah of the Tree of Life, associated with the astral plane. Its name means Foundation, for it forms the matrix from which the physical universe derives its support. It is associated with dreams and its colour is purple.

Yetzirah: One of the Four Worlds of the Qabalah. Yetzirah is the astral plane, and is especially associated with Yesod.

Yin, Yang (Ch.): Yin is the feminine, receptive principle related to: the moon, negative polarity, shade, water, contraction. Yang is the masculine, active principle related to: the sun, positive polarity, light, fire, expansion. The philosophy is Chinese by origin, and states that every object has a balance of yin and yang. For example, the sun is yang when compared to the moon, but yin when compared to the galaxy. It is therefore a relative concept.

Yoi (Jp.): In budo-kai, when a natural stance is assumed (standing normally with feet shoulder-width apart) and the mind is in zanshin.

Yoroi (Jp.): A type of Japanese armour, constructed from both leather and metal. Yoroi was extremely intricate; it had many sections, and each had to be bound to the body.

Zanshin (Jp.): Literally, "perfect posture." A state of perfect mental balance, of ultimate awareness of the environment, reached by utilizing the senses to their utmost.

Recommended Reading

Dennings and Philips. *The Foundations of High Magick:* Llewellyn, 1991.

———. *The Sword and the Serpent:* Llewellyn, 1988.

———. *Mysteria Magica:* Llewellyn, 1986.

Fortune, Dion. *The Mystical Qabalah:* Weiser, 1984.

Kraig, Donald M. *Modern Magick:* Llewellyn, 1988.

Regardie, Israel. *Garden of Pomegranates:* Llewellyn, 1970.

———. *The Golden Dawn:* Llewellyn, 1898.

———. *The Middle Pillar:* Llewellyn, 1970.

Stay in Touch

On the following pages you will find listed, with their current prices, some of the books now available on related subjects. Your book dealer stocks most of these and will stock new titles in the Llewellyn series as they become available. We urge your patronage.

To Get a Free Catalog

You are invited to write for our bi-monthly news magazine and catalog, *Llewellyn's New Worlds of Mind and Spirit*. A sample copy is free, and it will continue coming to you at no cost as long as you are an active mail customer. Or you may subscribe for just $10 in the United States and Canada ($20 overseas, first class mail). Many bookstores also have *New Worlds* available to their customers. Ask for it.

In *New Worlds* you will find news and features about new books, tapes and services; announcements of meetings and seminars; helpful articles; author interviews and much more. Write to:

Llewellyn's New Worlds of Mind and Spirit
P.O. Box 64383-355, St. Paul, MN 55164-0383, U.S.A.

To Order Books and Tapes

If your book store does not carry the titles described on the following pages, you may order them directly from Llewellyn by sending the full price in U.S. funds, plus postage and handling (see below).

Credit card orders: VISA, MasterCard, American Express are accepted. Call toll-free in the USA and Canada at 1-800-THE-MOON.

Special Group Discount: Because there is a great deal of interest in group discussion and study of the subject matter of this book, we offer a 20% quantity discount to group leaders or agents. Our Special Quantity Price for a minimum order of five copies of *Lilith* is $51.80 cash-with-order. Include postage and handling charges noted below.

Postage and Handling: Include $4 postage and handling for orders $15 and under; $5 for orders over $15. There are no postage and handling charges for orders over $100. Postage and handling rates are subject to change. We ship UPS whenever possible within the continental United States; delivery is guaranteed. Please provide your street address as UPS does not deliver to P.O. boxes. Orders shipped to Alaska, Hawaii, Canada, Mexico and Puerto Rico will be sent via first class mail. Allow 4–6 weeks for delivery. **International orders:** Airmail—add retail price of each book and $5 for each non-book item (audiotapes, etc.); Surface mail—add $1 per item.

Minnesota residents please add 7% sales tax.

Mail orders to:
Llewellyn Worldwide, P.O. Box 64383-355, St. Paul, MN 55164-0383,
U.S.A.

For customer service, call (612) 291-1970.

The Dream Warrior
Book One of the Dream Warrior Trilogy
a novel by D. J. Conway

Danger, intrigue, and adventure seem to follow dauntless Corri Farblood wherever she goes. Sold as a child to the grotesque and sinister master thief Grimmel, Corri was forced into thievery at a young age. In fact, at eighteen, she's the best thief in the city of Hadliden—but she also possesses an ability to travel the astral plane, called "dream-flying," that makes her even more unique. Her talents make her a valuable commodity to Grimmel, who forces her into marriage so she will bear a child carrying both her special powers and his. But before the marriage can be consummated, Corri escapes with the aid of a traveling sorcerer, who has a quest of his own to pursue...

Journey across the wide land of Sar Akka with Corri, the sorcerer Imandoff Silverhair, and the warrior Takra Wind-Rider as they search for an ancient place of power. As Grimmel's assassins relentlessly pursue her, Corri battles against time and her enemies to solve the mystery of her heritage and to gain control over her potent clairvoyant gifts...to learn the meaning of companionship and love...and to finally confront a fate that will test her powers and courage to the limit.

1-56718-169-4, 5 ¼ x 8, 320 pp., softcover $14.95

The Holographic Dollhouse
Part 2 of the Merrywell Trilogy
A Novel by Charlotte Lawrence

An ordinary woman's exposure to the occult intensifies when she discovers a door to the past in *The Holographic Dollhouse, Part Two of the Merrywell Trilogy*. Rian McGuire, New-Age bookstore owner and heroine of the trilogy's first book, *The Rag Bone Man*, is resuming her search of the past for answers to her true identity when she discovers that an heirloom dollhouse can provide her with vital direction—through the fascinating phenomenon of time travel!

An informative and entertaining read, *The Holographic Dollhouse* builds upon the trilogy's foundation of believable characters, fast-moving action, plenty of engaging dialogue and transfixing descriptions of the supernatural. If you've ever been curious about magick, myth, dreams, elementals, past lives, time travel, out-of-body experiences and more, *The Merrywell Trilogy* provides an excellent introduction to this fascinating world. Discover for yourself how the paranormal influences the most ordinary lives—both in and out of *The Holographic Dollhouse!*

1-56718-413-8, mass market, 432 pp., softbound $5.99

CARDINAL'S SIN
Psychic Defenders Uncover Evil in the Vatican
a novel by Raymond Buckland

Magical secrets found in an ancient grimoire hidden away in the Vatican Library... an insanely vengeful and ambitious Cardinal... fierce magical storms that take America hostage... sounds like another case for the Committee!

The story begins in the United States, where coastal hurricanes, flooding rains and tornados have cost the country billions of dollars and thousands of lives. As it becomes clear that these storms are not natural, the Committee—a covert group of psychically talented people formed by the U.S. government to neutralize malignant paranormal forces—joins minds to determine how and why these devastating, magical storms are being caused—and by whom.

Enter Patrizio Ganganelli, a crazed Roman Cardinal obsessed with avenging his mother's rape during WWII by American soldiers. As the Cardinal plunders the Vatican's secret magic library to evoke demonic forces against the United States, the Committee joins forces with a Wiccan Priestess to counter the Cardinal's attack. But the Goddess alone may not be able to defeat this evil entity—someone needs to die....

1-56178-102-3, 336 pgs., mass market, softcover $5.99

VISIONS OF MURDER
a novel by Florence Wagner McClain

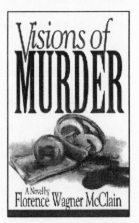

Set in a scenic Oregon resort town surrounded by mountains and vast natural beauty, this suspense novel delves into the real problems of New Mexico's black market of stolen Indian artifacts. *Visions of Murder* mixes fact-based psychic experiences with lively archeological dialogue in a plot that unravels the high toll this black market exacts in lives, knowledge, and money.

David Manning was gunned down in an execution-style shooting outside his office. Unknown to his wife Janet, David had just discovered evidence in his employer's data bank of money-laundering connected to a black market in Indian artifacts.

Janet embarks on a personally exhaustive investigation into the death of her husband when she unearths a kind of dirt she's not used to handling. Elements of the occult, romance, and murder simmer hotly in this bubbling cauldron of mystery that is as informative as it is absorbing.

1-56718-452-9, 336 pgs., mass market, illus., softcover $5.99